Hilton McCabe is a happily married man and the proud father of five children, who are now all adults. He has five beautiful grandchildren. He lives in Belfast, Northern Ireland.

He was a serving police officer in Northern Ireland from 1983–2010. During his service, he performed both uniformed and plain-clothed roles in both city and rural settings. Hilton experienced many of the province's atrocities first-hand, but also the marvellous spirit of its people.

He always wanted to write, but never found the time until the Covid lockdown arrived. The author hopes you enjoy his humble creation. He can assure you that this fiction is closer to the truth than one might think. This is not a book about politics, it's about people.

Mountroyal Pearls is dedicated to two very important people in my life. Without their encouragement, love and constant support at opposite ends of my journey, none of my anythings would have been accomplished. The Pearl is for you both, with much love. Firstly, my Uncle George Magee, sadly no longer with us, sleep well wee man. Then secondly to my beautiful mother-in-law Rachel Mallon, they say that angels walk among us, I can assure you that they do.

Hilton McCabe

MOUNTROYAL PEARLS

AUSTIN MACAULEY PUBLISHERS
LONDON * CAMBRIDGE * NEW YORK * SHARJAH

Copyright © Hilton McCabe 2025

The right of Hilton McCabe to be identified as author of this work has been asserted by the author in accordance with sections 77 and 78 of the Copyright, Designs and Patents Act 1988.

All rights reserved. No part of this publication may be reproduced, stored in a retrieval system, or transmitted in any form or by any means, electronic, mechanical, photocopying, recording, or otherwise, without the prior permission of the publishers.

Any person who commits any unauthorised act in relation to this publication may be liable to criminal prosecution and civil claims for damages.

This is a work of fiction. Names, characters, businesses, places, events, locales, and incidents are either the products of the author's imagination or used in a fictitious manner. Any resemblance to actual persons, living or dead, or actual events is purely coincidental.

A CIP catalogue record for this title is available from the British Library.

ISBN 9781035872466 (Paperback)
ISBN 9781035872473 (ePub e-book)

www.austinmacauley.com

First Published 2025
Austin Macauley Publishers Ltd®
1 Canada Square
Canary Wharf
London
E14 5AA

Thanks go to two amazing helpers. Firstly to my darling wife Kim, my beta reader, critic and liver punching straight shooter. Secondly to Mrs Patricia Diamond Buller, a close friend who brought a lifetime's editorial experience from her journalistic days working for Ulster Television. Ladies, I could not have managed without you.

Chapter 1
Last Night Of 'Nights'

Welcome back, dear reader, I've missed you.

The year is 1983 and we're languishing in the balmy month of July. It's approaching 3.30 AM on Saturday, the second of July to be precise. Yesterday's Battle of the Somme Commemoration Parade has passed without any major mishaps which is nice, a few bottles thrown, some bricks followed by the usual howling arrests and claims of police brutality. You do nothing, you're wrong; you do something you're 'wronger'. 'Hey-ho, dem's the breaks. Apart from that nothing much has changed in the province since 1969. 'The Troubles' as they're known by are still alive and kicking which suits the grim reaper just fine. You see, he does his utmost to please.

Death is served up in all shapes and sizes, from plain to panache. Some wait patiently for his gentle knock while for others, he came as quite a shock. He has no favourite way, with him there's no political affiliation nor does he give any credence to your faith. He cares not a jot whether you're a sinner or a saint or as to the quality of life you've led. His only concern is that it you're alive and not dead. Put simply, death lurks all around like a putrid stench. Death wants to plant you along with all the rest in his forest of forgotten souls. Spare a thought for those poor souls trapped in the path of his murderous scythe.

Tonight, or this morning, we find ourselves in the heart of East Belfast. It's deadly quiet as well as deadly and quiet. Only three types are out and about during these dark hours. The good, the bad and the milkmen. Ignore if you will, the incessant droning of the army helicopter hovering unseen from above, or its searchlight clawing at the darkness looking for trouble. We hear the thumping of its blades rising and falling on the night's breeze, a tinnitus like a bad hangover now accepted as a norm. Ignore the crackling of gunfire in the distance or the delirious howling of terrified dogs.

Now concentrate, YES, can you hear it now? That high-pitched harmonica sound, its humming calling from the black. It's that unmistakable sound of an electric milk float. There, look, over to your right, look harder, can you see it now, turning citywards out of Ravenhill Avenue into the Woodstock Road? Well, I'll be blowed, its driver is none other than the legendary Harry Dean or Deano as he's known and loved by all his acquaintances.

Deano hails from the Clonduff Estate which is not too far away, he's worked for the Dale Farm Dairies on the Castlereagh Road since the late forties. Deano's a confirmed bachelor never having found his Mrs. Right, maybe that's the reason why he's always so chirper. He's in his early sixties though a man on a galloping horse would couch him cosily in his mid-forties. He's of medium height, olive skinned with a full head of jet black 'brylcreemed' hair. Deano sports a wiry frame which is mostly down to his anti-social working hours, apathy towards good food and fifty fags a day.

He did his bit during the last war serving as a foot soldier with the Royal Ulster Rifles. He, like many of his peers, endured the horrors of North Africa and Italy. It was there Deano became heavily scarred and we're not talking about physical scars. It's probably the reason he became a milkman when he returned home. In truth, he lacks the in-depth acumen to figure all this out. He will never talk about his experiences; it's a sign of weakness, isn't it. Another thing the good folks of Northern Ireland have become good at. Post-traumatic stress disorder wasn't a thing then so he had to find his own way using his own coping tools. Life is now very precious to our Deano, simply put, he feels very lucky to be alive.

Deano enjoyed a bit of peace time delivering milk, but in the early seventies, when the 'Troubles' really kicked off, he had his milk float hijacked and burnt out. This trauma really hit him hard and he had many flashbacks to his wartime hell. If only the drunken hijackers had taken the time to explain to him their rationale? That their actions were solely to highlight the deprivation and suffering of the protestant people. I'm sure it was on the tips of their beer-stenched tongues. Apologies, did I say drunken hijackers, oops silly me. I meant to say Loyalist Defenders. Happy now, everyone? Deano reminisced about his wartime sacrifices as he watched his float go up in flames. Was it worth it, would he do it all again? Probably not. Between you and me, why anyone would hijack a milk float beggars belief. Talk about shooting yourself in your calcium deprived foot. Now let that be a lesson to you, British Government.

He looked quite resplendent in his Dale Farm uniform consisting of a white overcoat and equally white forage cap. Quite spectral for the hour, actually. If Heaven has milkmen and I can't for the life of me see why not, then I'm sure there wouldn't be much of a change to tonight's look. Deano just adored these solitary hours and the inner peace it gave him. He loved the sound of his bottles clinking in their crates, reminding him of a hundred chandeliers twinkling on a warm Mediterranean breeze. Now smiling, he doffed his white forage cap to the moon then playfully winked at the myriad stars. In the right light and behind the wrong eyes, there's more than a passing resemblance to his idol, Dean Martin. His laden float now hummed happily down the Woodstock Road, a gust from a warm breeze pecked him gently on the cheek.

That's his cue, not that he needed one, he theatrically leaned out to the side engaging in a huge lungful of air. There's no stopping him now as he bursts into song. Deano has a fine baritone, he's pitch perfect and his lyrics are on the money, sadly his diction could do with a bit of spit and polish. His entire performance is bludgeoned by his broad Belfast accent!

"When the moon hits your eyes like a big pizza pie, that's amore. When the world seems to shine like you've had too much wine, that's 'amor-ee'." In a flash, he's gone from his van and then he's back as bottles are lifted and laid from doorsteps with the devotion of someone who really cares.

Deano sang with a joy at odds with his present surroundings and the world of his past. He refused to kowtow to the Babylon of death and fear. Many locals would swear to hearing his voice in song on certain nights long after his passing. Drifting through deserted entries echoing through the sad cobbled streets, raising tattered spirits when hearts were heavy and moods were low. Tonight, moonlight bounces off those mischievous dark eyes as his chattering wagon drew closer to Mountroyal Police Station. It's his next port of call. He saw the station security barrier slowly rise as a mustard armoured Cortina entered. It passed a red armoured Cortina exiting. They're like two large growling cats eyeing each other up. Deano quipped, "Happy days!"

The red vehicle headed countrywards towards him and familiar waves are exchanged. Deano has a delivery to make and spied his opportunity. He's 200 yards away and closing in.

The mustard Cortina growled in a deep gravelly tone as it slid under the barrier and parked up to the side of Mountroyal Station. It contained the crew of AM70. Constable Gary Weaver is the 'Big O' or Observer. Gary's in his early thirties, a family man and sound operator. He's a solid six-footer and not to be messed with. His driver is Woman Constable Stephanie Gates or 'Heavenly' as in 'Heavenly Gates' as she's known by her section. Heavenly is a stunning beauty both inside and out. She's mid to late twenties, 5 feet 7 inches in height with masses of fine blonde hair which she kept enslaved in a bun. She's blessed with the fairest skin and the largest deep aqua blue eyes. Spending eight hours patrolling the mean streets of East Belfast on a night shift with her was more than a delight. Ok, so she didn't do football chat, nevertheless with her, time simply flew like water down a storm drain. She always left Gary feeling mentally cleansed and refreshed, a better version of himself.

The pair were in the station for their designated break. Just passing them and heading out in the red armoured Cortina was call sign AM71 containing Lionel and Arnie. They had been in from 1.30 AM. Quick waves were exchanged among the yawns as Gary lifted the mic, "Uniform AM70, code 50,73. Over."

The Belfast Regional Control (BRC) constable, the controller responsible for Mountroyal's calls responded, "AM70 from Uniform. Roger, out." If the gods were kind, that would be them in until 5 AM. Gary and Heavenly climbed out of the old mustard war horse in perfect tandem then shared a prolonged stretch. The tandem continued as the pair flipped their Kevlar flak jackets off and dumped them in the boot. They now felt light as a feather. It was still dark as a warm gust charged up the Woodstock Road flapping and blustering like stage curtains on opening night. They turned at the sound of the electric milk float whining towards them. They could hear the milk bottles clinking in the rattling crates as the float drew closer. Then came the unmistakable sound of Deano in full song.

The pair grinned as the float came to a clattering halt just outside the barrier. Heavenly giggled at the antics of the old milkman. Deano was leaning out the side of his float with a pint bottle of orange juice in drunken fashion. Both officers were now in hysterics.

Heavenly screeched, "Deano, what are you like man?"

Deano skipped lightly out of the float with bottle in hand, his white cap perched at a jaunty angle. Grinning like a teacher's pet, he then bowed in Knights of the round table fashion. "Ah my fair Heavenly, how beautiful you are under this starlight canopy tonight. Please deliver this orange elixir to Constable Tweety Pie as an expression of my eternal gratitude for that 25/1 winner at Kempton the day before last. Failing that, let me transport you away from all this madness in my electric steed." They all laughed as warm puffs of breeze playfully danced about them. Heavenly curtsied before her knight in shining milk float then took the orange bottle. "Anything moving out there tonight, Sir Deano?"

The milkman shook his head then lightly skipped back up into his float, "No my Queen, it's dead as Hector so it is and that's how we 'likes' it. If I see or hear anything you lot will be the first to know. On that, you have my word. Onwards and upwards my lieges, My Lady's Road and beyond." The float surged forward then bounced to a sudden halt after only a few yards. Deano's mask slipped for a fraction revealing a face that had witnessed much death.

"Stay safe kids, there's bad people out there. Now giddy-up old girl." The electric float sprung back to life with a high-pitched whine as crates jostled and bottles sang. It raced off down the Woodstock Road then disappeared into My Lady's Road. The old milkman was gone.

Gary grinning collapsed into a hijacked yawn, "Love old Deano, night shift wouldn't be the same without him on our travels. Plans, pard?"

Heavenly smiled mirroring the yawn giggled. "Aye Deano's a hoot. It's Bo Bo's for me, pard. Getting me hair done tomorrow at 10 AM A new Steph awaits. Need to get me some beauty sleep." Gary mused gazing at her gorgeous face. It had indeed been quiet last night. Nothing had stuck files wise as the pair climbed the steps to the front pedestrian gate. The gate buzzed open as they approached enabling them to glide straight through.

Gary passing peered into the sanger window where Wee John smiled back out at him. "Cheers, Wee John."

Heavenly followed with a tired smile and a wave with the hand carrying Tweety's orange elixir. Radio 2'S Night Ride was on and the strings of Mantovani serenaded the pair on their way to the main station entrance. As they approached, the huge bomb proof metal door hydraulically eased open allowing the pair to shuffle on in to the public reception area. To their right was the Enquiry Office. The reception area and the Enquiry Office were separated by a wall and a counter with a large reinforced window which ran the width of the wall. A small sliding hatch sat at the middle of the counter. This was used for inspection of paperwork and the like. Its fortified door was wedged open with a grubby grey green pedal bin stuffed with that day's garbage.

The pair looking in could see the Enquiry Office was busy, activity wise, anyway. Heavenly gently set the orange bottle on the Enquiry Office counter and along with Gary watched the scene unfold. Victor Snape, one of the Station

Guards or SDO's was at his desk. A tense atmosphere prevailed. Heavenly caught his eye and pointing to the bottle mouthed, "For Tweety, from Deano."

His forty-something face, a picture of concentration was obscured by a handful of playing cards held tight to his chest. Victor acknowledged Heavenly's last with an almost imperceptible nod and thumbs up as his eyes remained fixed to his cards. His partner, Harold Sweetlove or Tweety Pie was in the annexe adjoining, which was the radio room and firearms store all in one. It was like the black hole of Calcutta in there. Tweety wasn't visible but his feet were. A highly polished pair of black oxford brogues were propped up on an old office chair visible at the mouth of the store; he was in the coiled spring position. Classical music purred from its heart along with Tweety's bass baritone snoring. The genius was resting his eye.

Sergeant Tony Speers was sitting to Victor's right, knee deep in concentration. Tony was six feet plus with jet black groomed hair. Handsome with a capital H, he came with a fair complexion which housed a deep set of dark brown eyes. His cards appeared tiny in his large hands. His perfectly creased green shirt strained at the seams with his every movement. A physique hewn out of granite; gym crafted to perfection. But Tony was struggling, while at the same time humming the same line of an annoying tune everyone knew but couldn't place.

A state of double annoyance had set up camp amongst the unhappy campers. Tony looked the complete package which was not entirely his fault, mother nature had to hold her hands up and accept her share of the blame as well. You see, mental agility was just not his forte. Tony had to give 100% to scrape by on a full-on 'B' in both life as well as in the mental stakes. He was however a straight shooter, honest and fair and always had his section's back. Tony never shied away from proving he was less than perfect, another one of his unwitting endearing traits. He was most definitely eye candy to the female populace, one of whom sat opposite him pretending to take the game seriously.

Shelley McCann was one of the babies in the section both in age and in service. She was 23 years old and was in her third year of service. She was a good police officer with great social skills and could mould her personality to fit whatever situation was required. She was no shrinking violet and was more than capable in handling herself amongst the worst when it came to it; Shell was a looker in the Snow White cum Liz Taylor mould. She had thick black curly hair with a pale complexion and large mischievous blue eyes. Her lips were full, which she always kept scarlet. She was blessed with a curvaceous figure which came in handy on occasions.

Shelley now slightly agitated, whipped a fag out from her Embassy Regal cigarette box which sat on the desk beside her. Tapping it a couple of times on the desk, she allowed herself a tired stretch, arching her back and putting considerable strain on the buttons of her white blouse. If one of them had popped, chances were someone would lose an eye. Mouthing at the rest of the players, "Any fucking chance, skipper?"

Shelley then lit up. She inhaled with serious intent and exhaled long and slow, feeling the rush as smoke drifted in soft swirls over the table. Nobody at the table noticed. Not even a blink. "Any time today, you big hunk," she blurted.

Shell was tired and a hospital appointment with her elderly mum awaited her when she got home. She pushed that from her mind, noticing Heavenly and Gary watching quietly from the counter. She surrendered a weary smile and mouthed over to the pair, "I'm fucked so I am, honest to god," before jigging her eyebrows up and down at the female figure sitting to her left, then silently mouthed, "Romance brewing."

Heavenly chuckled silently at her 'bestie'. Gary nodded in agreement suppressing a tired giggle. Sitting beside Shell was the newest arrival in the section. Maureen Bennett.

Maureen was Stevie Uprichard's replacement following his arrest for a spate of vicious sexual attacks and the attempted murders of Heavenly and the Preacher a short while back. As it turned out, she was just what the section needed following the stink Stevie left. A real breath of fresh air.

Maureen was in her mid-forties and single. Maureen or wee 'Mo' as she was known, was for her vintage attractive. She had medium length nutmeg hair which framed her youthful 'pixie' face. Makeup was kept to a minimum; it would've got in her way. She wasn't short either standing at around five and a half feet, all lithe and sinewy. Mo didn't so much speak as much as squeak in suppressed tones. It was as if the greatest punchline ever was just about to arrive and she couldn't wait. She was a serial 'innuendoer' and devilment was never far away. Maureen gazed across at Vic who was oblivious. He was a very one-dimensional creature, lost in his cards. By the way, Beanie was the game they were playing. Played by police for as long as playing cards and police have been around. (Look it up).

To a man on a galloping horse, Vic could come across as slightly boring. He was quiet for starters though not shy. He kept himself to himself and minded his own business. To really get to know him, you had to put the effort in, dig around for a bit. Unearthed, Vic was a secret garden full of colour. A wonderful mix of quiet shades and hues. He could be funny on his own but also loved a laugh. He was never a leader or follower for that matter. A quiet strength in the section, much loved and much respected. When left alone, he would revert back into his hermit crab like shell, awaiting the next tide of trials and possibilities. His tide usually arrived in the form of his mentor and tormentor, Harold Sweetlove aka Tweety Pie.

Vic and Tweety were a band of brothers. Both had suffered serious injury due to the Troubles, Vic with his back and Tweety the loss of an eye, neither were expected to pull through. Maybe that was the way he was, or the way they both were. An unlikely pairing but they fitted perfectly. Vic the consummate professional and Tweety the genius. For their obvious differences which actually helped, both were very close.

Maureen adored Vic who didn't seem to have a Scooby Doo. All his silent qualities were a deafening chorus to her. The little things he did, the kindness he showed to the public, his casual indifference to threatening goons who arrived at the counter. Statements he would take for his colleagues and just the way he treated the lowest critter to the highest in the land. Vic was always just Vic.

In the briskest blink of an eye, Tony threw down, cards followed fluttering from all directions. Hands reached for more cards accompanied by mumbled cursing. At one point, Shell gasped in agony as if stabbed in the back by her vicar. Fuming, she picked up a clatter of cards from the deck.

"Tony Speers, you're one fucking bastard. How could you? I'd never do that to you"

Tony, laughing from ear to ear, sported his finest cherub face. "Aww Shell, it was nothing personal. They were all I had. I couldn't do anything else, honest!"

Vic then threw down quickly followed by Mo who leapt from her chair punching the air squeaking, "I'm out. Yippee. Victory's mine. Thank youse one and all. Awful nice doing business with yez. Oh, and by the way, YEZ WUR EAZZYY!"

Vic laughed, "You wee tinker. I never saw that coming. Well done, Mighty Champ!"

With that the 'party' was over. The weary warriors got up from their bear pit and quietly put the spare chairs away. Tony stretched out, "I'm retiring to my office to do some paperwork nudge-nudge, wink-wink. Only disturb me if the station's coming under attack and the Mongol hordes have breached the station walls!"

Tweety surfaced from his crypt, blinking on his seeing eye trying hard to adjust to the bright light. "Is it something I've said?" on seeing the office slowly emptying, his sleep gravelled throat rasping as thought he'd just swallowed a Farley's rusk.

Mo giggled with triumph, "Hard lines Tweety, you just missed me wiping the floor with these amateurs. I'm this month's Mighty Champ." Tweety blinked in bewilderment not that anyone would notice. It looked like any other of his blinks.

"Well done Mo, not that you had much competition." Tweety flicked the kettle switch coughing hard trying to clear his throat, "Tea, coffee, anyone?"

Vic gave a thumbs up. "Coffee, cheers Tweety." Vic pressed the partition door release button allowing the Sarge and his straggling entourage into the main building from the public reception area.

All were headed for their secret sleeping spots dotted around Mountroyal Station. For each of them, it was the end of a draining week of nights, much of it mugged by early starts. Such was a peelers lot during the 'Troubles'. Mo hovered at the main front door which was closed, smiling eagerly at Vic. Vic eventually twigged before pressing a further button fixed to the wall by his side. The huge metal door slowly eased open and a cool breeze crept in.

Mo smiled, "Sure it's all a bit of fun. I'm away to give Wee John his break and watch the sunrise. Catch you later boys." With that Mo skipped out in youthful fashion. Another buzz later, she was in the sanger passing Wee John who was heading for his secret scratcher, three loungers in the porta cabin gym located in the rear car park.

Vic settled as quiet normality returned. He lifted yesterday's copy of the Belfast Telegraph kicking his heels up on his desk. He'd been reading an article on the 1912 Titanic shipping disaster before the cards and was patiently searching from where he'd left off. Other hands had been on the local rag since then. Tweety, still coughing, plonked a steaming coffee beside him accompanied by a slice of carrot cake. Mo had made it and left it in the kitchen for the section to enjoy. Simple pleasures to cheer the spirits. Tweety sagged into his chair and got stuck into the coffee and delicious cake. He purred in appreciation before throwing his feet on top of his desk.

The police radio crackled, both ears pricked but it wasn't a Mountroyal call. Tweety growled, "Jeez, a domestic in Donegall Pass's patch. It's bloody four in the morning. Do folks have no beds to go to?" He rubbed his good eye gazing up at Her Majesty. *Bless,* he thought. *She never gets a day off here. The shite she has to listen to. I'd be looking for a new job if I was her.* Vic, still lost in the Titanic article, gave a reflex "aha" to Tweety's last. Tweety was restless. A genius in search of mental distraction. Looking over to the settled Vic, he verbally prodded, "Lovely bit of carrot cake there, Vic. Nice and moist just the way I like it."

Vic barely responded with, "Aha, moist."

Tweety kept on going, like a tracker trying to get the campfire kindling to catch. "I think there's a bit of orange zest in there which takes it up a level, don't you?" Vic was still lost in his article as he bit into the yummy slice and took a slurp from his mug. It was 4.00 AM and he was some 200 miles away from the safe harbour of Newfoundland, Canada. He was going down with the great ship as the strains of 'Nearer my God to thee' ached through the frigid North Atlantic air. Vic could see the black inky swell getting closer clawing at him as the great behemoth slowly descended to its watery tomb. Her Majesty was gazing over his shoulder: it was actually quite a good article.

"Don't you think, Vic?" Tweety repeated. Vic surfaced from the terrors of his imagination and took in a huge gulp of air. "Oh yes Tweety, orangey. Lovely, nice cake. Indeed."

Tweety now had Vic ever so slightly on the hook. He drifted over to the two-way intercom controls located on the Enquiry Office wall, coffee in hand. The intercom allowed for direct contact between the Enquiry Office and the security sanger. He quickly checked that the sanger switch was off enabling him to chat freely. Vic had returned to his sinking ship when Tweety struck again. "You know Vic, you could do a lot worse than Mo. She's a looker for her age and she's got the hots for you."

Vic lowered the rag momentarily exposing his fluster. "Tweety, what the fuck are you on about? Mo fancying me. Me and Mo. Mo, Mighty Champ Mo?" Tweety poker faced stared him straight between the eyes, "Yep, with bells on. Even I, with my one good mincer, can see it. Yez are the talk of the section. Her eyes are never off you. She hangs on your every word. Personally, I think you're a boring ugly bastard. However, there's no accounting for taste. Well, what do you think then?"

Vic tried hard not to wriggle uncomfortably in his chair but his fidgeting hands gave him away, "Tweety, are you trying to pull my plonker. Wee Mo. Me and Wee Mo?"

Tweety's eye lit up. Vic had now folded the paper and set it down. Tweety 1 - Titanic 0. Tweety laughed, "Jeez Vic, is that all you can say. You're like one of those kiddies speaking dolls, every time I yank your cord all you come out with is, Mee Mo, Mo Meeeeee!" Laughing now, "Or like AM70 heading to a bomb call with its blues and twos on, MEE MO MEE MO. Come on chum, life's too short, we both know that. Here, and she can bake as well. How about this? What if I arrange a wee coffee date for the three of us next Monday Rest Day? Say for around 11.00 AM. She's always harping on about SD Bells Coffee Shop on the Upper Newtownards Road. We all like coffee, sure where's the harm in it. She can only say no?"

Tweety stared the writhing Vic down. "Well what d'ya say?"

Vic wriggled some more, "Tweety, Mmm, do ya, it's just. Well, if you…"

Tweety clapped his hands, "Ha, well done, me old son. I knew you had it in you. Leave it with me, I'll sort it out."

With that, Tweety lifted the dirty mugs and plates borrowed from the canteen at Castlereagh Station years ago. Exiting the Enquiry Office door, he blurted, "Buzz me!" A shell-shocked Vic pressed the door release button.

Tweety glided through the reception area and out into the main building mugs and plates a rattling kitchen bound. Vic crashed back into his chair, his face resembling something close to a state of terror. How the fuck did that happen? One minute he was happily ensconced in the final moments of the Titanic, the next he was in a threesome with Tweety and Mo. Vic returned to that familiar sinking feeling again. Was Tweety serious or just winding. Could the lovely Mo see something nice in him? He'd taken more than a shine to her. Yep, she was a honey. Had a great way with her, oh and that squeaky mischievous voice. "Dare to dream, Vic me old son, dare to dream."

Tony took a right and dandered down to his office. His pre-set bed of three chairs like ducks in a row awaited. They were strategically parked up against a radiator in the darkest corner emitting deep sleep-inducing heat. He grabbed a purple velvet cushion all battered and bruised from his desk drawer and collapsed in a heap. Perfect. He was asleep in seconds. Heavenly trailed after Gary along the downstairs corridor but paused at the foot of the stairs as Gary plodded on up to his boudoir in the male Cons Locker room. She smiled hearing the click clack of a typewriter, heavily thudding in the Cons Workroom. She had a fair idea who it was and could never resist a quick chat. After all, he had saved her life once. She entered quietly seeing the large figure with his back to her, brutally typing away at an accident report. A tape recorder was on and weird jazz was whizz banging filling the small space.

Oh, how yuck, Stephanie thought. Smiling at the broad back and mass of light brown curls she whispered, "Hard at it are we, Constable Majury?"

The Preacher turned and offered up a smile, "Ahh, Constable Heavenly, good to see you. Fate has conspired to keep us apart this week." Heavenly smiled, her heart beating a little faster, "Them's the breaks. By the way, your music's horrendous!"

The Preacher winced, "If you prick us, do we not bleed? Anyhow, nearly done. You not going for a bo bo?"

Smiling back, "Yep, just calling to see how you were. Getting my locks cut tomorrow. A new me, a different look." The Preacher tried to hide his surprise, "Oh, nice, I shall look forward to seeing the new you, though I didn't mind the old you either. Nothing too drastic please. The punk look wouldn't do you any favours."

Heavenly rolled her eyes then clipped the top of his head while reversing out. "Don't you be working too hard, Mister. Bud will be expecting his morning dander around the Majury estate when you get home! Looks like it's going to be a nice morning."

Bud or his official title, Golden Orient the Third, was Pete's golden retriever dog. They were lifelong companions and lived in a cottage slightly off the beaten track wedged between Comber and Killyleagh. "Ouch" Pete returned to his heavy-handed typing as Heavenley floated up the stairs. "Sleep well princess," followed her on her way. She smiled widely knowing no one could see. Her heart was all of a flutter as she quietly entered the women's locker room. A smell of confused fragrances met her as she unzipped her Dartex jacket then removed her tie. (Women police officers were not granted firearms until 1993). Three armchairs sat in the corner and had been there for years. A cheap yellow pillow was lifted from her locker and within a minute Stephanie was in slumber. Gary was in a similar state in the men's locker room at the far end of the corridor. The fragrances there were less confused, stale sweat with a dash of Brut aftershave.

Downstairs, the Preacher bashed on in his attempts to thump the life out of the typewriter. He was slowly winning his duel.

Mo was on high alert in the sanger with the week's Woman's Own on her lap as John Denver serenaded her with "Perhaps Love" from the old Bush radio in the corner. The police radio had been silent for over twenty minutes as soft morning light began to slowly frame the edges of the retreating night. "Beeeep" went the pedestrian buzzer like an electric shock, Mo jumped, completely caught off guard. "Shit." Who the hell was it?

A big smiley face beamed in at her. Mo recognised the mug. "Jeez Bob, ya gave me a heart attack. What the hell are you doing out this time of the night, or is it morning?" Bob Harvey was a member of C Section, a good cop with nearly 20 years done. Bob was a bit under the weather having consumed too many sherbets the previous few hours.

The big beaming face remained as he spoke in a very slow and deliberate pissed fashion, "Sorry Mo love, I've had a few too many in me. Completely outta order, I'm sure. I was partying up the road you see and, well, I didn't want to take the chance and drive. My missus would kill me so she would, hic, if I ever drove home drunk. Sooo, I'm a wondering could I come in and for someone to call me a taxi? I've tried to wave a couple down but they wouldn't stop on account of me being, well, pissed"

Vic and Tweety had watched the performance via the station security cameras and were having a good laugh. Tweety buzzed through to the sanger on the intercom, "Hi Mo, that's grand. Let the drunk fart in. We'll get him sorted."

Bob on hearing Tweety's voice roared, "Aww Tweety. Top man, I owe you one, me old son." The pedestrian gate buzzer went as the main station door slowly eased open. Bob began making his way in resembling a sailor top deck in a trawler caught in a north Atlantic storm. Two steps forward, one step back and several from side to side. He eventually made it into the reception area and staggered up to the counter. Tweety stood patiently at the open Enquiry Office door beaming from ear to ear, "Jeez Bob, you're pissed as a fart."

Bob laughed, "Aye Tweety and you can throw forty sheets to the wind in there for good measure. What's to be done with me, Tweety? Can I go sleep it off in the cell?"

Tweety pondered, "Nope Bob, too risky. Careless talk and all that. We've got to get you offside and home safe and sound. Is your car tucked away safely?" The drink was beginning to die in old Bob and sleep was setting in. He barely managed a weary "Yusss" before nodding off on the metal bench screwed to the reception floor.

Tweety looked back at Vic and rolled his eye. Cringing, he whispered, "Better get the skipper up!" The next thing Bob knew, he was being prodded awake. He had in fact been asleep for over twenty minutes. Standing over him was a smiling Sergeant Tony Speers, Constables Weaver and Woman Constable Gates. Tweety the prodder was standing behind him. Tweety got down on his hunkers and spoke softly to Bob, "You're going home now, chum. We've found your address from the officer's contact list. Young Gary and Stephanie here have kindly agreed to drive you home to Bangor on their break. Sergeant Speers has agreed to all of this. But if you're ever asked, you must promise to say it was because you were unwell. Got it. You were unwell! That's what we're all putting in our notebooks. Control has been informed so everything's cushti. Do you get the picture, Bob?"

Old Bob was a tired mess. His bolt was well and truly shot. Looking around at the blur of faces, the grin returned. Then slowly nodding, his eyelids struggling to stay open Bob blurted out, "Shanks everyone, shanks very much. I'm sick so I am. Awfully shick. Oooops, I think I am going to bee siic…"

Tweety, in a flash, got a paper bin tucked under Bob's quivering chin just in the nick of time. Bob began to chunder his all. The Gag Reflex Quartet surrounding him began to feel themselves go in sympathy. But for Tweety shooing them all outside into the fresh air things could have gotten messier. Bob was by now a very sorry and tired boy. A few minutes later, he was gently placed into the back of the AM70 vehicle as if he were an unexploded bomb. Bob was going home.

Chapter 2
'Arson' About

It was always a strange feeling when you left the confines of your patrol area which was in a sense your world. Mountroyal's was a small one of only around 4 square miles consisting of shops and houses. Other Sub Divisions were larger, some offered a hundred miles of mainly farmland and green fields to get lost in. It was the luck of the draw where a police officer finished up.

Old Bob was a spent force. Heavenly gave a quick check in the rearview mirror and could see that he was in deep slumber. Gary chuckled, "Poor Bob, I don't fancy being in his head tomorrow. Ouch! Tweety said his missus didn't sound best pleased when he rang. They've got the grandkids tomorrow or should I say today. His good lady is for showing him no mercy. He'd promised her he was only going out for one or two."

Heavenly shook her head, "Aww, poor Bob. I've always found him to be a decent spud. Hopefully a few hours' kip will sort him." There were next to no cars on the road as they exited the Dee Street traffic lights and cruised up the Belfast to Bangor carriageway. It was like a small treat for the pair, driving through a different world enjoying some coastal views as well as green fields and cattle.

It was now shortly after 5.30 AM and the night was spent. The palette of colour for that hour of the morning could best be described as umber as a weary sun struggled to get out of bed. They arrived in Bangor. A picture-perfect coastal town in the County of Down. It's located some 12 miles away from the city of Belfast and was considered a safe haven for police officers and their families to live. Several minutes later, Gary took a left into Clandeboye Drive, a well healed neighbourhood consisting of mainly detached dwellings.

Looking across at Stephanie he whispered, "How are we going to handle this, pard? Oh, and what number are we looking for again?"

Heavenly whispered back, "Number 22. And what do you mean?"

Gary sighed, "Well I don't particularly want to speak with his good lady and cop an unwarranted earful from her. After all, we're the good Samaritans here. But for tired Bob here, we should be heading out from our break and doing the final lock up checks now."

Gary looked back at the cherubic face of the softly snoring Bob and continued, "I say we assist him out of the vehicle, get him up his driveway. Lean him up against his front door, ring the bell and run like fuck. We'll be gone before his good lady gets to the door. What do ya say, pard?"

Heavenly gazed at Gary with a mild frown on her face. It was as if he'd made an indecent proposal. Gary pressed on looking to close the deal. "Come on, pard. Good deed done. I'll have us back in the station before quitting time and that's us for the long weekend off. Let's just do it?"

Stephanie sighed, "OK, let's get on with it then."

Gary left the engine running while suburbia slept on none the wiser. After gentle shunting and shaking Bob slowly stirred mumbling, "Wha, where the fuck am I? Who are youse?" When the penny dropped, contrition set in, "Oh Jeez, I'm awfully sorry guys. Yez are the best!"

Bob was still very drunk or as we say in Belfast, "the drink was dying in him." Heavenly and Gary soon had him hoisted by each arm and gently nursed him up his slightly elevated driveway. As they approached the pale blue front door, Bob paused then straightened up, he took a man-sized gulp of fresh air then whispered to his carers, "You know guys, I'm well and truly fucked. Her indoors is going to kill me!"

Heavenly gave him a small hug and a quick peck on the cheek, "You'll be grand, Bob, let me get the doorbell for you. Steady now, that's it, grab a hold of the front door. That's it, you're doing great."

Bob swaying like a mighty oak in a storm clung hard, his knees occasionally buckled beneath him and gave way. Heavenly gazing across at Gary with a conspiratorial look nodded tight lipped before pressing the doorbell once long and hard. "So long Bob, see you back at work next week. Your good lady should be with you soon."

With that both officers fled the scene in a fit of juvenile giggles. Neither looked back or wanted to for fear of Mrs Bob. Like ninjas, they slipped into their wagon and were gone. The residents of Clandeboye Drive were none the wiser. Gary smiled into himself a minute or so later before yawning quietly. He enjoyed driving their armoured Cortina and loved the growl of its powerful engine. Right then, it was purring like a large cat as it cruised through the desolate streets of Bangor. He looked across at Stephanie and was happy. Her eyes were blinking heavily and a bit of rubbernecking was going on. She had maxed out with all the nervous tension and excitement.

Gary whispered to himself, "Home soon, wee pard." Their vehicle was now slowly gliding by the Bloomfield Shopping Centre, the cosmopolitan pride and joy of the slightly yuppie Bangor. It was an American mall type affair full of shops and eateries. The natives loved it. It made them feel very chic, hip and trendy.

It was now just short of 6.00 AM and daylight with flittering blinks of sunlight had arrived. What was that? The faintest of sounds pierced the calm of his thoughts, or was it? Gary tilted his head to one side questioning his hearing. No, there it was again. He could barely make it out above the growl of the Cortina but then his ears caught a far-off ringing noise. It was the sound of a security alarm and it was coming from his left; it was coming from the shopping centre. Heavenly stirred, feeling their vehicle slowing to barely a crawl.

"What's up Gary?" She said, clearing her throat. "What's that ringing noise?"

Gary gazed across at the shopping centre trying to establish where the alarm was coming from. "Over there, Heavenly, look." Gary pointed to small plumes of smoke coming from an office attached to the Texas Home Store Outlet. Heavenly nodding was now on the same page.

"Jeepers, Gary, the place is on fire. What are we going to do? We're well out of our patch. So much for our wee hush hush job?"

Gary nodded. "Call it in Steph, with bells on. If that fire caught, the whole mall could be destroyed along with millions of pounds worth of damage."

Steph nodded and quickly picked up the mic hastily changing their Mountroyal radio channel to the Bangor setting. "Uniform from AM70. Urgent assistance required."

The G Division controller covering the Bangor net responded immediately, "AM70 from Uniform, you're a long way from home but we can talk about that later, send over." Steph was flushed with adrenaline, wide awake and fully focused. "Roger Uniform, we're at the Bloomfield Shopping Centre. There's smoke coming from a downstairs office in the Texas Store. Its audible alarm's off. Urgently request fire crews and local police back up."

The Bangor controller responded, "Good work guys. Roger on your last, wilco. Uniform out."

Heavenly looked worried, "Gary, what are we going to say to the Bangor crews when they pitch up?"

Gary yawned trying to appear more confident than he was, "The truth, pard. We were running a sick colleague home on our break. Our bosses were aware and had granted permission. Even our own controller was awa…"

Suddenly a male burst through a thick hedge to their right some ten yards ahead. Gary yelled, "Fucking hell!" slamming hard on the brakes. The male's face registered complete surprise as he froze to the spot directly in front of them. They faced each other for what seemed like ages. In reality, it was a split second but more than enough time for the Mountroyal crew to get a good look. The male was around 5 feet 8 inches in height and was in his late twenties to early thirties. He was a shade short of olive skinned and possessed an average build, blemished by a small beer keg of a belly. Heavenly couldn't get over how perfectly round his clean-shaven head was and was also struck by the size of the male's large circular brown eyes which bulged. Or was that to do with his shocked expression? His nose and ears were tiny in contrast which drew her eyes to two large piercings. Both were rings. One in his right nostril and the other on his left ear lobe. His lips were non-existent and his mouth resembled a tear on a page. The male wore a grubby cream top and dark bottoms. The farcical freeze frame continued.

Then Heavenly spotted the male toss something small away. It was light blue in colour and had been jettisoned backwards from his right hand. The object bounced and spun before rolling into the grass verge to the side of the road. Suddenly he broke hard to their left.

In one unathletic leap, he awkwardly vaulted a barbed wire fence landing clumsily into an overgrown field which was on a lower level. His right arm got snagged and he had to rip himself free from its clutches. Then he was gone. Disappeared. Gary motored on towards the smoke. Heavenly gripped her mic again and circulated the male as suspicious. He was to be stopped, searched and questioned in relation to the suspected arson at the shopping centre. The message was transmitted for the attention of all Bangor mobile call signs.

Gary was trying to stay calm, cool and collected as their vehicle sped into the Bloomfield Shopping Centre car park. Its wheels spun hard on loose gravel as they powered in towards the flames. They could see the fire beginning to billow and rage and as they drew closer. The sound of the alarm became deafening.

"Fuckety, fuck, fuck me, Heavenly," yelled Gary. Then he spotted something on the ground ahead. He sunk the boot pinning Heavenly back into her seat and drove as close to the blaze as he could. A breeze was buffing heavy smoke and myriad acrid fumes in their direction.

Heavenly coughed as black fumes began to surround them. She spluttered, "Gary, what the?"

It was like a scene from Dante's Inferno. Gary flung his driver-side door open and grabbed a large plastic evidence bag from the boot. "Back in a mo pard," he yelled covering his mouth with his sleeve. With that he was gone, disappearing from view. Now surrounded by the pulsating heat and thick churning smoke, Heavenly screamed after him, "For God's sake, Gary be careful!"

In the distance, she could hear sirens getting closer against the din of the clanging alarm. Heavenly pulled herself together. Time for some positive action. She dashed round the back of their vehicle and climbed into the driver's seat, then in an instant she turned the grumbling beast for a quick getaway. Gary was now staggering towards the burning office; the heat was becoming unbearable. He could feel his eye brows singe and his eyes stream. Visibility was now becoming more difficult between the smoke and his teary eyes. Coughing wildly against the thick hot smoke Gary realised that if he hunkered low, he could avoid the worst of it.

"Two more steps," he gasped as he approached the side of the Texas Office building.

Gary could see that a window had been smashed but there was little in the way of broken glass on the outside. Flames and thick billowing smoke were snatching out at him like a cobra striking at its prey. Gary determined, lunged with his biro pen at a clear plastic bottle lying on the ground by the window. Using its point, Gary carefully picked the bottle up by the nose and placed it into his evidence bag. He quickly scanned around. No sign of the bottle top. Job done! "Pronto Tonto!"

Gary turned away from the inferno and blindly began to stagger back through the thick smoke. Heavenly had activated their sirens and flashing lights creating a sensorial route back for him. Gary focused all his energies on both the lights and sounds as he inched his way out of the black inferno. He was never so relieved when he saw their vehicle with Heavenly sitting in the driver's seat. She was waving at him furiously urging him to get in. Gary clambered on board bringing a blast of heat and stinking smoke with him. His face was black and his hair charred with both eyebrows singed. Coughing heavily, he slammed the door hard, throwing his exhibit back over his shoulder. Heavenly, her face like thunder sunk the boot, the old war horse responded and immediately burst forward powering its way out of the inferno. At that moment, gas bottles and other combustibles erupted causing a huge fire ball of an explosion. They'd made it, just in the nick of time.

Gary exhausted, sagged back in his seat coughing and gasping for breath. He looked across at his pard, "Phew, Heavenly. That was close. We were nearly toast there." He grinned wildly looking strangely comical. Stephanie was not amused. To say she was furious with him would be an understatement.

No one had ever heard her swear but, "Fuck you, Gary Weaver. You nearly got us both killed. All that for what, a lousy plastic bottle! What about Irene your wife and wee Maddie, your beautiful daughter. I hope you think it was all worth the effort, Captain Courageous?" Gary was stunned.

This was most un-Heavenly like. Then he spotted her tear-filled eyes.

Looking down he nodded.

"Yeah, you're probably right, pard. I spotted the bottle and thought of the evidence. I didn't want to tarnish the Mountroyal name for missing out on the evidence." Heavenly now had her act back together as they approached an oncoming fire engine. "Understood, Gary, but remember they can rebuild a shopping centre, they can't replace a husband and a father."

The fire tender with lights flashing and sirens blasting sped into the shopping centre car park. The senior fire officer in charge pointed across the car park to the burning office. He yelled to his driver noting the direction of the wind, "Pull her up over there, Chris. Right lads, we haven't got much time here. If we don't get that fire out the whole shopping centre could go up. Back up crews are on their way from Donaghadee. This is a biggie. You know your roles, good luck." Suddenly his jaw dropped open in amazement. An armoured police vehicle was driving out from the smoke at brake neck speed heading towards them. "Good God Almighty, where in the name of… have they come from?"

Then the huge explosion. "Jesus, someone's watching over those peelers today!" Moments later, the police vehicle was with them screeching to a halt.

A vision of beauty swung the driver's side door open and yelled out to the fire chief, "Morning Sir, I'm Constable Gates. We came across this and called it in, looks suspicious! The seat of the fire appeared to be the Texas office. A window's been smashed. Looks like some sort of accelerants have been used. We've seized a plastic bottle from outside the window as evidence. It may be crucial. Oh, and good luck. Hopefully there's still time to save the place."

The Fire Chief nodding growled, "You pair were lucky there. Another couple of seconds and you were in the obituaries!" Now spotting Gary, he laughed, "Jeez luv, yer partner's already done on one side!" The tender crew erupted in laughter. Heavenly looked across at her pard who resembled a Victorian chimney sweep and nodded contritely. With that the fire engine sped on.

Gary glanced over to Heavenly still feeling slightly in her dog house. "Do you want me to drive, pard?" He said meekly.

Heavenly smirked, "Eh no, not if you're going to drive me into the fiery pits of hell again!"

Gary laughed, "PAARRRDDD."

Heavenly turned to him and laughed. Soot was smudged on her forehead and on the tip of her delectable nose, "Gary Weaver, you'll turn me into a nervous wreck. Every time I'm out with you I age ten years. No, I'll drive. That goon you nearly ran over threw something out of the back of his hand before he bolted into the field. It was small, light blue in colour. Let's go see if we can find it. I'll bet he had something to do with the fire."

Gary nodded, "Sorry, pard, I missed that bit. Let's go take a wee looksee."

As they were driving out of the shopping centre entrance, they met a Bangor call sign coming in. They stopped for a quick chat or de brief.

Gary knew the driver of the Bangor crew very well; they were best mates. They happened to live in the same street and had been squad mates together, "Well I'll be blowed, if it isn't me old mucker Tommy McClelland. How's it going bud?"

Tommy laughed seeing the state Gary was in. "Gary, son, much better judging by the cut of you. Golf Mike 70 at your service. We're here to preserve the scene for the CID boys and SOCO (Scenes of Crime Operatives.) Oh, and to keep the nosey bastards out or should I say the press at arm's length."

Tommy gazed over to Heavenly and smiled. He was instantly attracted, obviously. Tommy was single and in his early thirties. He was average everything. Height, weight, intelligence. Regarding his looks, slightly below average but his rapier wit and easy-going manner usually got him to where he wanted to go. Gary seeing what was going on gave him the old 'Out of Bounds' stare to which Tommy reluctantly alluded.

Just as they were parting Tommy leaned out of his vehicle and whispered theatrically, "Word to the wise, chums, beware of our inspector. He'll be all over this like a rash. Loves himself. Himself is his favourite subject. He'll do anything to get to the top. He'd even ride his granny. Watch out for him, especially your wee partner there."

Gary nodded. "Cheers Tom, what's he called?"

Tom laughed, "Apart from pain in the arse, we call him 'Dashingly delightful Damien Dalzell' or 'Double D', take your pick. You'll get my drift when you meet him. Tread carefully guys, don't fall for his silky suave demeanour. He'd fillet you as quick as look at you. Bye naeee." With that, Tom or should I say GM70 and his vehicle were gone, headed for the smoke, sirens and countless activated burglar alarms.

It took just another 30 seconds for them to get to the spot where the bulgy-eyed male had appeared then disappeared before them. The road was light with morning traffic as the pair got out of their vehicle. Gary's appearance attracted the attention of the early morning commuters, most giggled at the cut of him. He looked a mess, totally filthy. He felt ten times worse. Heavenly, his partner on the other hand, in spite of all she'd been through still looked well. She hopped out first followed by the wearier Tony then made for the grass verge. The image of the pale blue object was still fresh in her mind.

"It was over here somewhere Tony, I'm quite sure. There, there it is. I'm right!"

Heavenly leaned over a spot at the verge fixing her eyes on it, "It's a pale blue bottle top, pard. I'll wager it's a match for your bottle in the back seat. Grab me one of your small exhibit bags from your big fancy case and I'll bag it up for forensics."

Tony was happy, no searching required as he trudged wearily back to fetch the exhibit label from his bag of tricks. While he was mid-rummage Heavenly shouted out, "Make that two bags, please. He's left us a piece of fabric on the barbed wire fence when he made his leap for freedom. Whose been a silly Billy then?"

Gary was amazed at how perky his partner was as he handed her both exhibit bags allowing himself a full-on yawn and stretch. She bagged both then spotted a pale blue coloured Ford Escort vehicle slowly approaching them from the direction of the shopping centre car park. It stopped a few yards behind their wagon. Gary spoke from between clenched teeth, "Heavenly, could this possibly be?"

Finishing his sentence before he could, she went on whisperingly, "By Jove, I think you're right. It's the dashingly delightful Inspector Double D!"

Both watched as the lone figure applied the hand brake before pausing momentarily to check himself out in the rearview mirror. He then stroked his hair carefully over to one side before a further final check was made. Gary raised his comically singed eyebrows at Heavenly who fought hard trying not to laugh out loud. The driver-side door opened very precisely and the male alighted ever so lightly. Double D straightened himself up to his full glory. He stood at 5 feet 11 inches but claimed 6 feet plus. He was of average build and was tennis come squash fit depending on the seasons. The fact that he couldn't beat his way out of a paper bag was more to do with his self-adulation and the preservation of his gorgeous features than anything else. He was reasonably attractive for his 28 years and had dark brown shiny hair with pale blue eyes.

A sun lamp at home and a proliferation of carotene tablets gave him that all-year-round tanned glow. His teeth were pristine courtesy of private dental work. Capped off as they were, and pardon the intentional pun, with the final touches of vanity bleaching. When Double D smiled, which was usually a calculated move and a means to an end, the whole room would light up and bask in his resplendent gorgeousness.

He placed his forage cap on as if he were getting marks for excellence then looked across at the motley pair with a steely glare leaving them in no doubt that he was really important. He would have much preferred it if they'd taken a knee. He smiled coolly at them on purpose, reinforcing a mastery over the pair he immediately sought. He was after the master, slave relationship straight away. Double D was fishing for a weak link between the pair and was surprised at how easy he found it. Fixing Heavenly with a superior glare brought no rewards. This one was beautiful, just his type. However, she returned his glare with cool indifference just falling short of a sneer. Not the usual he was used to and preferred, all fawning and preening at his feet.

He then fixed his icy glare on Gary, his mouth set with the mock smile. Like a gunslinger in a show down Double D began to slowly make his way towards him. Heavenly was fighting hard not to laugh at the jumped up plonker. Gary on the other hand was drowning in all the horrors of his hidden insecurities. For Gary was a man troubled by his past and his dearth of formal educational qualifications. This was the skeleton in his padlocked cupboard, his very own Achilles heel. He had to sit a written exam to get into the police because he didn't possess the necessary grades to walk in. And there it was, the sum of all his worst fears.

His nemesis was slowly approaching, magnificently packaged or so poor Gary thought.

A dashingly handsome high flying young inspector. He was everything Gary wasn't. His star was on the rise, his future limitless. He came fully loaded with qualifications, a veritable Encyclopaedia Britannica of all matters legal and now Gary stood before him.

Gary gulped, "Good morning, Sir."

The inspector raised his eye brows in mock surprise having been spoken to without express permission. He purposely stepped into Gary's comfort zone, leaning his face to within inches of Gary's. Gary could smell his high-end aftershave and felt all the dirtier for it.

Tilting his head slightly to one side Double D continued eyeing him with a somewhat pained expression, much as a gorilla would at the sight of its first human. It was as if to all the world that Gary was the strangest thing he'd ever seen and that he just couldn't get his head around it. He took a deep intake of breath then snatched a quick peek at the stoic Heavenly who could see right through him as a fraud.

"Mmm. Good morning, is it, Constable? Mmm, is it now? Not so very good for the Texas building ablaze across the way, is it? Not so very good for our valiant fire crews trying to put the blaze out. Mmm, not so good for the good folks who are probably looking for a new job after this. Mmm, good you say. And who exactly might you be Constable?"

Gary gulped looking slightly downwards, "Constable Gary Weaver Sir. From Mountroyal in East Belfast Sir." His eyes still locked on Gary's, he whispered, "Well Constable Weaver, it's been a while since I've seen an officer as shabbily turned out as you. My God man, you look like Stig of the Dump! Mountroyal, you say. You're hardly a standard bearer for them in the turn out stakes. If you were a Bangor man, I'd have you on report!" A small sneer surfaced from the edges of his cold smile. "And you?"

Heavenly knew the question was being rudely directed at her so chose not to answer. A chilled silence took place as the inspector continued with his eyeballing of Gary whose knees were knocking. Then again, this time with a raised voice, "And youuuu?"

Heavenly continued with her silence. No one ever had the right to address her in that fashion. She had too much self-respect. The standoff ended when the inspector released Gary from his glare and turned to Heavenly. He was livid. His voice trembling with rage he hissed, "And you Woman Constable, who might you be?"

Heavenly smiled, "Woman Constable Stephanie Gates, (long pause.) Sir. Good morning. And you?"

The inspector turned purple with rage, "WHAT did you just say?"

Still smiling, almost grinning Heavenly repeated now with notebook in hand, "AND YOU? Who might you be?"

Gary was going to throw up. What was his partner doing! He snatched a quick look over in her direction and noted the steel in her eyes? She raised herself up to her full height and calmly walked over to the arrogant ass nearly stepping on his toes. She then leaned her face right into his, "AND YOU?"

On seeing the notebook brandished in her hand and a beautiful face staring hard and unremitting had the effect of a rug being pulled from underneath his dazzlingly polished feet. This woman was a force to be reckoned with, while he was a mere popinjay, a narcissist child, a bluffer in a police uniform. In fear of a complaint against him and his untarnished record he went into full-on survival mode. Let the charm offensive begin.

As different as chalk is to cheese or as night is to day the glacier glare melted and a warm summer smile appeared. "Why Woman Constable Gates, I'm Inspector Damien Dalzell, Duty Inspector for Bangor this morning. I just called out to see that the scene over there was being properly managed. Eh, excuse me, what are you writing in your notebook there?"

Heavenly continued writing for some thirty seconds, head bowed and unresponsive. Double D was left hanging and anxious. When Heavenly next raised her head, she looked the creep up and down considering what crumbs she would throw at him. "Mmm, I'm perfecting my notebook entry relating to this morning's fire. You see we, that is me and Constable Weaver came across it. We called it in. We called for the fire response. We called for CID and SOCO. We circulated a suspicious male who appeared out of that hedge over there and dived into that field there. He threw a pale blue bottle top away which we've recovered, as well as a torn piece of fabric from that barbed wire fence he left for us. Constable Weaver or as you referred to him as Stig of the Dump, at great personal risk to himself recovered a clear plastic bottle at the scene of the blaze which may be connected to the bottle top thrown away by the suspicious male. AND YOU, is that a sufficient enough response for YOU?"

Dashingly Dazzling Damien Dalzell was crushed. Bangor Station and the Shopping Centre were in the Mountroyal's pair's debt. He looked at her and started with his "Mmm..."

Which she hijacked with her own, "Many thanks would be nice, Inspector Dalzell and an apology to my partner!"

Double D snapped at the chance and grabbing Gary by both arms, "My dear fellow, I can't apologise enough. I should've realised. My mistake 100%, please forgive. Well done, great job and many, many thanks from us all at Bangor."

Double D shot a glance seeking approval from Heavenly. None came unless you called a raised eyebrow of admonishment as a royal pardon. Gary's pocket mic crackled into life, breaking up the newfound love-in. It was a Bangor crew, GM73, looking for a 'RV' (Rendezvous) at Ward Park less than a mile away. They had stopped a suspicious male matching their earlier description and requested their attendance to positively ID him.

Heavenly sighed and looked over at Double D. No rest for the wicked inspector. We've got to dash and catch a criminal for YOU! Oh, and would you please let the boys from CID know about this place. It wouldn't hurt for a wee attendance of SOCO and Photography here as well. Better to have the answers now than looking for them 12 months down the line at the Crown Court. Right Stig?" Stephanie was most definitely the master of the three. Gary. "Yes HEAVENLY!"

Double D nodded and bowed, "Absolutely. Wonderful. Thanks to you both again. Oh PLEASE, don't forget to do out your witness statements for the chaps at CID before you leave. They'll need them for their interviews later."

Heavenly spun around and set him free with one of her dazzling smiles, out-dazzling the Dazzler himself, "Why Inspector Dalzell, we're from Mountroyal in East Belfast, that's how we roll!"

A minute later they joined the Bangor crew at Ward Park. Yep, it was the same man, of that they had no doubt. Their eyes met and he coolly blanked them. Heavenly gave a thumbs up to the Bangor crew who duly did the honours in arresting him. A minor scuffle occurred as Mr. Bulgy Eyes briefly protested his innocence before being placed into the back of the Bangor vehicle. Their short journey back to Bangor Station passed uneventfully or so they thought. The Bangor crew made two serious omissions. They failed to search Mr. Bulgy for evidence relating to the arson when they arrested him at Ward Park. Secondly, they missed him secretly squirrelling a pair of rubber gloves from his trousers and wedging them down the back of their police vehicle. These gloves would be discovered many months later by a professional cleaning firm and disposed of quite innocently. Such are the twists and turns of fate in the real police world, sometimes resulting in letting a punter loose other times the gallows and the noose!

Gary gazed across at his partner utterly knackered. His adrenalin tap had been on and off all night. In wrestling terms, he just wanted to tap out. "Jeez, pard, I'm Daffy Ducked. Oh, and by the way, what was that all about with Dashingly Dazzling Inspector Dickhead back there. Where did that come from, I didn't know you had it in you, girl?"

Heavenly laughed which collapsed into a long-tired yawn, "Yeah, and don't you forget it, Weaver, this angel's got claws." A long sigh followed. "Last lap, Bangor Police Station, statements for the CID boys, then home and bed. I'm wrecked!"

At Bangor station, they found an empty interview room and got their hands on some blank witness statement forms or 38/36s. They were in the process of starting when they overheard a Tannoy announcement. "Would any member of the Mountroyal crew make their way to the Enquiry Office. Telephone call waiting!"

Heavenly rolled her eyes as she got up like an old woman, mock sobbing, "I just want to go home Gary." Moments later, she was in the Enquiry Office where an old guard nodded her in the direction of a phone sitting off the hook. He gave her a reciprocal thumbs up while chomping on some toast. Effective communication at its best.

Returning the gesture with a smile Heavenly lifted the receiver, "Hello?"

A familiar voice greeted her from another planet, "Bout ye Heavenly, what sort of handling have you pair gotten yerselves into? Jeez, you were only meant to run old Bob Harvey home on a mission of mercy. Not get involved with Bangor's biggest fire in thirty years?"

Heavenly laughed, "Tweety, are we lucky or what. Our hands were tied honestly. We just came upon it on our way back to base. The punter involved leapt out in front of us close to the blaze, our Gary nearly ran him over. A real weird looking bloke. He gave us both a heart attack."

Tweety laughed, "Aye, I've read all about it on the Bangor log. You pair are bound to get a commendation for all your heroics. Apparently, his clothing was covered in minute particles of broken glass which would tie in with the smashed window at the Texas Office. Make sure you give the fullest account of what your man looked like and what he was wearing. These cases often boil down to pure recognition, identification and circumstantial evidence. Listen to your Uncle Tweety now."

Heavenly nodded and yawned heavily down the phone, "Aye Tweety you're probably right. We positively ID'd him to the Bangor boys at Ward Park. It was definitely him alright; I guess it wouldn't hurt to get a closer look at him for our statements. Good thinking, he's getting booked in now down at the cells."

Heavenly could hear Tweety yawning down the phone at her and giggled, "Cheers chum. Be off with you now. See you Monday for 'Lates'."

Tweety mid-yawn struggled to get out, "Okies. Oh Heavenly, just to be on the safe side, stick in your notebooks that you made out your statements in different rooms. These things make sense in the long run. Fuck me, I'm full-blown cream crackered. See you Monday."

Two minutes later Heavenly and Gary bounced into the cells where the prisoner was being processed. Strictly speaking they had no business there. A Sergeant was processing the paperwork along with the arresting officer. Inspector Double D was there basking in all the glory. He was going to be the teller of great tidings to the Bangor Divisional Commander when he rolled into work. It was as if he had made the arrest himself. Another gold star awaited his portfolio.

"Shit!" gasped Gary clutching tight on a scrap piece of paper and pen in his right hand. "Not him again!"

Heavenly straightened up, "Leave him to me, he's all mine. Just you start getting old Bulgy's description down tight for our statements."

Double D turned on hearing them enter. Heavenly who had just refreshed her face with a hint of mascara and the faintest hint of lippy gave him her fullest of smiles lighting up the room. Double D was dazzled by her radiance. He looked heavenward, now totally distracted and thought, *Thank you God.*

Heavenly jumped in eyes all a flutter, "Yes Inspector, you wished to see us regarding our statements?"

Double D looked puzzled, "Mmm, no. I don't recall Woman Constable Gates? Eh, apologies. Perhaps you could enlighten me? When did I say about the statements again?"

Gary stood in the shadows hastily jotting down all of 'Bulgy's' distinctive features. From his earrings down to his clothing and designer trainers. Heavenly went on, "Don't you remember Sir. (giggles) You asked to see our statements before we left?"

Double D bemused but relishing the fawning adulation couldn't help thinking this one might just be the one for him. Perhaps a romantic candlelit dinner for two, yes at the Culloden Hotel beckoned, with this gorgeous beauty on his arm. What a pair they would make. What children they could create togeth… Gary barged into his palace of dreams like a whoopee cushion at a confessional.

"Woman Constable Gates, I think what the Inspector meant was for us not to leave Bangor without doing witness statements out for the CID boys. Isn't that it, Inspector Dalzell Sir?"

Double D was gazing at the pouting beauty before him lost in less chivalrous thoughts, "Mmm, crudely put Constable, ehhhh, Constable eh…"

Heavenly jostled in. "Constable Weaver Sir, it's Constable Weaver." Double D kept his eyes on the woman constable. The way he felt now, a blow torch couldn't prise them off. He eventually gathered himself. "Constable Weaver, good man yourself. Absolutely correct. What you just said there."

Heavenly glanced over her shoulder offering Gary her Zsa Zsa Gabor pout, then a quick wink. "Oh Inspector, how silly of me. I feel so stupid now. We'll get them done now as requested. Bye the way, nice to meet you. Ever so glad we could help our colleagues out in good old Bangor sur la mer!"

The pair were fit to explode as they returned to the interview room. Gary gasping with suppressed laughter, "Oh Inspector, my head was all a dither when first we met. How do you do it, woman? When I first met you, I thought butter wouldn't melt in your mouth. How wrong can a bloke be?"

Heavenly offered a shy innocent face, "Oh Gary you've only just scratched my surface. Did you get a good description of old Bulgy?"

Gary laughed, spreading the sheet of paper on the desk before them, "All here, let's get our statements done and into the lads at CID pronto. We'll take photocopies of them and update our notebooks separately so that we read differently."

Heavenly nodded, "Agreed Gary. Tweety's also advised us to stick in our notebooks that we completed our statements in different rooms. I'll say I did mine in the Cons Workroom."

Gary hummed, "CID Office for me then. Tweety's the man."

Stephanie nodded mid-stretch, "More haste less speed. Let's get these done, then home. Jeez it's well after 7 bells, I'm getting my hair done in a couple of hours. I'll be asleep in the sink!"

The pair handed in their completed statements to the gang at Bangor CID who received them with all the joy of someone getting an eviction notice from a bailiff. Gary and Stephanie were two tired troopers as their Cortina grumbled its way out of Bangor Police Station. Heavenly caught a glimpse of a tendril of smoke from the blaze in the distance and muttered softly, "Good riddance."

Gary said nothing, allowing himself a tired smile as their vehicle eased on to the main Bangor to Belfast carriageway and cruised the easy 10 miles back home to Mountroyal. No bunting greeted the heroes of the Bangor inferno upon their return. Their own section was long gone and as far as the Early Section were concerned, they were late for the vehicle handover. Gary got ridiculed for the state he was in by the Early Crew then bollicked by the Early Sergeant for not leaving the vehicle full to the neck with petrol. This chore was unofficially the night crew's job for the incoming 'Earlies'. Radios were signed back into the radio room with little chat. The Early Section were already up to their ears in morning calls. Their final act was to sign off with Uniform. Upstairs, they quietly changed into their civvies like a pair of interlopers before shuffling down the stairs to their cars and home. It was 8.10 AM on a lovely summer Thursday morning. Their long weekend off lay ahead. They were not officially due back until the following Monday at 3.00 PM. Oh sorry I forgot. Gary was on a Security Patrol on Saturday night from 7.00 PM to 3.00 AM while Heavenly was down for an Orange Order Band Parade that Sunday afternoon from 11 AM to 5 PM if things went quietly. Fingers crossed for the pair. As far as the Bangor affair was concerned, they had done well, very well.

Such was the lot of a police officer during those times. The pair would quickly forget the fire as other challenges forced their way in along with the long stressful hours. As far as they were concerned, it was all in the past. It was their present where their worries lay.

Sometimes however, the past has a habit of coming back and biting you just when you least expect it or want it!

Chapter 3
Pearls of Wisdom

It was 11.00 AM on Monday, 2nd July 1983. The sky was a gluttonous grey all heavy with rain and rumbling thunder. Outside it was hot and muggy with oxygen in short supply. A heavy downpour was hovering side stage awaiting its curtain call. Splatting pips of rain began to dance off the hot dry pavements like tiny flower girls ahead of the bride.

George Sewell swung his be-socked feet up onto his mock walnut desk. He sighed heavily, rubbing his temples. Nothing helped. "Problems, problems, problems. Lucky George!" A portrait of the young Queen Elizabeth looked down at him from the cream-coloured wall facing his desk. She never looked particularly amused at him; in fact, he had become accustomed to her scowl. He swore he could read her expression which was always somewhere between 'Charming Bullshitter' and a total waste of space.

Three reports in varying degrees of thickness stared up at him. He had read each from cover to cover several times. He was now at that stage of, "What to do, what to do?"

George Sewell was the Sub Divisional Commander of Strand SubDivision located in East Belfast. This placed him in charge of both the Strand and Mountroyal Police Stations. Strand Police Station was the more dangerous of the two. Mountroyal was located half a mile or so up the road heading away from the Belfast City Centre. It was definitely the safer posting with regards longevity and aspirations of grandchildren.

George stood at six-foot and had thick, well-groomed grey hair. For a man of 62 years, he was very trim. He had never married; the job was his mistress, lover and wife. He was distinguished looking and from behind the right eyes was attractive. George was always immaculately dressed and today he was in his deep blue and grey suit, the jacket of which was hung up on a newish coat stand located beside 'Her Majesty'. He was also wearing the faintest pink coloured shirt and a classy silk striped tie of dark blue, pink and white. A silk hanky peeked out of his breast coat pocket. George in Belfast parlance was a 'Dapper Dan'. He was in his plush fourth floor office based at Strand RUC station which was like a fortress at that time.

It had garnered the deserved reputation of being the most attacked police station in the world. It rested on the outer edge of a very nationalist stronghold where the police were hated. Its outer blast walls were pitted with bullet strikes and petrol bomb scars. Nationalist or Republican murals and graffiti fought for any remaining space all aspiring for a United Ireland, 'Brits Out' and 'Up the 'Provos.'

George could be easily distracted especially when he was agonising over his "What to do, what to do's." He prolonged matters with a wee procrastination 'eeny meeny miney moe' moment when suddenly the station tannoy blared, "Sergeant Norwood to the station yard. Sergeant Norwood to the station yard PLEEAAASSEEE."

George's ears pricked. Firstly, because he despised Sergeant Norwood who he considered to be an out and out buffoon. Everyone in the subdivision unaffectionately referred to him as Sergeant Plank, a derivation of Norwood then All Wood to Plank. Secondly the voice on the Tannoy sounded like Donald Duck with a hangover. The tannoy mics hung all around the station. They were in the Enquiry Office, security sanger and in every corridor on every floor of the place. There was even one in the station canteen. This message could have originated from any of them.

Something was afoot and George was happily distracted. He skipped over to the window, his socks prancing through the pink shag pile and looked down into the station yard. A Hotspur, a grey armoured police land rover was idling with a crew on board, its engine growling as the accelerator pedal was being flared. George could see its two rear doors were slightly open. A full-time reserve constable on station security duty was standing by the station gates wearing a huge grin which quickly vaporised as Sergeant Plank walked out from the Enquiry Office. Sergeant Plank was a legend in his own lunch box. He was as skinny as a pipe cleaner. He was 23 years old and had a bum fluff moustache which made him feel manly. When he spoke, he had a high pitched North Down accent which to Northern Irish ears comes over as posh. He was big headed, arrogant and knew way less than he thought. His men had two major worries in life, one was staying alive in spite of the Plank and the other surviving the Provos. They viewed both these adversaries in the same vein. One was trying to get them killed by sheer stupidity while the other was trying to get them buried by means of cunning and guile.

George at this moment was happily enthralled. He watched on as Sergeant Plank bellowed at the security man, "Well, who's looking for me?"

Then something caught George's eye from a third-floor window directly below him. A large metal bucket full of water slowly eased out directly above Plank's head. George gulped, this was going to be good noting that the security guard was trying hard not to laugh and could see both him and the bucket.

"Go on, go on," whispered George to himself. Then it happened. The master of the Plank's fate tipped the pail in one sharp flip releasing freezing water like a clump earthward. The Plank was mid-finger wag when the frozen water crashed onto him. A screech of shock turned anger erupted from the drowned rat then rage as he stomped around the yard yelling, "BASTARDS, FUCKING BASTARDS! I'll get you for this." He then stormed back into the Enquiry Office drenched, still effing and blinding.

George laughed out loud then heard the clatter of tiny feet clanging down the emergency metallic stairwell located at the far end of the station, the culprit appeared in hysterics. In a flash the heavy gates opened as he bounced into the back of the land rover and with a final flare of its powerful engine it roared out of the station into Madrid Street and was gone. Then the heavens opened and everything turned slate grey. Hard rain began to pound off the hapless pavements. George however wasn't finished yet. He jogged out of his office into Debbie's. Debbie was his long-suffering secretary.

George was smiling from ear to ear sticking his tongue out as he trotted by and out into the main corridor. Debbie shook her head in despair. "Jesus George, there's wiser eating grass!" George laughed and gave her the thumbs up.

He swiftly arrived at the tannoy on the fourth-floor corridor and after checking the coast was clear held the mic to his lips and in his finest Reginald Bosanquet tone uttered, "Sergeant Norwood to the sub divisional commander's office immediately, if not sooner!" Chuckling hard, he returned to Debbie's office. Debbie was never surprised by George but the mischief in his face said it all. Debbie was a classy thirty something, a single blonde bobbed beauty. Always stylish, highly professional and much sought after by the Neanderthals below. The pair had formed a close working relationship together during the past six years. Debbie could read him like the Daily Telegraph. She had developed a listening ear and was his proverbial unseen shoulder to cry on. Shaking her head and trying hard not to laugh she said, "What now, George, I'm up to my ears at the moment and it's no thanks to you?"

George laughed, whipping a silk handkerchief from his jacket. "Right Debz, get the waterworks on. The Plank's been effin' and blindin' in the station yard for the whole world to hear and you and all the other ladies in the station have been most upset by his guttural outpourings. I've received the complaints and we are not amused. George looked up at Her Majesty and gave her a wink. For a moment she looked as though she was about to giggle."

That was good enough for George. Debbie stared up with a bewildered look on her beautiful face, "But George I didn't hear anyth…"

Then several knocks were heard coming from Debbie's office door. George fixed Debbie with a wink. "That will be the Plank, don't let me down now Debz, your finest Olivia De Havilland if you please."

George scurried behind his desk and tucked his be-socked feet out of sight then looking at the door he bellowed in his finest 'Olivier', "ENTER." Sergeant Plank nervously opened the door and meekly shuffled in. He was like a drowned rat. His hair was soaking wet, swept back as if fresh out of a barbers' sink. Sweat and water began trickling down his slender brow. His shirt, soaked, clung to him like an anxiety attack. Looking ahead into the boss's office, he could see the back of the lovely Debbie Dean his glamorous secretary. He definitely had a crush on her. Horrified, he saw her back going up and down uncontrollably. And then he heard the sobbing between the stuttering as she blew her nose into a silk hanky.

The Plank gulped as Superintendent Sewell fixed him with his infamous death stare, then spoke, "Ah Sergeant Norwood. How nice of you to join us. Are we finished terrorising the station party with your disgraceful language and behaviour? I've received numerous complaints especially from our female counterparts, including Debbie here who was most upset by your language."

At that, Debbie swivelled around on her chair. The Plank's jaw dropped. Debbie gazed up at him with tears running down her mascara smudged cheeks. "Please Sir. Let me explain. You se…"

Debbie blew hard once more into the silk hanky then sobbed quietly repeatedly dabbing her tear-filled eyes causing George to wince. That silken beauty was all about show and no blow. He had paid a small fortune for it a few years back from Gieves & Hawkes Tailors, Savile Row, London. Debbie was having a blast or three. George hastily continued in fear for his hanky's life.

"Miss Dean, I cannot apologise enough for this officer's behaviour and as for his general appearance, what kind of example must that set for the men under his command. Well Sergeant Norwood, what do you have to say to poor Miss Dean?"

The cat got the Plank's tongue as he stared at the pair of faces looking back at him. He was doomed.

"Sorry," he squeaked, giving Debbie a pleading expression for forgiveness. "It won't happen again. I promise."

George raised a condescending eyebrow. "Mmm. We'll see about that. Now help poor Miss Dean to her feet Norwood, there's a good chap."

The Plank approached her all dripping wet offering a damp hand, Debbie took it with the hand containing the crumpled and stained hanky. George cringed. She forced a smile at the Plank, then pushing her swivel chair back towards her office grinned broadly behind the Plank's back at George. The silken hanky was given one final trumpet extraordinaire. George squirmed as Debbie or 'Olivia' quietly closed the door behind her. George and Sergeant Norwood were now alone.

George gave one of his famous head to toe glares all the while sighing heavily. "Sergeant Norwood. You've been with us for several months now and during that time, all I've received is one complaint after another. You inherited a fine section who were always one of the top producers in the sub. Now they're the worst. I have three transfer requests from three senior Constables who all state you're hell to work for. They say you're arrogant, petty and apparently hell bent in getting them all killed with your ridiculous patrolling patterns. They say you're like the 'Olympic Flame' because you never go out! You know they call you the Plank?"

Sergeant Norwood gulped as a blob of water slid off the tip of his long beak-like nose before disappearing into the pink shag pile. He stammered back, "Well no Sir, I didn't know Sir."

George humphed, "Well I'm no expert but I think they are inferring that you're stupid. There's no hint of respect or hero worship there. When I had my sergeant's stripes on many moons ago in Lurgan, the men in my section called me the sheriff. (George puffed his chest out like an old silver back.) Sheriff Sewell me. I ran a tight ship there. Firm, mind you, but fair. No Planks to be seen anywhere there, Sergeant Pla… Sergeant Norwood. You're now in the 'Last Chance Saloon' with me, if you'll pardon the pun. I'll give you a month and I don't give a flying fig if daddy knows the Chief Constable.

Three things I want to see. Firstly, a big improvement in your appearance and language. Look at you, man. You're a disgrace!" The plank looked down at his feet. A large damp area had appeared on the carpet as he stood steadily dripping. He felt lower than a snake's belly. "Secondly, I want you to win your section round. I know them all personally, and some for many years. They're a good bunch, cut them a bit of slack, encourage them, buy them s some buns now and then, try leading by example for goodness' sake. Finally get your woeful figures up. Remember this, a happy section is a productive one. It's not rocket science man. Have I made myself clear to you Sergeant Norwood?"

An awkward silence followed before the Plank slowly lifted his head and nodded, "Yes Sir. Apologies for everything."

George gave him one final death stare for good measure then sighing heavily said with a wave of his hand, "Dismissed, go on be off with you."

As his office door closed quietly, George leaned back on his chair and contemplated. He still held some faint hopes for Norwood or the Plank. He was masquerading at being an adult and failing miserably. George had seen this dance played out many times during his career. Something had to give, a maker or breaker of the man. George hoped earnestly for the former.

Where was he again, ah. "What to do, what to do?" They hadn't gone away you know. The three files taunted him from his walnut desk. Outside, the rain battered hard against his security windows. He could see nothing to further distract him other than wet sliding blobs. His telephone shrilled causing him to jump. It was the internal ring as opposed to the external one. George picked up the receiver, "Hello, Superintendent Sewell."

A female voice came back all soft and sultry. "Your toasted crumpet awaits. Do you wish me to bring it to you, Superintendent Sewell?"

George laughed recognising Debbie straight away. "Perfect Miss Dean. Care to join the old codger?" The line went dead and seconds later, Debbie appeared with tea and crumpets for two. As she entered, George thought to himself, this is why I haven't retired. She was gorgeous, intelligent and funny. She had the power to lift him up when he was down as well as bring him down when he was too far up himself. If only he was twenty years younger.

Debbie smiled widely at him while she did the needful. She had remembered the lemon curd marmalade for her boss. Points up. Her makeup was still a bit smudged from her award winning 'Plank' performance but on the beauty stakes, again no points lost. The pair laughed raucously as they replayed the earlier events while enjoying their tea and tiffin. George caught 'Her Majesty' frowning at him from behind Debbie's shoulder but carried on regardless.

Debbie caught George eyeing the three files and could see the anxiety. "Well Big Boss Man, what's been keeping you up these nights. I thought we had learnt our lesson from the Stevie Uprichard's escapade?"

George shrugged and smiled, noting the concerned face opposite him. She should have been a master carpenter for she always hit the nail clean on the head. They had no secrets between them which was their wee secret.

Rubbing his temples and looking over at the rain splattered window he whispered for no apparent reason for no one else could hear, "File number One, from Special Branch, a senior officer from our subdivision is being heavily targeted by the Provos. The intelligence is high grade. We're talking about an imminent hit. They're trying to put more meat on the bones but as yet 'Nada'. I've had Janet O'Loan in, you know, the subdivisional collator. She's been instructed to brief the troops and advise on the usual. Check your vehicles for UVIEDs (Under Vehicle Improvised Explosive Devices.), to change their daily patterns where possible and to report anything strange or unusual. There's little else they can do. I've also let the duty sergeants and inspectors in on the full SB threat.

"File number two, fucking drugs, Cannabis to be precise. It's like vine weed. Once it takes hold you can't get rid of it. It's running amok on both sides of the fence and is in plentiful supply. Again, I've got Janet briefing the sections and refreshing them on their Stop and Search Powers under Section 23 of the Misuse of Drugs Act 1971. It's vital we get to the bottom of this before someone dies or we have a turf war on our hands. With a bit of luck and graft, we can flip a user into talking."

Debbie nodded. "Not good George, not good at all."

George took a sip from his QPR bone china mug. The one with the legendary Stan Bowles image on it. Smiling over at his glamourous chum he said, "Stuff you've never come across before, Princess?"

Debbie's eyes bit back, "Yeah old timer, nothing like getting me some Bamba, Bobo Bush, Ding, Gonj, Instaga, Reefer, Sinister Weed or as they say in good old Norn Iron Wacky Backy! I was young once, George and attended Durham University. That shit was on tap. I think 'The Troubles' have kept a lid on it here up to now."

George nodded with a smile, so many strings to her beautifully put together bow. "Apologies 'hard core', we'll just have to capture this 'Magic Dragon' and slay it!"

Debbie's eyes smiled back from behind her huge pink Care Bear mug. George always felt a tinge of guilt when he viewed the mug in Debbie's delicate hand. His well buried grubby mind always surfaced screaming Care to Bare before George had time to shoo it away. He didn't have to look. Her Majesty was definitely NOT amused.

"Finally. File number three. A bit of reported 'Perving' going on in Mountroyal's patch. We've had several calls from irate parents that some old timer is exposing himself to their kids."

Debbie giggled, "You mean his 'Wee Willy Winker' or his …?"

George butted in, "Yes Debbie, spare us the other hundred names you call the male 'Todger'. If it's anything like your knowledge of 'Weed' names, we'll be here all day!"

Debbie shrugged, slighted at being nipped in the bud. "What's he doing then? Could it not be different old timers needing a pee and caught short, relieving themselves up an entry or wherever. You know, the old prostate issues. Why George, you spend half your working day going to or coming from the loo. Look, the carpets are worn bare."

George found himself looking. She'd mugged him. Debbie screamed with laughter. George shook his head slowly. Her Majesty gave him a 'Serves you right, perv' look. Then out of the blue in the twinkling or should I say tinkling of an eye, George felt a very urgent need to pee. Had she prompted his prostate. Nudged it awake. Was that even possible? No! Not in front of Debbie. If he had a leather strap he would've bitten on it, such was his angst. Please no. Not after all the carpet mockery. Not now, shoo go away. But his bladder alarms were now screaming in his ear. A body language expert would have picked up on the miniscule rocking and rolling. But he couldn't, he dare not. He was going to have to hang tough and put his urges behind him. Or TRY!

Debbie continued, "You know George kids are everywhere. Maybe it's all a big mistake."

George smiled, draining his mug while trying to hide his grimace. He carefully brushed rogue crumbs from his desk onto his side plate as Debbie gathered up. "I wish. Sadly, the descriptions given of him are all a basic match which is worrying. The children he's exposing himself to are all female. Ages from ten-ish or so up to twelve or thirteen. Pubescent girls!"

Debbie frowned as she recovered the silk hanky from her skirt pocket, "Dirty bastard, pardon my French George." Then tossed it over to him with a "that will teach you buster" look. It was a mess.

George shrugged, his body anguishing, his mind agitating. "Oh, and while we're on the subject of kids, the wee bastards are thieving bacon, sausages and the like from all the Spars and Co-ops and any place that sells meat in Mountroyal's patch. A plague, a fucking plague that's what they are. Do we have any clues as to who? Answer, nope, not a one!"

Lifting the tray, Debbie made her way towards the office door before pausing, "Dirty bastard, what makes a man do things like that on a child?" She then skilfully hooked it open with her foot. Looking back over her shoulder Debbie fixed him with a dazzler and laughing said, "No finer man for the job than our very own Superintendent George Sewell, now get cracking."

George was now bursting to pee. His spider plant pot looked inviting. "No, don't be daft. Say someone walked in!" He decided to give it another five then he would make a break for it. He glanced out his window as rain scurried on by heavy gusts arriving in waves adding to his torment. Her Majesty was enjoying every second. Wriggling in his seat, he picked up the phone and rang a familiar number. Several moments later a deep voice answered.

"Hello, Mountroyal CID. Cliff Boomer speaking." A few 'aahas' later, he shouted into his boss's office, "Hey, ya wee shite. The boss wants to know are you free for a wee Hop House conference tonight at seven?"

From behind the door marked Detective Inspector Archie Brown squealed, "Does a bear shite in the forest?"

By the way, show a bit of respect to your betters, you fat bastard."

Big Cliff spoke again to George. "Yep, sounds like a plan. I'll see if Tweety's free as well." George smiled from the other end of the line. Pinky and Perky at their best, another reason he hadn't retired.

Standing as he hung up his need to pee became critical. He began gyrating like a professional Hula Hoop champion come Irish Dancer. His bladder was about to explode. "Enough. Fuck you Debbie Dean!" He paused for the split second he didn't have at his office door.

A man woefully trying and failing to gather himself. Still no good, in fact worse. Sweeping it open he entered Debbie's domain. Her head was down typing hard. George feigned a casual stroll towards the corridor door. His eyes were bulging and his steps were becoming shorter and knotted. To coin a derivation of his own previous phrase, he was now in 'Last Pants Saloon!'

Debbie looked up and cocked an eye and said in matronly fashion, "Hurry up George, you're going to wet yerself!" He just about squeezed out a strained "Oh my God, is that the time?" before hurtling out of the office and down the corridor towards the men's loo. Time was of the essence as he sprinted through the loo doors. Fortunately, there was no one on the other side or they would have been killed. George gave heavenly thanks as he arrived at the Armitage Shanks porcelain urinal. Some things in life were definitely better than sex as far as he could remember.

Moments later George casually strolled back into Debbie's office, a more relieved man on the planet did not exist. Smiling at Debbie, he chuckled, "Silly me. That appointment's not 'til tomorrow."

Debbie raised her head, cutting her boss a bit of slack, "Aww good George. You were in an awful panic there!" Her infernal eyebrow told another story. Returning to his office he paddled over to his beloved window. The rain had ceased and the grey was gone, all was shimmering in the summer colour. The heavy mugginess in the air had lifted and the world seemed a happier place. George reluctantly returned to his desk and his 'what to do, what to do'.

Her Majesty was NOT amused!

It was just past 7.00 PM and George was sitting in his favourite armchair in the corner of the snug. The snug was situated upstairs at the Rosetta Bar, located on the Rosetta Road, Belfast. East Belfast that is, just on the outer limits of Mountroyal's patch. It was a safe haven for police and was very pro police. It had plenty of cameras and there was only one-way in. As a building, it was an eyesore, basically square cement with tiny windows to the front. Over time, a mutual adoption had occurred between it and security force members. It was known affectionately as the Hop House an abbreviation of the House of Pain. A joint where peelers could go and have a good moan and drown their sorrows in relative safety.

Paddy the faithful barman, a man somewhere in his sixties and part of the fixtures and fittings watched on. Like Vivaldi's four Seasons he had seen all of George's. He was luxuriating in the midst of a bleak midwinter that evening. Paddy went for a distraction. Sometimes that helped.

"Hey George, do you want the television on? Corrie's about to start. I don't usually watch it but it's quite good at the moment. Len and Rita are…"

George raised his hand to his lips with eyes closed tight stopping Paddy dead in his tracks. Smiling gently, he whispered, "No, Paddy. A few of the crazy gang will be here shortly for a wee chat. Another Bushmills please, if you can spare the time."

Paddy laughed, "Spare the time George, there's only me and you here." The door whipped open and in breezed Tweety resplendent in a grey fedora and matching sports jacket. Underneath was a green silk shirt, khaki trousers and brown polished brogues. He wore his deep blue lensed glasses masking the fact that he only had one good eye which he now used in Paddy's direction.

"Evening to you, Paddy me old son, café con leche y Soberano con hielo aparte as per usual (coffee with milk and a Spanish brandy.). Many thanks!" Paddy laughed, "Evening Tweety. Hey, do something with your man over there. He looked like a man what's won first prize at a raffle. A one-way cruise on the Titanic."

Tweety gazed at George who was staring blankly at the ground. Two empty glasses sat on the table in front of him "Evening sunshine!"

George looked up, "You ok to run me home after, my car's back at the station?"

Tweety nodded, "Abso, how did you ge…"

George butted in, "Debbie, she's collecting me in the morning. She's a wee darling so she is."

The door of the snug burst open like in a western saloon. Like a whirlwind full of sound and fury appeared the two amigos. The dynamic duo the dream team. Perky and Pinky in that order. Big Cliff Boomer all 6 feet 7 inches of brick shit house and sartorial elegance closely followed by his perfect foil. Wee Archie Brown, 5 feet 8 inches, billiard ball bald and bespectacled. Pipe cleaner thin, resplendent in 30 shades of brown. The pair of legendary Detectives had arrived and the world became a safer place for the smiling George.

Big Cliff boomed rubbing his shovels with excitement, "Evening all. Hey Paddy, any fucking chance? My head thinks me throats cut. Two pints of the black stuff and one for yourself if you're feeling that way inclined."

Paddy smiling gave a thumbs up. The party was getting started. Archie cut in, "Aw now cunty ballicks that wasn't very nice, the way you spoke to Paddy there. Be nice now."

Big Cliff spun around, light as a feather as any former rugby international would. "Fuck off wee man that was me being nice! Hey Paddy, me old son, awful sorry if I upset you there."

Paddy laughed, "Go fuck yourself, Boomer!"

Cliff gazed all the way down to the wee man, "Are we happy now, you wee gobshite?"

Archie laughed, "Ecstatic. Hey Cliff, look at the cut of those two sad bastards sitting in the corner. They haven't got a smile between them. You pair, where's the funeral?"

George and Tweety broke into a grin at the advancing pair. George spoke, "Is Derek coming?" Tweety replied, "Not the night. He's ironing or flower arranging or something. He's not the drop of a hat kind of guy. More of a long-distance diary type attender."

George shrugged, just in time for Paddy to arrive with the happy juice. Tweety now rubbing his hands with glee said, "What's the damage Paddy, me old son?"

George nudged in, "My treat lads. Stick it on my tab Paddy, I'll settle at close of play. Did you get one for yourself?"

Paddy nodded, "Cheers George. A wee pint. I'll have her later before closing. No worries. Enjoy Gents."

The next five minutes went by in silence save for some mellow supping, an unofficial tradition which had evolved way back. None of the gang knew exactly when but it just had.

Eventually Archie broke the ice, "What's eating at you, George? You promised after the last fiasco with that bastard Uprichard you'd be more chilled, more ehh…"

"Philosophical!" Finished Tweety. "Aye, that. What Tweety said."

George looked up and smiled. To him, Archie always looked a tad comical, his slight frame made his suits appear just a half size too large while his shirt collars resembled a yolk on a cow. Then there was his highly polished bald head, slightly tanned which housed his tiny brown inquisitive eyes. These wee beads appeared huge behind his milk bottle lenses. Finally, his high-pitched nasally machine gun voice. A thousand words a minute, Brown. Archie was a star.

George spoke, "Archie chum. I don't know where to start. Is it just me? Am I getting too old for all this shit? I spend all my working hours worrying about everything around me. This threat, that threat. There's intelligence in that they're targeting one of us senior rankers with a view to a hit. Then there's this crime trend or that crime trend. The sub's awash with drugs on both sides of the fence not to mention the bacon thefts by the wee nippers. I can't get a wink of sleep at night worrying about the safety of you lot as well as the lads on the ground. Oh, and there's one in particular who's proving himself to be a real ass-hole. I'm tired chewing him out. Sergeant fucking Nigel Norwood aka the Plank. I swear it's only a matter of time before he gets himself killed or one of his section. Spinning plates, fucking spinning plates syndrome. I'm shit scared that one day they'll all come crashing down around me! And as for the bombs, it's only a matter of time before we cop a big one."

Big Cliff drained his pint and gave Paddy the thumbs gesturing for the same again. Tweety grabbed Paddy's attention motioning, "none for me."

Cliff gave George a compassionate smile then spoke, "Aye George, we've all had the pleasure of Sergeant Plank. I'm trying to find something nice to say about him but I can't come up with anything."

Arnie was stoking Woody his pipe up. A soft St. Bruno haze drifted across the bar, its aroma massaging their frazzled senses. From clenched teeth he remarked, "Yep, he's a piece of work so he is. Little wonder everyone hates him. Tweety, any thoughts or opinions you'd care to share?"

Tweety took a swift nip of his Soberano followed by a sip of coffee. The combination of the two as they slid down his pipes were divine. "Mmm, Sergeant Norwood. Tony Speers hates him, you know." Archie plumed then fumed, "Answer the question, you genius ballicks?"

Tweety raised his eyebrow, the one above his good eye. "Ouch wee man. Well for the Plank, it will end only one of two ways. He will die a horrible death due to his stupidity and arrogance orrrr…"

George snapped, "Or fucking what Tweety?" A knowing smile arrived.

Tweety continued, "Or gentlemen, he will receive a shock which will turn his life around. The full package. The complete 360 degrees. We've all witnessed the effects of trauma negatively impacting on a good soul, turning a solid peeler into a nervous wreck incapable of performing the simplest of tasks. We've seen them forever on the sick or hiding behind the drink as a means of escape. (The gang recognised that trait, maybe a bit too close to home.) The boffins are now calling it post-traumatic stress. The yanks created the term following the Vietnam War. But it's been with us long before that. You only have to look at the mental car wrecks from the first and second world wars. I'm of the opinion that a traumatic jolt can also have a positive effect. Be the awakening of a narcissist soul. Shake the self-indulgent mirror out of his clammy hand if you like."

Big Cliff rumbled, "I'd like to give that wee creep some trauma and shove his wee self-indulgent mirror right up his as…"

Tweety went on, "As I was saying lads we can't control the actions of others. If a bomb comes, it comes. If the Provos carry out a hit, well so be it. Bad news for you, George. You see, you're simply not God Almighty and the great see-er of all things. By worrying yourself to death isn't going to stop these horrible happenings happen. This is the world we live in today. We can only do our best with whatever tether remains within us. What happens when a sponge is full? It can no longer function, well not as a sponge anyway. It loses its reason, its sole purpose. That for which it was meant to be!"

George gulped hard on a whisky and gave Paddy the faintest twitch. Paddy winked and quietly got another one in. Nodding at Tweety, he said, "Perhaps you're right Tweety, I think I'm just about at the end of my fucking tether. In your speak, me sponge's full."

Tweety smiled, "George, maybe we're all just about there. The two Great Wars, eight years in total. Look at us lot, we've been in these trenches for nigh on 23 years. The bastards are killing us in our homes and in our work. We've been burying friends and colleagues all this time. As for the Provos, the rules don't apply to them. Is it any wonder we're all doolally!" Paddy arrived quietly placing two stouts and a whisky on their table.

Big Cliff hoisted a fresh pint to his lips and closing his eyes took a long sip. "Ahh Paddy me old son, nobody can pour a pint of the black stuff quite like you. You're an absolute legend in my eyes."

Paddy laughed, "Crawling bastard!"

Archie, lifting his newbie pint, laughed, "'Bout right Paddy, he's been kissing ass for as long as I've known him."

Cliff growled, "How do you fancy my toe up your ass you wee shite." Tweety shook his head and glanced over to George who was now smiling. Was it the whisky or was it the friendship? Probably 'Yes'. A tired yawn engulfed his face. "That will do me Tweety if you're happy enough."

Tweety nodded. Pinky and Perky were now glued to the tele. They were frozen in time, pints in hand. Paddy's back was to them at the bar. The old barman was polishing a wreck of a mirror, his face pointing elsewhere. All three hardened veterans of 'The Troubles' were glued. Len Fairclough had just snogged Deirdre Langton up an entry behind the Rovers Return. Such deceit. Poor Rita. With that the classic cobblestones music jumped in. Wee Archie's mouth hung wide open his pint pausing against his lips. Big Cliff looked as though he was going to burst into tears.

Paddy spun around, "I told yez lads, that Len Fairclough's one dirty bastard. He'll never change. Every time Rita gives him another chance, the bastard goes and does the dirt on her."

George quietly mouthed at Tweety, "Wiser eating grass!"

Big Cliff drained his pint then growled, "I know what I'd do with him given half the chance."

Paddy spouted, "You'd be behind me in the queue, Cliff."

Archie roared which sadly sounded like a squeak, "And me as well Paddy. I'd knock his ballicks in."

At that everyone burst out laughing much to Archie's annoyance. George laughed as he headed for the door, "Thanks lads. Just what the doctor ordered. I needed that. Oh, and by the way, I still hate his fucking guts!" He was met with three blank expressions.

Big Cliff went, "Wha…"

George sighed pausing by the door expelled in exasperation, "THE PLANK. THE FUCKING PLANK!"

Chapter 4
Holy Mo, No!

Maureen had lived happily with her boyfriend or should we call him her partner for over 15 years. During all that time she had stuck steadfastly by him as his career in the police progressed. She was his rock and helped him through all of his studies. She was always there for him especially during those dark days when his fragile confidence took a dip. He was a slogger come plodder academically but don't tell him that. Compared to our Tweety, tortoise versus racehorse would be a fair comparison.

Sorry, how rude of me. Let me introduce you all to 'J'. Well, that's what Maureen lovingly called him and who are we to argue. J was a man with very few friends of either sex. He looked fine enough on the eye, it's just that he had no real personality. Men found him to be not quite manly enough. He was most conspicuous by his absence when the physical macho stuff was called for. He just wasn't built physically or emotionally for all that rough and tumble. Women found him to be a bit awkward as well. Was it that high-pitched shrill of a laugh he had or maybe his wet lettuce pat, pat patting when he was around you. Ugh, a real turn off. J was also a little too light on his loafers for the normal punter, not that he'd realised, noticed or particularly cared. You see while J was not really a hit with either sex, he was his very own greatest fan.

I guess you could say Maureen or 'Mo' as others referred to her, kind of mothered him. He was definitely a typical 'mummy's boy' having been an only child. As a child he was spoiled which nurtured his selfish and controlling side. What he wanted he got. Prior to his parents passing, he had been placed on a pedestal. Maybe we can't apportion all of the blame on him. You could argue he knew no other life. Maureen simply took over the reins where his doting parents left off. Off being when they shuffled off their mortal coils!

Then there were his little selfish traits that would peek out every now and again. Behind closed doors mini tantrums would flare up over the silliest things, like the TV remote control not being in its usual spot or who had dared handle his personal items. He was very touchy about his things which brings us nicely around to a hobby J got interested in. His photography. He was very, very precious about his Kodak EK300 instant camera. He wouldn't allow any other mortal near it. I believe they're top notch not that I know anything about them. He kept his beloved camera in a secure cupboard in their box room. It was left on the top shelf right at the very back. He also kept sets of images in separate envelopes there. J went on to convert the box room into his own personal dark room and all that it entailed.

He enjoyed looking at his images when no one was around. A bit weird really but then again J was a bit weird. The cupboard was always locked and J was the keeper of the only set of keys. Maureen used to wonder what the point of the camera was but never interfered. J seldom had it out save for the occasional jaunt. There was never any rhyme or reason to these occasions as far as Maureen could see.

For all his quirkiness, as Maureen referred to his little ways to the outside world, they had made a great team. They appeared to mirror each other in almost every aspect. J definitely liked to have Maureen close by especially during those crowded public engagements. She was a real head turner on his arm. It gave him that manly look he sought, wanted or perhaps needed.

They lived in a charming house in Moira which they put together with simple touches and charming taste. The décor was pastel shades of mainly peaches and pinks. J just loved those colours. Though to his credit Maureen got all the accolades. He insisted. How very kind of him Maureen would think. They had the perfect little life together and were every neighbour's favourite neighbour. The loving couple would get around to a wedding someday which is what Maureen yearned for the most. J insisted there was no real panic. It would just be a matter of time. Maureen anguished quietly in his shadow, for her body clock was going "tick tock, time's marching on and it's getting late!"

Maureen had been a popular classroom assistant in the local Primary School where she worked at P2, P3 level. The kids simply loved her. She had a lightness of heart and was caring and compassionate and was always sensitive to their needs.

Years swept by as Maureen supported J as he progressed at first awkwardly through the policing ranks. With each promotion, a small part of him evolved and changed. From the shy awkward constable, his confidence slowly grew. With rank came power and with that power, he discovered the secret pleasures of control and manipulation. Those same pleasures he had enjoyed as a child but now on a much larger scale. He found untold delight at being cruel in the most circumspect of ways. Always in the shade, hidden behind the might of his classic fountain pen. J would choose his unwitting victims for no other reason other than idle curiosity. Just how far could he bend that branch before it snapped. He particularly despised the popular souls. People that could light up a room by their very presence. People with an abundance of personality, promise and bon vivant.

People in reality who were polar opposites to him. He once ruined a career, though keep this under your hats by virtue of a smiling, "Hello!" in a corridor. The poor individual never could figure out how his career went west much like himself. He went from the leafy suburbs of Helen's Bay to the killing fields of West Belfast quite out of the blue. I think he was blown up a while back, buried in the Clandeboye cemetery. Lovely send off.

J discovered that with very little effort he could make people's lives a misery. He would turn men and entire sections against each other. Strip a man of his dignity by making an example of him endlessly in front of his peers. He created his own personal pets or snitches who themselves were terrified of him. These minions would report back on an officer's personal or private comings or goings as directed by their master.

Maureen noticed the change but put it down to the job creating a more professional product of the once awkward man. She knew nothing of his cruel side.

J eventually scaled to the dizzy heights of Chief Inspector. He was thrilled when posted on promotion to Complaints and Discipline Branch or C&D as the unfortunates called it. C&D handled certain internal police complaints as well as complaints made by members of the public against police. This could be to do with the general handling of a case or against a specific police officer. C&D was based out of Lisnasharragh Police Station, East Belfast. His career progression by this time showed no signs of slowing. The move to C&D was akin to giving Fatty Arbuckle the keys to the Pie Factory. The lives he could destroy. He could have men sacked or blocked to the far-flung corners of the province. Marriages ruined. Wives in despair would contact him pleading their husband's cause.

Some would even offer themselves, if you know what I mean and he absolutely loved it. Normally, these distressed damsels would be way out of his league. A double whammy if you like. Wreck a life or have his wife. It was at this time that his hobby, if that's what you could describe it as, really flourished.

J enjoyed these little 'amuse-bouche'. He really had become a creature void of decency or compassion. I suppose in today's fancy lingo our J would comfortably recline and luxuriate in the armchair of the classic narcissist. He certainly held an inflated sense of self and his own importance. He had a complete lack of empathy and exploited others with a total absence of any guilt or shame. A bully's bully in every sense. As far as the job was concerned, he was exemplary. He was respected and revered. No one ever wanted to get on the wrong side of him.

The unsuspecting Maureen carried on in sublime ignorance; she even encouraged him with his hobby. Photography was a pleasant distraction from his busy police work. Bless, he was too shy to show his pictures to her. J assured Maureen that when he developed the right images to his own exacting standards that she would be the first to see them. Everything he said was still a work in progress and well, poor Maureen believed him. One day Maureen arrived home from a hectic day at school. She was dog tired and felt a little grubby after helping out with the P7 Netball practice. A good shower is what she needed. Mo had the house to herself. A hastily scribbled note left on the hallway table informed her that J was called into work on an urgent matter. It told her he would be back shortly after 6.00 PM. She smiled at his handwriting which for all his achievements was still really quite Neanderthal. She peeked at her watch, he would be home in an hour or so.

"Aww, bless. He works so hard."

Her form was excellent as she skipped upstairs and popped the shower on before heading into their bedroom. She began stripping off recklessly humming away at some random tune she'd heard on the radio that wouldn't let go. This was no sensuous striptease, more of an agricultural disrobing. She caught herself standing naked in the full-length mirror. Giggling, she gave herself a quick wink, she was alright, no, better than alright she was damn hot. Happy, she skipped towards the bathroom but stopped suddenly in her tracks when she spotted the box room door lying slightly open. This was never usually the case. She knew the curtains were always closed so naked she tiptoed in. She felt like a trespasser in this low light. This was his inner sanctum. She gasped. The sacred cupboard doors were also lying open. This was her chance to finally see what photographic gems he had stored away.

She reached up into the upper shelf and carefully lifted several envelopes. She noted that each envelope had an individually handwritten mark consisting of two letters followed by a series of random numbers then one final letter. It was his clumsy scrawl alright. A feeling of guilt briefly stopped with her but was quickly shooed away by her complete curiosity. She would never get another chance like this. His forbidden fruit beckoned and the urge was too powerful. She made a note of which order they were in then darted back into their bedroom. Maureen plonked herself down on their bed like an excited cherub. Nervously biting her bottom lip as she cautiously opened the first envelope, her mouth dropped open in shock. "Oh my." Then the second all the way to the fifth envelope. "My, my!" What she saw and the betrayal she felt disgusted her. Each image she looked at bore the same pattern of letters and number as its corresponding envelope.

For some unknown reason, she nervously selected one image from each envelope and placed them all carefully in the zipper section of her hand bag. Maureen then got herself up and made her way to where she had stood before. Naked and trembling, she stood herself upright in front of the large bedroom mirror. She was gasping and felt sick to the pits of her stomach. She could see the free-spirited sprite had gone. She felt degraded and dirty. She needed to cover herself. Sobbing, she quickly turned away.

J returned home shortly before six. His form was uber good. He reminded himself to get more film for his camera. He needed it the following Thursday. He called out for Maureen. Strange, no reply. He then came across the scribbled note left on the kitchen table. Frantically, he headed upstairs where he discovered all her belongings gone. It was then he spotted the box room door and cupboard open. His mouth became dry as he checked the cupboard and its contents. Nothing had been touched, everything was in place. With his hands now shaking, he locked the cupboard and then the box room door. The note was explicit. He was never to make contact with her ever again. He had a feeling, a bad feeling. It would be wise for him to let this sleeping dog lie. He never saw her again.

It was definitely well and truly over.

Chapter 5
The Delivery

A weak morning sun struggled to its knees then slowly rose above a cloudless Mediterranean horizon. A soft haze had freshly formed and was shimmering off the weathered stone harbour walls. The surrounding sea was clear all the way to the bottom. Old men perched like crows sat on ragged stools, casting their lines into the early morning blue. A chapel bell chimed in the distance heralding another hot day. Life was slowly stirring at the Port of Mersin located on the southern tip of Turkey. It was the shipping gateway to the north eastern coast of the Mediterranean and the European ports beyond.

The Oceana Perla slipped quietly out of port barely causing a wake. Gulls swept back and forth across her weathered bow angrily squawking and squealing. There was no rush for this 13-year-old voyager or its tiny but capable crew.

The Oceana Perla or 'Ocean Pearl' was around 430 feet in length with a 33-foot draught. In layman's terms she was a container ship. She wasn't the prettiest craft on the ocean by any means. A complete overhaul was long overdue but she was a busy ship that just kept on going. The Pearl was owned by the MSC Trading Services, a global trading enterprise and was one of their work horses. In vehicular terms she hadn't been rallied or raced. The Pearl was officially classified as an Intermodal Freight Transporter and was responsible for transporting and carrying Intermodal Containers. These containers came in only two sizes, 20 feet or 40 feet in length. A standard 10 feet in height and 8 feet of width.

Lars Vilfort, a rugged 58-year-old Dane was The Pearl's Captain; he had spent all his working life at sea and was never happier when he was in her embrace. Lars was just over six feet and came with a slim build. A man full of wiry strength and agile vitality. He had a full head of wavy steel hair accompanied by a 'Fisherman's Friend' styled beard. Lars had captained The Pearl for the past 9 years and knew every square inch of her. The sea was in his Viking blood and held no fears for him. Truth be told, Davy Jones's Locker would be his final bed of choice and with each rocking wave he was heading there.

Lars was popular with all of his crew who respected his knowledge and vast experience of all things oceanic. He was proficient in most international languages thus enabling him to communicate effectively with Harbour Masters the world over. He was a firm Captain and the standards he expected of others he kept himself. When Lars took his Captain's hat off, he was very much one of the boys, a serial prankster with a wicked sense of humour. Socially he enjoyed the movie nights and impromptu quizzes with his crew. On such occasions, he would partake of a bottle or three of ice-cold Danish beer.

His number two and close friend was Dimuth de Silva, a Sri Lankan. Dimuth had been with Lars on The Pearl for the last seven years and was a handsome 48-year-old with typical Sri Lankan features. He was 5 feet 4 inches and carried a slight paunch. He was softly spoken bordering on reverential with faltering eye contact. This was borne from a childhood stammer long past. Like Lars, he was multilingual and the pair could trip off into German, French or Russian or whatever tongue or nationality was called for or required. Dimuth, the quieter of the pair, was a practising Buddhist who enjoyed the company of a good book or quiet meditation. He shared his Captain's values and was equally respected and loved by the crew. Dimuth, like Lars, loved life on the ocean wave and its simple overtures. The real world was too hectic and demanding for him.

As The Pearl eased into open waters, Lars smiled broadly at Dimuth and handed him a cup of steaming hot coffee with a wee bit extra in it. It was their tradition in the hope for fair weather and calm seas. From the Captain's Bridge, all they could see was the aqua blue of the Mediterranean shimmering in all its beauty ahead.

"That's us now Dimuth, the world can't touch us here. Tell the boys in the engine room to trim her up to 20 knots for the foreseeable. The charts are there, you take the first four hours and I'll take over the next four. Any problems holler."

Dimuth took a sip from his steaming mug and smiling broadly at the taste nodded, "For sure, Captain Lars. The sea is like a billiard table. I don't think there will be any hollering today. I shall see you whenever."

With that, Lars disappeared en route to the Captain's Quarters and a bit of shut eye. Dimuth gave the orders to the boys in the engine room and felt The Pearl's speed increase as it eased up to a comfortable 20. She had 25 knots in her, at a push.

The Pearl was heading for the port of Rotterdam a distance of around 3,755 nautical miles. Lars had reckoned somewhere in and around eight days for the trip. There he would deposit most of his container load for onward transmission to mainland Europe. The final leg of the journey would be a 700 nautical mile two-day jaunt into the Port of Dublin. Fifteen containers were to be deposited there, three of which contained high-end ceramic bathroom wares all from the same company, Vitra Ceramics from Bozüyük, Turkey. Of the three containers, one was destined for the south of the island and the other two for the north. Everything about them was ship shape and squeaky clean. The accompanying paperwork was all in order and the sight of The Pearl was usually taken as a given that everything about her manifest was straight.

On the morning of the third day at sea a bewildered Dimuth was paged urgently to the ship's galley. Something or someone had turned up uninvited. As he stepped into the spotless cook house he could hear raised voices, one he was all too familiar with. If you closed your eyes and didn't have a Scooby about the German language, you could forgive yourself for thinking you were listening to Der Fuhrer, Adolf Hitler giving one of his rousing speeches at the Reichstag. Gunther, their Head Chef was in a rage. Bad form and a large chip on his shoulder (not the eating kind) was his usual form of choice. This volcanic rage was just a minor step up from his Germanic norm.

In cheffing terms, Gunther felt that he was too good to be a chef on a container ship; after all he had received classical training in London under the renowned Roux brothers. All of his yellowed teeth had been cut at their three-star Michelin restaurant 'Le Gavroche.' They had parted company when the brothers realised that his abilities were mediocre at best. Gunter fell short of the levels required for cheffing in the big leagues. He had been mortally wounded by Albert Roux's comments when on his last evening at 'Le Gavroche' his puff pastry, like himself had failed to rise to the occasion.

Snapping at Gunther's final straw, Albert Roux yelled, "OUT, OUT! I cannot make the silk purse out of this sow's ear!" With those cutting words ringing in his ears, Gunther left the super league of cooking forever. Aspirations of his own Michelin star 'Uber Eating House' evaporated down the sink hole of his pipe dreams. Gunther in Beau Geste fashion ran off to sea to forget the cruel twists and turns that cheffing life on land had dealt him.

Gunther Draxler was a native of Berlin. A man in his early forties who had been savagely mauled by the premature ageing gene. A passing glance would have nailed him down for mid-fifties. He was 5 feet 8 inches or so in height but looked much shorter by virtue of his stooping gate and his walrus wobbling waist. He had fine shoulder-length flyaway hair and large huckleberry hound doleful eyes. These mirrors to the soul had a tendency of making him look much sadder than he really was. Gunther was a chain smoker and marginal junkie. His 'hobby' hadn't helped with his blotchy complexion or his flaky skin. He always kept a supply of his 'kiffen' (cannabis) or as he would openly refer to it as "das grass" in his cabin.

There was nothing more Gunther enjoyed than a good spliff at the end of, or even at the start of, or now that I come to think of it any time of the day. Oh, and most nights as well. The problem with this particular voyage was that Gunther had forgotten to bring his life support system of Wacky Tabacky.

Dimuth, the peacemaker approached the Teutonic diva with platitudes and calming tones, "Gunther, Gunther. Beruhige dich, was ist los mein Freund?" Or in English, "Calm down, what's up, my friend?"

Gunter in hysterical Germanic English railed back, "Look what I am finding in my vegetable store behind the potatoes and the carrots. I am nearly having a heart attack from the fright he gives to me. Get him out, get him out, Schnell Schnell!" Dimuth raised an eyebrow recognising the all too familiar craving signs of the once promising chef. Gunter's eyes flashed this way and that as his cold sweats took grip. His cold turkey had nothing to do with that day's menu.

Cowering in the corner of the store was a young male all skin and bone. He was no more than 16 years old, with swarthy skin and tight black curly hair. He was wearing a faded sun-stained khaki jacket which drowned him, a blue t-shirt, canvas jeans and a pair of tattered trainers. His black eyes were like saucers, saucers that had witnessed much sorrow in too short a life. Dimuth shot Gunther a glance as if to say, "Enough." Smiling at the young male he spoke softly, "Hello, my name is Dimuth. Do you speak English?"

The trembling male nodded, "A little Sirs."

Dimuth smiled, "Up, up with you now, no harm will come your way.

Apologies for my friend, you gave him a scare that is all."

Gunther harrumphed and stormed off in the direction of the walk-in freezer, his jets needed cooling. "Come with me, I will take you to see the ship's Captain, he will know what to do with you." The young male nodded, slinging a bleached duffle bag over his shoulder then meekly followed.

A few minutes later after shuffling along dark corridors and scaling several flights of clanging metal stairs the pair arrived at the Captain's Quarters. Dimuth respectfully knocked and waited. "Come in, come in," came the reply.

The young male was led in. He was instantly amazed by what he saw, the Captain's Quarters was huge, it was bright with walls of a soft lemon hue. Several prints by the artist Cezanne hung tastefully in competition with garish pieces of pottery. These quirky items dazzled on light enhanced shelves. In fact, they were original Clarice Cliff pieces which Lars had fallen in love with and had added to over the years. Mozart was playing softly from a stylus and to the young male this was the most splendid room he had ever been in.

The morning's events were conveyed to Lars who sat quietly behind his desk nodding and gently drumming his fingers. He eyed the young interloper whose head was bowed. He noticed that his hands fidgeted nervously deep in his oversized jacket pockets. Dimuth spoke softly in his usual straightforward fashion. Lars got to wondering what his story was, what series of life's twists and turns had placed this barely young man in his path? His eyes could see a helpless fear wrapped up in a parcel of dusty and dishevelled hope. Dimuth's eyes mirrored his own with compassion.

Releasing a heavy sigh, Lars rose from his old hacked leather chair, it always creaked, creaked in protest at being bolted to the floor. Lars would often chuckle at their similarities. Both firmly bolted, the chair to the floor and Lars to the sea. As he made his way over to the fridge Lars briefly glanced through his porthole, seeing the timeless ocean and feeling the powerful engines beat beneath his feet. Lars became more relaxed, more himself. He found himself quietly humming to Mozart, realising he had plenty of time to think all this through; after all nobody had been killed.

Lars reached into his fridge and gathered three bottles of ice-cold water. He returned to his chair placing them on his desk motioning the pair to take a seat. Lars smiled then calmly leaned across his desk and offered a hand of friendship. Excitedly the young stowaway sprung to his feet. Anxiously, he thrust his right hand out of his pocket, scattering poppy seeds all over the cabin floor. Panicking, he fell to his knees frantically apologising, "I'm very sorry, Sirs for this. Please forgive me."

A smiling Dimuth joined him on his knees and the pair quickly gathered the seeds up. When finished he took comfort from the smiling Captain, worse things had happened at sea. The pair then shook hands. The Captain spoke, "Hello young man, my name is Captain Lars Vilfort. I'm Danish, I hope you can understand me. I am Captain of this lovely old ship the 'Oceana Perla' or The Pearl as we call it. Dimuth here is my number two. Poppy seeds I see, if that's all you've had to eat you must be starving as well as thirsty. You have caused quite a stir this morning. Gunther our sensitive chef, was most surprised by your appearance in his vegetable store. He is very precious about his greens as the British would say. Please, please have a drink. Are you hungry? I'm sure you're hungry?"

The young male tentatively looked up nodding his head. He then grabbed one of the bottles on the desk. In a flash, he had unscrewed its plastic top and began gorging the freezing water. Lars casually lifted one of the two remaining bottles and lobbed it into Dimuth's lap subtly winking. He then lifted the remaining bottle for himself carefully unscrewing the top before taking a measured sip.

When the young male had drained the bottle, Lars spoke again, "I hope you don't think me rude but I was just wondering, apart from how you got yourself on board, just what are you actually doing here?"

Laughing he went on, "You see none of us were expecting you. Perhaps you would tell us in your own good time who you are and what your future plans are for us?"

Lars then returned to his fridge and retrieved another bottle of water. His guest who was clearly parched feverishly unscrewed the lid before taking another huge swig, some of which went down the wrong way. Retching hard, he coughed several times before looking over to Dimuth and then up at Lars. With an embarrassed expression, he falteringly spoke, "Captain Lars, I thank you for your kindness. My name is Ozan Karaki. I am 16 years old and the last of my family. My mother died giving the birth to me and my father died at sea when I was a baby. I was raised by my grandparents up to now. My grandmother she died two years ago and my grandfather, well he died three weeks ago of a fever, but he was very old. I'm thinking he stayed alive so long just for me. That is to say for my sake. We lived in a tiny flat in Mersin, it was rented you see. So, when he died, I of course had to leave, I had no places to go and that is why I am here. Oh, (giggling) and how I got on your lovely ship, that for me was easy. I followed behind the vegetable men when they boarded the ship with their supplies. They thought I was crew and your crew thought I was one of them. When they left, I hid in the store." Now smiling, "I'm glad I was found, I was so hungry. All I had to eat were those poppy seeds!"

Lars felt a great pity for the boy with sad eyes. He gazed across at Dimuth. His head was bowed. "Ozan, I'm sorry for all your sadness but how do we fit in with your plans?"

Ozan grinned, "Captain Lars Sir, I believe you are sailing to Ireland. I too wish to go there. I hear it's beautiful and green all of the year. When I get there, I will get a job and live a happy life. If God is willing, maybe even meet a beautiful Irish girl with the red hair, then we fall in love and have many beautiful children. It will be perfect, you will see. God will take care of me."

Lars sighed an agonised sigh, "Ozan my friend, it's not quite as simple as that. To even get into Ireland you need a passport. To work there you need a work permit, then you need their government's permission to reside, that is to live there. I take it you have none of these things?"

Ozan looked crestfallen, then his eyes suddenly widened and his face lit up, "I am thinking I could sneak into Ireland with no passport or papers. I know of many Turkish people there; I will find them they will look after me. Please Captain Lars, there is nothing left for me in Turkey. Can you not help me?"

Lars gazed into the pleading eyes, his stomach churning. Every ounce of his being wanted to help Ozan but the stakes were too high. If caught he would face a huge fine and maybe even jail time. He didn't need to seek Demuth's opinion. The pair thought too much alike, the risks were too great. Lars returned to his battered leather seat, plonking himself down with a tired sigh. He looked Ozan in the eye and spoke from the heart, "Ozan, Ozan, my hands are very much tied. Maritime Laws are very strict on these matters. The International Maritime Organisation stipulates that all stowaways must be reported to the relevant port authorities. Regarding you, that would mean the port of origin in Mersin. Our next port of call is in Rotterdam where you must be medically examined."

Ozan interrupted, "But Captain Lars, I am not even sick. I am very well as you can see."

Lars frowned, "But these are the laws upon which we are bound. I would even have to report your presence to the port at Dublin, even though you wouldn't be getting off! My crew now knows about you. If any of them reported me trying to help you, my career as a ship's Captain is kaput! You're young, your whole life's in front of you. I'm getting on, a man nearing his sixties. If I were caught my life in effect would be over. I'm sorry, but I just can't help you."

The room fell silent. Ozan nodded slowly, his eyes watering, "Captain Lars, I'm so sorry. I never realised my actions would cause such much trouble to you. You must take me back to Mersin, of course."

Dimuth sighed, "Ozan, we understand you meant no harm. We'll take good care of you until your return, it's also our legal obligation to you. We have a spare cabin which I will make ready. First, I will have Gunther prepare you something to eat, don't mind him, his bark's worse than his bite, you'll see. Now please, come with me."

The pair left, closing the door quietly behind them leaving Lars alone with his thoughts and the soft strains of Mozart. "Decisions, decisions. When to make my report, that is the question. For the poor boy's sake."

Lars however was completely unaware that Ozan was the least of his worries on board The Pearl. Located inside one of the two containers marked for Northern Ireland were three innocuous cases. Each contained 300 lbs. of tightly wrapped cannabis with a street value of three million pounds, one million pounds a case. Deals had been done in the shadowy underworld and the appropriate palms had been greased, no finer place to hide this deadly stash than the good old Oceana Perla.

The Oceana Perla would continue on her journey to the port of Rotterdam. This would take her another five days or so. Following Rotterdam another two days would see her berthed in Dublin. The weather would be kind to The Pearl as the old work horse creaked and groaned steadily onwards. Dropping containers off and picking containers up, all done with the minimum of fuss by her very proficient Captain and crew. She was like an old dowager doing her rounds. All in all, she would be back in the Port of Mersin with Ozan in just under a fortnight. Fingers crossed!

Chapter 6
Bomb Scares, Who Cares!

It was Friday, 6 July 1983 and an unofficial State of Emergency wasn't announced. The skies were a brilliant blue and void of any clouds which were on a 24-hour strike. The sun had its shades on and sat all buffed up as if on steroids. Swallows soaring high above would appear at breathtaking speed darting this way and that relishing the abundant heat currents. Today would turn out to be the hottest day of the year. With little or no breeze, the temperature rose to a perilous 26 degrees centigrade. It was seriously hot and the natives normally as pale as ghosts were turning a lovely lobster red. They were way out of their comfort zone and simply not coping.

At 11.30 AM, a cream-coloured armoured Cortina trundled slowly through the main entrance of Ormeau Park. The old park was sandwiched between the Ravenhill Road and Ormeau Road of South and East Belfast.

Old folks sat on park benches sweltering with knotted hankies perched atop their eggheads, gasping and nodding with tooth gapped smiles as tomorrow's world raced by. Children screaming like banshees ran topless amongst the glossy hedgerows and colourful shrubs, much to the chagrin of those high-brow readers seeking the quiet shade of a mighty oak.

Both the driver-side and front passenger doors of the crawling armoured Cortina, hung lazily open in an attempt to attract cooler air in. These war wagons were fitted with air con but these units seldom if ever worked. The choice was blasting hot air or dusty dry hot air. Today its lucky officers controlled the width of the open doors by their outer foot and arm, both easing their door in and out as necessary, narrowly avoiding hapless pedestrians from getting clobbered as they slowly trundled by. The vehicle on that particular scorcher was AM70 driven by the glamourous Woman Constable Shelley McCann, 23 years of age with three years' service under her narrow belt. Her work partner and designated Observer was Constable Arnie Savage, they were an unlikely pair.

Arnie was the Senior Man in A Section; he was an experienced officer at 47 years of age, with 22 years on the job. Arnie's belt wasn't quite so narrow which had bothered his wife enough to bring it up at and now enough for the ruffled Arnie to do something about it.

Shelley began to purr strangely, "Mmm…" A puzzled Arnie stirred from his double-glazed gaze looking over at his driver. Her face was a picture of unbridled pleasure. Ahead the sight of a yellow and white bandstand slowly came into view just beyond a copse of languishing copper beeches. Arnie suddenly screamed out, "Watch out Shell, for fuck's sake!"

With the reflexes of Nelson Piquet, that year's Formula One champ, Shell flicked her wrists without blinking, narrowly missing two old dears shuffling along on walking sticks.

"Ohhh bless us all," one cried out, turning white with fear. Her elderly bestie froze to the spot, convinced she had just caught a glimpse of the grim reaper.

Arnie leaned his portly frame out and treated the pair to his movie star smile. Waving at the two old biddies he purred, "Smashing day for a 'wee' dander ladies, enjoy." He then sprockled himself back into his bucket seat as beads of sweat glistened off his furrowed brow.

Shell remained glacier calm and focused though her breathing was becoming heavier. "Mmm. I can't wait to get my hands on you, I'm going to have all of you, I'll not be denied a second longer."

Arnie's jaw dropped trying to find the words to come out, but his brain had turned to mush, "Sh, Sh, Shel, but, but Shell, eh, what?" Had he just died and gone to heaven?

Shelley still purring eased their armoured vehicle between the side of the yellow bandstand and a dense mass of overgrown laurel hedging. She licked her cherry lips then skipped out to the rear of their vehicle flipping the boot. She then hastily undid the straps of her heavy flak jacket and in one heave pulled it over the top of her head and tossed it in the boot. Shelley allowed her back a long stretch, freedom, released from her Kevlar prison for a few short minutes. Arnie could hear the purring as she scurried back in the driver's seat. The next thing was Shelley smiling wildly and licking her young lips at the recoiling Arnie.

With flickering eyebrows, "Well, shall we then, pard?" Arnie was scared, very scared. He heard a mouse-like squeak reply, "Shall we what, our Shell?"

Shell's eyes widened, "Get stuck in, Arnie." Arnie didn't know whether to laugh or cry. Shell expertly threw her left arm backwards in the gap between the two front seats and after a quick feel around retrieved a white paper bag which had been hiding under her raincoat. "Ta daa, check these beauties out, made fresh this morning, two amazing ham, egg, lettuce and tomato floury baps from White's Bakery just below the station. They've a thin skimming of garlic mayo, that's their hidden secret. They're scrummy, just what the doctor ordered."

Shell grabbed one and without further ado launched her mouth at it trying to force it all in at once, she threw her head back as she munched on in ecstasy. For sure her cheeks were going to explode. Arnie couldn't quite believe his eyes. For one so beautiful she sure could pack it in. Shell returned to the present and attempted to speak, much like a chubby bunny. "Wha… you 'avin?"

Arnie assumed a righteous tone, "Me. Well Shell, I'm on a special chemical diet. To help me shave those few spare ounces off and get me back to my fighting weight." Shell had just about adiosed her first bap and had the second one in her hand. Nodding, she gulped down the last of her first and quickly gave a swift burp. Her mouth temporarily empty was free to engage, "Arnie love, chemical diet. What the fuck are you on about?"

Arnie, slightly wounded, continued, "Wait to you see what I've got here wee pet."

Arnie did his own reaching into the back seat and pulled out a cream plastic lunch box. It used to be white but he'd had it for nigh on 20 years. Excitedly he removed the lid in triumph, "Well Shell, what do you think?"

Shelley had her second bap up to her lips but was forced to stall at the sight of the contents in Arnie's box. The sight alone made her retch. "Arnie love, sweet mother of God. What the good fuck is that. It looks yucky and stinks to high heaven?"

Arnie oblivious smiled, he was now holding a fork older than himself. "Prunes and cottage cheese wee love, prunes and cottage cheese, guaranteed to lose a stone in a week, a week that is."

Shelley retched as Arnie speared a prune drizzled in purpley stained cottage cheese.

"Yum, yum, it's tasty. Want to try some, wee partner?" Shelley lurched out of their wagon and parked her backside on the front bonnet. She was now facing the Ormeau Golf Course on the other side of the park fence. Biting into her second bap she mumbled, "No thanks, pard. I'm all good here. I'll watch me some golf while you knock yourself out on your chemical diet, Mmm. NOT!"

Tony Speers and Derek Grant were slumped on two knackered chairs in the station yard to the rear of Mountroyal Station. Both were topless, soaking up the rays and lapping up any breeze that came their way. They'd been working out in the station gym located in a huge portacabin in the rear car park. It was half gym, half changing rooms; this area was also allocated to the part-time reserve police officers, in their support of the full-time members during those darker days. The gym bit consisted of a creaky running machine which despite its abuse, age and total lack of maintenance never broke down. It could be heard running all through the day and into many nights helping the gang with their general fitness and aching stress, an enemy from which they could never escape.

The gym also housed a vast assortment of free weights, these had been left, donated or abandoned by former members of the Mountroyal party. If you knew what you were about there was enough there for you. Derek had been on the runner and had just blitzed three miles. Tony had been on the weights, it was his arms, back and shoulders day. His arms were buffed and looking mighty fine. Derek described them to Tony as "His guns of the Navarone." They shared a chuckle. Resting on the ground beside them was a Motorola hand-held police radio which their ears were glued to.

That day's vibes were taking a downward turn. The radio was full of bomb alerts and bomb scares in the Belfast City centre. The Belfast crews were being stretched with one alert after another. DMSU call signs (Divisional Mobile Support Units) used for public disorder and rioting were deployed and, on the ground, it was a frantic race to clear buildings of people and save lives. Most times the Provos would let the security forces know what vehicle the bomb was in so a deadly game of cat and mouse would follow, not discounting the 'come on', where details of the vehicle would be a hoax in a bid to lure the security forces into a deadly trap via other explosive devices or a sniper attack. The radio crackled with strained transmissions as crews responded to their deadly tasks. From where Derek and Tony sat, they could hear multiple sirens wailing in the distance as Belfast City Centre was being reduced to a virtual lockdown. It only took one huge bomb to go off and the loss of lives for the Provos to achieve their goal. Global attention for their bloody struggle.

Derek gazed across at Tony, "Not looking good today, Tony, son. It's only a matter of time before those bastards bring a bomb into the East!"

Tony ran his fingers through his black hair. He had never been involved in a bomb scene and was happy to wait a while longer. Holding his finger up to his lips went, "Shhhhh, they can hear you!"

The rear station door flew open and out bounced Tweety carrying a tray load. "Behold, I come bearing gifts for my masters. Drag another couple of chairs there, lads, Aggie's joining us." Derek's face lit up like an orphan on Christmas Day as he dragged two chairs over from the side of the building. "Tweety you're a wee bastard, I've just run three miles, what you got there?"

All of a sudden, a deep boom could be heard coming from the city gripping at their insides. Reports of an explosion outside the Littlewoods store started to come through. They all looked city-wards and waited as a pall of thick black smoke slowly rose into the clear blue summer sky. Tweety stood rigid, tray in hand through clenched teeth snarled, "Bastards!"

Aggie the 70-year-old plus VAT cleaner trotted out from the kitchen in an agitated state. "Dear God fellas, what in the name was that? It sounded awful close?"

Derek smiled, "Nothing to worry about, Aggie. A wee bomb in town. Littlewoods has taken a bit of a hit but the boys had the place cleared before it went off. So far so good, no injuries reported."

Aggie sighed then smiled, "Aww, that's good news at least Derek, though I was planning to return a pair of trousers to them the marra. Just a bit too tight around my backside, too many buns and cakes. No thanks to you Mister Tweety Pie!"

Tweety laughed, "Aggie love, if you cut me, do I not bleed? Come here and take a seat before this lot melts, it's your favourite, strawberries and ice cream with strawberry and chocolate sauce. Oh, and a couple of wafers. Enjoy!"

Aggie erupted with her infectious laughter, "Oh I think I've just died and gone till heaven. All this and two topless hunks sitting in the sunshine. As for you Mr. Tweety, you're the worst thing what's ever happened till me. You and your home-grown strawberries, an inch on my lips and a mile on my hips, heaven bless us all."

They all laughed and got stuck in trying to feign nonchalance as the hand-held radio continued with more bomb calls and frantic radio transmissions coming from all corners of the city. It all felt strangely surreal. Aggie got up, "Right fellas, give me them plates, I'll tidy up. Back till your work nae. Be on with yez."

Derek laughed, "Who needs me when you're in charge Aggie. OK Tony, a quick shower then back to the grind. Cheers Tweety, just what the doctor ordered."

Tweety nodded, "Welcome boss and thanks for doing the dishes, Aggie."

Ten minutes later they were all back at their work. AM71 crew consisting of Heavenly and the Preacher were at the Shelbourne Road, a classier side of the patch, a well-heeled sought after residential area. It came at you all tree lined with detached Victorian dwellings. Its long driveways usually displayed the latest wheels that status could afford. If you lived there, you had definitely arrived. Heavenly stood just outside number 33 biting her bottom lip, her face a picture of concentration. She had a 55/22 (a) booklet in her hand known as the Road Traffic Accident (RTA) booklet force-wide. This little gem led the officer dealing with a road traffic accident by the nose. From A all the way to Z, missing nothing out. It covered every aspect of his investigation in a sequential fashion. It was a life saver for the junior ranks.

She was intently finalising a sketch of the scene of a road traffic accident as though her life depended on it. The actual accident had occurred the previous week and she had recorded all the vital measurements then. These related to both vehicles involved including points of impact and what manner of debris was caused. These measurements were all taken from a focal fixed point. On this occasion, a lamppost located just outside number 33. Today was all about the basic topography of the Shelbourne Road, width of the road, width of the pavement, road markings, traffic signs and street lighting.

The Preacher was standing nonchalantly under the shade of an old Acer, a purple Japanese maple tree. His arms were folded, quietly watching his pard hard at it. A pale blue RUC issue tape measure was cupped in his large hand should the need for any further measurements arise. He had a lazy ear on the hectic goings on in the city centre as a deep *Boom!* was heard. Heavenly looked up with raised eyebrows.

Preacher responded, "Littlewoods. They got everybody out in time. Any number of bomb scares on the go at the moment." Heavenly nodded with a relieved expression and carried on with her sketch. Preacher had snatched a quick peek; it wasn't the greatest he'd ever seen. He could have done a better job in a tenth of the time, but hey ho nobody's perfect. Though in the Preacher's eyes, she just about was.

A warm breeze pitched a faded bunch of pink blossoms and lazily tossed them up the street. The heat was clambering up to unbearable, especially for Heavenly and the Preacher wearing their dark green heavy woollen uniform. Heavy flak jackets didn't help their cause one bit. What the Preacher wouldn't give for a nice ice-cold glass of water, or a jump off the pier into the freezing waters of Strangford Lough. Naturally no jump would be complete without his golden retriever dog, Bud. His heart ached for his bestie who was probably dozing on their weathered porch that very moment.

"Wish I was there with you bud," he whispered into the blossomed breeze.

"Are we well, Constable?" The Preacher jumped, spinning around instinctively feeling for his handgun. Relieved, he found a miniscule elderly lady standing beside him. She was holding a silver tray containing two sparkling tumblers of lemonade clinking with heavy ice. She must easily have been a woman in her eighties and no more than five feet in height. Her silver hair was swept back tight in a bun held together by a beautiful coral hair clasp. She was elegantly attired in a splendid blend of plum and silver hues. On her feet were a simple pair of brown leather sandals.

Gathering his composure, the Preacher engaged, "Afternoon madam, it's a hot one today."

With sparkling eyes and not without a hint of devilment she giggled, "Precisely Constable. Why do you think I'm standing here with these two tumblers of homemade lemonade? You pair looked as though you could do with the refreshment. Come, come join me in the summer house for five minutes. The job can spare you that much." No second invites were needed, within a minute the pair were sat on two huge wicker recliners, heavily padded and worn from many summers of sweet repose.

The summer house was located at the far end of a mature back garden. It was a large wooden framed structure, matt white in colour with huge glass windows. Borders edging an immaculate lawn were in a spectacular blaze of summer colour. The young police officers sat in silence lost in their vista and the chorus of the industrious worker bees. A large marmalade coloured cat cruised lazily through the flower beds.

Heavenly leaned forward and smiled at the old lady, "How very kind of you for this lovely treat. We don't get these perks every day. I'm Stephanie and my partner is Peter by the way. We're stationed at Mountroyal Police Station." Pete nodded realising he hadn't made the introductions. He would pay for that.

The lady looked at the pair and laughing said, "Well how nice to meet you both. If you don't mind me saying you make a lovely pair. (Pete's heart flipped.) I'm Nancy Flynn and I've this whole place all to myself, since my Vincent died seven years ago. He was a surgeon at the Royal Victoria Hospital you know and a very good one at that. Well, it's just been me and Montague, the cat or Monty as I call him. We're both getting on a bit, wondering which one of us is going to go first. Oh, I do hope it's going to be me."

Nancy gazed wistfully down the garden lost in memories of summers past. "Come to think of it, the garden was Vinnie's little treasure. Everywhere I look, I see him smiling at me. Whether it be in his glorious dahlias or the splendour of the cascading purple campanula down there in the shaded border. Look, just down there, tucked in behind the cherry blossom."

Just then, Monty slid into the summer house unperturbed like a confident thug. He was in full purr mode softly gliding across the floor before carefully dumping his furry frame on Nancy's feet. Nancy giggled infectiously and rubbed Monty's exposed belly hard eliciting even louder purrs of joy. Looking seriously at the pair she exclaimed, "Losing Vincent was horrid, but to lose Monty would be quite unthinkable!" Stephanie shot Pete a glance, laughter wasn't very far away.

Less than half a mile away Gary Weaver and Wee Mo were in deep cover. They were lying low at the Malone Rugby Club neatly tucked away in Gibson Park just off the Cregagh Road. It's a large family friendly club with a modern club house purpose built for viewing club matches from the comfort of the first-floor bar. The club was founded in 1892 and is steeped in a rich rugby tradition, it's a focal point for rugby followers in East Belfast.

During the winter months, it would be a hub of activity, serving beers, burgers and hot stews to rugby lovers young and old. Outside in all weathers its five pitches would be in full swing. For 80 minutes, opposing teams would go at it hammer and tongs. Sometimes punches would fly and dark arts performed as teams fought for the upper hand. Come the sound of the final whistle it was all handshakes and back slaps and a piping hot communal shower followed by the hug of a cold pint. That was the winter past, now it seemed a world away. Today in the off season, the shutters were down and all was quiet save for the hot summer breeze and excited bird song.

The pair had just bought two ice lollies from the BP Garage at Ladas Drive. Local knowledge had taken them up Daddy Winkers Lane and on to the familiar quiet of the pavilion.

Tony Speers had detailed them as a beat patrol that morning. Wee Mo was beyond excited. For her it was a day of freedom from the security box. Their designated call signs were AM30 and 30 Alpha. Their duty on paper was to patrol the main Woodstock, Cregagh and Castlereagh Roads for clues relating to the ongoing spate of thefts, thefts of the frozen meat by youths in the area. All of this looked fine and dandy but in reality, there was nothing going on. That morning, the pair had engaged with the good folks of East Belfast trying to pick up any snippets as to who the kiddy thieves were or who was behind it all. Sometimes all it took was just one whisper but it was finding that whisper, the whisper wouldn't find you. This is when their superior social skills came into play. As far as public relations went Wee Mo and Gary were right up there, they were points up, this pair could bullshit for Ireland.

With their flak jackets off, they sat on freshly mown grass beside number one pitch. They were well out of the sight of any prying eyes. Gary was listening in on all the chaotic radio transmissions coming from the heart of the city. He had an earpiece attached to his radio while Wee Mo for those few moments, had her radio turned off not wanting to give their location away. Gary glanced at Wee Mo raising his eyebrows.

"Any second now, pard... One's due to go off at Littlewoods. Meanwhile we're here basking in the summer sunshine. Me with my 'Porky Pineapple' and you with your 'Joker'. At times, it just doesn't seem fair."

Wee Mo nodded, screwing up her nose squeaking the way her voice came over, "Aww Gary, fair's got nothing to do with it. Some folks are hell bent on death and destruction and the rest of us are trying to stop it. Today, the city centre crews are getting it, tomorrow it might be us. Hope not though!"

Giggling, she accidentally bit off a huge tip of her 'Joker' and was hit with an instant brain freeze. "Ugh, Oh my Gog Gary. I've got me some grain feeze goin' on!" They laughed.

BOOOOOOOOOOOM!

No words were needed. Gary shook his head as tension gripped his stomach and his chest tightened. "Fuck!" Anxiously worrying about the innocent souls caught up in the blast Gary mumbled, "Poor sods."

Their radios crackled into life. The velvety soft tones of the king of controllers, Wes Lamont, calmly came through, "Any Alpha Mike, Alpha Sierra call signs to respond to an urgent CODE 25 bomb warning! Recognised codeword's been used. Wyse Byse, Cregagh Road. Blue transit van, we're looking for a blue transit van, boys and girls. Look out for the 'come on'. Beware of the 'come on'! They've given us 30 minutes before she goes off, repeat 30 minutes!"

A split second later the air waves were alive. "Uniform AM70 responding!" Shell and Arnie sped out of the Ormeau Park with their blues and twos in full song. "Likewise, AM71 Uniform."

Heavenly's transmission was flat calm mirroring the Preacher's expression. Their vehicle tore off down the Shelbourne Road with wheels spinning heading in the direction of the Cregagh Road. Nancy stood at the end of her drive as the armoured Cortina sped off. A soft cherry blossomed breeze stroked at her cheek. She was cradling Montague and absent mindedly swaying from side to side. The comfortable silence of the street returned. Nancy suddenly became overcome with emotion and felt herself well up.

Burying her head deep into his furry chest, she sobbed, "Please dear God keep that lovely couple safe. Keep them all safe!" She turned and slowly made her way back to her summer blooms, bees and bird song.

A thin nasally tone quickly followed in.

"Uniform from AS19, responding (Sergeant Plank.) Call signs AS50 and 51 will put in traffic diversions at the Cregagh Road, Ardenlee Avenue and Woodstock Road, Ravenhill Avenue junctions. They will divert all city and country bound traffic away from the Wyse Byse Store on the Woodstock Road. My call sign will try to locate the blue transit van. Out."

Wes Lamont calmly responded, "Excellent AS19, AS50 and 51 many thanks and out."

Tony Speers and Derek Grant burst out of Mountroyal Station in the red supervisory armoured Escort. Derek, who was no mean pilot, was driving. Tony shot Derek a glance, "I hate to say it but the Plank's come good."

Derek laughed, "Give him time Tony lad, he'll find a way to fuck things up. He's a natural!"

Gary and Wee Mo fled the rugby club and were now dashing down the Cregagh Road. They could see the Wyse Byse premises some 300 yards away. Gary panting, made a radio transmission, "Uniform from AM30, me and my partner are on foot. We're on the Cregagh Road heading city-wards, Wyse Byse is a couple of hundred yards away, we'll start clearing the buildings and carry out any suspicious vehicle checks while we're at it. We could use a hand with the buildings." The heat, the heat. Gary was sweating hard, his heart thumping, a blend of adrenalin, anxiety and fear.

Wes was already a step ahead like a soothing balm. Molasses.

"AM30. Roger on your last. Silver Section Mobile Support Unit are on their way from the city centre. That's six Land Rover crews at your disposal."

Derek Grant and Tony arrived at the Woodstock Road, Ravenhill Avenue cordon. The AS51 crew had just arrived and got set up. They were swiftly diverting all country bound traffic away from the Wyse Byse premises and down Ravenhill Avenue. Time was not their friend. Although the traffic was now being diverted, the natives of East Belfast were still casually drifting out onto the Woodstock Road from the adjoining side streets oblivious to the danger at hand, to them it was just a delightful summer's day. There were eight streets in all within the cordoned off area of the Woodstock Road.

Their radio crackled. "Uniform from Silver 1. Silver India transmitting (Inspector). Arrival Woodstock Road, Ravenhill Avenue cordon. Instructions please."

Derek leapt out of their vehicle and placed his forage cap calmly on his head. He had danced this deadly dance once or twice before. For Tony, this was his first time, his nerves jangled and his brains scrambled to a gooey mush. If he wasn't careful, he could find himself in full-on flap mode. He decided to stick tight to his boss, who appeared to be totally under control. Just then six grey Land Rovers appeared powering up the Woodstock Road. They were in full blues and twos mode. All lights flashing and sirens blaring. The Land Rovers screeched to a hard halt at the cordon. Their powerful engines snarling acrid fumes into the heavy air. A helicopter overhead added to the already pulsating volume.

Derek went to his pocket radio, "Uniform from AM5, arrival Woodstock Road, Ravenhill Avenue cordon. Roger Uniform can you confirm A.T.O have been tasked and are on their way? (Ammunition Technical Officer or Bomb Disposal Unit)"

Uniform responded immediately, "AM5, Uniform. Roger on both your last. Out."

The front passenger door of the lead Land Rover, Silver 1 swung open. A slight male figure alighted popping his Inspector's hat on, slightly skew-whiff. Derek smiled, it was his old golfing mate Stevie Campbell or should we say Inspector Campbell, 48 years with 23 years' service. Stevie was their man in charge. The head honcho of the Silver Section Mobile Support Unit. Derek went to his radio again, "Silver 1 from AM5, eyes left!" He watched as Stevie glanced over.

Seeing Derek, he gave a quick thumbs up and dashed across. The pair were great friends but this was no time or place for jokes or idle chit chat. Stevie puffing hard barked out, "Lovely day for it, fellas. Now what the fuck do you need?"

Derek laughed, "Stevie son, we need plods at the side streets within the cordon to keep the bodies back. Two of your crews should do it. The rest of your troops to clear the shops, businesses and private dwellings. By my reckoning, we have about 15 minutes. Got it?"

Stevie nodded, "Have we identified the offending vehicle yet?"

Tony yelled pointing above the din, "Aye. We think it's that blue Ford Transit up there facing the Wyse Byse Store. They're checking it out now!"

Stevie nodded again, "No worries, we'll copy on your last. Catch yez laters. I've got things to do, places to go and people to see."

Shouting over his shoulder as he dashed back to his unit he shouted, "Stay safe y'old bollocks."

Derek laughed and returned, "You too, Stevie!"

A minute later the street cordons were in place. The Woodstock Road suddenly became eerily deserted save for the police on the ground ushering the good folks to safety. Gary and Wee Mo arrived puffing and panting at the Cregagh Road, Ardenlee Avenue cordon. Suddenly AM71 roared in on full blues and twos screeching to a halt on the other side of the road. The Preacher and Heavenly leapt out.

Gary shouted across at the mobile patrol pair, "We'll take the country bound side, you two do the city bound side. The guys from the Silvers are working their way up towards us from the other end. Good luck!" The Preacher gave a thumbs up and the pair dashed into the large front windowed Wyse Byse store.

The Wyse Byse store was a stylish affair. It sold all manner of goods relating to the home. Items of household furniture such as suites, beds, fire places, mirrors, stools, pots and pans, cutlery, vases, you name it they had it. Oh, and in the right season, as this was, clothing for that special day at the beach or that ramble into the glorious countryside. A carefully placed group of mannequins or shop dummies to the rest of us was presented stylishly at the shop entrance. They were wonderfully clad in the latest summer fashion portraying the perfect family. Minus, of course, the shouting, bawling, coke and ketchup strains of brats who didn't want to be there. Shopping and shedding cash was what Wyse Byse was all about. A magical shopping experience heightened with the twinkly hits from the seventies sung, not by the original artists, all good quality at affordable prices.

The Preacher burst in yelling at a young cashier who had been absorbed with the state of her fingernails and absent mindedly worrying a chunk of Wrigley's gum to death. "Page me the boss please. It's urgent!"

The young woman jumped with fright causing a bubble she'd carefully been nurturing to explode all over her moon cratered face. Seeing the Preacher's expression through her bubble gummed lens she knew better than to ask why. She reached straight for the pager and comically bellowed, "Mr. Prentass to the front counter urgently please. Mr. Prentass please!"

The Preacher momentarily marvelled, for this, bubble gummed face and all, was the broadest Belfast accent he'd ever heard. He'd never heard a twangier one. Meanwhile Heavenly briskly closed down all the other check outs, calmly ordering the dismayed shoppers to set their shopping down and proceed to the rear of the store. There was STILL no sign of Mr. Prentass.

Somewhere inside the Preacher snapped. Normally he was a man for all seasons and all occasions. In the right setting, he could come over as the sweetest of the sweet, beloved by children and little old ladies. In a different setting when the stage lighting cast a darker mood a more dangerous creature lurked, cross the Preacher at your peril. Unbeknown to Mr. Prentass, he had inadvertently crossed the Preacher's Rubicon. He had unwittingly passed the point of no return. A full minute had lapsed and in that day's currency a minute was a long time.

Looking at the young assistant, he growled, "Hand me that pager please Miss, then go get the rear of the store opened up. We've got to get these people out."

The young assistant's mouth opened in terror, "But Mr. Prentass doesn't allow anyone…"

The Preacher raised his hand signalling her to stop. He then reached across her counter and gently peeled her small hand from the pager. He could see the horror on her face and mouthed at her, "It will be OK. I promise." She still looked mortified.

The Preacher then raised the mic to his lips and relayed the following message, "This is an urgent police announcement. There is a suspect device outside which we are treating as serious. The IRA have claimed the device and have given us a recognised code word. Would everyone in the store please leave what you are doing and make your way to the rear of the building in a calm and orderly fashion. The rear door will be opened whereupon you will all exit. Please stay well away from the Woodstock Road until advised otherwise. We only have a few minutes to spare. Thank you."

A mild state of hysteria ensued with shoppers of all shapes and sizes bouncing each other out of the way in a scene resembling that Hollywood Classic, 'Rollerball.'

"Out of the road, you fat bitch." rang out in screeching tones, as well as, "Who the good fuck do you think you're talking till busted bake!" Hilde Garde dump tackled raging Isolde in hair nets and carpet slippers. A few ended up on their backsides. Others now on their knees kept on going. These Wagnerian heroines eventually arrived at the back of the store puffing and grunting hard. There the young assistant nervously stood by the large rear exit door, key in trembling hand, blocking their flight.

A dark brown wooden door flew open barely hanging on to its hinges. An austere name plate attached rattled bearing the name ANDREW PRENTASS. Out from a fussy looking office flew a raging inferno of a man. The young assistant nearly wet herself. "Mr. Prentass. I'm awful sorry but it's the police…"

Screaming banshees were wailing from the back of the store, "Hey Prentass, get your ass in gear. There's a fuckin bomb about to go off outside. Hurry the fuck up! My hubby's in the UVF!" and "Aye, mine is in the UDA. If you like your knee caps where they are open these fuckin back doors. Pronto Tonto!"

Heavenly watched on, as curious as she could be under the circumstances. Mr. Prentass stormed out, a grandiose figure just into his mid-fifties. His silver hair was a tad too long and reckless. It flounced in a new romantic style which didn't fit well with his advancing years. He was plump but not in the 'pleasantly' category. His once attractive face was a ruddyish complexion favoured by the heavy smokers and closet boozers of the day. His jacket, shirt and tie combo were fine, corduroy, cotton and silk. He sported a pair of plum flannels which fluttered. Sadly, and most nauseating of all, a pair of pale grey mock leather moccasin shoes. The Wyse Byse store was his jungle and in it, he was the king.

The Preacher stood at the empty tills calmly absorbing this ridiculous clown. Wondering for the life of him how these creations were ever allowed to develop, how they'd ever managed to survive in the real world. With a confidence borne from many years terrorising at the top, Mr. Prentass was unaware that he was about to outreach his capabilities. Storming up to the Preacher with his neck and chest puffed out in true 'Silverback' fashion, he bellowed, "What the devil's the meaning of this, Constable, do you know who I am??"

The Preacher smiled, no not that one. Heavenly knew his nice smile. This was the other one, the one that made the hairs on the back of your neck stand up. The smile that said you are not long for this world!

"Judging by the plastic badge on your cord jacket, you're Mr. Prentass. Where have you been, Sir? We're dealing with an emergency here and lives are at stake. Now open the back doors or else?"

Mr. Prentass was totally blind to the fact that at that very moment he was walking through the valley of the shadow of death. "Constable, I demand to speak with your supervisor. I shall certainly not take orders from the likes of you. Now run along. Go fetch, do you hear!"

The Preacher sighed then in one swift movement lifted Mr. Prentass clean off his feet, it was as if he were a rag doll. He then marched him like a marionette down to the back of the store. The Preacher was holding him by his jacket collar and his trousers belt. This effect had resulted in the squealing Mr. Prentass receiving a substantial wedgie. He wasn't quite sure which was going to pop first, his bulging eyes or his sugar plum fairies. The Wyse Byse staff giggled uncontrollably as the Preacher marched past them with his nice smile and a wink. When they arrived at the back of the store the Preacher looked at the keeper of the keys and quietly said, "Open!"

Mr. Prentass was all gassed out and exhausted. He resembled a set of bagpipes the morning after Hogmanay. Seeing the state he was in put her troubled mind to rest, she promptly opened the rear doors and the gaggling shoppers hurriedly slipped out the back and to safety. Mr. Prentass was clearly out of condition. He stood at the rear of the store with his hands on his knees puffing and panting coldly eyeing the Preacher. He discretely unwedged himself before shuffling out to join the rest.

Outside the back of the store the Preacher got on to his radio and updated Control (Belfast Regional Control) that the Wyse Byse store had been safely evacuated. Mr. Prentass felt a gentle tap on his shoulder and immediately recoiled. When he looked up, he saw Heavenly smiling down at him, she had a tumbler full of ice-cold water.

"Here, take it, have a sip. It will bring you around."

Prentass took the tumbler and drank, all the while quietly watching the Preacher. He had felt his power and never wanted to go through that again. Draining the glass, he shook his head in dismay. The same person was on his pocket radio calmly relaying the facts, smiling and totally at ease. "Remarkable."

Mr. Prentass numbly handed the tumbler back to Heavenly. "Ah yes, thank you very much. Indeed." He gave her a quiet nod and then a brief smile. Several of his staff were standing in a smokers' huddle. One nodded over at him, she looked as though she was going to burst out laughing. That was the final straw. Prentass fumed, glaring over at the man responsible. This wasn't the last there would be of the matter. No, not by a long shot!

The pressure he felt was intense, no it was unbearable as Sergeant Nigel Norwood lightly jogged down the Woodstock Road towards the blue Ford Transit Van. No manuals had prepared him for the way he was feeling, no Force Orders had described his present terror. He found himself tip-toeing towards his own demise then pulled himself together. As if tip-toeing up to a bomb was going to make any difference. He had to get close enough to get a read on the vehicle registration number for a radio check. The van was parked tight between two other vehicles making a read on the number plate from distance impossible. This was his moment to shine, the one he'd dreamt of all of his short 23-year-old life. To be the man. To be the hero. The man in the big picture. 'The Duke.'

John Wayne was his lifelong hero. He would have lit up an old stogie then casually strolled all hen-toed down the middle of the Woodstock Road. Nigel pictured the scene, the Duke's little red neck scarf fluttering in the summer's breeze. Forever cool, forever nonchalant. His dusty Stetson parked just at the right jaunty angle. Sneering, yes sneering folks into the jaws of death. But the Duke never placed himself in the way of a 200-pound bomb going off. For it would be his colleagues picking up pieces of him all over the road. Shop, windows, trees and hedges. Oh, and the crows and magpies would be there as well, to lend a hand in all the clearing up, feathers flapping, all fighting and squabbling for a nibble of the Duke's snarly bits!

Nigel was now twenty yards or so from the van and edging ever closer. The heat was intense. His heart was pounding like a symphonium kettle drum and his mouth was as dry as an Arab's flip flop. The sound of sirens and flashing blue lights accompanied by the helicopter's blades chattering from above added to his strain. He was scared, very scared. How he wanted to run, let someone else do this. But he couldn't. His eyes caught a flash some 100 yards down the Woodstock Road.

"Aww Jesus to fuck. The press boys. Here to film me getting blown to kingdom fucking come! Pull yourself together, Nigel, son. We can get through this."

Closer, ever closer with every step. Would the next step be his last! Then there it was, the full number plate before him. He clicked his transmitter then croaking hoarsely, he spurted, "Uniform AS19. Urgent Victor check, over!"

The response was immediate. "AS19. Uniform. Send. Over."

Terrified, Nigel blurted on, "Details please on XRAY, INDIA, JULIET figures 4208. Over."

Gary and Wee Mo's last port of call was the Spar Essentials store facing Wyse Byse.

Gary burst in shouting, "Police, police. We've no time, folks. Suspect device right outside. Everybody out the back. NOWWW!"

Mrs. Stewart a 60-year-old verging on battle axe, screeched long and hard out in her finest Hammer House of Horrors soprano, "Arrgghhhh." She ran the tiny shop and usually took no prisoners. "I'm going to have a heart attack so I am. Oh, sweet mother of God, protect us all. Please let it not be my time. I'm for Benidorm next Thursday, full fucking board and all! Yes, yes Constable right away. OUT, OUT, all of youse. Drop whatever you've got and out the back nae. NAE, I'm telling you! Oi. You kids down there. Drop them bags and out with yez!"

Three little urchins, two girls and a boy all in and around the 11 years mark giggled with excitement and bolted passed Maureen. "Yeowww, a bomb. Magic. Hope it goes off. Let's go watch it!"

Mo caught sight of a co-op plastic bag abandoned by the fresh meat freezer. She made a quick mental note; 30 seconds covered the evacuation from top to tail. Belfast folk were top evacuators. They were World Champions in all of its disciplines.

A bead of sweat was slithering down Derek Grant's skeletal brow. He was impervious. His eyes were glued on Norwood or the Plank depending on how he stood in your affections. "Jeez Tony, what the fuck's the Plank playing at? He's standing there like he was glued to the spot. If that's a bomb and it goes off, he'll be fucking mayonnaise!" He reached for his pocket radio. "AS19 from AM5. Take cover, take cover, OVER!"

Sergeant Norwood leapt back at the sound of the sudden transmission and went ass over tit. But he had the wit to keep on going and scrambled his way back behind the cordon at the Cregagh Road end. The AM70 vehicle arrived at the Woodstock Road cordon. Arnie Savage bounced out of the front passenger seat and joined Derek and Tony. Shelley nervously waited behind the wheel. This was her first bomb and she was now worrying a bazooka joe bubble gum to death. All eyes were on the blue transit van.

Their radios crackled into life. "AS19 from Uniform. Your victor check comes back as a blue Ford Transit Van. Registered owner is a Mr. Stanley Lockwood, Electrical Contractors. Number 8, Cregagh Road. Comes back fully taxed and all regular. Over!"

Sergeant Norwood heaved a huge sigh of relief. He would see another sunrise. The blue transit was parked right outside number 8. "Uniform AS19. Roger on your last. Many thanks. Out."

Derek became aware of the blob of sweat on his brow and wiped it off with the sleeve of his white shirt. Turning to Tony and Arnie he blew a silent whistle, "Phew. Thank God. That's it then a fucking hoax. Shower of bastards, I'll close it off then…" But Derek was beaten to the draw.

"Uniform from AS19. This would appear to be a hoax call. The blue transit comes back as all regular and is parked legally outside the owner's home address. I propose we lift the cordons and all diversions and let things get back to normal."

A short pause followed. "AM5 from Uniform. Are you happy with the lifting of the cordons and returning things to normal as per AS19's recommendations?"

Tony watched and waited as Derek weighed up his next move. He wanted this all to end. The heat, the noise, the flashing lights, the worried faces. Most of all the weight of tension. He craved normal, he yearned for it. Inwardly he was pleading with Derek, "Come on Derek, close this one off."

Out of the blue he heard a grim and determined growl. "WAIT, Inspector!" Arnie Savage was staring hard at the transit. The gravy was pouring from his wrinkled brow. "Something's not right here. I've known Stan Lockwood for years, he's one decent spud so he is. He's done work at the station as well as my place. In all my years here I've never seen the blue van parked out the front of his place. As well as all of that, there's been no answer from his front door when the place was being evacuated. I think he's got his lot down at the caravan at Ballyhalbert around this time of the year. Jeez Sir, just look at the fucking suspension, the springs are barely off the ground, there's got to be some weight pushing them down. Give me two ticks."

With that, Arnie trotted off towards the blue transit. His left boot lace had come loose and was dancing like a Mayfly. Derek yelled after him above the hellish din, "For fuck's sake Arnie get your ass back here. That's an order." But Arnie was gone, he was a man on a mission. A deadly mission.

Derek agitated, went to his pocket mic. "Uniform from AM5, re. your last. Another couple of seconds please. A colleague is checking a final matter out. Over."

Arnie got to the front of the van in seconds borne on the wings of adrenaline and fear. He tore at the number plate which came away with ease revealing another number plate beneath. Arnie got the picture instantly and yelled down his mic. "Uniform AM70, URGENT Victor check. Over. On the following. Papa, India Juliet figures 9, 8, 8, 2. Over."

Arnie didn't wait for Uniform to respond. He began running back as fast as his burly frame would carry him. It felt as though he was running with diving boots on. By this time, Shell was out of their vehicle and had unceremoniously shoved Derek and Tony aside. Her beautiful snow-white face was frantically screaming "RUN, RUN Arnie. Hurry HURRRRY!"

She along with everyone else watching were now fully aware what the false number plates brought to the table. Arnie had never run so hard. Everything was becoming a surreal blur, like one of those slow-motion dreams. He had made thirty yards from the transit and all he could see was Derek, Tony and Shelly waving frantically for him to get back.

He could make out Shell's words as they fell in slow motion from her mouth, "RUUUUUUN ARNIE, RUUUUUUNNN!"

Arnie was gasping for air. His head was fully back in 'Chariots of Fire' fashion as his arms and legs thrashed for all they were worth. His bastarding flak jacket was trying to decapitate him with every bounce while his left boot lace cracked like the whip in 'Rawhide'. Then fate struck suddenly as sometimes it does, his right boot trod boldly on his flying left lace causing Arnie to trip in the most acrobatic of fashions. He left the ground like a hippo on wings and landed face down between two parked cars. To say Arnie was winded would not be accurate for he had no wind in him.

He let out a long "Fuuuccckkk!" then gritted his teeth and whispered to his God, "Be home soon, Molly love!"

KABOOM!

When a huge bomb goes off as this one did, for a few seconds everything stops. Meanwhile the human brain tries to take it all in, tries to rationalize, tries to make sense of it all then tries to deal with it. If the brain had hands on such occasions, they would be full. Maybe a bit like Harrod's as the doors swing open for the January Sales. Total and utter chaos and surreal madness happening all at once from every direction.

Every sense screaming, "TOO MUCH DETAIL CANNOT COPE, CANNOT COPE!"

The ears have to deal with the sound of the explosion which is the loudest sound they will ever hear. The eyes will have to deal with the brilliance of the blast followed by millions of particles of debris flying off in all directions, most of it deadly. The body depending on its proximity in relation to the explosion can be thrown like a rag doll in all directions. Limbs can be severed, shredded or torn, severe burns can be inflicted with its softest breath and last but not least, the mind can be irretrievably lost. Not nice! And then the night terrors entering your citadels of sleep and forever haunting your quiet moments and peaceful thoughts. As you grow old in pace with father time, the bomb blast remains like a nasty brat ever young, ever vivid, ever goading you.

"REMEMBER, REMEMBER."

Shelley, Tony and Derek were thrown off their feet. The blue sky of that summer's day was lost, replaced by a thick black fug of billowing smoke and carnage. At the Wyse Byse store a second makes all the difference. One second, all was quiet save for the tick tock of myriad clocks faithfully marking time until… The good folks were now out the back none the wiser and safe. Safe by the margin of 23 seconds. Tick tock, tick tock, the tiny clocks whispered as the countdown continued, fate and destiny holding hands as one skipped towards the here and now bearing gifts. When the bomb went off, a raging thump of energy and power bashed all the windows in, sending daggers of glass in all directions.

The tick tocks stopped as the tiny time pieces became fiery balls of metal shooting off in all directions. The mannequins were obliterated as heads and limbs were torn and ripped off. Fires started and alarms wailed for help. Had human life been present, the results would have been utterly catastrophic. An office door had been torn from its hinges and lay on the ground smashed and charred. A name plate with letters missing clung tight in ruin. The remaining letters showing were AN_ _ _ _/_ _ _ _ ASS.

Thirty seconds after the blast debris still fluttered earthward. Derek could feel his body shaking uncontrollably as he tried to get to his feet. His body was in a state of shock, his white shirt covered in his own blood caused by tiny shards of glass now happily embedded in him. Tony was thrown back into Shelley, inadvertently shielding her from the blast. His ears were ringing and all sound to him was a numb muffled hum. His eyes were streaming encased in black soot. It was then he noticed blood on the right side of his collar. His right ear drum had burst and blood was slowly trickling out. Tony kept opening and closing his mouth in a yawning fashion willing the sound to return as he wandered aimlessly over broken glass. A soft sweeping breeze cleared a sight line through the smoke. Shelley screamed from deep within, "ARNIE, ARNIE PET!"

All she could see were Arnie's shredded boots peeking out from between two badly wrecked cars. The Preacher and Gary were there with him. Shelley found herself running hard towards her wee pard who only moments before had been laughing with her in the Ormeau Park.

Sobbing and fearing the worst, she screamed, "PRUNES AND FUCKING COTTAGE CHEESE WEE PET!"

Arnie's pocket radio went off. "AM70 from Uniform. Re. your last Victor Request on Papa, India, Juliet figures 9, 8, 8, 2. This vehicle was reported as hijacked from the nationalist area of New Barnsley in Belfast yesterday morning. Treat with utmost caution. Repeat, treat with the utmost of caution. AM70 from Uniform did you receive my last over?"

A few seconds of silence was eventually broken.

"Uniform from AS19. Disregard my last. A huge explosion has just occurred within the cordoned area. The blue transit van containing the bomb was a ringer vehicle on false plates. Urgently request ambulance and fire service personnel along with CID and SOCO. Make the Press Office aware for media release. Thankfully we had cleared the area prior to the explosion. Will update you regarding the injuries sustained. This could have been a lot worse. Over!"

Arnie slowly began to come around. Although heavily concussed he opened his eyes and smiled meekly up at his two section mates Gary and the Preacher.

His errant boot lace had saved his life. Shelley arrived, the tears tripping her. Her face one big gooey mess caused by tears, mascara and the thick belching smoke. Arnie had just managed to sit up with help from the Preacher. Every part of him ached. Had he not been wearing his flak jacket, well things may have been a lot different. Gary had left to get him a glass of water. He was slowly coming back to life when Shelley launched herself at him thumping back against the pavement. He moaned quietly for that was all he had in him.

"Arnie, Arnie, you wee bastard. I thought we'd lost you. I thought the blast had taken you. Never ever do that on me again you wee bollocks even though now you're a big-time hero. Do you promise me now?"

Shelly now cradling Arnie, began to shower him with hugs and kisses. Arnie was helpless to do anything about it. He had no strength left in him. This certainly wasn't the salacious image he'd imagined between Shelley and himself an hour or so ago. He looked up at the smiling Preacher and felt safe. Chopper blades above thrashed out a morbid drum beat jigging with the wailing sirens below. Raising tensions, raising fears, it was like a scene from Dante's Inferno. A living hell.

Arnie felt a fullness as he slipped in and out of consciousness. A real sense of pride. With every painful rocking motion and the feeling of Shelly's salty tears on his cheeks, he knew that if he never achieved anything else in his ordinary life and policing career, well today, what he had done had really mattered. Arnie was no saint but folks what is a saint? Today, Arnie was prepared to make the ultimate sacrifice. He was prepared to give up his life for his colleagues and his people. The Good Book covered it well, I think.

"Greater love hath no man than this, that a man lay down his life for his friends" – John 15:13. Three hundred police officers both men and women did just that during the province's dark shameful past.

Derek and Tony appeared hovering above Arnie, their faces fraught with worry. For Arnie it was wonderful as their shadow momentarily blocked the sun from his eyes. They all gawked, registering the horror on each other's face. Arnie smiled at Derek and then at Tony. Both were looking more like chimney sweeps from Mary Poppins than police officers, except these sweeps were splattered in blood. He began to chuckle then laugh hysterically which became infectious, for they had all survived, thanks to an errant boot lace.

Shelley found herself giggling from a state of howling tears and sniffled, "What the fuck do you lot find so funny, WELL?"

Arnie patted her on her raven hair and winced, "It's just that Shell, I just can't remember the last time we all looked so well. A sharp turn out or what!" More laughter.

Arnie looked up at the punk Snow White. "Oh, stop Shell, please. I'm ever so slightly in agony. My wee ribs can't take it no more."

Shelley released him gently from her bear-like hug and wiping the tears away giggled, "Oh my God Arnie, what am I like!"

Derek regathered himself realising his injuries were superficial. Like a well-oiled machine the officers around him were doing what needed to be done; helping any injured, assuring the elderly and scared, performing minor first aid until the emergency services arrived. He spotted Heavenly with a sobbing child, Gary was clearing a pensioner's doorway with calm assurance, the Preacher as only he could with his wide smiling face and calm demeanour, was shifting the agitated media further back up the road. None of these acts were to be found in any training manuals but were there in abundance in the cup of human kindness and public service. The explosion would greet global audiences within the next few hours until the next major incident knocked it off its perch.

Sure, there was always some goat mouthing off with the likes of, "Why don't yez go and catch some terrorists, you black bastards", somehow blaming the police for all the province's woes but they were well used to it. They had been taking the same crap from both sides of the community for years and still paying the ultimate sacrifice with their lives.

The annoying helicopter suddenly disappeared allowing Tony to assess where his hearing was. It wasn't too bad but still not good. The sun that day, unlike the bomb blast, never loosened its grip. The officers were parched, not helped by the smoke and churning dust. Derek smiled at the coming together of the community.

Cregagh Methodist Church stuck in the middle of the hellish cordon opened its doors, its stalwarts offering a seat, a cup of tea and a hug to whoever needed one. Old dears were out with trays and plastic cups of water for the officers at the scene. Next the arrival of the ambulances for whoever needed one. Arnie was whisked off to the Ulster Hospital as a precaution and under protest. Tweety had contacted Molly Savage, Arnie's beloved and reassured her that it was just a precautionary measure and that her Arnie was quite the hero.

CID and SOCO came next with door-to-door enquiries regarding the blue transit and whatever forensic analysis that could be done. Finally, the clear up squad appeared supplied by the Belfast City Council and the DOE, a highly professional and well drilled outfit of clearer uppers, a mix of sweepers, carpenters and glaziers, launched themselves in military fashion firstly clearing all the debris then either boarding up properties or reglazing them; bomb zone, to open for business in a couple of hours.

Derek remained at the scene updating Uniform at every stage for their log. He was a rock of assurance to his men around him. He calmly remained at his post until all that could be done was done. Finally, he looked over to Tony and said, "That's us, Tony. I'm closing the scene off, apart from a bit of sweeping up that's it. When we get back to the station, you're signing yourself on the sick book as well as the Injury on Duty Log. Then get your ass straight up to casualty and get those lugs looked at. You don't know how these injuries play out twenty years down the line!"

Tony nodded and replied with a thumbs up and a raised voice due to his ears, "No worries, Inspector, but don't forget, I've got me a doctor at home!"

Derek laughed, "Ahh, Doctor Chloe. And there's no need to shout you wee bollix."

Tony laughed, put his hand up to his bloodied ear and went, "Whaaa!"

Inspector Stevie Campbell appeared beside Derek, "Jesus, look at the cut of you pair. Did a bomb go off or something?"

Derek laughed, "Fuck off Stevie."

Stevie smirked, "Couldn't resist. That's us done with your permission. Are we good to open the road up and lift the cordons?"

Derek nodded, "Aye Stevie, that'll do. Tell your crews thanks from us at Mountroyal, great job done." Stevie gave a mock salute and laughing hysterically said, "Jesus, Derek, those Mountroyal women of yours are a tough bunch. Look at your woman constable up there standing outside the Spar Store gassing away with the owner. Not a care in the world. She's only went and got her shopping in. Hard as nails or what! Anyhow, we're off. Hope not to see yes too soon boys. Byeee."

Derek's mouth dropped open. Was he shell-shocked? There was Wee Mo sauntering back towards Mountroyal Station carrying a plastic bag full of shopping. Her beat partner Gary was on the other side of the street totally unperturbed. He looked over to Tony and said, "Tony lad. Please tell me I'm dreaming all this. Tell me this ain't happening. Tell me, my eyes are fucking deceiving me!" Tony gawped in wonderment. His flabber had never been so gasted!

George Sewell stood stiffly by his office window watching the filthy smoke rising menacingly into the East Belfast sky. His chest was tight and his breathing short and snatched. His mouth had never been so dry, a large tumbler of whisky rested in his right hand. This would be his second in as many minutes. He had listened on his pocket radio as the scenario played out but still jumped in horror at the heavy sound of the BOOOOOOOOOOM. All he could think about were the casualties and then his very good friends and colleagues, all caught in the middle of it. Tears started to wander aimlessly down his cheeks. His friends, his friends. His tear-filled eyes looked up at the portrait of a young Queen Elizabeth the Second. George would have conversations with her from time to time and always referred to her as "Her Majesty."

Taking a long gulp, he raised his golden goblet towards her and quietly sobbed, "Well, Your Majesty, who'd be a boss? You have us all to worry about. I only have this wee patch of about five square miles. I don't know how you stick it because at this very moment in time I'm struggling really hard, just saying, Your Majesty."

At that moment he heard a knock at his office door which then opened quietly. Debbie Dean entered head bowed. They looked at each other, seeing each other's tears. Debbie spoke, "Sir Jack's just off the blower (John Hermon, the Chief Constable), I told him you were understandably busy. Well, he sends his support. He says whatever you need, just ask. Thoughts and prayers. Thoughts and prayers."

Like a light switch moment in one's life, the blast had triggered a chemical transformation within Sergeant Nigel Norwood. Who could figure it? From pain in the arse policing by numbers, a bullying cretin to a man utterly and completely altered. Had the cordons been lifted as he had requested many people would have perished. Men, women and children, young and old. Tears of personal survival and tears of gratitude began to flow. He knew then that he had been given a second chance. Arnie's actions, the tubby little constable he had always talked down to, had in fact brought him salvation and precious time. Time to change. He had been spared as the lives of others had been spared. He had been shown mercy and now realised that life was the most precious gift of all. Nigel made himself a promise that horrifying day, he would become as good a man and a Sergeant as he could possibly be. The Plank, like Elvis had left the building, he was gone never to return. A new name slowly evolved and slowly took favour amongst all who knew him and worked with him.

From Sergeant Norwood to the ever popular and highly respected Sergeant, 'ALL GOOD.'

Chapter 7
Wee Geordie Magee The Pearl Street Pearl

Dense drizzle swirls through dazzling floodlights casting a soft pearlescent shimmer.

A very good evening to you all. It's Friday, 4 May 1990 and local time shows, let me see now, yep, it's just gone 9.00 PM. We have an amazing setting here at the spectacular San Siro Football Stadium in Milan, Italy. The conditions could be better though. This heavy rain's putting a dampener on tonight's proceedings. It's relentless, like a nagging toothache and shows no signs of letting up. The temperature pitch side is hovering somewhere in the low twenties making life for our footballing gladiators hot, sticky and energy sapping.

The 80,000 excited fans packed inside the ground are undeterred by the soak. For them, like the rest of us, it's a privilege just to be here. There's an amazing energy about the place, as swathes of emotions are fed like steroids from the fanatical fans crammed in the stands to the players on the pitch. As a football fan myself, I couldn't be more excited, you see tonight's only about one thing, as the world holds its breath and watches on. In footballing parlance, it's The Holy Grail. The ultimate dream. Welcome friends, to this year's European Cup Final and footballing immortality.

Bayern Munich, last year's champions, are looking to retain the trophy. Manfred Beer at 74 seasoned years is their wily manager. In footballing jargon, he's been there, done that and got the T-shirt. Up to now he appears to be holding all the cards, most of them aces. Bayern's running the show with a swagger though miraculously it's still nil all at 83 minutes.

Beer smiles across at the opposition dug out. His eyes light up at what he sees. His opposite number and his larger sidekick are having a proper rant. Their ageing team are chasing shadows and are all but out on their feet.

The Ace in Manfred's star-studded pack is a certain Maxi Danner who at 27 years is a footballing superstar. Der Adler or the Eagle as he's known, simply has it all. Maxi is German born and bred, the archetypal Arian superman. The term "Vorsprung durch Technik" could also be said of this glorious specimen. Maxi imposes at a muscular 6 feet 3 inches and is blessed with movie star good looks. Outside the footballing stage, Maxi is a modern-day playboy who's never short of a date. From 18-year-old models to 60-something celebs, he's not fussy. Age is just a number, right? Maxi loved everyone and everyone just loved Maxi. Tonight, Maxi or Der Adler has been giving a footballing master class, the San Siro is his stage and he's tonight's star billing. His blonde mane rides the sodden air in foppish fashion as he orchestrates the match from midfield. My knees turn to jelly at the very sight of him. He's just too quick, too strong for the opposition. Maybe they're just in awe of his aura.

Careful now, don't be fooled by his wonderful physique, good looks and disarming charm, our Maxi given half a chance will happily break your leg at no extra cost. Occasionally he waves out to his female fans from both sides of the supporting divide. Quite incredible really. What a star, what a showman. He treats them to one of his sexy winks followed by his trademark dazzling smile. He does a toothpaste ad, you know. Oh, apologies dear football fans, how remiss of me, I've been 'Maxied'! This year's opposition are the mighty Red Devils of Manchester United and right now they're hanging on by the finest of threads.

The crowd suddenly gasps, sounding like a crack of thunder as Dickson the United keeper pulls off another miraculous clawing save, his every sinew straining as he tips a powerful volley delivered by our Maxi just over the bar. Excited applause follows from both sets of fans. Dickson's having the game of his life and he's the only reason we're still at nil all. Maxi smiles, waving an admonishing finger at the United keeper, ever the showman.

As if things can't get any worse, Jimmy Millar, the United centre forward, suddenly raises an outstretched arm towards the bench. This doesn't look good. Jimmy's clutching at his right hamstring. His face is a picture of heartbreak and agony. The United fans concede a collective groan. He'd been a doubtful starter for this one and sadly tonight Jimmy was a ghost of his former playing self. How we'd love to have seen him here in his prime. Age can be a cruel mistress and she's denying him his final hurrah. Beer covered his mouth and smiled, United are all out of options. Their gamble has failed to pay off. He knew their bench is a weak one. To the best of his knowledge, they have no recognised strikers apart from some kid from Belfast. Beer flicks through his meticulous notes.

He sniffed then shrugged. "Must have plucked him from their youth squad. Nothing on him." The stadium warmly applauded as Millar left the stage for the final time. A new career in football punditry awaits this popular icon.

The United manager Bobby Milligan is apoplectic. He's a 63-year-old footballing legend, an international player in his day and now a wonderful hands-on man-to-man manager. Bobby hailed from a working-class Geordie background. He's a charmer and raconteur if you catch him in the right mood and right now Beer can see he's most definitely in the wrong mood. As for apoplectic, that word's not to be found in his limited vocabulary. Our Bobby's blowing his top with bells on. The pinnacle of his managerial career is sinking fast just like the Titanic. His number two and sidekick is Malcolm Fenton or plain Mac. Mac's a scouser, a former player himself though not in the same class as his boss. Mac's in his mid-fifties and is seen as the calming influence in this dynamic duo. Mac would also be a bit more camera shy. The pair are a little and large combo, Bobby being the little to Mac's large. Let's have a listen in shall we, I'm sure they're discussing tactics, team formations and the like.

"Mac, you wee bastard. You've really fucked me up this time. Why, why dear God did you have to do it here and now. Of all the places to finish me, you choose the San Siro Stadium in Milan and the European fucking Cup final. Even worse against them bloody krauts. This here was supposed to be our greatest moment together. Now you're telling me that the only fit striker we've got is that lily white boy sitting over there. Jesus Mac, he's just over 5 foot. Look at the cut of him. He's away with the fairies mon. Aw, and he's just a bairn for fuck's sake. Movie Star Maxi out there will have him for his tea. He'll destroy him!"

Mac tried to get a word in but Bobby was in full flow. "Yes Mac, I know the boy's good. But it's too soon. Way, way too soon. I'm just saying Mac, it's not fair on the boy. He only heard he was on the bench this after bloody noon, after Carlos what's his name went down with the shits. Fucking Mediterranean diet. Worst thing ever I say!"

Mac glanced over at the youth sitting on the bench. He's the picture of calm but inwardly ready. His life's been a hard one and if you looked a little closer you would catch a glimpse of the steel in his eyes. Bobby pulled the silk hanky from his drenched jacket and mops his sweaty brow then blows his nose hard.

The hanky was a match for his commemorative tie and was to be auctioned off for charity at a later date but, "Hey-ho, Dem's de breaks!"

A United player took a knee feigning cramp. He's playing for time. The Russian referee checked his watch and condescendingly waves a trainer with the magic sponge on, the crowd groaned, fast becoming restless. Beer the Bayern manager is a picture of stoicism as Maxi gathered his team at the halfway line for a final pep talk. Victory is surely within their grasp.

The drizzle now turned to heavy rain and faint sounds of rumbling thunder stoke the San Siro cauldron. Mac gazed across at the 18-year-old Belfast boy and smiled. He's been holding him back but a talent like this can't remain a secret forever. Mac has never seen a better player ever. It was his time. The boy gazed at the ground with his feet crossed, lost in another world. His socks are down round his ankles and his arms are folded. He simply waited. A picture of ice-cold calm in this swell of jangling emotions. Mac smiled at his boss, he already knew the answer but asked anyway.

"Well Bobby, are you letting him on or are we just going to lie down and get humped by these kraut bastards?"

Bobby laughed probably more in delirium. They're both now drenched and resemble drowned rats. A roll of thunder cracks and rumbles in the sodden sky. He nodded, "Aye get him on. It's all duck or no dinner time. Last chance saloon for us and our lot, Mac."

Mac smiled and caught the boy's eye pointing him in the direction of the pitch. He shouts out above the clammer, "Son, it's your time to shine. Stay in their half and ruffle a few feathers. Feel free to score whenever you like. You're ready to rock and roll. Go make your people proud."

The boy nodded then stood up. He smiled over at Mac before allowing himself a stretch. He's short, maybe 5 feet 8 inches at a push but blessed with a bovine frame. His legs are like tree trunks all hacked and scarred like a butcher's bench. Mac noticed for the first time that he has a back on him like a docker. The boy's a ball of explosive power. He mouthed back to Mac, "Ta, now" and headed for the touchline. Beer gazed across at the opposition dug out and is surprised to find Bobby and Mac smiling over at him. Something had suddenly changed. A roar from the United fans rang out as the substitution is announced over the tannoy. The referee again checked his watch, 10 minutes to go then extra time if necessary. He waves the boy on as fans and commentators alike scramble to their programs to see who this individual is, Number 7. MAGEE.

Saturday 30 June 1983. BUMPH. Like the sound of a mallet hitting a mattress. The boy always jumped at that sound; it wasn't the surprise; it was pure terror. He started rubbing and scratching away at his hands. He had no idea he was doing it. Then came the squealing followed by the pleading hysterical cries from his mother. His father Stan was in one of his drunken rages and had just started. The boy bit on his bottom lip as the sound of the pounding strikes continued. His heart was thumping and his tiny scratched hands were trembling. He had to get out, he had to escape. He eased the front door open then gently crept out. The foul-mouthed rage continued behind him like a violent thunderstorm.

At first, he began to quietly tip toe but then an adrenaline surge kicked in and he found himself running wildly with his heart bashing. He had made it out this time, released from his horrors. He was free. His best friend was tucked under his arm. His beloved football. He had fetched it out of the Connswater River with an old broom shaft a couple of months back. It was well battered and bruised much like the boy himself, but still danced and swerved at the behest of his magical feet. This boy was special. He had been blessed with a talent only God could bestow.

Wee Geordie Magee was just over 11 years old and lived in a wreck of a terraced house in East Belfast, Number 4, Pearl Street to be exact. He was 5 feet tall, all skin and bone with fine dark brown hair which languished all streaky straight. He was a translucent white in colour with tiny slits like daggers for eyes. On closer inspection they were a bland grey, the steel was yet to form. When Geordie spoke, which was rare, he sounded much like how you would imagine a teletext machine would sound if it could speak. A careful steady stream of only what was essential would come out of his tiny mouth. He always spoke the truth. Wee Geordie was not backward in coming forward, if you know what I mean. He called it as he saw it. It was in his DNA if folks had known about it back then.

He attended Nettlefield Primary School located just off the lower Woodstock Road. Wee Geordie was popular with both teachers and pupils alike. As far as his learning was concerned, he was steady rather than spectacular. His spectacular he saved for the football pitch. Out from the roughest of working-class areas where even the faintest of praise was rare, tongues began to wag excitedly like water crashing over a dry riverbed following a furious downpour; news to lift the spirits of those working-class souls, something to help them forget their surroundings, their money worries and all about The Troubles surrounding them. For a few moments, they could forget about the bombs, the bullets and all the engineered sectarian hatred and the hopelessness of their situation. Their excited jabber was all about a special talent rising out from under the shadow of the mighty Goliath, a huge yellow crane housed at the world-renowned Harland and Wolff Shipyard. Goliath is the iconic symbol of East Belfast.

Crowds began to turn up at the matches to see what all the fuss was about. No one was ever disappointed. Footballing Scouts came from far and wide to watch the young prodigy. Wee Geordie thrived on all the pressure and adulation. He mesmerised his adoring fans for that's what they all soon became. To them he was 'Wee Geordie Magee, the Pearl Street Pearl'. They marvelled at his touch, his control, his blistering pace and unerring accuracy in front of the goal. Sometimes he would score just for the fun of it reducing the touchline crowd to gasps of amazement. Whether by head or foot, it all came with supreme ease to him. His future was assured and it lay at the end of his tired and well-worn boot laces.

One of his biggest fans was Malcolm Mackie, the male half of the cleaning staff at Mountroyal Police Station. Malcolm was in his early forties and single, a painfully shy soul who lived in Roseberry Gardens with his elderly mother. Malcolm was her sole carer. Malcolm first came to notice the boy around three years ago. He spotted the child kicking an old battered ball against a wall with a sublime artistry that took his breath away. The pair got to know each other and over time became unlikely friends. They would always stop for a quick chat or a chuckle. A pair of odd balls completely at ease in each other's armchair. Malcolm would watch the boy in awe for ages dreaming of a world he knew he could never enter. A mystical world where only the greatest of the greats were permitted.

Geordie's parents never made it to the matches, they never witnessed his sublime gift. One person was responsible for that, wee Geordie's father Stan, a hateful thug and a wife beating drunk. He supped at the Longfellow Bar located at My Lady's Road, East Belfast. The Longfellow was a UVF Bar and Stan was a fringe UVF player. He was a 'roid' taking goon who collected debts and ran messages for his beloved firm. Stan terrorised the neighbourhood and would think nothing of thumping you if you looked at him in the wrong way. He bitterly resented his young son's rising star. Any chance he got he would beat him mercilessly, for Geordie was everything Stan wasn't or ever would be.

Geordie was always a mass of lumps, bumps, swellings and bruises. The beatings and the injustices created an inner toughness and strength of will in the Belfast boy. He knew what unfair looked and felt like. Thanks to his loving mother, Daphne, he was also quietly receptive to goodness and doing the right thing. One night after another cruel beating with his mother sobbing by his side, Geordie lifted her life-hacked hand and gently placed it against his heart. He fixed her with his narrow eyes and said words she would never forget:

"Mammy, one day I'll take you away from all of this. You'll have all you could ever wish for. A fancy house and car. You'll have your hair done every day and only have the best of clobber. No more charity clothes for you mammy. We'll leave him behind where he can't hurt us. Just keep going mammy, keep on going for us. It won't be long. I promise." Daphne nodded as tears were shared.

Geordie made himself keep two simple promises. Firstly, he was never going to turn out like his father. Secondly, he was never going to get involved with anything that was going to bring trouble to his mother's front door. For a Belfast child at that place and time, both promises were a fairly tall order.

Geordie raced into his haven, a disused builder's yard. A heavy metal sign dangled from a single rusted chain bearing its previous occupier's title, 'Edgars Builders'. It clanged forlornly just above the entrance pleading for attention. The abandoned site was located just off the London Road. Here the boy felt safe, here was his Theatre of Dreams. Geordie was in his favourite top, a red jumper all tattered and stained. Like his treasured ball it had seen better days, but it was Geordie's footie top and he was allowed to abuse it. He was a Man United fan through and through. They were the only team for him.

'One day maybe', he thought. Then with a quick skip, he was off, dreaming dreams and beating the best, for in his mind he was the best. He felt exhilaration and release as he began thrashing his ball hard with his right peg into the far yard wall. The same was repeated as the ball came back at him at breakneck speed but this time it was smashed with his left foot. The power and accuracy had to be seen to be believed. Then he was off dribbling with the ball. Feigning this way and that, breezing passed old bins, discarded pallets and empty paint pots. Here he was free and here he would stay until the light fell in all days and in all weathers. Wee Geordie versus the ball, the wall and the world.

"Fuck, fuck, fuck. I'm fucked and gasping for a fag," muttered Constable Arnie Savage as he made his way lumpily on foot down London Road heading towards Ravenhill Avenue. It had just gone 5 .00 PM. He was hot and bothered like a suckling pig on a rotisserie. Like a bad swimmer, plenty of thrashing about but very little movement. His personal issue flak jacket weighing in at around eight pounds was doing him no favours. It cruelly bobbed half a beat out catching him in the throat and neck with his every choppy stride. Ahead of him by 20 yards on the other side of the street was his pard for the day, the Preacher. That was the section nickname given to Pete Majury.

The Preacher bit was all to do with his Christian faith. Pete was just over 30 years old and at 6 feet 3 inches was supremely fit. He glided on ahead oblivious to poor Arnie's struggles. Arnie was 47 years old and was the senior man of 'A' Section stationed at Mountroyal Police Station. He had over 22 years' service. A good guy and a steady peeler. He was packing a few extra pounds and had recently curtailed his heavy drinking following friendly advice from his new Sergeant Tony Speers.

Arnie kept a little secret known only to his good self and his long-suffering wife. His secret was that he was 100% ginger. This he cleverly disguised by means of a black hair dye. Everything was jet black which included his swept back receding hairline, thick bushy eyebrows and his Tom Selleck moustache. That's where Arnie and Tom's similarities ended, for Arnie was no Tom Selleck. Unless of course, Tom was secretly ginger all over and wore six-inch-high heels while on set. They were probably near the same weight though, if you chose to overlook the wobbly fat versus Hollywood grid iron muscle. Poor Arnie was gasping and out of puff. Looking ahead, he could see the Preacher slowly pulling away from him.

This dynamic duo was out on a detailed beat patrol. Their call sign that day was AM30 and AM30A. They would walk on opposite sides of the street or at a distance from each other as a safety measure. Two police officers walking side by side were easy pickings for the terrorist gangs of the day. In fact, it was seen as a disciplinary matter within the force, the risks being so high. It was Saturday, 30 June 1983 and they were on the late turn which ran from 3.00 PM to 11.00 PM. "Aw fuck nooo, please God nooo." Arnie gulped as he saw potential disaster looming. Just ahead, he spotted 10 hairy arsed gorillas. It looked to Arnie as though they had just returned from out of the mist, the Maze Prison type mist. This group of chattering primates had positioned themselves out in the street just below the Longfellow Bar. It was a pleasant afternoon and they were enjoying warm tins of Harp stashed in their plastic 'Mace' bags. A ghetto blaster was powering out 'The Number of the Beast' by Iron Maiden. A dreadful racket thought the panicking Arnie. In Belfast terms they were having "a wee sesh."

A drinking session. Judging by the empty cans strewn around they were well on their way. "No, fuck, Preacher NOOO." Arnie upped his pace to a trundle. Any faster and his flak jacket would have decapitated him. He groaned as he saw the Preacher casually crossing over to the group who were visibly straightening as he approached. The Preacher was smiling as he always did. The gravy was now tripping down Arnie's furrowed brow as he watched his version of the Titanic sailing full steam ahead towards the iceberg. Impending disaster was approaching!

"BEEEEEEP!" Arnie leapt as his thumping heart jumped up to take a peek. A cream-coloured armoured Cortina had glided beside him. It was the main Mountroyal response crew for that shift, AM70. The driver-side door opened slightly and a wide grin greeted him. Behind the grin was Constable Lionel Graham. An ash laden fag hung precariously from his bottom lip. "Nice day for a wee dander Arnie me old son. Jesus, you look fucked."

A gorgeous female leaned forward from the front passenger seat. It was Constable Shelley McCann the main Observer and responder. Her fag was held daintily in her beautifully manicured left hand. A 23-year-old raven haired beauty with huge blue eyes and 'Betty Boop' lips.

"Hiya Arnie love. You're looking a bit hot and bothered. What's up, pet?"

Arnie was hyper. "Call for backup. He's going to get me killed. So much for my cosy wee beat."

Lionel looked at Shelley and the pair burst out laughing. Lionel noted the seriously pissed expression on his senior man's face then cleared his throat still trying hard not to laugh. "Apologies, senior man. We'll remain with you and see how this all plays out." Arnie couldn't bear to look as the Preacher ambled like lambsy into the lions' den. The group slowly surrounded him until all they could see was the top of the Preacher's cap.

Arnie snapped. "Call for backup. They're going to kill him. JESUS!"

Lionel and Shelly were totally focussed on the scene before them, high above the birds sang on. Lionel whispered softly, "Just a few more seconds, Arnie. Keep the faith me old son." And then it happened, the group erupted in laughter and then more laughter as some peeled away and began gathering up their empties, then the volume of the ghetto blaster reduced. The Preacher was now relaxing against a lamppost laughing loudly as one of the group regaled the others with a funny.

Arnie gazed in at the pair, his eyes wide in astonishment. "I mean he doesn't drink; he doesn't smoke and he doesn't swear. How the fuck does he do it?"

"AM70 from Uniform!" Shelley rolled her eyes heavenward lifting the mic to her beautiful cherry lips. "Uniform from AM70 send."

Uniform tasked their call sign to the Co-op store on the Beersbridge Road regarding youths stealing sausages and bacon from the freezers. This was becoming an increasing occurrence. Shelley sighed. "Roger Uniform. Out." She looked up at Arnie with a puzzled expression. "That's my third call regarding these types of thefts within the past couple of weeks. The wee shits are lifting £50 quid's worth at a time."

Arnie nodded, "Agreed our Shell, I've attended similar calls at the Spar on the Ravenhill Road as well as one at Iceland on the Cregagh Road."

Lionel nodded, "Me three. A pain in the ass pattern developing here, looking at Shelley. Shall we proceed thither Oh Mighty Observer?"

Shelley nodded regally, "Drive on, humble driver." With that, the driver's side door closed with a heavy clunk. A quick wave from its occupants as the deep two litre engine grumbled then growled, before moving off slowly down the London Road then taking a left onto Ravenhill Avenue before disappearing.

Arnie's jets had cooled by the time he caught up with the Preacher who had just left his new buddies laughing and in high spirits. They shouted over to Arnie as he waddled passed them on the other side of the street.

"Afternoon Canstable. Lovely day for a wee dander." Arnie nodded back eyeing the cans of Harp very much like Eric Morley would eye a Miss World Contestant. He had a familiar drooth on him but had given up on his bad old ways. At least when he was at work.

The Preacher called over from the far side of the street, "You OK, pard? Do you need a wee fag break?" Arnie loved the Preacher. He was smooth as molasses and took everything in his stride. A class act and a great peeler but cross him at your peril.

Arnie smiled. "Cheers Preacher, we'll take a wee quickie in the disused builder's yard down there on the right." It was then they both heard the steady and rhythmic thumping of a football.

London Road was bathed in late afternoon sunshine. A soft haze shimmered off the pavement as the strains of Iron Maiden faded into the background. Arnie walked underneath the dangling 'Edgars Builders' sign as he entered the old yard while the Preacher was forced to stoop. "Look out Cappers. I didn't see yez," yelled a high-pitched scream coming from a scrawny youth wearing a shabby red jumper.

A battered football was travelling like a bullet towards them. Arnie was blessed with the reflexes of a sloth on beta blockers. His blotchy face had an imminent date with the ballistic missile. He froze terrified on the spot making his outcome more definite. A split second later and just before disaster struck, his partner's left foot appeared from behind him stopping the ball in its tracks. A flick later the ball was nudged deftly 10 feet in the air. Then the Preacher appeared. His flak jacket, gun belt with radio and forage cap were placed carefully over an old upright pallet. As the ball fell earthwards, he trapped it on his chest then eased it onto his right knee then left and then began a game of keepy-uppy with the rest of his body. At no time was the ball in any danger of hitting the ground.

Preacher smiled at the youth who laughed back hard. A look between the pair was enough as the ball was deftly lobbed back at the youth who in turn began his own display of keepy-up. The Preacher cheered and the youth again laughed out loud. Arnie for the second time that day was gob smacked.

When the youth finally stopped Arnie shouted, "And who might you be cub?"

From behind them a familiar voice shouted, "It's wee Geordie Magee the Pearl Street Pearl. He's brilliant lads, isn't he?"

Malcolm Mackie entered the yard smiling at the youth and his two police officer friends. Malcolm shared the Mountroyal cleaning duties with Aggie Patterson. Both were vital members of the station personnel and very popular. Malcolm was laden with shopping bags but could never resist a wee peak at the child prodigy.

Geordie smiled broadly at Malcolm and shouted, "Bout ye Malky, hey yer big Capper's nearly as good as me!"

They all laughed, none more than Preacher. A happy five minutes passed while Arnie sucked the life out of his fag. Time was soon up and the Preacher slipped his rig back on. Finishing, he propped his forage cap back on his head. Smiling at Geordie he said, "Nice meeting you, wee Geordie. You've some talent about you. Keep it up. Catch you later, Malky."

As they left the yard, Arnie turned to Geordie and shouted, "I'll second that wee man. You're a smasher, a real prospect. Try to avoid the tackles a wee bit better son. You're all covered in bruises so you are. Catch yez later."

With that, Arnie and the Preacher were gone. Malcolm smiled down at Geordie. "Well, what did you think of those guys wee man, they're here to look after us and that includes you?"

Geordie stared past Malcolm deep in thought, trying in his own mind to make sense of things. Finally, he looked up at Malky, his chest still racing, "Aye, they were dead on I suppose. Actually, quite nice. Here that Constable Preacher, he's some player, he could walk straight into the Glens. They're busting for a striker so they are." (Glentoran Football Club is the top semi-professional football team in East Belfast.) Malcolm laughed.

"You're right there Geordie. Just remember if you ever need any help for any reason, you can call any one of us. Do you hear me know?" Geordie stared on. Malcolm gazed at the mass of cuts and bruising on the boy and winced. They hadn't come from any football pitch. No one could get near him on the pitch. They had come from his brute of a father. Malcolm ruffled Geordie's hair and made his way out of the Theatre of Dreams. He stooped slightly as he passed beneath the 'Edgars Builders' sign and out again into the real world. He worried for the boy. Then the thud of boot to ball to wall began again. Malcolm crossed his fingers and toes for the exceptional wee critter.

Geordie Magee, the Pearl from Pearl Street.

Chapter 8
Bud's Tale

The lush dewy grass was nudged aside by a large wet black nose all searching and sniffing. It had rained heavily the night before, leaving the sky a luminous blue and the morning air as light as a feather. Bud just loved his down time first thing in the morning, sunrise was his very own 'pawsonal' alarm clock. There was always so much to see and explore around their gaff, the tiny rustic cottage. It had hidden itself untroubled and undisturbed for generations behind a small wooded area quietly looking out onto the beautiful Strangford Lough. Bud shared his home with his master and best friend, the Preacher. It had just eased past 10.00 AM and the magnificent golden retriever had been lolloping around since sun up. He'd taken up position behind an old tree stump now smothered with ivy. It was one of his favourite spots to chill and observe. His head turned suddenly as his twitching nose picked up the smell of bacon frying, aha his master was up, another few minutes and he would get the call.

A large bowl of dry kibble awaited him followed by their bacon game. A few offered paws then a roll over or three ending with the counting routine where he had to bark out the answers. You know the game, one bark meaning one, three barks meaning three. Bud could count really well, especially when he was counting on the bacon sitting on the kitchen table. This performance usually secured Bud a few extra rashers of the fattest fatty bacon. Bud's eyes smiled. His master just loved those times. Who was he to spoil them?

Back to business, his long tail began to slowly swish at the sight of three baby rabbits. They had appeared from the woodland behind him and had tentatively hopped out onto the shorter grass leading down to the shore. Bud had remained unseen with the soft breeze blowing against his thick damp chest. Bud smiled, softly panting, his long sloppy tongue out. He had always had that curious pup-like quality. He watched with tail wagging pleasure as the rabbits nibbled greedily on the masses of clover and weeds. Bud was in doggy heaven. Things for this special dog just couldn't get any better.

"BUUUDDDD!" Oh, but they had just got better, a lot better. At the sound of his master's voice, the startled rabbits scurried back into the woods. Bud released a woof of pure joy and excitedly bounded back towards the two things he loved the most, the fatty bacon and his master.

About a mile further up the shoreline, two figures supped coffee from a thermos. Both sat at a picnic bench like two blank canvases, with their hardened features snarling at each other. Neither was interested in the wonderful views on offer or each other's company for that matter. They were at a prearranged meeting in a location both men considered safe. Armed goons lurked close by affording them that extra protection if required.

Their meeting point was the ancient Nendrum monastic site located at Mahee Island, a local beauty spot just a few miles beyond Comber in County Down. The site was founded by Saint Machaoi in the 5th century and has links with Saint Patrick the patron Saint of Ireland.

Nendrum is surrounded on three sides by Strangford Lough and is accessible by only one narrow road. Its elevated aspect and tranquil setting afford breathtaking views making it a must see on anyone's bucket list. The site is lovingly maintained by the National Trust and is a popular tourist and family attraction. It's also a twitchers' paradise as well as an ideal hook up spot for any other nefarious liaisons, if you catch my drift!

Here two of Northern Ireland's biggest criminals sip coffee and discuss delicate matters of a business nature. On one side of the frosty bench, we have Martin Rooney, he's 44 years old from 3, Vulcan Court, Short Strand, East Belfast. Martin choses to live in the area that Strand Police station luxuriates in, like an irritant boil on the backside of his community. He's the IRA Commander for both the Short Strand and Markets areas of lower South and East Belfast. Both these areas stare across the River Lagan at each other while guarding the entrance to Belfast City Centre in a snarling pit bull fashion. His stomping ground is a staunch Republican stronghold and easily identifiable by Irish tricolour flags and anti-British graffiti daubed on many of its prominent walls. These charming logos offer little cheer to 'The Troubles' weary commuters heading to and from the Belfast City Centre.

Looks can be deceptive, can't they? Outwardly Martin appeared, well, rather nondescript. He stood at no more than 5 feet 6 inches and came with a somewhat jolly roly-poly frame, pudgy if you like. His hair is ginger, curly if left to its own devices but cut stylishly short, as you would if you were a man who cared about his appearance. This coiffured mop sat atop a gammon-coloured face. Stay away summer sun if you please. He's long sighted so spectacles are a needs must, 'Heinrich Himmler' in style if you're interested. These classics cling forlornly to his little oinky nose, not that he's 'noseticed'.

Handsome is not a word to be used when describing our Martin. He comes at you with an educated Belfast accent giving you the impression that you're chatting with a bank clerk or civil servant type. Martin lives alone but has male friends if you catch my drift. If you see him about, he'll stop and pass the time of day with you.

The females in his manor think he's great and very down to earth, you know the type, "Never has a smile off his face!" Rookie cops are taken in by his easy charm, some even think that he's their friend never realising that when they're passing the time of day, he's offering nothing about himself. It's about them. He'll talk to you about cars, holidays, girlfriends, wives and lovers.

Anything really. "Where's the best place for a pint, is that handy to where you live? Oh, you live there, do you? It's lovely up there I'm told, wish I could afford it. I had a mate who lived in this street, is that near you? Oh, I see, yours is the next one down. Lucky you. Wish I was on your wages. Must go now, all the best to you. Cheerio."

BUT Martin hated everything about you! His hatred is a generational one. As my fathers hated you so I hate you. His hatred ran deep and is unquenchable. He's incapable of seeing his world in any other way. Friendly Martin now knows what street you live in and what type of car you drive right down to the colour. He knows where your wife works and where your kids go to school. Martin wants you planted. He wants you dead.

Martin didn't become head honcho of the Provos in the East for being nice to little old ladies though I should comment that he is. He's been an active volunteer for many years. Word has it that he's been responsible for several police and army killings. He's also spent five years in Long Kesh Prison on explosive charges. There he garnered major respect from his peers on the Republican wing. His mantra within Republican circles was and is, "The bastards will never take me alive!" So far, they haven't!

On the opposite side of the frosty bench sat Darren Boyd or "Dazbo" to his inner circle. Dazbo is the main man of the East Belfast UVF (Ulster Volunteer

Force). Dazbo is 38 years old and single. He saw himself as a bit of a 'Don Juan' and very much likes the ladies, anything from barely teens to the nearly twenties variety. He stood precariously on stork like spindly legs at a gangly 6 feet 2 inches. His greying hair's a nicotine colour matching his gold capped teeth. Personal hygiene is a complete stranger to him. He's all into his denims and oh, before I forget, he's also heavily into the 'roids', steroids that is. His arms are buffed up huge and veiny, and are pitted like pin cushions. His left upper arm sports a 'Red hand of Ulster' tattoo while a 'FTP' (Fuck the Pope) is crudely etched on his right forearm. He acquired this objet d'art on a drink and drug fuelled break in Bangkok many Lolitas ago. Intellectually he's no match for our Martin who he's now eyeballing as a queer fart.

Our Dazbo however has something in common with Martin, maybe about the only thing now that I think about it. He's also done a bit of bird. No, not the underage variety this time. We're talking about his prison time on the Protestant Wing in Long Kesh, three years at Her Majesty's pleasure for firearms offences. All to do with a robbery at a 'bookies' that went terribly wrong. Today, he would love to have a one on one with Martin and knock seven bells of green shite out of him. But not today Dazbo. Today's all about business.

Martin gazed up at Darren who's giving him a 'Queer bastard' contemptuous glare. "What's up. Everything ok at your end?"

Dazbo snatches the verbal faux pas and sneers, "Oh aye Martin, my end's just fine unlike yours I'll bet. Busted cigar springs to mind!"

Martin shakes his head while removing his glasses. He calmly wipes the lenses with a clean white cotton hanky. When done he perches them precisely back on his tiny oinker then coldly hisses, "They get filthy, so they do. Especially when there's a pile of orange bullshit flying around. Now cut to the chase, you stinky orange prick. What do you want?"

Dazbo bit, he was a gift. "Fuck you, ya fenian bastard, people have died for less. Anyhow, there's a wee job needs done. Urgent like."

Martin shrugged, "A wee job?"

Dazbo leaned his face right up to Martin's introducing him to the joys of his personal stink, a gross cocktail of stale booze and heavy nicotine. In a wheezy whispered tone, he continued, "A wee hit on a peeler what's been causing us all a shit load of grief. He's taken the war to our drugs racket. Dealers' doors are being smashed in and our shits being seized. I'm telling you it's only a matter of time before he arrives on your side of the fence. The bastard's costing us a small fortune so he is."

Martin contemplates quietly for a moment before gently easing the stink away. "A wee hit you say Mr. UVF Boss, are you lot incapable of doing the dirty deed yourselves? I mean to say, it's only a peeler for fuck's sake. You're holding all the cards. You choose the who, the how and the when. Jesus Christ, half the time, they're not even carrying. Let me think about your generous proposition for a moment. Shucks, didn't even need that long. Fuck off with bells on. I'm not risking any of mine, not while your lot are sitting at home scratching your ball bags. That said, crack on Dazbo, you have my fullest blessing. If some black bastard is throwing a spanner in the works, erase him, take him out."

If looks could kill, they'd both be dead. Martin glanced at his watch then took a deep breath from the side. "Now are we done here because you're one stinky bastard?"

Dazbo snarled, he really wanted to end the fenian prick. He subtly felt for his Walther PPK pistol stuffed down the back of his jeans. Martin was freaking him out, or was it the drugs dying inside him. "OK, OK, hear me out. If us lot do the hit, the cops will know it's all down till the drugs, which, let's face it, neither of us want. They'll get really pissed at us. Next thing is they'll be all over us like a rash, smashing doors in, raiding pubs, you know what they're like. Not good for business, not good at all. However, if your lot kill him and claim the hit, it'll look like a regular Provo hit on police. Fuck's sake, you lot are plugging the bastards all the time. Come on Gaystein, use your brains."

The Provo Boss let that one go; he'd learnt from experience that temper wasn't your friend when faced with a problem. Nodding slowly, he gazed up at the smell, "By the by, when's the next shipment in?"

Dazbo sensed a slight shift. "Arriving in Rotterdam in a couple of days. Should be in at the Port of Dublin by Saturday at the latest. That's providing everything runs smoothly, of course."

Martin nodded still deep in thought. His cogs were now heavily engaged on the peeler proposition. "The usual routine, Dazbo?"

Dazbo nodded, "Aye. The old Turkish ceramics gig, it's not failed us yet. Three cases of wacky, two for us and one for you. The lorry driver at the Dublin end's a Scottish 'melter' but sound as a pound. We call him the Postman, he's cheap as chips and never fails to deliver."

Martin smiled or was it a grimace. "So, when do we need this peeler sorted?"

Dazbo sensed that Martin was slowly coming around. How he'd gloat to his lackeys at the Longfellow that evening, the Provos carrying out hits for the UVF. Trying to contain his excitement he whispered sincerely, "Oh, as soon as Martin. If the peelers flip one of our dealers we're fucked."

A young male appeared from behind a pile of stones nattily labelled as a monk's former Des Res. He tapped Martin on the shoulder. Martin turned nonplussed. Dazbo missed the familiarity. "'Scuse me mate. You dropped this back there so you did."

The male winked as he waggled his finger over his shoulder. Dazbo still wasn't on the correct page, his was a few pages ahead, at the Longfellow Bar in a few hours' time. Martin took a brown envelope from the male and smiling said, "Jeez chum, I didn't even realise it was missing. A life saver, that's what you are. A fucking life saver."

Dazbo stirred now back in the present. What a dick Martin was, losing stuff and him a boss. He wouldn't last 5 minutes in the UVF, he'd have had his knee caps done for that one. It was then he noticed the other bloke for the first time; now he looked as though he could handle himself. He had that ease about him, the one that let you know he's not to be messed with. He was early twenties and around 6 feet tall. A good-looking kid with dark hair and brown eyes, pity about his busted nose. His weight, hmm, he was a trim and athletic 168 pounds give or take a pie or two. In boxing parlance, a light heavyweight perhaps.

Dazbo clocked his knuckles which in places were depressed. Martin reached for his wallet tucked away inside his jacket pocket, "Here mate, here's a fiver, go get yourself a pint with my undying thanks." His back was to Dazbo and a smile played on his lips as he slipped the male a wink.

The young male chewed a smile. "Nahhh mate. You're all good. Let's call it my good deed for the day. I'll just stay here and admire the view. It's lovely this time of year, don't you think?"

Martin nodded, "Lovely. Sure, where else would you be on a day like this!"

Dazbo was now bored titless. "Ok Gaylord, any fucking chance, some of us have places to go and people to see."

Martin spun around, "Aye and school girls to ride, you sick bastard!" In a furious rage, Dazbo snapped and made for his gun, then in an explosive second he found himself pinned down with his face pushed hard into the bench. His right arm was wrenched halfway up his back in an agonising twist.

Screaming in agony, he yelled, "Aww, fuck yez, me arm. You're breaking my fucking arm!"

The young male had saved his boss. Another powerful move had Dazbo flipped leaving him panting and pinned down by his wrists. For all his efforts, he couldn't budge. It was then his brain registered that his own back up had disappeared. Apart from another one of Martin's goons standing over at the pedestrian entrance they were the only ones there. Frantically he stared over at Martin. The Provo boss was ice-cold staring at the ground impassively. Panicking, he gasped as terror gripped him, "Martin, what the fuck!"

Martin snarled with a casual contempt. "Didn't want you getting yourself killed before our wee meeting was over DAAZZBOO."

Dazbo's heart was bashing. His every twist and grunt proving futile, he was heavily out muscled. Then he felt his Walther pistol being removed from the back of his jeans. I t was handed over to Martin who deftly ejected the magazine which he casually tucked away into his jacket pocket. The Walther pistol was then set on the bench beside him.

Martin gave the stinky Prod a warm smile, the one reserved for the little old ladies. "Settle petal, you're going to do yourself an injury there. Now then, what's the story, morning glory. Who's the peeler and where's the best place to have him whacked?"

Martin gave a faint wink and Dazbo's wrists were released. Panting hard, he nervously sat up. His mouth was parched as he struggled to get the words out. He placed his hands on the bench and began rubbing at his tingling wrists and then he noticed the trembling. Martin smiled up at Slugger, his young minder. Dazbo was in no doubt that he was at Martin's mercy. He heard himself speak. It sounded like an adolescent boy whose voice had just broken.

"What have you done with my boys, you fenian bastard?"

Martin sighed; his patience was beginning to wear thin. It would be nice to top this smelly wanker with his own gun, but not today, business before pleasure. "Not nice, Dazbo. Don't be speaking to your business partner like that. Your boys are having a wee chill, you can go get them when we're all done here. Word to the wise, when you're choosing your heavies, I'd be looking for blokes that can actually handle themselves in a tight squeeze. Those pair of dicks were as handy as a whoopee cushion in a minefield." Slugger sniggered.

Dazbo nodded clearing the feathers from his throat, his overwhelming hatred of Martin had been replaced by abject fear. "OK, OK. His name's Grant, Derek

Grant. He's your Mr. Golden Balls. He's an inspector at Mountroyal and the one behind all the operations against us. Word has it he's nearing retirement, but that's no good to us now. He attends the Free Methodist Church at the bottom of Castlereagh Street every Sunday morning, never misses. That's the one facing the Mountpo…"

Martin butted in, "Mountpottinger Road, Short Strand. I know. I do live there." He was beginning to see the possibilities.

Dazbo continued, "Sorry Martin. Well, you see, he drives a maroon Volvo Estate TIJ9016 or something like that. It's a mix of 1690 (The year of the Battle of the Boyne celebrated by Loyalist Orangemen every Twelfth of July). But the TIJ bit is spot on.

His Church kicks off at 11:30 AM. Grant gets their 'peeler' punctual between ten and a quarter past and parks his wheels up in the exact same spot in 'The Mount'. That's the street 50 yards above the church. He's so fucking predictable. I'm telling you; a blind man could nut him with his eyes shut. The only people up that hour of the morning is the 'churchies'. As hits go, Grant's a fucking gift!"

Martin sat with his head bowed, nodding slowly. True, Grant had to go, there was too much cash at stake. But what to do with Dazbo?

He could, of course, make Dazbo and his pair of goons quietly **disappear**[1] forever, the thought appealed to him, it would be nice getting rid of the smell once and for all.

Martin dragged himself back from his wishful thinking and returned to his now. As for Dazbo's proposition, Golden Balls Grant would be easy, sure he came practically gift wrapped for his young minder and protégé. Slugger here had been champing at the bit to prove himself. This would be his first kill. Martin

---

[1] *People disappeared in Northern Ireland every day. It became a legacy of the Troubles. Saints and sinners alike all clumped together in a box labelled 'THE DISAPPEARED'. That same box was then stuffed in the attic of our collective consciences and left there unopened and undisturbed. Everyone carried a fear of falling into it. The police then were up to their eyes with daily murders, shootings and explosions. Someone reported missing came way down in their list of priorities. Of course, there would be the initial flap from family and friends and the wringing of hands. But life and a lot more deaths in the province went macabrely on. It would take but a few days, a few murders and atrocities to have them completely forgotten about. The legacy sadly remains. A blight on the province's conscience.)*

had no doubts as to his ability or to the success of his first mission. But back to Dazbo? Decisions, decisions. It was a hard life being an IRA Commander.

It was like an epiphany. A curlew swept by overhead releasing its lonely call. A soft breeze made its way through haggard creaking pines and brushed against his yellow jaundiced cheeks. He squinted as white clouds slipped past the summer sun like an old slide show at your favourite aunties. Light, shade, light shade. Live or die, live or die.

Dazbo sat in silence rubbing at his wrists which was now more of a nervous twitch. He anxiously watched on as the queer bastard pondered. Little knowing that his life at that moment was hanging by the finest of threads. Then for the first time, Dazbo began to take in the beauty of his surroundings.

The sun flashed bright through a gap in the clouds as Martin lifted his head like a man reborn. "OK. We'll do it, and it will all happen this Sunday. It will be done 100% my way, do you understand?"

Dazbo nodded. "Mr Feel the Love will pick up the drugs in his shiny green van Saturday night, Sunday morning at the usual border spot." Dazbo interrupted him there, "Martin, it's Fields the Love, that's what's on the side of his van." Martin nodded. "Whatever, we'll pick up our share of the drugs and top Golden Balls, all at the same time on Sunday morning. Have Mr Feel the L…"

Dazbo interrupted, "His name's Oli, Martin." Pet hate, Martin hated being interrupted. He had been working on his anger management but Mr. Stinky here was tapping all his buttons, hammering them actually. "For fuck's sake, Dazbo just shut the fuck up and listen."

Dazbo nodded contritely, secretly enjoying being a pain in the arse. Martin took in a deep lung full of air then slowly exhaled. "Shall we continue? Instruct Oli to park his van up, unlocked at the mouth of **Cluan Place**[2] shortly after 11.00 AM on Sunday morning, have him leave our case of goodies in the back." Martin looked at Dazbo, "Are you with me so far, fuckwit?" Dazbo nodded, smiling from behind clenched teeth.

---

[2] *(Cluan Place is a tiny working-class cul-de-sac street. It rests against a massive peace wall with further high security fencing dividing two very differing communities. Come the marching season, it became a veritable Beirut of hatred and tribal activity. It's located 20 yards above the Mount on the other side of the road of Castlereagh Street. If you ever stumble into Cluan Place you are left in no doubts as to which side of the political divide you are in. Its red, white and blue curb-stones and Loyalist murals are a dead giveaway.)*

Martin continued, "Oli will then leave his van and make his way out onto Castlereagh Street.

Have him position himself so that he's looking up into the Mount, have him wear a green Glentoran footie top and have a newspaper tucked under his arm. While he's at this my boys will collect our case of 'wacky' from the back of his van.

When Grant arrives and parks up in the Mount, have Oli open his paper and pretend to read it. That will give us the heads up so to speak. When the bastard walks out onto Castlereagh Street, have Oli cross the road and tail him for about 20 yards then leave. That's him finished, all done, he can fuck off in his shiny green van. You got all that. Do you need me to write it down for you shit for brains?" Martin laughed. Dazbo nodded, "Aye, sounds like a plan."

Martin grinned at Slugger and winked. "We'll take it from there won't we Slugger?" Then turning back to Dazbo, he growled. "Remember. NO Glentoran man. NO HIT! Comprendi?"

Dazbo nodded, "Right you be Martin. Sure thing."

Martin beamed, "Well thank fuck for that. It's just that you're one stinky bastard isn't he Slugger?"

The young minder grinned. Dazbo inwardly raged. How he'd love to see those two begging for their lives in a Loyalist romper room. Martin got to his feet tossing Dazbo's gun at his young minder. Slugger caught it then wedged it down the back of his sporty chinos. He grinned at the Prod, "Hope not to smell you too soon, Dazbo."

Martin then casually headed for the small secluded car park as the sunlight and breeze danced with the summer leaves. He smiled as he approached Slugger then paused suddenly as his piggy little eyes detected something. Martin closed into Slugger's personal space making him feel uneasy. He then critically tap-tap-tapped at Slugger's light-coloured top.

"Bit of ketchup there, kid, those kind of stains are the devil to get out so they are!"

Slugger raged, "For fuck's sake. It's only just on me, boss."

Dazbo inwardly seethed as he slowly followed Martin out. He watched the little performance imagining how he'd kill the poster boy first, right in front of his master before nutting him as well. But for all that, he was now physically and emotionally spent. Their little business meeting had been one hell of an experience and yes if truth be told, the UVF boss was still very scared. As they approached the car park, Dazbo froze.

"Right, you shower of shites, joke's over. Where the fuck's my wheels?" Martin walked on towards a black Ford Mondeo idling quietly in the otherwise empty car park. Its driver was immaculate, another poster boy, thirty something, spray tanned, lean and muscular. His hair was dark, medium length greased back in Calvin Klein fashion. To complete his look, he was wearing a white cap T-shirt. Bach was playing softly from the music system. His eyes remained fixed staring straight ahead. Slugger opened the rear passenger door for his boss and waited. The remaining goon on the hill nipped into the front passenger seat and was impassive. Martin's crew could've passed as a boy band.

Just before popping himself into the vehicle, Martin turned and grinned at the flummoxed UVF prick, "Ooops, silly me, totally forgot in all the excitement, this is yours I believe!" He reached into his jacket pocket and pulled out the brown envelope from earlier. Dazbo, puzzled, took it from him and tore it open. He screeched as a set of car keys and a human index finger fell to the ground. Both were covered in blood!

"Ahh, you crazy bastards. Yez are all sick fuckers." The four Provos burst out laughing as Dazbo's bladder suddenly betrayed him. A dark stain emerged on the front of his jeans. More hysterical laughter followed. Martin gasping raised his arms signalling for calm. "Enough lads, enough now. Ok Mr. Pissy Pants, it's like this, your wheels are?"

The driver spoke up, "Quarter mile down the road on the lough side planted up a lane boss. A lovely red Vauxhall Cavalier, might need a wee deep clean though!"

Dazbo yelled, "Yez bastards. What about my crew? They better be alright or…"

Martin laughed, "Or what, big-time Charlie? They're alive. One of them is resting his eyes though, his reflexes weren't up to scratch, hey Slugger?"

Slugger laughed, "He had the reflexes of a sloth on beta blockers. I sparked him with a feather duster right hook!"

Dazbo gasped at the finger, it was now an oyster blue hue gathering dirt. He stammered, "Whose finger is it then?"

Slugger spoke looking at Martin. "That's Mr. Pointy boss, you know who I mean."

Martin nodded. He did indeed. "Aye, we've been looking him for months. The legendary Mr. Pointy. What do you call him then Slugger. I take it, he was in chatty form?"

Slugger smiled now holding up and waggling an attractive gold coloured cigar cutter. "Well boss, after a little gentle persuasion he told us he was a Magee, a Stanley Magee. Once we lopped his pointer off, he was fit to tell us anything. Jeez I never met a grown man who cried as much. Click, Click! Like a knife through butter it was, and here's everyone telling me he was a hard man!"

Dazbo gulped, he was now in a bit of a quandary. Should he pick it up or choose to forget about it? He heard himself scream out. "Fuck's sake lads, what did our Stan ever do to you lot?"

Martin glared, "Plenty. These last few years he's always about the interface, come marching season, stirring the shit. He's the sheriff of the orange brats goading them into chucking bricks and the like into the Strand. Our pensioners are terrified every summer, terrified of getting their windows put in. Aye, then there's the petrol bombs and the free for alls in no man's land. He's always there, hanging around like a bad smell. Bit like yourself Dazbo except you actually do smell. Listen here, someone's going to get killed sooner or later, you mark my words. We call him Mr. Pointy because he's always pointing over at our lot inviting them for a dig. Trouble is, it's only to the kids he's making the offer. Some fucking Prod hero. NOT!"

Dazbo bit back, "Hark. Listen to Mother fuckin' Theresa. Your lot are just as bad. We're always on the wrong end of beatings walking past the Strand after a night out in the city. When we're stopped it's all about knowing the words to your 'Soldier's Song'. When we don't know them, it's a trip to the Belfast City Hospital A&E with broken bones if we're lucky!"

Then the penny dropped as Dazbo eyed the red stain on Slugger's top. "That's not fucking ketchup!"

Martin laughed, "No shit Sherlock, it's Stan Magee's finest claret. No more pointing over at us this marching season, not with that finger anyways. You tell him from me he's lucky to be alive. He's a dead man if he shows his face at the interfaces again, comprendi? We're off now. People to see, places to go and peelers to plug. Don't be letting us down on Sunday. Bye now and have yourself a nice day DAZBO!"

Dazbo was shattered, he didn't know which end of him was up. "Lads, at least give me a lift to me car. Sure, look at the state of me and I've got to pick that thing up."

Suddenly a huge black backed gull swept in from behind him all squawking and flapping, its timing was perfect. Dazbo screeched, cowering like a whipped pup, then he felt his bladder squeeze out one final encore. In a single sweeping stall, the bird plucked Stan's pointer from the ground then effortlessly took off into the clear blue sky. The group watched on open-mouthed as the gull slowly disappeared from view over the vast watery expanse. Martin burst into unbridled laughter. His crew all joined in.

"Aww, Dazbo, you're too much. Our sides are splitting. Pure genius. Please stop now. We've had enough. Could our day get any better? Could yours get any worse?" And with that they were gone. Wheels spun hard against the silence, throwing up dust and dirt onto the solitary UVF boss. He watched shell-shocked as the Mondeo powered off down the road at breakneck speed. He knew they would be laughing all the way back to the Short Strand or the Shit Strand as the prods called it.

Dazbo let out a huge sigh then muttered to himself, "Some fucking crew. Some back up those jokers turned out to be. Arseholes more like." They were in for it. He was going to… Then he forlornly gazed down at the front of his piss-stained jeans. If he'd paid more attention at school he would have noted a striking resemblance to the map of China. Sadly, he hadn't and what should have been a magical moment passed him by. It could have been worse though, he could be dead for that matter and yes, looking at his hands he still had all his fingers, he supposed. He began slowly walking down the empty tree lined road in search of his red Vauxhall Cavalier. What sort of carnage was he going to find?

Bud licked his chops. He could barely move a paw. His master always gave him too much meal, and as for the rashers of fatty bacon grrrrr, 'pawradise'. He had gotten himself round to the front porch where there was a little shade from the heat of that day. Plumping himself down facing the lough gave him the views and the soft cooling breeze it had to offer. He slowly relaxed as his old muscles sagged into sleep mode. His inquisitive eyebrows like showroom shutters began to close and then he was gone. Dream world. "BUDDDD, come on fella. Last one in's a rotten tomato!"

Bud stirred, if dogs could smile, he was. "WOOF." Shuffling up on all fours, he had already lost 15 yards to his master who was sprinting effortlessly towards the old wooden jetty. "WOOF, WOOF!" Bud set off like a runaway train slowly gathering speed. He wasn't the speed machine he once was but he could still turn a paw. Closer ever closer to his master and the jetty. "WOOF."

They arrive at the end of the jetty at the same time, Bud never for once considering that his master had sneakily slowed up in deference to his advancing years. "YEEHAW! WOOF!"

Both leapt off together, one of life's most beautiful sights, the unconditional love between a man and his dog. *Splash*, it never lets you down. The water was freezing cold. Every sense, muscle and sinew received an explosion of stimulation, it was great to be alive.

The Preacher swam out a bit, slowly becoming accustomed to the chill with Bud paddling serenely in tow. Bud was more elegant on water than he was on land. The Preacher stopped for a bit as he usually did and began treading water. This is where he liked to chat about the personal stuff. Bud was an attentive listener.

"Bud fella, I have to confess. There's another pulling at my heartstrings." Bud had already picked up on that one, the beautiful blonde. He liked her too. She was nice. She had a good heart. "I'm giving you fair notice so no moping."

"WOOF!" Bud's eyes lit up. "Her name's Stephanie, Stephanie Gates.

You've met her before. You both seem to get on. Someday I'm going to ask her out on a date. But I think she sees me just as a friend. What should I do and how do I do it?"

Bud thought about it then went, "WOOF WOOF." In doggy language meaning, "Does she like bacon!"

A great time was had and the Preacher found comfort in their heart to heart. "Come on fella, let's get back. You're not getting any younger and I've got me some shirts to iron for work tomorrow." The offshore breeze had kicked up resulting in tiny slapping waves and soft spray, a perfect end to their swim on that hot summer's day. High overhead a black backed gull was struggling with something in its long sharp beak. A gust of wind later and Stan Magee's index finger fell earthwards, splashing lightly into the pale green waters of the lough. Mother nature would dispose of it from there on in.

Dazbo looked down the overgrown lane and spotted a gateway to a large fallowed field, and there they were, his wheels. The red Vauxhall Cavalier with the fine white stripes up its sides. He checked the front of his trousers; China was slowly fading but still there. As he neared the vehicle, he could hear muffled moaning. Shuffling up to the side, a quick look inside revealed two bodies in the back seat lying hogtied. One was out for the count. Stan Magee was the other. He was a man fully 'compos mentis'. Stan was wriggling and writhing with one of his ankle socks stuffed in his mouth, his torturers had been kind enough to tie a cotton hanky over his index stump which pleased the squeamish Dazbo no end.

Dazbo assumed the UVF Commander mode striking his best Mussolini pose. Hands on hips he angrily glared down at the unfortunate Stan. Stan finally noticed his boss mid-writhe then caught a glance of his China. His eyes widened in horror followed by a, "Ewwww!"

But Dazbo was too tired. He opened the car door and pulled the socks out of Stan's muffled mouth. A torrent of verbal expletives followed. "Fucking sneaky bastards, they snuck up on us while we were having a quick fag break. Untie me for fuck's sake!"

Dazbo gazed over at the sleeping beauty beside him. "What about your mate there?"

Stan sat up rubbing his wrists and then began untying his feet "Who Oli? That fucker's as much use as an ashtray on a motorbike, thought you said he was a boxer? The other fella barely touched him and he went down like a sack of coal. Good night, Irene. Here, did they give you my finger back? I hear tell that it can be sewn back if it's not off too long?"

Dazbo shook his head. Stan was a bollix. An out and out wanker but they'd been friends all their days. "Stan mate, I don't quite know how to say this to you other than you'll not be doing anymore pointing with that finger ever again." Stan paused, "What the fuck do you mean, boss?"

Dazbo squirmed a little, "Well, you see it was last seen in the hands of or should I say the beak of one huge bastard of a seagull making off over Strangford Lough. It's gone for evermore me old son. Its pointing and nose picking days are over." Stan nodded resigned to his digital dearth and death.

Dazbo patted him on the shoulder, "Stan, you'll just have to learn to point with your other hand." Dazbo found himself annoyingly chuckling. He couldn't stop.

Stan grumbled. What's so funny, pray tell?"

Dazbo was losing control. "Mr. Pointy. The bastards call you Mr. Pointy, oh and by the way Stan, your interface days are over. If they catch you there again, they're going to kill you and that's from the horse's mouth! Apparently, you told them where you lived and what you had for your breakfast!"

Stan held up his pointer-less hand. "Maybe this had something to do with my need to express myself at the time!"

Dazbo nodded. "Fair 'nuff Stan, here, give him a wee nudge. Wake sleeping beauty up there. The only good thing that came out from all of this is they're going to plug Golden Balls this Sunday coming."

Stan nodded, slightly bewildered. "How do you mean?"

Dazbo stretched, "I can't be arsed telling you just now. They took my gun, what about yours?"

Stan shrugged in defeat, "Aye they got both ours."

Dazbo groaned, "We've got some story to concoct among ourselves. Let's get the fuck out of here and back to the East. I need to change these pissy pants and you need to get yourself up to casualty!"

Stan winced, feeling some phantom pains, "Will you not come with me?"

Dazbo laughed, "Dead right on that one Stan. What do you say I drop you off at the Ulster Hospital on the way back? How's that for First Class service? Oh, and I'll big you up to the lads at the Longfellow, I'll make you out as the big hero taking on six of the bastards. We'll say your finger was shot off in heroic circumstances. What do you say?"

Stan liked that very much, "And I won't tell them you pissed your pants Dazbo!"

Dazbo laughed, "We've got ourselves a deal, Stan the man. I'll tell all about the Sunday hit later on the night at the Longfellow. Right Stan, wake up crystal chin in case he needs some casualty treatment!"

Stan nodded and held what used to be his finger but now a space up to his mouth in a shhhhh fashion. Dazbo did all he could not to laugh. His lips trembled as he feigned a cough come splutter. He set the key into the ignition and started her up. Soon his team were on the road for Comber and heading home to the mighty East Belfast. Downtown Radio was on as Stan gently shook the unconscious male. "Oli son, wake up. Come on now."

Eventually Oli stirred like a fairy tale Prince who had been asleep for a thousand years. Groaning to himself he slowly sat up. He winced as he patted at his swarthy face. "Jeez boys. Where the fuck am I? Arrgh, I think me jaws broke." Oli Fields head was thumping, his chiseled jaw now resembled the winner of a chubby bunny contest.

Oliver Fields was a thirty-something useless boxer from East Belfast. He lived with his mum at 12, Ampere Street and was spoiled rotten. A mummy's boy I suppose. If truth be told there wasn't a bad bone in his body. He looked the part alright at 6 feet 3 inches and was hewn out of gym sculpted granite. Oli was naturally swarthy with thick black hair which he always kept just so. He had large deep set chestnut eyes which the chicks found irresistible. There could well have been a bit of Sicilian in him for his mummy had entertained many nationalities in her hedonistic youth. In short, our Oli was a real live babe magnet. When he wasn't masquerading as a UVF goon he was a painter and decorator by trade and a good one at that. He had a professional side to him and was very particular about his work. There were never any complaints on that score, nor the other goodies he bestowed on females who were lucky enough to benefit from his extra strokes.

His pride and joy was his Ford Escort van which he'd painted a brilliant chartreuse green. It stuck out like a sore thumb, a bit like himself in the looks department. To the sides of his van was painted 'Fields the Love. Painter and Decorators. Satisfaction guaranteed.' This was delivered in a white swirly style. He was a natural heavyweight but had been cursed with one fatal genetic flaw, it was his Kirk Douglas dimpled glass jaw. The softest tap would lay him out in slumber mode. Smart asses would tease him that he was the only boxer ever to have advertisement space on the soles of his boxing boots.

A bit harsh on our Oli who in truth was more of a lover than a fighter.

Dazbo looked over his shoulder, "You're all right champ? Let's get you home 'til your mammy. You've a couple of important wee jobs coming up."

Oli nodded, rubbing hard at his ruffled hair now standing on end. He then smiled goofily rubbing his chin in a rather comical manner. Where had Dazbo seen that done before? Then he remembered as the crackling black and white music from the 1930s began to play in his head!

Jesus he should have seen the signs. His two minders, his two heavies, STAN and fucking OLI! Or, OLIVER and HARDY!

Chapter 9
Black Bart

Derek's paper knife swiftly scythed open the buff envelope addressed to the Station Inspector, Mountroyal. Removing several sheets of documentation some stapled others paper clipped, his trained eye made for the top right-hand corner giving the address from whence it came. Complaints and Discipline Branch, Lisnasharragh Police Station, Montgomery Road, Belfast. A "Bastarding fuck" escaped from his usually eloquent mouth. Through pursed lips, he began to mumble, come read through several pages marked for his information and attention. Another "Bastarding fuck" came when he read who was overseeing the complaint. Detective Chief Inspector J. Bartholomew known and feared throughout the force simply as Black Bart. A noted slayer of police careers. If Black Bart was on your case, you were in a serious hole. The black bit was all about his black heart. Fact and fiction danced a merry 'Paso Doble' merging as one as tales spread as to the cruelty of this smiling assassin.

Derek sighed knowing full well that his role in the matter was to serve a formal complaint on one of his men. A written complaint by a member of the public had been received for some alleged transgression or another. In police jargon he was going to have to serve a Form 17/3.

Up to that point, Derek was having a fluffy day. Classical strains had been seeping like honey on hot toast from his old faithful Panasonic radio. It had perched on the window ledge behind him for years, a light dusting wouldn't have gone amiss. Baroque as opposed to hard rock kept his mood light and his mind clear. After two hours he had arm wrestled his in-tray into submission as he slowly cleared his busy diary. Apart from this newly arrived 17/3, everything on his desk was in order. Derek fidgeted then checked his watch, 9:20 AM time for action. Tea with the boys in the Guardroom! This was more of a minor head in the sand manoeuvre, for Derek needed to get his thoughts in order and his little mental ducks all in a row.

He slipped out of his office taking a right quickly arriving at the partition door separating the main building from the Enquiry Office and public reception area. He pressed an electric door release button which buzzed letting him into the main reception area. Derek found it empty save for Malky, the station cleaner, who on seeing him practically stood to attention beside his mop and bucket.

Malky's tape recorder was playing the latest of his favourite tunes, "Beyond the Sea" by Bobby Darin.

Malky panicking made to switch his music off but Derek gestured him not to bother. He sauntered on into the Enquiry Office with a nonchalant swagger.

"Tea anyone?" The two guards looked up feigning astonishment.

Vic looked over at Tweety reaching for his heart, "Jesus Tweety, put me on the sick. I think I'm losing my facilities. I thought I'd heard the Inspector offering to make us a cup of tea!"

Tweety laughed, "Me too. What about you, Malky me old son?"

Malky fidgeted uncomfortably, banter wasn't his thing. Derek shook his head at the two old stagers, "Bastards. Last chance you pair. Do you fancy a cuppa yourself, Malky?"

Malky fidgeted some more. "Well like, I'm awful busy so I am …"

Tweety grinned, "Yes Inspector, we'd all love a brew. Vic's got the custard creams in; you know how we take it, don't you?" Derek gave a thumbs up and pointed for a buzz of the partition door. Tweety obliged. The door buzzed and Derek disappeared into the main building en route to the kitchen.

Vic continued their heated debate, "I'm telling you Tweety, George Best is the best there's ever been. Sure, look at his flair, his skill, no one dribbles like him!" Vic left it hanging there.

Malky hopped in, "Specially after a couple of bottles of champers." Malky chuckled to himself. Vic and Tweety looked at each other flabbergasted. Malky had cracked a funny, that was one for the vaults.

Tweety regathered, "Pele for me every time. What an athlete. 21 years at the top and 1279 mesmerizing goals. Your Bestie was amazing but he falls way short of my man, Pele."

Tweety glanced up at Her Majesty hanging on the wall. She had a disapproving look on. Tweety thought to himself, "Eh, Your Majesty, I know, it's Jimmy Greaves for you. Yes. I get it, when he played for the Hammers and not the Lily Whites. Check the stats out, Your Majesty, they never lie."

The intercom linking the Enquiry Office to the security sanger buzzed. Wee John threw his hat into the ring, he'd been listening in while watching diligently up and down the Woodstock Road. "Cruyff for me. What a player. Total football. Played for Ajax, Barcelona, a couple of yank sides finishing up at Feyenoord. Scored loads and made even more. He won the Ballon d'Or three times and captained the Dutch team to a World Cup Final in 1974. How do you like them tomatoes Tweety Pie?" Tweety nodded.

Maybe Wee John had him there, "Mmm, not bad Wee John. What about you Wee Mo. Any thoughts on the matter?"

Wee John responded, "Just me in here. Wee Mo's on files in the Cons Workroom and Billy Porter's out."

"Sweeping!" rhymed Vic and Tweety. Vic stretched back in his creaking chair, "Over to you, Malky. Who is the best you've seen?"

Malky loved his football. He supported Glentoran, the East Belfast Giants and the Red Devils, Manchester United. If footie was on the tele, Malky would be in front of it. He knew his stuff. Malky ummed and ahhed. He knew he was about to get slaughtered but he had to call it as he'd seen it. "Ok youse pair, I want no slagging. Do yez promise me now?"

Tweety and Vic nodded. Wee John piped in from the sanger, "Go ahead Malky son, we're all ears."

Malky took a deep breath then blurted, "Wee Geordie Magee, the Pearl Street Pearl. He's the best I've ever seen." Silence followed.

Malky went on, "I know yez are dying to laugh, how can a child of 11 be better than all the others. I've watched all the greats in my lifetime but this kid will take all your breaths away. He does stuff with the ball that hasn't been invented. He dribbles like Best and shoots like Pele, I'm telling you, watch this space fellas. I may be just a lowly station cleaner but when it comes to football, I knows my stuff!"

Tweety's vast database could find nothing on a Geordie Magee but he saw something in Malky's eyes which made him a reluctant believer. It was a debate ender all right. Tweety nodded, "We shall wait with eager anticipation then Malky me old son."

Derek breezed through the Cons Workroom, he had to, to get to the kitchen. He noted Lionel and Wee Mo were on files. "Morning team, hard at it?"

Lionel paused typing. "As ever Inspector. I'm responding to your queries regarding the Ormeau Golf Club assault file. I got a wee statement from the barman as requested."

Lionel smiled, he could see the blank expression on Derek's face, he hadn't a Scooby Doo. Derek gave a quick "Aha then, very good Lionel, keep the good work up. Eh, leave no stone unturned and all that." He then nipped into the kitchen and quickly filled the kettle and got the mugs sorted.

Realising he should have asked, he shouted through to the workroom, "Do you pair fancy a cuppa?" Both declined, which suited him fine. Derek popped back into the workroom while the kettle was boiling and shimmied over to Wee Mo. He noticed she was chewing anxiously away on her Bic biro. "A little bird tells me you've single-handedly cracked the bacon theft crime wave in the patch. All wee kids stealing to order, I believe?"

Lionel looked up from his clattering typewriter and smiled. He was happy for her; she was one of the best. Wee Mo was in awe of Derek Grant who was none the wiser. "Well Mo, tell all, how did you crack the case?"

Lionel butted in, "Top police work Inspector, top police work!" Derek smiled, giving Lionel a blind side wink as the kettle in the kitchen began its final squeal.

Mo gulped and let out a squeaky cough, "Eh, you see it happened like this…" Derek knew exactly how it happened, Tony Speers had briefed him on her excellent work a couple of days ago. He also knew Wee Mo was looking to get into the regulars and work like this would help her cause no end. Maureen had been given the names and addresses of the children by Mrs. Stewart who ran the Spar Essential Store on the day of the bomb blast. It had then been a straightforward matter of matching the frozen goods in the abandoned shopping bag with the local stores from whence they came. Formal statements of complaint had then been taken which included dates, times and places the goods had gone missing as well as their value.

Derek nodded repeatedly feigning fascination and admiration. In reality, he was really wondering as to how a woman in her mid-forties had suddenly decided to change career paths, from the safety of being a Primary School Classroom Assistant to the dangers of being a serving police officer in Northern Ireland. What had been her reasons, what journey through circumstance had taken this lovely elfin faced creature to this place? "So, that's about it, Inspector," she squeaked, forcing a smile. To Derek, she looked more like Santa's favourite helper.

Derek returned the smile. "Excellent work. Most excellent work Wee Mo! Oh, that's the kettle done boiling. Come see me in my office in 20 minutes or so, bring all your paperwork with you. I have an idea how we can progress this investigation."

Mo nodded. She needed help. This one had given her sleepless nights. She had never arrested anyone let alone interviewed a suspect. Her stomach churned some more as Derek disappeared into the kitchen to make the tea. A minute later he returned kicking the kitchen door open carrying a mock wooden tray and four mugs of tea. Mo leapt up and opened the Cons Workroom door for him. "Cheers Mo, you're a star. Don't forget 20 minutes, my office. Hoy, lads. Hit the partition buzzer for me." The buzzer sounded as he shuffled down the corridor and then disappeared through the buzzing door.

Mo looked over to Lionel who was thuggishly battering the keys on the old dilapidated workroom typewriter. Here was a man lost in creative writing. Lionel could be very, very creative when the need arose. "Oh, Lionel love, I'm really dreading all of this this. What if he thinks my work's rubbish? What if I blow the case? I'm going to have a nervous breakdown so I am!"

Lionel looked up smiling, "Are we shitting ourselves then wee partner? Ok, bring it all over. I'll give it the once over."

Wee Mo heaved a sigh of relief, "Oh would you Lionel love, that's awful kind of you. You see I'm trying to get ..."

Lionel interjected, "Into the regulars. Yes, we all know Wee Mo, come on now, let's see what you got." Lionel pushed himself away from his desk and reached for his fags sitting handily in his in-tray. Mo nervously placed her file before him while Lionel plucked himself a fag. Seeing the state she was in; he offered her one for her nerves.

Mo shook her head at him disapprovingly, "Lionel love, you know I'm trying to give them up, aw but, Jesus. My nerves are pure jangling. Give us one then."

Lionel lit them both then began slowly going through her paperwork. Mo sat in agonised silence dragging hard on her fag, all the while gazing into Lionel's stoic face. He made her start when an involuntary cough escaped like a thunder clap but then quickly resumed his dead pan stoic. He began to hum an annoying tune while all the while his tired eyes remained focussed. He said nothing from the first page to last.

The kitchen door flung open and Tony Speers sauntered in. He was glistening and puffing hard from a session in the gym. His knackered black T-shirt was soaking in sweat; his red cotton shorts were straining to contain his thick muscular thighs amongst other things. His trainers had seen better days but they still worked fine as far as Tony was concerned. He smiled seeing the two lovebirds enjoying a wee fag together.

Lionel looked up, "If you don't mind me saying skipper, you look Daffy Ducked!" Wee Mo looked the other way. Too much testosterone on show. Tony took a final swig from a water bottle he was holding then shook the last few remaining droplets over his black hair.

"Too right, Lionel, the cardio kills me every time. Everything ok with you, Wee Mo?" Tony was oblivious to the effect he was having; he didn't see himself as others saw him, the others meaning mainly the woman folk.

Mo was forced to look up, "Aye, yes Sarge. The Inspector wants to see me in his office in 15 minutes, to do with the bacon thefts, Lionel's just going over my statements and stuff. He's a wee pet."

Lionel smiled through a fag clenched mouth. "Her file's as tight as a duck's arse skipper. Nothing to worry about."

Tony smiled at Wee Mo, "No more than I expected Constable Graham. I'm away for a shower before I stink the place out. Good luck Mo." Tony shuffled out of the Cons Workroom, wearily climbing the back stairs heading for the male showers.

Fifteen anxious minutes later or as near 10 AM as made no odds, Wee Mo was stood outside Derek's office door. She'd always found herself tip toeing past it like a headmaster's office. She took a sharp intake of breath and knocked, a voice from the other side shouted, "Come on in!" Maureen entered.

Derek was on the phone; his face exuding one of pure delight. Chuckling, he motioned her to take a seat. "So, you lot are happy enough to take this one on. Brilliant. Wee Mo will be even happier. Haha. And you can fuck off with bells on you big useless ballicks. What's that, your boss is going to sort me out? Ooooo, my knees are knocking. Right Cliff we're on our way up. Yep, I hears you. You pair have to be at Castlereagh Holding Centre for 11.00 am, Terrorist interviews. No finer men for the job. This won't take long, just the formal handover of paperwork and any loose strings. Think about what this will do for your shitty crime stats this month. I'll have you pair soaring like eagles. Yep, get the kettle on, Archie has the recipe written down somewhere. Aye right. Dead on. What's that, Catherine the real boss has got a lovely apple tart in. We're on our way. Up in two ticks. Bye, bye now."

Derek pushed himself back from his desk trying to wipe the foolish grin from his face. "Ahh, Wee Mo. Good news, if you're happy with it. Pinky and Perky are happy to take your major investigation off your hands. You'll still share in all the credit, make no mistakes about that. They're upstairs waiting on us for the formal handover. The kettle's on and a slice of apple tart awaits. What do you think?"

Relief like a tsunami hit Mo who shrieked with delight which to Derek sounded like a high-pitched squeak, "Yessss oh Inspector Grant, that's brilliant news. Absolutely terrif…"

His phone rang which cut her off mid-flow. Derek mouthed "Sorry. One second," as he lifted the receiver. "Good afternoon, Inspector Derek Grant. Ah, Detective Chief Inspector Bartholomew from Complaints and Discipline. How may I help Sir? Ah ha. Yes, I received the paperwork this morning. No, I haven't served the complaint on Constable Majury as yet. He's out on the ground, I'll see him before he terminates duty. You want a wee chat, is that not what we're doing now Sir? Oh, my covering report as to Constable Majury's overall performance and fitness for duty. Okay, when? Tomorrow morning at Mountroyal 10.00 AM. I'll let the boys on security know you're coming. What's your car? Eh eh. A blue Rover Vitesse, registration LIJ 2418. Fine Sir, see you then."

Derek set the phone down gently. He stared blankly at the wall over Wee Mo's shoulder, his previous sunny disposition had been angle ground off by the call. Mo could see that he was troubled. Smiling at Wee Mo he said, "My time has come to eventually meet Black Bart, the smiling assassin of C&D fame. His infamy precedes him! He's the only man I know that takes pleasure in wrecking a police officer's career and his life, for that matter."

Maureen's joy slammed to earth like a train crash. She looked up at Derek who caught a strange expression in her eyes. "Sorry Sir, but what was that name again?"

Derek frowned, "Bartholomew, why?"

Maureen nodded slowly; her usual upbeat perkiness gone. "Ah ha. Sorry Sir, and his first initial please?"

Derek, puzzled by the request, had to find Black Bart's first initial in the paperwork sitting before him on his desk. A quick shuffle through and he raised his head like a question mark on a page, "Maureen. His initial is a J. It's a J. Bartholomew. My advice to you as far as the job is concerned is to avoid him like the plague. He's coming in to see me tomorrow at 10.00 AM. You lot are on I believe. Here's his vehicle details. Give him the 5-star treatment, not because he's nice. Nope, because he is a bastard of the highest order and he's gunning for our Preacher and we can't stand by and let that happen now, can we? Oh, and please keep all this under your hat. I haven't told the poor sod yet!"

Wee Mo looked as though she had been hit in the face with a shovel. She gulped and under her breath she whispered, "J." Derek stood up, "Sorry Maureen, I didn't quite catch that?" Maureen pulled herself together and smiled her cute Mo smile.

She squeaked, "No Sir. We can't have him gunning for our Pete Majury. I'm sure you'll do your best for him. Shall we get this show on the road with the gang upstairs then?"

Derek chuckled, she was something else, a rare blend of innocence and kindness that had survived the savagery of life. Derek glanced up at Miriam's photograph, his heart suddenly ached, for his true love had passed three years ago. Then looking back at Wee Mo, the old inspector smiled. They were two peas in a pod. How he missed her. He gathered up her paperwork and bundled them into a blank green DPP folder cover.

"Absolutely Mo. We'll have a giggle, a quick cuppa and a slice of tart with the boys. Oh, as well as clear up a major crime wave in our area. To the victors the spoils!"

Derek and Maureen were welcomed with open arms by the CID gang upstairs. Catherine Mercer the stylish Office Manager had the refreshments ready and waiting. The handover took five minutes and the tea and tiffin a further ten. For the pair it was just what the doctor ordered, their party ended when Pinky and Perky reluctantly dragged themselves away for their scheduled terrorist interviews at Castlereagh Holding Centre. This was a policing norm of the time. Wee Mo laughed at Derek's dry wit and mischievous eyes as the pair left the CID Office. She now realised that Derek was quite wonderful, he was kind and had a heart of corn. For people like Derek, you went the extra mile.

They said their goodbyes as Derek returned to his office and Maureen headed for her second home, the security sanger. As she approached the sanger door, a thought gripped her, she urgently needed to pick the mind of another. The brilliant mind of Harold Sweetlove known to all in sundry as Tweety Pie.

It was 2.00 PM later that day when Derek's office door knocked. He felt his chest tighten and teeth clench. He knew who was on the other side. "Come in, come in." The door opened gently and Pete Majury entered stooping under the door frame. Derek looked up, standing before him was 6 feet 4 inches of lithe muscle and natural good looks, all capped with curly rebellious hair. The Preacher was one of the police officers of any rank he admired the most. A thought flashed in, out of the blue. If he could look like any man on the planet! Derek was fixed with a large pair of glacier blue eyes, eyes that viewed life from a different perspective. "Good afternoon, Sir. You wished to see me?"

Derek smiled, "Good afternoon, Peter. Sit yourself down. Here, take that big hulking flak jacket off. Tea, coffee perhaps?"

The Preacher smiled, slipping his flacker off. Something was up. "Don't touch the stuff Sir, I'm fine thank you."

Derek's tummy tightened as he clumsily lurched to the point. He was like a teenage learner driver taking his first lesson in daddy's new car. "It's a 17/3 on you Peter. I'm sorry but I've been sent this 17/3 to serve on you by C&D, that's the Complaints and Discipline Branch. A member of the public has made a formal complaint against you. I'm sorry, Preacher, really, terribly sorry!"

If Derek could see himself now, he wouldn't have been too impressed. He was flapping about like a vicar in a strip joint. The Preacher however was cool as. The Preacher quietly nodded. Derek stumbled on, "It's all to do with the day of that fucking bomb. You and Heavenly were in the Wyse Byse store evacuating it. Remember?"

Pete nodded, "Yep, we got the place cleared just in the nick of time!"

Derek nodded. It had been a close-run thing from many angles. "Absolutely Preacher, no one knows that more than me. However, a Mr. Andrew Prentass, the store manager has alleged that you assaulted him. There's five corroborating witness statements from staff members supporting his allegation. Please tell me you made a notebook entry?"

The Preacher nodded, retrieving his notebook from his shirt pocket. He quickly leafed through it, stopping at the opening page of that day's events. He handed it across the desk to Derek who was anxiously fidgeting with various loose statements. "There you go Sir, that's my Wyse Byse notebook entry."

Derek read through the Preacher's entry several times then exasperated, pushed the notebook back at him. Sighing he groaned, "I'll need a photocopy of your minimalist masterpiece. You see Pete, let me be blunt. What you've recorded in your notebook there, is totally fine but perfunctory. The bit you've put in about assisting Mr. Prentass to the rear of the store doesn't tally up with the witness statements I have in front of me. They're all saying that you grabbed him by the collar of his jacket and the back of his trousers and basically frog marched him all the way down to the rear exit. The man's obtained a doctor's statement. (Which Derek was now waving in the air like an act of surrender.) It said, now let me see, scratches to the neck, eh, sore neck. Strained lower back and eh, (Derek coughed!) swollen nether regions.

"He's got all of this recorded and fine-tuned in his statement of complaint while all you have in your notebook entry is that you ASSISTED, I repeat again ASSISTED him to the rear of the store. Preacher, I'm sorry but if this takes a turn for the worst, we're looking at a charge of Assault Occasioning Actual Bodily Harm at the very least. It could even be argued in a certain light as a Section 18 or Section 20 GBH. (Grievous Bodily Harm). It's not looking good, not looking good at all. Do you have anything to say about these allegations then?"

Pete shrugged, slightly bewildered. This had hit him like a bolt out of the blue. From hero to zero! He spoke, "Inspector, we, as it turned out, had little or no time. The man refused to leave. He was demanding to see my superior officer. I made the call. Preservation of life came first. Did you see the damage to the store when the bomb went off? It was a mess? We got everyone out just in the nick of time. People would have died if I hadn't done what I did. Would or could I have done things any differently? I guess not Sir."

Derek sighed, rubbing the top of his balding head. "Is Heavenly about?" Preacher whispered, "She's on files this afternoon Sir."

Derek nodded and picked up the phone quickly dialling an all too familiar number, "Hi Tweety. Would you mind paging Heavenly to my office. Get your ass down here as well, that's if Vic can spare you? Okay, thanks now."

Derek hung up and looked across his desk. Constable Majury wore the expression of someone waiting on a bus, a bus due in twenty minutes on a soft summer's afternoon. Derek seeking a modicum of approval, "Hope you don't mind. We could use all the help we can get?"

The Preacher noted Derek's anxiety, "No Sir, not at all. I appreciate you're trying to help."

A soft feather light knock came from the other side of the door. Derek looked up. He knew who it wasn't. "Enter Woman Constable Gates." The door opened and in she glided, her soft eyes darting as she weighed up the situation. It didn't feel nice to her. The strained calm was broken by the clattering storm of Harold Sweetlove. He bounced in like a force of positive dynamic energy. He looked down at Derek who looked sheepishly up at him. Tweety beamed from behind his dark blue lenses. "What's up. Bit of bad news, I take it?"

Derek nodded and handed the paperwork over to his favourite genius. The reading began. Tweety had all the law degrees there were to have. He knew the police codes verbatim chapter and verse. He could apply them meticulously with all the ease of a man sipping a glass of sherry at his favourite aunties. Two minutes later he looked up.

"Notebooks please, yez pair of galoots!" He held his hand out as the notebooks were gingerly surrendered. First the Preacher's and then Heavenly's. A further two minutes passed as Tweety stood motionless absorbing all there was to know about the events of that fateful day. The only thing moving was, as he called it himself, was his 'All Seeing Eye'. Derek's office took on the feel of a holding cell before a murder verdict. All present were anxiously waiting for the maestro to resurface. Hopefully with some promising news.

After an agonising wait, he placed the paperwork back on Derek's desk and then returned the notebooks. Tweety then cracked a smile, "Nat a problem, folks. Comments for future reference. Pete, you were a bit light on your notebook entry. I know time was of the essence and you saved lives which really is the nuts and bolts of the matter. In future take the extra time to protect yourself from the likes of Mr. Prentass-hole. Your notebook should have reflected he was being obstructive and you were considering arresting him for the same but time was not your friend. Your notebook should have reflected him struggling and verbally abusing you and in doing so perhaps injuring himself."

The Preacher meekly nodded. Tweety as usual was spot on. "Ouch, but noted for next time, Tweety."

Tweety winked which looked like a regular blink. "As for you, Miss Heavenly, your notebook entry is just what the doctor ordered. Everything boy blunder here has omitted you've included. Well done!"

Pete gazed across at Stephanie looking slightly crest fallen and mouthed, "Thanks partner." She was suddenly all consumed with a need to throw her arms around him and give him a big kiss. Her 'Aslan' looked for all the world bound and helpless. If only he knew! She looked back at him and mimed, "you owe me a coffee for that, you big tube!" The Preacher nodded and gave a secret thumbs up.

Derek felt a lot happier now, "Okay Tweety, what's your plan? Black Bart is coming in to see me tomorrow."

Tweety grinned. "For starters, Derek, he's coming in tomorrow to get you on his side, to be a member of his lynch party. He's a bully and is looking for an armchair ride. Tell him nothing, agree to nothing. Preacher, I'll write your statement of evidence for you and also act as your '**friend**[3]' during your formal interview with this despicable man."

The Preacher nodded, "Thanks Tweety. It's not all doom and gloom though, is it?" Derek blustered in, "Absolutely not, Preacher, nothing to worry about. Northing at all". His eyes however told a different story. Heavenly smiled up at him, then bit her bottom lip in a subliminal act betraying her feelings. Nothing was lost on him.

Derek smiled, "Well once again apologies Preacher, not a task I relished. That's Mr. Prentass' formal complaint served on you. There's your copies for your records. For our notebooks sake shall we say complaint served at 2.05 PM?" Pete nodded as they all slowly eased out of the office.

The office door closed gently leaving the popular inspector alone and in silence. He opened his desk side drawer and removed a silver cigarette holder. It was highly polished and bore three engraved crowns to the front. Two crowns at the top, one at the bottom. He smiled at the Grant coat of arms while his tired eyes read two lines of familiar engraving. Derek then glanced up at the framed photograph he kept in his office of Miriam, his wife, lover and best friend. She had bought the case for him when he was promoted to inspector way back. The engraving had been added when she passed. He no longer smoked but kept it as a keepsake.

It also housed something precious to him. Miriam was smiling back at him from their past, a beautiful brown-haired brown-eyed woman who had gently kept Derek on the straight and narrow over thirty years of marital bliss. She had passed three years now and the pain of her loss was still there. Derek lifted her photograph and smiled before gently dusting it and replacing it. His pain was

---

[3] *A "Friend" is someone who can accompany a police officer at any conduct or any investigatory interview. He is entitled to give advice regarding all relevant Police Conduct Regulations to that officer. The criteria for being a friend is that you must be a serving police officer or police staff member.)*

never that far away which was how he wanted it. It was approaching the anniversary of her passing and he had a trip planned. It was the same trip that he had taken the previous two years. It was a trip where he could be close to her. A trip that no one was aware of, not even Tweety. It was Derek's secret. Returning to his desk he noticed that his fists were clenched tight and his mouth was dry. Tomorrow was another day. Then, thinking about another day without Miriam he wearily got up from behind his desk and once again touched the framed image.

Leaving his office he whispered, "Not long now, my love."

Walking through the Cons Workroom, Derek nodded at the Preacher, Heavenly and Wee Mo. "Lovely people. Lovely people to work with," he thought to himself. He then entered the kitchen, first turning the cold tap on before hunting out a respectably clean looking tumbler. Some looked as though they'd been there for centuries. Most were a dull translucent yellow. Piss coloured actually. Derek selected the lightest tumbler he could find and held it under the crashing cold water tap. He allowed himself a greedy glug then topped it up again before switching off the tap and heading out the back door into the rear station yard. He had the tumbler with water sploshing everywhere in his right hand.

The beautiful summer's day hit him like a slap. He took a deep breath then smiled for no explicable reason then began to gaze about the station yard. Derek's squinting eyes took in the cars in the car park noting some new faces and trying to remember those that were no longer there. "Hmmm, who has got new wheels then?" He mused, playing a game of elimination with himself, knowing whose cars were still there against the missing ones and then trying to put a personality type beside the new unidentified owner's wheels.

"Mmm, wee Shelley, no sign of her clapped-out rust bucket of a Fiesta. Ahh, a lovely new Ferrari red one where she normally parks." The strawberry air freshener and the tiny teddy bear cutely placed on the rear parcel shelf was the clincher for Derek. "Bingo, I should have been a detective!"

Derek made his way for the old clapped-out armchair permanently abandoned in the station yard. It was positioned for maximum exposure to the sun. Everyone in the station used it from the smokers to the taking five minutes out of the stressful day brigade. Derek at that moment belonged to the latter group.

"Fuck it, I'm the Station Inspector. I'm entitled to a break like anyone else."

He collapsed into the old chair and felt its hug. It shouldn't have felt good but like a lot of things in life it just did. Derek took a final glug, his thirst quenched, then set the old tumbler down on the ground. Wearily, he stretched back, hearing his back creak. Crossing his legs, he then threw his hands behind his head and closed his eyes, enjoying the feel of the warm sun and soft breeze on his face. "Mmm, just five minutes dear God, without any distractions please."

Sadly for Derek, God must have been sitting on his own beaten-up recliner at the same time taking his own almighty five. His chill out was shattered by the opening of the huge rear metal gates allowing vehicles in and out of the station yard. Reserve Constable Billy Porter could have shown him a tad of consideration. There were two ways of opening these massive gates. The correct way was to keep a hold of them and walk with them as you opened them, this would result in a quite considerate and controlled manoeuvre. Then there was the violent I'm cool as fuck and don't give a shit way. This way the gates are hurled open in a hands-free slinging manner, thus creating untold aggravation, clattering, banging and screeching of metal on concrete before finally shuddering to a halt.

Derek was not in the slightest bit surprised when Billy chose the cool as fuck gate slinging method. He was the fastest slinger in the East! Billy looking about noticed Derek for the first time and in his high-pitched cheese grater voice yelled, "Fuck me. It's lucky for some basking in the sun all day. I haven't stopped!"

Derek noted Billy wasn't carrying his sweeping brush. Giving Billy the thumbs up and feigning that he was very relaxed he mumbled to himself, "Must have been surgically removed from the wee toe rag. I know where I'd like to shove it this very second. Wonder when his contract's up for renewal? Awww noooo, please God noooo!"

The slate grey CID Ford Orion slid into the station yard. The driver was massive and his front seat passenger was tiny. Derek considered running for it but he'd been spotted. Well and truly rumbled. It was too late. "Anyone but Pinky and Perky!"

Derek looked up to the heavens shaking his fists, "Dear God Almighty, five minutes. Could you not give this poor sinner just five minutes' peace and quiet in the sun? Do I not pay my taxes, Lord? I attend church every Sunday, Heavenly Father. Just five fucking minutes please!"

His two mates dismounted from their vehicle. A deep booming laugh rang out, "Well if it isn't the sheriff of Mountroyal snatching a few rays. Thought you were up to your eyes in crime!"

Big Cliff laughed again looking down at his side kick and boss, Detective Inspector Arnie Brown. Arnie was chewing down on Woody his pipe trying hard not to laugh. "Aye you're right there, Big Cliff, while we've been at Castlereagh Holding Centre this morning interviewing terrorists, were they Prods or Catholics today, Cliff, I can't remember?"

Big Cliff nodded, "Can't remember and it doesn't matter wee man. Carry on."

Arnie continued, "Aye, anyway. He's been out sunning himself like the Queen of Sheba."

Big Cliff shook his head and sighed looking at Derek slipping him a wink. "For fuck's sake, wee man, is that the best you got. Who writes your material?" Derek found himself chuckling. They were so bad it was good or was he just becoming delirious. Billy Porter slam-dunked the gates shut once more causing Cliff to duck. He gave them all a cheery wave then warbling returned to the sanger. Big Cliff had known Derek long enough to know when he was frazzled and frazzled was what he was looking at now.

"Come on son, want a wee chat with you about an operation we're planning. Shall we call it operation 'Piggly Wiggly?' We need to borrow a couple of bods with your permission. We've sausage rolls and 'cream Charlies' in for lunch, there's plenty, you're joining us." Derek knew that Cliff knew or could see the shape he was in. He got up out of the battered chair like the tired old man he felt like. "Sounds good to me, chums."

Derek attempted a jog come shuffle catching up with his two CID friends as they disappeared back into the station. That's the way it was then. One day your colleague was down and you picked him up. The next day it was your turn to be picked up. That was how they coped. That's what it was all about.

Back in the Cons Workroom, Wee Mo was tidying up her paperwork at one of the old rickety desks. Pete and Stephanie were directly in front of her gabbling away while placing paperwork into their in-trays. Each officer at Mountroyal had their own designated cubby hole where their in-trays were housed. These cubby holes sat in a huge open fronted wooden cabinet and were earmarked from left to right A-D sections.

Each officer had their own slot located below their section heading. In A Section for example, Arnie Savages' in-tray was top of his section by virtue of his being the senior constable. Lionel Graham's would be directly below his and so on with Shelley McCann, the junior constable sitting at the bottom. Below Shelley, the full-time reserves' in-trays started again with seniority. It was actually a good system, with officers' in-trays being easily located with regards to post both internal and external.

Wee Mo couldn't help but hear or maybe if truth be told, she could have tried a bit harder not to hear or maybe the conversation was for public consumption. Stephanie nudged Pete causing him to shuffle, come stumble to the side, "You okay, pard? Have you recovered from the complaint being served on you?"

Pete sighed looking across at her. He knew she was trying to cheer him up. "Yea, I'm fine. Just a bit peeved. I thought I did ok at Wyse Byse on that crazy day. Like, it wasn't as if I had any choice in the matter. Mr. Prentass was unwittingly trying to get us all killed. That's the thanks you get. Tweety was right though, I should have stuck more in my notebook. I left myself wide open there. Thanks to your good self and your sparkly notebook entry I might just get away with a **block** [4] to the wilds of Pomeroy or the like!"

Stephanie laughed, "Don't be daft. It won't come to that. Sure, our man Tweety's on the case. As 'friends' go you couldn't have better."

The Preacher nodded, "I guess so. I'll just have to prepare myself for all eventualities. It's just I'm happy here as well as loving my life down at the lough with bud. Fingers crossed. I'm a bit wary of this Black Bart though. Infamy…Infamy…they've all got it in for me!"

Stephanie cringed, "Jeepers the old one's are the best. Where did you unearth that one, Noah's Ark?" Stephanie then noticed a sheet of paper half crumpled, tucked away at the back of her in-tray, "What have we here now. Where have you been hiding then?"

Pete looked over. Wee Mo looked up. "Oh, well I'll be. It's a Crown Court Summons for next week. Mmm. Judge and jury trial. Downpatrick Crown Court. Nice wee drive with a bit of 'smileage' and a lovely old historical building thrown in. What's it for now? Ah ha. It's the arson at the Bloomfield Shopping Centre in Bangor a while back. Old Bulgy eyes himself. Denis McNeice. So

---

[4] *(A block in those days was a form of punishment by the authorities. The block could be for any number of reasons whereupon an officer would be transferred from his present station to a less favourable or more dangerous one.)*

that's what you call him. More like Dennis the Menace if you ask me. Gary and I were at that. We done good too! Uggh, yuck. Then there was that horrible so and so of an inspector. What did you call him now? Ah yes, D.D., Double D. Damien Dalzell, useless twerp. OK. Fine. The case is all forensic, glass fragments. Lovely, I'm just a walk on extra if anything at all. Suits me to a tee. A chillaxing few days ahead. A week of lie ins. Those Crown Courts don't start until 10.30 AM. Yippee."

She looked around her face beaming, "Oops, sorry folks. Was I blethering out loud?" They all laughed. Stephanie really was just 'Heavenly' thought Wee Mo as she got to her feet and placed her in-tray into her own personal cubby hole. She smiled at the golden couple as she slid out of the Cons Workroom whispering under her breath, "Gotta speak with Tweety, gotta speak with Tweety." She wanted Tweety. She had a strange tale to tell him relating to her previous life!

At 9.55 AM the following day, a blue Rover Vitesse pulled up at the barrier. It was expected of course. Billy Porter was on the buttons and ready. The usual game was played out with 'unfamiliar' vehicles. No warrant card. No entry. Black Bart though pissed off, leaned across to his front passenger window and presented his card. The barrier lifted upon proof and the vehicle slid in and parked up at one of the outer parking bays. Had Billy not challenged the strange vehicle make no mistakes about it, Bart would have 'blocked' him for a breach of security regulations. Billy then leaned across to the tannoy mic and gave the signal. A sharp double click. Derek lifted his head from his office. A minor flurry occurred in the Enquiry Office with, as in theatrical parlance, everyone scurrying to their places and taking their marks. Bartholomew arrived at the pedestrian gate and looked up into the security sanger window smiling. He was carrying a large expensive looking black leather 'Berluti' briefcase, a £3,000 symbol to himself and others that he was important and classy. He feigned an impassive expression as he held his warrant card up beside his face and was quickly buzzed in. Billy sighed, his monumental task was over. He had survived the Angel of Death. Bartholomew didn't have to break stride as the huge metal bomb blast doors glided open in expectation. He entered the public area, his steel heel taps clicking authoritatively giving him a sense of presence and importance. He was a classic narcissist and paused for a second taking in his surroundings. A tall swarthy individual wearing dark blue glasses was standing at the counter waiting. A smaller figure was in the background, darting half in and half out of the radio store. It was Wee Mo. Bart failed to notice her but she noticed him. Another officer was at his desk on the phone. The officer with the dark blue glasses smiled at Bartholomew.

"Morning Sir, how can I help you?" Bartholomew smiled back through clenched teeth and held his warrant card up to the glass window. "Detective Chief Inspector Bartholomew, C&D. I've an appointment with Inspector Grant at 10 AM." It was then Bartholomew first noted the man opposite him had only one eye. How unfortunate, he thought. Tweety could see his cogs whirling. "Yes Sir, absolutely. I'm to take you on down."

Tweety left the Enquiry Office on his escorting duties followed by Bartholomew casually click clacking behind. Vic buzzed the partition door. He must have hit that door release button a thousand times a day. Tweety quietly led Bartholomew down to Derek's office and knocked on the door gently. He waited until Bartholomew disappeared inside then returned to his domain. He was puzzled by the worried expression on Maureen's face as they passed each other in the reception area.

Derek had cleared his desk of all unnecessary paperwork. His portable radio was off and in his cupboard. All that he had in front of him was his notebook, a jotter and copies of the Preacher's 17/3 and the associated witness statements. In a moment of blind panic, he scribbled wildly on the back page of his jotter, just to make sure his biro worked. He wasn't going to leave any openings to Black Bart. Derek took a deep breath and then a final glance at Miriam's photograph for courage. He cleared his throat then feigning a calm authoritative tone said, "Come in please."

Tweety opened the door and ushered Bartholomew in. In Derek's office, the mood immediately turned sombre. It was like the scene from the movie 'Gunfight at the O.K. Corral', both men eyeing each other closely looking for that blink of weakness. That tiny moment when a twitch would indicate who was the master and who was the slave. What Derek hadn't acutely noticed was that while Bart was taking him in, he was also taking in Miriam's photograph. Darkest thoughts and seeds of plot and planning were forming in the dark melting pot of his mind. It was then that he smiled which Derek reciprocated. Derek couldn't deny it. Bartholomew the man was impressive to look at. Mid-forties give or take, around six feet tall with a medium build. Definitely not gym fit though. He had a good head of slightly wavy blonde hair which framed large glacier blue eyes. Glacier, Derek mused for they were cold, ice-cold. Handsome?

Not quite, but power and money could take this man to wherever he wanted to go in the romance stakes.

Bartholomew was dressed immaculately. He could give his boss George Sewell a run for his money. He was wearing a tailored dark blue pinstripe suit with a pale pink cotton shirt. His silk tie was a blend of pinks, peaches, blues and whites, not stripes or patterns mind, it was like a mix of all those colours swirled in a paint pot. Derek hated it on sight and then gradually he wasn't so sure. Oh, but he did hate his shoes which completely ruined the look, or was it meant to appear that way? Large brown alligator skinned shoes with the steel heel taps. They were way too pointy for Derek, like a Texan oil billionaire would wear. They obliterated his suave look, but the preening narcissist didn't give a jot. He did everything for effect right down to his outrageous steel heel taps.

Eventually Derek broke the frigid silence. "Well Sir, you requested this meeting. Shall we get a move on?"

Black Bart smiled, if that's what it was. "Cut to the chase you mean? Well Derek, (a subtle effrontery. Feathers successfully ruffled.) not to put too fine a point on it, your Constable Majury is in a bit of a pickle. I find myself a bit like the great Houdini in that my hands are completely tied. We need to find a way out."

Derek noted the 'we' bit but his face remained poker calm. "We have a clatter of statements from members of staff all saying the same thing. Majury assaulted their wonderful boss."

Derek broke in, "I see it was your good self that recorded all these witness statements Sir and if you don't mind me saying, they are all very samesy. I mean none of them digress to mention the circumstances involved, there's no mention as to where they actually were when all this was going on. There's no mention as to what was said between the pair, it all reads a little too stacked for my liking. Stacked against Constable Majury that is."

Inside, Derek was at exploding point. Black Bart nodded thoughtfully reflecting upon the veiled criticism. "Mmm, but those are their signed statements nevertheless, Inspector Grant." Derek continued but was slowly coming to terms that he may as well be banging his head against a brick wall and it hurt.

"Sir, with respect, the facts are clear, they were all within seconds from being blown to kingdom come. Prentass their beloved boss was doing everything within his power to facilitate this. Constable Majury saved many lives that day by his swift actions."

Black Bart remained calm while Derek was slowly falling apart at the seams. "Inspector Grant, I'm fully aware of the circumstances but the level of violence used was wholly disproportionate. Why a court could well draw an inference by his, shall we say very basic notebook entry, particularly the "ASSISTED" passage. There was nothing assisted about all of this. I see from our records that Majury is a martial arts expert as well as a supremely fit individual. His list of sporting achievements went on and on ad nauseam. All that brute power against an elderly man. How unfortunate for poor Mr. Prentass."

Derek felt the sweat trickle down the back of his shirt, "Well what about Woman Constable Gates' notebook entry? She outlines the circumstances very succinctly. Very succinctly indeed. Under the circumstances he had very little choice in the matter!"

Black Bart smiled and slowly shook his head from side to side, "Misguided loyalty. I see it every day. A sense of us against the rest of the world, for all we know she's terrified of him or even worse besotted by him. If I'm guessing correctly, he's made her embellish her notebook entry. Could it be Inspector Grant that he's taken you all in and that you have a monster in your midst."

Derek could now see very clearly the canvas Black Bart was trying to paint.

He threw him a crumb. "Interesting Sir. What do you suggest WE do then?" Black Bart eased back into his chair exuding the faintest whiff of triumph.

Holding out his right hand he began to smugly examine his fingernails tilting his head this way and that. He was now king; he was now the master. "First rule is always to apologise. Apologise unreservedly for your actions. That done, I'll write up my final report and I'll see what I can do for him."

Derek gripped tightly at his chair handles and nodded trying to look impassive. He was anything but. "So, you're telling me that if he apologises, you'll caution him, slap his wrists?" Black Bart left Derek's crumb where it was. His nails were fascinating him. It wouldn't be long now. We'll see what we can do for him, won't we? But I need that apology in written statement form. Shall we make an appointment for say, this time next week? That's next Thursday, here, at 10.00 AM. A formal interview with your Constable Majury. I do hope he sees sense. My patience only goes so far. We would hate this matter to go the whole way wouldn't we. You know what I mean, Inspector Grant. A DPP file (Director of Public Prosecutions). The Crown Court. A criminal conviction resulting in loss of gainful employment or maybe, even worse, jail time?"

Derek nodded, "You know Inspector Bartholomew, he's a good lad is Peter Majury. He wouldn't hurt a fly."

Black Bart stood up briefcase in hand and made for the door. He was wearing a stupid painted on smile. On opening it, he paused and turned around, "It's not the flies we're worrying about. This day next week. 10.30 AM sharp. Statement of apology. Good day, Inspector Grant." With those words ringing in his ears, he left. Inspector Bartholomew had an urgent pedicure appointment to attend.

Derek was mentally shattered. He got up out of his seat and paced about his office for a few seconds. He retrieved his radio and stuck it on. "Thank you, God."

Brahms was playing. He then gazed up at Miriam's photograph. She smiled at him from behind the glass plate. "I'm getting too old for this, my love. I've lost my toughness, my mental edge. That bastard wiped the floor with me with one hand tied behind his back." The smile remained constant and gave him strength, "Keep going. Trust in the right. Trust in the good. They need me. The Preacher needs me."

"Justice, it's all about justice."

Chapter 10
The Not So 'Legit' Gertrude Liggett

Euston Parade sat like a thick rasher of fatty bacon in the middle of a soft and sumptuous O'Hara's bakery bap. It nestled between Euston Street and the Castlereagh Road in the heart of East Belfast, actually it's only about five minutes easy dander from Mountroyal Station. It's a quirky little street built in the early 1950s. It would never be described as a head turner, probably more of a 'Drive on James, and don't spare the horses' kind of street. If you live in the parade, you're definitely working class and for those with ambitions of betterment in society, it's a mere hitching post.

The dwellings at Euston Parade are not overly attractive, which is as nice as I can put it. Basically, they're an eyesore of a square box with a flat roof. A front door sat bang in the middle of the box with square windows straddling either side and above. What more can I say about the parade other than its grand designs were probably scrawled by a five-year-old architect huffing in the naughty seat for not eating his greens.

However, it's a close-knit wee street where everybody knew everybody else's business. This closeness can be a good thing or a bad thing depending on what your business is.

One end of the parade took you to Euston Street where you'll find yourself looking at Euston Street Primary School. The school's quite pretty to look at and was constructed in 1925. It's a happy place and very much part of the community. A clatter of its students play a part in this tale. Are we all sitting comfortably? Then let's get started. Our tale revolved around the comings and goings at 14, Euston Parade and its stellar resident. Look, there she is now, standing out the front of her gaff smoking a fag minding everybody's business. She's sweating so she is, this one just can't stick the heat. Just look at the bake on her, she looked like a Rottweiler chewing a wasp. Without further ado, let me introduce you all to the matriarch of Euston Parade, please give it up for Mrs. Gertrude Liggett or Gertie as she's known by her very few acquaintances. Oops, that's her away back inside. Nice touch, Gertie, the way you flicked your fag butt out onto the pavement while coughing your lungs out. Well, it's coming tea time and the old dear's starving. Let's follow her in, I'm sure she won't mind.

Looking about me as I follow her into her palace, I can see décor wise, it's a bit tired. It has the stamp of someone that doesn't really give a shit about colours, style or cleanliness. The front living room door is open, ah, the racing from Kempton's on the box, bless. There's a wee betting slip sitting on a grubby coffee table just beside a Carlsberg ashtray, oh, and an open box of 20 Embassy Regal. The ashtray's overflowing with cigarette butts and resembles the great pyramid of Giza. Gertie has every race covered. A 50 quid betting slip to boot. Gertie love, that's some people's life savings there.

Basic, Basic, Basic, everything about this room is Basic with a capital B. Her walls are a nicotine shade of cream, the carpets and curtains are knackered and done in plum. Aww now, come on Gertie, all three bars are on from the electric fire and you've opened the windows to let the heat out. Go on then Gertie, just toss your hard-earned money right out the window.

A battered armchair beside the coffee table is all there is, it's positioned so Gertie can watch the telly as well as all the comings and goings in the street. Whoa, what's that above the fireplace? It's that famous painting, you know the one, 'Girl with a Pearl Earring' painted by the great Dutch Master Johannes Vermeer.

OK, so it's not the original as it's valued at somewhere in and around the ten million mark. A tad out of Gertie's reach, I think. Oops, I nearly missed it, a small polaroid photo sat upright on the mantelpiece, a picture frame wouldn't have broken the bank. Let me see now. Oh, it's Gertie all right, standing with a very slight figure of a man. Don't they make a lovely pair? Ok, so I was stretching it a bit. Remember it's nice to be nice. Maybe taken around ten years or so ago. You still had the weight on then I see Gertie. He's not doing you any favours there, my love, perhaps he should have stood slightly behind you. Just saying. Moving on, oh, what have we here? Something's written on the back. Give me a tick, the writing's very spidery, ok, here it is, a literary masterpiece. "Me and Reggie. Donard Park 1967."

Just by the by, Donard Park is located in Newcastle, County Down. It sits at the feet of the Mourne Mountains; you all know the song, 'Where the Mountains of Mourne Sweep Down to the Sea..' Newcastle is a stunningly beautiful coastal town and well worth a visit if you're ever by that way.

Back to the photograph. Our Reggie doesn't look very happy in this pic which made me wonder were there any smiling photos of him knocking about. Then I look at the 'bake' on Gertie and think to myself, maybe not. Reggie was Gertie's insignificant other half. He was a former welder by trade and worked as so many did at the world-famous Harland and Wolff Shipyard. The pair had been unhappily married for thirty something years and were childless; children would have involved loving feelings on Reggie's part and physical exertion on Gertie's. They lived quite separate existences during his last few years. He holed up in the back room with his stamp collection and his historical books while Gertie sat in the front room nosying out and living off the tele.

They should have been divorced years ago but what was the point, they had no other places to go to and no one better to be with. You see, neither were particularly easy on the eye, or stimulating after dinner conversationalists. A state of 'Entente Cordiale' existed until Reggie passed away from terminal apathy some five years ago. They say he died with a smile on his face. Some say death came as a sweet release. For Reggie, it came as his very own 'Get out of life free card!'

Our Gertie's on the move again. We're now in the hallway, kitchen bound, slow down they're giving me a stitch. I see Reggie's rear living room door shut tight, too many painful memories for the old dear, bless. Into the kitchen we go and it's humble pie time for me and a Findus chicken curry micro-ding dinner for her. It's out of the box and into the microwave in a flash, a button's pressed three times for the requisite three minutes nuking. Gertie's done this rodeo before. She's now got the cold tap running and reaching for a solitary tumbler sitting by the kitchen sink. She sloshed it to the brim, that's her drink sorted. I grudgingly have to admit that her kitchen's spotless. Respect Gertie, that oven looked as good as the day you bought it 11 years past. Not a mark on it or in it. This is how you must spend your days then, keeping the kitchen 'maculate'. What's your secret?

Let's describe our Gertie in a little more detail then, shall we? She's a rather overweight unattractive looking 67-year-old woman shuffling through life at around 5 feet 3 inches in height. She's been blessed with thick wiry silver hair resembling a Brillo pad in both substance and style. Her face is large, lunar large and came with huge flapping jowls. Her suspicious eyes appear tiny, sat just above her button nose and thin-lipped mouth; features all but lost in her vast facial landscape. Would it be too cruel for me to say that she bears more than a passing resemblance to "Jabba the Hutt" of Star Wars fame? Well, if these extraterrestrial events are actually going on all around us then I'm a believer. Who knows they may even be related.

To describe Gertrude as being overweight by several stones would not be the polite thing to do, but her doctor, a Doctor Navid from the Templemore Avenue Clinic has done. It was his job you see, "in his professional capacity" is the way they put it. She had attended his practice last May for a full check-up and had failed her health MOT with flying colours. She tipped the scales at 14 stone, a good 3 stone overweight. Her blood pressure was through the roof and her lung capacity was miniscule. I suspect the 40 fags a day had something to do with it, allied to her Olympian diet of micro-ding meals, boiled sweets, Tayto cheese and onion crisps and pints of her favourite Smithwick's red ale.

Doctor Navid, following her examination, removed his trusty gold rimmed glasses then began polishing them carefully with his white cotton hanky. A man deep in thought. He was trying to find the right words to say while the impolite one's were trying their damnedest to escape. Sighing he cast his tired eyes over the unhealthy lump sitting and staring blankly before him. In his rich Bengali baritone with more than a hint of Belfast twang, he finally found his voice, "Gertie my love, you are the walking time bomb. You must urgently change your lifestyle or you will be dropping dead on the spot. No more fags. No more of the Smithwick's, sweets and the Tayto potato chips. Join the Weightwatchers classes, along with all them other fatties. Ooops, I am so sorry, my English, sometimes it deserts me. I meant to say along with all those other fuller figured women of the East. Will you not try for me Gertie, please, before it is too late?"

Gertie smiled, not a pretty sight and wheezed, "Ah ha Doctor Navid, will do, Thank you nae."

In reality, she was thinking, "Hurry the fuck up, the horse racing's on in 20 minutes and I haven't got my bets on yet. Mmm, then a few fags, a glass of ale and a packet of Tayto cheese 'n' onion. Smashing!"

Gertie Liggett, the woman we see standing before the microwave, is one of life's survivors. While others toe the line and receive no thanks or reward, Gertie has all her days toed her own line. She has lived her life by this simple mantra "MINIMUM EFFORT, MAXIMUM RESULTS."

Oh, we're on the countdown, last 10 seconds and 3, 2, 1 and beep, beep beeeep. Classy Gertie, as she gathers her steaming hot curry out of her dinger.

She then let out a chesty cough's contents into the sink. Yuck Gertie, at least rinse it away. Contentedly she lifted her water then shuffled back to the front living room just in time for the TV to shout "And they're off!"

That's the 2.30 PM from Lingfield Park by the way. You see folks, none of this happens by chance. Gertie never took her eye off the ball. Whether that's balls bouncing around the street, the Racing Post or what is the latest gossip. She also has a keen fascination with the easiest way of making a few quid. For Gertie is a slave to no one. She is an island fortress and kept her existence simple. Me, I, myself and I don't mind if you do too. Knock yourself out! Wow! that didn't take long. Quite the speed eater, aren't we? Easy girl all that bouncing up and down on the old armchair's going to do you an injury, "Fucking great. Fucking amazing. Another hundred quid for my holiday fund." That's Gertie speaking by the way. It's a husky, somewhat chesty voice. That'll be the fags, of course. Maybe a bit of Marlene Dietrich going on there, what do you think? Oh, please yourselves then!

Gertie's chuffed. Could her day get any better? Yes, it could. She heard three loud knocks on her back door. Two quick knocks then a pause for a couple of seconds then the third knock to be exact. Gertie smiled as her nicotine-stained dazzlers appear. A huge grunt of effort followed as she sprockled herself up and shuffled down towards her kitchen door shouting, "Hold on to your horses love, I'm coming now, with you in a wee second." She opened her back door without checking who the caller is and is already making her way towards the rear living room, remember, the one where the door was closed, Reggie's old room.

A young boy followed her inside carrying a rucksack. This is actually his school bag, it contains no books today, yet it's surprisingly full. Gertie entered the room with the young boy in tow. She made for a stool and plonked herself down. Looking about the room there's nothing left to suggest that Reggie was ever there, gone and completely forgotten, hard lines, Reggie, old boy. The room is spartan to say the least, it made her front room look like the Palace of Versailles in comparison. Gertie now sat in comparative darkness as all the light from the outside world has been eliminated by thick dark drapes.

Two huge chest freezers take up most of the floor space and hum contentedly as our Gertie caught her breath from all the exertion. The freezers' green power lights cast a soft iridescent glow illuminating Gertie's huge panting face. Maybe Gertie is Jabba the Hutt after all.

The boy's been running hard and his tiny lungs are grabbing for air. He struggles due to the heavy fustiness shrouding the room. A large plastic sweetie jar sat on a lonely shelf on the back wall. A white sheet of paper has been sellotaped to it with a crudely scrawled 'FUNGEROLA FUND" written on it. Gertie smiled at the young boy who is one of her many 'wee partners in crime' as she called them. Young boys and girls all of a similar age that she has shrewdly recruited over time. This particular partner is wee Jude Campbell. He's nine and a bit, bright as a button and sharp as a paper tack. Jude's like a little whirlwind and came at you full-on, a child that always has to be somewhere else five minutes ago. He sat with a beaming smile, bright ginger hair and large blue eyes.

Jude's a wee heartbreaker, he lives in Vicarage Street. His dad's in the Maze Prison on the Prod Wing. His pretty mum Gracie works behind the bar at the Welders Club in Dee Street, not out of choice more out of necessity. All in all, Jude is left to his own devices for long stretches of the day, not necessarily good for one so hyperactive and clever. He was lured into a life of crime by the 'Faginess' and a promise of easy money a while back.

Gertie smiled, not a good look, I don't think she has one. Am I bad? "Well handsome, what have you got for your Auntie Gertie today then?"

The boy returned the smile while pouring the contents of his bag on top of one of the chest freezers. Gertie's eyes light up. He's done well. "Got you this lot. Like what you said you were short of last time Gertie! Packets of maple cured bacon from the Iceland, Denny's Pork sausages from the Mace on the Ravenhill Road and these lot (chicken breast fillets) are from the Co-Op on the Cregagh Road. Oh, and I got these packets of pork chops from there as well. Nearly forgot, close your eyes and hold out yer hands, Gertie."

Gertie giggled; he really was her favourite. She felt ice-cold plastic being gently placed there. "Here you wee skitter, that's freezing."

Jude giggled, "Right open them then." Gertie opened her eyes with excitement, "Aww you wee darling. An eight-ounce fillet steak from Marksies (Marks and Spencer). From the one on the Ormeau Road, I see? Sure, that's too far away for them wee legs of yours, but thanks anyway, wee Jude. I take it you're wanting paid for this lot?"

Jude nodded, "Aye, something like that." Gertie reached up for her Fungerola jar and dramatically unscrewed the lid for her boy. All in all, she had around

£600 quid there made up from a clatter of cash and coins. Jude had delivered between £50 and £60 pounds' worth of frozen meat and Gertie would have no bother shifting it on. Her grape vine was well established. She plucked a tenner from the jar and handed it to her wee carrot top.

"Good work, wee son. More of the same for next time please, and for god's sake, don't be going and getting yourself caught by them police. God forbid son, but if you do, keep me well out of it. We don't want you spoiling it all for the rest of the gang. Now run along now. See you next time."

Jude beamed, "No worries, Gertie. I'm off to Eddie Spence's Chippy for a pastie supper with tons of ketchup and a can of cokie. Yum-yum." And with that, the little whirlwind was gone leaving just a trace of sparkle in the humming green gloom.

Gertie smiled as the silence returned to her world like a summer sunset. It got her thinking. If she could have had any child, it would be wee Jude Campbell. Gertie began shuffling back towards the front living room while doing crude maths in her head. She felt gassy and burped. "Oh. Give over, bloody heartburn!" Then prompted by her greedy gland, her beady eyes lit up and she burst into song, "A hundred on the gee gees and fifty on the frozen food. A hundred and fifty smackers profit today. Oh, we're off to sunny, sunny Spain, Y viva Espana. Fungerola all the wayyy, Y viva Espana."

Gertie was on cloud nine. Earlier it had been liver and onions for tea but that was then. "Filleto steakeo for meoo, Y viva Fungerolaaa."

Gertie love, sit yourself down and catch your breath. You're going to do yourself a mischief getting on like that. Remember what the good Doctor Navid said?

A wheezing Gertie plonked herself down on her armchair. "Rennies or a fag?" Bearing in mind what the good Doctor said and after a bit of soul searching our heroine popped a fag in her cake hole. She was just about to light up when her front door bell screeched at her like a banshee. Gertie jumped. "Eeeek." Yelling, she expelled the cancer stick out from her paper-thin mouth, it was last seen rolling under the TV cabinet, never more to see the light of day. The door bell had to go, every time it rang the shock of it nearly killed her. "Jesus, God my poor chest. Can't a woman have five minutes? Alright, alright I'm coming."

Gertie swung the front door open with a face on her like thunder. A young woman was standing there furiously chewing gum. Gertie took her all in. Nice looking wee critter, mid-twenties, thick black wavy hair and a pretty face. She looked to be well on in the pregnancy stakes though, her tattered overcoat could barely disguise the bump. A gasping Gertie snarled, "Yesss?"

The young woman's face had now disappeared behind a huge pink bubble which suddenly burst. Gertie was becoming pissed as she watched the gum being gathered in again for more furious chewing. "Any chance bazooka joe. I don't have all fucking day."

The young woman broke into a nervous laugh, "Sorry Missus, I'm trying to remember the password. Right, got it. Bacon and eggs. Am I right, I'm right, aren't I?"

Nervous giggling followed by more ferocious chewing. Gertie shook her head, "Aye, yer right. You're also a right pain in the ass. Come on in. What are you looking?"

The young woman followed Gertie into her rear living room.

"Don't know yet. All depends. Depends on what you got?" Gertie lifted both lids of her chest freezers releasing an icy breath into the fusty gloom. "See for yourself. Here, haven't seen you before, what do they call you and how'd you get to know about all of this?" The young woman's head was now buried in one of the humming freezers, she began feigning a pretty good New York accent. "Very noice, very noice indeed mam."

The head popped up with a sparkling smile, "Oh, I'm Rachel, Rachel Beattie. Folks call me Rae."

Gertie nodded. "And the rest?"

Rae shrugged her shoulders and giggled. Gertie mused, dizzy wee trollop, probably a floozy as well! Rae went on. "A girl from the Ashmore Street Hostel up the Shankill told me. She arrived the day I was leaving. Her bastarding boyfriend had been knocking the bejaysus out of her. Don't ask me her name or anything because I haven't got a clue. I could barely remember your password for fuck's sake. (Giggles) Well, my turn, and what do they call you then Missus?"

Gertie was now weary and her chest was giving her the gyp. Young Rae was too full-on for her liking. "I'm Gertrude Liggett or just plain Gertie (sighing). Here love, do you want anything or are we just chin wagging?"

Rae went all Bronx again, "Sure do mam, give me three packs of your good ole streaky bacon and two packs of your finest Denny's pork sausages, the 12-pack variety if you're catching all my drifts."

Gertie nodded through clenched dentures, "Six quid to you love since you're in the family way. There are plastic bags in the corner under the shelf. Knock yourself out."

Rae gasped, "Cheeky cow, I'm not pregnant. Where'd you get that from?"

Gertie blustered, "Aww sorry love, no offence meant, must be that big overcoat you've got on. It's not very flattering, maybe it's the colour, Jesus God, it's drowning you."

Rae broke into her familiar chuckle, "Aye Gertie, I get where you're coming from, I suppose I'm a bit chubby on it as well. A slave to my takeaways and the odd custard cream so I am."

Gertie couldn't quite figure this one out, she gave no signs of being stupid, quite the opposite in fact. Gertie watched as she nimbly scraped a collection of coins from a tatty purse. Grinning wildly, she poured six quids worth of shrapnel into Gertie's outstretched hand. Gertie rolled her eyes dropping the mountain of change into her pinny pocket. "Thanks for nothing, Carnegie! Now let me show you out."

Rae skipped out the front door carrying a Co-Op bag containing her purchases. "Cheers, Gertie pet, maybe catch you out and about on the road. Laters."

Gertie grunted under her breath, "Not if I see you first fatso. Oh, my poor chest, where's them Rennies? Oh, just a wee mo! There's me fags. Well, it would be rude not to." Rachel Beattie, larger than life, wasn't she? A bit hurtful there, Gertie with your final comments by the way. Wee Rae wasn't the worst, you know."

Gertie wearily slumped back into her faithful armchair. Time for that much needed fag, her Rennies would have to take back seat again. She lit up and inhaled a huge satisfying drag. Gertie sighed contentedly, her chest softly rattling in the quiet of her room.

"That's nice now." She winced, "Ohh, me fucking heartburn. It's pure agony this day!" She watched with idle curiosity as the smoke slowly curled out of her mouth and rose like an arty dance before fading into her yellowed ceiling.

"That's me, no more work toda…" The doorbell exploded into life again!

Gertie screeched only louder this time nearly swallowing her billowing fag. "That fucking door bells for the bin. I'll get me one of them musical ones from the Wyse Byse store tomorrow. Hold onto your horses. I'm coming, I'm coming!" She heaved herself up as Rae's shrapnel sloshed about in her pinny.

Whoever it was was going to get the sharp end of her tongue. Gertie swung her front door open with a murderous expression yelling, "Wha… for fuck's sake?" She could be quite scary at times, she had the face for it, especially at Halloween.

Standing at her doorstep was a quirky looking middle-aged man, he was wearing a flat cap with dark blue glasses, he was in and around six feet tall and swarthy. Mr. Quirky was drowning in a huge khaki trench coat that had seen better days, its better days being from around about the First World War. Flapping grey flannels stuffed down his bright green welly boots added to his allure, more of a Giggles than a Flight Commander Biggles. He was clinging on to a dilapidated black bicycle which looked fit for the skip. The man now clearly scared stuttered, "Cheese on toast, love."

Gertie rolled her eyes and began to slowly close the front door, the male panicking yelled, "Scrambled eggs on toast? Aww fuck's sake, my mammy's going to kill me. I knew I should have written it down."

Gertie mouthed at the agitated gent in her Bronx best, it was becoming contagious, "Laters." She had just about closed the door when he yelled, "Sausages, bacon and eggs love." She looked at his pleading face then noticed he only had the use of one eye. A ripple of sympathy appeared, nowhere close to a wave but nevertheless it had the desired effect. Gertie sighed with fag propped precariously on her bottom lip. "Close enough, Einstein, in you come. Leave your bone shaker out there, nobody will touch it. They know better. What you looking for anyways?"

Einstein smiled, "Pork chops if you've got any love. I'm Mervyn by the way, Mervyn Maitland. We live in Cherryville Street just opposite the Chippy. Me and my mammy that is. I'm sorry about all those shenanigans outside, I'm not the sharpest tool in the box. You see, me mammy sent me, I've not a clue how she knew about your place. She knows a lot you see. She's old I'll grant you that, but she's still in full possession of all her facilities."

Gertie chewed a smile. Mervyn wasn't the worst. "There's pork chops in the freezer to your left, Mervyn, son, take your pick." Mervyn smiled all the while nodding furiously, "Right you are Gertie, thank you now. Thank you, thank you."

Mervyn continued bobbing all the way to the freezer leaving Gertie feeling like royalty. He lifted the freezer lid and quickly found what he wanted, an Iceland pack of four. The price tag showed £2.00. "These here will do her lovely. How much do I owe you, Gertie love?"

Gertie eyed the poor critter who looked as though he didn't have two shillings to rub together. "I'm a sucker for a sad face, hand me a quid. Tell me this Mervyn, what age is your ma by the way?"

Mervyn smiled, handing Gertie two fifty pence pieces. "Aww, smashing Gertie. Thank you now (more bobbing and bowing). Mammy, well she'll be 78 next month. She spends her days in bed. Bad heart and poor circulation you see."

Gertie nodded, smiling, "Well her teeth must be working just fine if she's going to handle all them big thick chops."

Mervyn laughed rather embarrassed, "Aye, she's still got the appetite but with regards the heavy chewing well, you know (more nodding)"

Gertie actually didn't know, "Sorry Mervyn, I don't know. What?"

Mervyn became bright red and continued with the bobbing and mouthing silently "You know, you know."

Gertie now low on patience, shouted, "Spit it out for fuck's sake, Mervyn."

Mervyn jumped back like a frightened child, "Well I have to do most of the chewing for her you see or else she'd choke." Gertie felt a chunder coming on and quickly eased the bobbing customer out the front door. "That's lovely of you, Mervyn. (A chundery burp tried hard to escape.) There's not many sons would do that for their mothers, I'll give you that! All the best now Mervyn, love. Hope to see you again."

With that, she closed her front door and slowly shuffled back to her front room mumbling "Disgusting. How yuck. Chewing his ma's chops. Jesus, God! Thought I'd heard everything." Gertie watched from her front living room window as Mervyn and his dilapidated bike disappeared right at the end of Euston Parade into Euston Street. She wearily eased back onto her armchair slowly shaking her head.

"Fuck me, that's disgusting. Can't get over it so I can't. Ew. At least Mervyn's as stupid as they come, probably helps being a little thick when you're in his position. By the sounds of her she has him tortured. Aw, poor wee Merv"

The doorbell screeches having the usual effect, it was to be the straw that broke our Gertie's back. "No more I'm telling you, I've just about had enough of this caper."

Gertie made it to her front door with a face on her like thunder, "If it's that numpty Mervyn again, I'll…" She opened the door to the rest of her life and gasps. Standing there with a smile set in granite is an enormous figure of a man, he must be at least six and a half feet and built like a brick shithouse. He's nattily dressed though, a nice brown flecked woollen blazer, white shirt and a navy tie with red hands sprinkled throughout. Dark brown slacks and brown brogue shoes. Very shiny. Gertie's mood swing swung. A real handsome bastard with a thick head of silver hair and an all-year-round outdoorsy tan.

Yes, he would do, thought Gertie, "That hunk could park his slippers under my bed anytime. Sorry about that Reggie love, you're out of circulation in more ways than one! Imagine me and him swanning down the promenade at Fungerola, oh just smashing."

The hunk spoke with a deep cultured drawl, "Bacon and eggs, love?"

Gertie smiled coyly, "Yes please Mister, sorry, I mean that'll do. Come on in big fella, mind your head under the door frame, I'm sure you hear that a lot?"

As the hunk entered Gertie gasps, for when he moved, she saw a woman police officer in uniform standing directly behind him. She paused feeling her clammy hands shaking. Swallowing hard, she whispered, "What the fuck's happening here. What's going on?"

The man smiled then whispered, "Let's go into your front room, Gertie (He knew her name, not good), I'll explain everything to you in there." Gertie led the way then wearily took a seat. What a difference a few moments can make in someone's life. Her stomach lurched as a grey police Landover pulled up outside, its crew remained inside waiting for a nod.

The leviathan spoke, "You're Gertrude Liggett, I assume that's correct and you're the sole occupant here?"

Gertie nodded, "Aye, that's right. Folks, just call me Gertie. I'm a widow woman since Reggie passed. I live here alone on me pension and that."

The gentle giant nodded. "I'm Detective Sergeant Cliff Boomer and my colleague here is Woman Constable Morrison. We're from Mountroyal Police Station." Gertie gave the policewoman a polite nod noting that she appeared nervous. He continued, "Gertie, it's to do with a spate of thefts, thefts of frozen meats and the like by young kids from this area. Been ongoing for a month or so now. They've been thieving from all the major outlets. We've had a couple of the wee skitters in the station with their parents and they've bubbled on the rest. We stopped Jude Campbell as he left your place today, caught him with the tenner that you gave him. His mummy wasn't best pleased at having to leave the Welders Club to fetch him from the station. He's told all you know. Right down to your fillet steak from Marks and Spencer. (Cliff smiled.)

"My colleague here has recorded 40 odd statements of complaint from these places, each statement covering all the various dates, times and places, what was taken and values lost. Roughly they're several thousand pounds out of pocket. We've also had a couple of test purchases by undercover officers earlier, that's more statements being lined up against you, Gertie love."

Gertie's jaw dropped, her dentures nearly popping out. Big Cliff smiled across at Wee Mo and continued, "Having said all that, I'm here to ask you how you want this all played out. Oh, and before you ask, I have a Search Warrant signed by a local Justice of the Peace. We're entitled to search for stolen goods and or the proceeds of alleged crimes. My "Bacon and eggs" at the front door was my wee joke. Sorry."

Cliff looked at the old Fagin seeing the despair in her eyes. Gertie nodded, "Fair enough. Yez have got me bang to rights. Isn't that what they say in the movies? Follow me and I'll show you where the action is." She led the pair into her Aladdin's Cave.

The crew from the Landover were quietly waved in and began their official search. On inspection of Gertie's freezers, the officers logged the frozen items cataloguing them as evidence. These perishables would be disposed of, they could or would not be fit for resale. Everything was done in a convivial manner with a light sprinkling of quiet banter. Cliff was good at that. For Wee Mo, it was an education in social skills. Gertie knew her number was up and the peelers were being decent enough with her. Big Cliff gathered her 'Fungerola' jar from the shelf and entered into the Spanish spirit. He gave the jar a shake as if it were Maracas and chuckled, "Ole!"

Gertie found herself giggling. "Cut it out, Senor!"

Seeing that it was burgeoning with cash and coins, he shook his head disapprovingly, "Not this year, Gertie love and while we're at it let's be having the rest, Mrs. Bojangles", eyeing her pinny pocket. Gertie rolled her eyes as she handed the tide of small change over, "Fuck's sake, leave me with something would ye big man."

Wee Mo appeared from the hallway and whispered into Cliff's ear. He shook his head again allowing himself a deep chuckle before giving Gertie a disappointed frown, "Follow me, Gertie my love." The hallway cupboard under the stairs revealed that her electricity meter had been tampered with, it was crawling at a slug's pace. Gertie gulped and looked to the ground. Cliff sighed,

"Abstracting electricity, Gertie, well there's another misdemeanour to add to our list. Have you anything else to tell us before we find it?"

Gertie shook her head, her jowls waving in surrender, "No Cliff love, that's it all, I promise." Tears began to well. Cliff smiled at the old Fagin. "Aww Gertie, when your catched your catched. No more tears now, let's get you down to the station and grab a few lines of a statement from you. If you've thrown your hands up, I'll see you right."

Gertie nodded, "Well there's fuck all else I can do now is there. What's that you just said there, when you're catched?"

The bear laughed, "You're catched, Gertie love."

Gertie chuckled wincing, "Fucking chest. Give over now." Gertie was taken back to Mountroyal in Cliff's CID wheels; she sat in the back like royalty as you would expect.

Back in the Parade, tongues wagged furiously with all the commotion. Eyes spied from behind drab net curtains as the booty laden land rover finally trundled out of their street. No more cheap meat.

Gertie was weary with all the excitement and stress but remained upbeat throughout. She had that innate survivor's instinct. She participated in a written question and answer style interview. This was all done under caution. A solicitor was offered to her but she declined. What was the point? In short, a full and frank confession was made. At the end Gertie was invited to read her written account and was told that she was able to correct, alter or add anything she wasn't happy about. Gertie was happy and signed. She was dog tired now and could barely keep her eyes open. For Gertie's level of fitness, this had been a very long day. She just wanted home and a feg. Big Cliff smiled as they wrapped things up.

"Thanks for that, Gertie. We'll deal with this by way of a report to the DPP (Director of Public Prosecutions). There's no need to charge you by virtue of your age and flight risk. You won't do a runner on us now, Gertie, will you?" Gertie laughed, "Not to Fungerola any ways, you big ballicks. I was looking forward till it." Wee Mo burst out laughing, it was the first time Gertie had seen her anything other than stressed out. Gertie smiled. Big Cliff lifted the paperwork and slipped it all into a blank green DPP file cover. "Give me 15 minutes, Gertie. I'll get my boss to agree with how your case should be dealt with, then we'll get you home. Don't panic, he's not the worst. Maureen here will take you out to the public waiting area now. Give me two ticks."

Gertie smiled at Cliff, she appreciated he had made this as pain free as possible for her, "Thanks love. Oh, what about the kids, will they be in trouble? All this was my doing. Some of their families don't have two pennies to rub together."

Cliff knew where she was coming from trying to protect them. "Gertie nothing will happen to any of the kids under ten. They're under the age of criminal responsibility. Any of them over 10 will go onto our Juvenile Liaison Scheme. As it's their first offence, they'll receive a caution but must stay out of trouble for the next few years. Now will that suffice, Gertie?"

Gertie's chest felt tight but to her that was a relief. "You lot aren't a bad bunch after all."

Wee Mo showed her into the public area where she took a seat. "Can I get you a cuppa Gertie. I'm sure all of this has taken it out of you?"

Gertie smiled, "Aye love. That would be nice. Milk and two sugars please."

Wee Mo squeaked, "Not a problem."

As she was disappearing towards the kitchen, she held the partition door open for two uniformed officers heading the other way. Tweety and Shelley dandered out and were taken aback at the sight of Gertie sitting there. Gertie took a double take, "Rae? Mervyn? Youse pair of skitters. Jesus you're not fat, not at all love, you're a wee stunner so ya are!"

Shelley laughed, "Awk sorry Gertie, we were just doing our jobs. My real name is Shelley McCann. That was a cushion stuffed up his old smelly overcoat." She pointed into the Enquiry Office where Vic was on the phone. He smiled and gave a thumbs up pointing to his own portly tummy. Gertie looked up at the smiling Tweety. "And you, Mervyn. I ought to give you a clip round the ear, chewing your mother's meat. What a yarn and I fell for it."

Tweety laughed, "Gertie love, I'm Harold Sweetlove, I normally work in there with him. I couldn't help myself, awful sorry so I am, (Nodding and bobbing away.) Guys like me don't get out much, see him in there, he keeps me right. You see I'm not the sharpest tool in the box."

Shelley laughed, raising an eyebrow. Gertie laughed, "You can say that again Einstein!" They all laughed.

The two officers left leaving Gertie alone with her thoughts.

Boy was she tired, and as for her chest! Yawning, she wearily looked about her. It was nice and warm in there. She liked the pale green walls in the station.

Her tired gaze spotted the portrait of the young Majesty smiling down at her from the far wall. Smiling back, she whispered, "Sorry wee love."

There was definitely something soothing about this place. A happy vibe, what with the telephones ringing and the ushered tones and then the police radio transmissions crackling back and forth in the background. In a way she was relieved, happy even, glad it was all over. She had been on a gravy train she knew she shouldn't have been on but didn't quite know how to get off. Something had to give, and today for our Gertie it did. She would be home soon for a wee whisky and a feg. Gertie sat back, closing her eyes allowing the background noises to wash over her. "Just for a wee moment to myself. Where's the harm in it?"

Then she quietly drifted off into a peaceful slumber. Moments later she coughed with a pained expression, then whispered, "Aw Reggie love, is that you? I've missed you!" The old Fagin let out a long sigh as her weak lungs heaved their last. A smile was playing on her thin lips. "Beam me up, Scotty and don't spare the horses! Reggie! Come on now, stop your faffing. We'll be late!" With that, she drifted off to a new dimension, never more to return.

Wee Mo burst into the CID Office as white as a sheet. Cliff humming a Dean Martin classic was just finishing off the paperwork. A long EEEK followed, "She's gone Sarge, she's gone!"

Cliff leaned back, carefully replacing the lid of his parker fountain pen. His chair creaked for mercy. Looking puzzled was his specialty, "Eh, what you mean Wee Mo. Thought we were giving the old girl a ride home?"

Mo eeked on, "Cliff, she's left us, Gertie's dead. I left her in the reception area, you know, to get her a brew. She seemed fine then. I was away only a couple of minutes, when I got back, she looked like she was having a wee nap to herself. Then when I tried to wake her, she wouldn't respond. I shook her gently, that's when I realised, well, that she was gone."

Cliff's face was a picture of shock and sadness. He gently closed over the green DPP file cover, "Poor Gertie. Well, that's that then."

Mo nodded, "Yes Cliff. That's that. They've closed the Enquiry Office to the public and are diverting calls to Strand Station. The boys in the Enquiry Office have placed a blanket over her."

Cliff saw tears in Maureen's eyes and swallowed hard. He was a man after all. Maureen whispered, "Tweety was awful upset, you know."

Big Cliff smiled then softly growled, "Aye Tweety can be funny that way. He sees things the rest of us don't. Thank God perhaps."

Mo was slowly settling down. "Eh, her doctor, a Doctor Navid has been contacted. He's seen her within the last 28 days. She wasn't in the best of health you know. He's on his way now to pronounce her life extinct and issue a death certificate." Cliff nodded. "Gertie wasn't the worst you know, robbing the rich to give to the poor, with a wee trip to Fuengirola thrown in every now and then. One of life's characters!"

Wee Mo laughed or eeked in her squeaking way while gazing at Gertie's sweetie jar. 'FUNGEROLA', aka Fuengirola, Costa del Sol. Spain. "She was a character wasn't she Cliff?"

Cliff nodded, "That she was Wee Mo. That she most certainly was."

Gertie was gone, she had well and truly left the building. She died as she lived, always on her own terms. Would the world be any worse off from her passing? I think so. I can't quite put my finger on the answers or give any of you exact reasons why for that matter. We all of us have our Gerties. She was a bit like that annoying itch we all get every once and a while, you know the one you can't quite get at, and then when the itch eventually leaves us, we kind of miss it. These moments of enlightenment usually arrive during a pause when we feel for the itch in our hearts they used to fill.

The frozen food caper had come to an abrupt end. Something new would appear on George Sewell's walnut desk to revive his own personal heartburn. Some new catastrophe for the popular Sub Divisional Commander to worry about. Wee Mo had done very well indeed. She would get her gold star and life in Euston Parade without our Gertie would go on.

I however with your kind permission like to picture our Gertie flashing through the universe in her very own spaceship. She's with Reggie and another by her side. They're seeking out hither to undiscovered galaxies and civilisations. She's every bit the modern-day time traveller, space explorer and of course opportunist. I can picture the three of them Jibba JABBERING with fegs dangling precariously from their flapping mouths. Reggie, he's at the wheel, then there's our Gertie, she's cosying up to her brother by a different mother.

'JABBA THE HUTT.'

Sale on Princess Gertie and "May the force be with you."

Chapter 11
Shocking Revelations

It was just after 10.00 AM the following Wednesday morning and the Enquiry Office felt like Dante's Inferno. A freak heat wave was pummelling the province, shooting temperatures well above the seasonal norms. The air was stiflingly hot and clammy, what breeze there was came at you like a hot slap. Threats of water shortages and hose pipe bans were all the talk. Considering it rains in Northern Ireland 360 days a year these portents of doom were a tad pessimistic, to say the least.

Inside the station the central heating was inexplicably on, making life a living hell for those trapped inside. The phones in the Enquiry Office hadn't let up either. The C6 or the Occurrence Book was getting a real pasting from our two guards Vic and Tweety. Calls were flooding in; road traffic accidents, my cats gone missing, my giro cheque's been stolen so it has, I wish to report my husband beating me up, I've had enough. He's one two timing bastard, so he is. I want for the police to call and arrest him - to name but a few. On and on it went like a slow and agonising ligature.

It was days such as this, that 'Her Majesty' hanging from the Enquiry Office wall yearned for a breath of fresh air. Just for once to be taken out into the station yard and set somewhere quiet. Far From the Madding Crowd or the maddening gang at Mountroyal for that matter. After all, she had been hanging there for nigh on thirty years never once looking a day over twenty.

Aggie, the elderly station cleaner was in their midst quietly mopping around the frazzled pair. Her head was bowed as she mopped in a smooth and swaying motion. With each sweep of her mop, she released a thick lemony bleachy aroma. The sharp smell snatched at the nostrils and crashed into the back of their throats. She hummed tunes softly to herself as she worked steadily in their background picking up on the strain in the air. Life had taught Aggie to keep her head down on days such as these.

Derek Grant entered through the thick front blast proof door. It gently swung open belying its great size and weight. The Inspector's head was down and his face wore a serious expression. He was wholly preoccupied with the complaint against Constable Peter Majury. This was a nasty one and the inspector was well aware that a very nasty individual was gunning for the popular constable. Derek had no time for his usual frivolous chat or easy banter. Vic nodded unnoticed while buzzing him through into the main building.

It was Tweety's turn on their shared radio. They switched every two hours. He loved the classical stuff while Vic loved his Radio 2. Tweety's latest classical offering was going down like a fart in a space suit. Classical punk jazz was blaring like chalk on a wet blackboard. The racket would have tried the patience of a Tibetan Monk.

Vic whose forehead was swathed in sweat shot Tweety a pleading glance mouthing, "Any fucking chance partner, that's doing my head in!"

Tweety nodded back, "Absolutely Vic. Pure shite. A disgrace to music. Sorry!" He leaned back towards the radio store which was directly behind him. Without looking he stretched his long sinewy arm over his head into the gloom, a flick of a switch later and the funky junky jazzy punky screeching was no more.

Complete silence followed like a muted explosion; their phones stopped ringing as the radio transmissions on the ground went dead in tandem. It was freakish. Vic thumped a full stop which echoed around the office closing off his latest entry in their C6. Wearily, he shoved the large black and red tome away allowing himself a long stretch. A blackbird could be heard in full song filling their lemony fresh silence, it was glorious. Looking over at Tweety, he raised his eyebrows in amazement, shocked by the sudden and unprovoked calm. Tweety smiled.

"What's just happened there Vic?", shrugging his round shoulders while dabbing at his moist brow.

Vic chuckled, "Long may it continue, partner. Fuck this heat and them radiators. They're on full blast so they are, feel them. They're on all summer and off all winter. We're melting in the summer and freezing in the winter!

Sorry 'bout your tunes, but that was fucking awful. How can anyone think that's nice?"

Tweety now had his blue lensed glasses off and was gently wiping them with a clean hankie. He was quietly zoning out, he nodded over at Vic. "It was pure shite Vic, that's what it was." His green eye looked tired and his thick black greying hair looked for all the world a bit dishevelled. Sometimes Vic had to remind himself that this special individual was also a mere mortal. Tweety had no need for gainful employment. He had more than enough money in the bank what with his stocks and shares, yet here he was steadfastly in the service of 'Her Majesty'. Vic glanced up at the wall catching 'Her Majesty's' eye but she blanked him as usual.

Aggie finished up her mopping with a final swish at their doorway. She plunged the mop head into her steaming metal bucket in an act of closure. "There nae, that's me done for the day. Cuppa tea fellas, I've some lovely lemon cake in with me the day?"

Tweety smiled at his pard, feeling the lemon bleach hacking at the back of his throat. "Aggie love, you're a Godsend. Lemon cake, lovely, just what the doctor ordered."

Aggie beamed. "With you in five boys."

Vic buzzed her into the main building. He heard her shout, "Cuppa tea for yourself Derek love and a wee slice of cake?" Vic began coughing and spluttering then chuckled. "Lemon cake. Only our Aggie?" The lemon fragrance slowly lost its snarl and filled their space more pleasantly. It then danced a jig with the birdsong creating a moment of mini euphoria. A collective sigh followed as the pair slowly cooled their jets.

"BUZZZZZZZZZZZZZZZZ, BUZZZZZZZZZZZZZZZZZZ!"

They jumped. Both released from their nirvana with a bang or should I say a loud "BUZZ!"

Vic mouthed, "For fuck's sake." Then hit the speak button on the intercom joining the front sanger with the Enquiry Office. "What!" His heart gripped when he heard Wee Mo's squeaky tones. Tweety, eyebrow raised wagged an admonishing finger. Vic returned it with his own victory V.

Both listened in, "Hi Vic, would you ask Tweety if he's free for a quick chat. I need his expert advice on something. It's really quite important?"

Vic shot Tweety his own raised eyebrow which translated into, "Well?"

Tweety hollered at the intercom, "How you fixed now, Mo?" An excited eek drew grins from the two guards. "Aww thanks, Tweety love, you're a star. Two ticks."

One and a half ticks later, Maureen stood in the Enquiry Office. Vic could see she looked agitated; something was definitely bothering her.

Looking at Tweety she squeaked, "Vic I have to speak to your man Tweety in private. I'm awful sorry." Vic smiled. His heart was all mush. Wee Mo was now unwittingly squatting in the fortress of his once impregnable heart. He nodded over at his pard, "Take the bottom interview room. I'll double click if I need either of you. Hey, and no hanky-panky with that one. He fancies himself as a bit of a player."

Wee Mo squeaked. "Oh Vic, you're terrible. I'll try and keep my hands off him. Tell you what, I'll make us all a cuppa when we're done. I've a wee madeira in."

Tweety whooped, "More cake! Now we're talking, onwards and upwards, Woman Constable Morrison. Let's get whatever's bothering you off your chest. Life's too short to be worrying over stuff." Vic buzzed the pair out into the main building. What in the world could be bothering his Wee Mo.

Tweety sat on the desk in the interview room. It was even hotter there than the Enquiry Office. He could feel his shirt sticking to his back as dust particles danced like nymphs in the scorching sunlight. A worried looking Maureen stood before him. The atmosphere in that particular interview room was always formal and imposing. It was a part of the station which in personality always felt at odds with the rest. Tweety noticed that Maureen was gripping a large brown envelope as if her life depended on it.

"Ok Maureen, what's got you all of a tizzy, surely it can't be as bad as all that?" Mo fidgeted and strained then the words erupted from her mouth like a mini volcano. "Oh Tweety, this could be something or nothing. If it's nothing, I'll feel like a real fool, you understand, don't you?" She burst into a flood of tears then suddenly threw herself at him.

Tweety was caught completely off guard. Sobbing she continued, "Go on then, look for yourself, Tweety, tell me what you think? I think they're disgusting. I feel disgusting. For taking them, then keeping them all this time. Don't ask me why I did it because I haven't got a clue. What I can tell you is that I've been tormented by them ever since." More sobbing.

Tweety awkwardly patted her on the back. Close contact and comforting came unnaturally to him. "There, there now Maureen. Let me take a wee peek at your envelope shall we. Like I said, it can't be all that bad?"

He eased Mo over to one side then gently opened the envelope. Mo watched on as he examined each of the photographic images with his slowly blinking green eye. Finally, he looked up trying to mask his disgust.

"Ok Mo, I'll have to hang on to these. You were right, these images are disgusting. Disgusting and cruel. It's their helpless faces staring back at me. It makes me so fucking angry seeing them posed like that. Now tell me how you got them?"

Maureen nodded, straightening herself up. This secret had weighed her down for several years. It had controlled her happiness and her ability to move on. She smiled at Tweety praying that he could release her from their evil grip. She then began her unusual story. Tweety listened quietly, never interrupting once. Wee Mo's power of recollection was mesmerising. When she was finished, Tweety nodded then smiled.

"Thank you, Maureen, that was excellent. Speak of this to absolutely no one. I need time for a little digging but I think I know where I'm going with this. Now do you promise me pet?"

Maureen nodded, already looking happier. "Absolutely Tweety. I promise, you can keep the photographs if you like." Tweety shuddered.

They were all sat in their usual spot on the first floor of the Hop House that evening. The House of Pain. That was their code word come nickname for the Rosetta Bar. It was located on the Rosetta Road on the more upper-class outskirts of Mountroyal's patch. It wasn't much to look at, basically a grey cement box with tiny elongated windows. Its front door was secure and monitored by a security camera. You had to be buzzed in to gain entry then bypass the burly doormen whose size had more in common with the Neanderthal man. The underwhelming sensation continued when you stepped inside. Maroon walls, carpets and matching drapes greeted the thirsty punter. Even the seating in all its forms was maroon. Setting aside all these plusses, this was a police-friendly bar and had been for as long as anyone could recall. Many thousands of Her Majesty's pounds had been spent there over the years.

The usual suspects were in attendance which wasn't very unusual except that Tweety had called for an urgent AGM. The attendees knew this had to be serious for Tweety had never ever called for such a meeting. The golden rule was as always honoured, no business until the first pint was sunk. Oh, apologies, how very rude of me. Let me introduce the select gathering to you. In no particular order for in the Hop House your rank was left at the front door. George Sewell,

Archie Brown, Clifford Boomer, Derek Grant and Harold Sweetlove. Resting at the front door were the following ranks: Superintendent, Detective Inspector, Detective Sergeant, Inspector and Constable of the genius variety.

Paddy the elderly bar man sashayed down from the bar with the next round of drinks on his old battered metal tray. Four pints of Guinness, his speciality, and a white coffee and a glass of Soberano brandy with a rock of ice in it for Tweety. Paddy, a man in his age defying seventies was in his usual sparkling form and was a delightful whistler. I fancy Paddy was a tit-warbler in his previous life. He was whistling 'Nellie Dean' as he served the assembled group. This was in direct competition with 'Top of the World' by Karen Carpenter playing from the crackling speakers dotted around the bar.

George clapped his hands like a youngster on Christmas morning. "Cheers Paddy son, right maestro, this better be good. Who's shagging who then, that we didn't know about? Has our Aggie got a new man in her life! Well, pray tell boy genius, what's with the urgent AGM?" Tweety smiled though it took some effort. He then took a sip of his brandy followed directly by the coffee. The flavours met and mingled like a modern-day romance. It was all too glorious.

He eyed the expectant faces then began, "An urgent operation is called for and we have less than a week. Everyone here present will be vital to its success or failure for that matter. Secrecy and discretion are the key." Archie Brown aka Pinky was furiously stoking up on Woody his pipe and a soft Saint Bruno whisper wafted across their nostrils. "Discretion assured, Tweety, did you get that, you big tube?"

Big Cliff rolled his eyes for the millionth time. Everyone laughed. Derek couldn't contain himself, "Yes Tweety. Got it. Absolute discretion with bells on. Pray continue, we're all ears." Tweety nodded. "We're waiting on one more to make up the dream team. The classiest of classy ladies is required. She's to be the female foil of a crack interview team, ah ha, here she is now." All eyes looked to the doorway.

Paddy the barman stopped mid-warble as the vision entered, and how she entered. Soft shoulder length jet black hair framed a stunning face. Her eyes were heavily mascaraed and a brilliant turquoise, her lips were full and a scorching scarlet. When the usual suspects managed to peel their eyes off her gorgeous face and move in a more southerly direction, they were rewarded with a shimmering green silk blouse tucked into a pair of skin tight blue jeans. These were equally tucked into a pair of black patent boots. Tweety smiled as the beauty approached their snug. On seeing him, she fired back with her own smile which lit up the room.

"Aww Shelley pet, thanks for turning up, what's your pleasure?"

Shelley plonked herself down on a stool then leapt back in shock when she realised the company she was in. Her boss then her boss's boss then the gods from CID.

"Holy fuck Tweety! What's going on here? Oh, sorry Sir. I mean Sirs. Oh, fuck me. Sorry to the lot of you again. Will that do? As for you Tweety Pie, fuck you for getting me into this pickle. Sorry again you lot. Oh, and since my career's ruined, mine's a vodka and diet coke. Cheers!"

A moment's silence followed the mini maelstrom then they all burst out laughing. Derek looked across at George and mouthed "Classiest of classy!" The big boss smiled. He had a lot of time for Shelley McCann. Shelley's vodka arrived and was downed before Paddy had made it back to the bar, another was quickly ordered.

Tweety continued. First came the photographs which were met with shock and disgust. Then he conveyed Mo's story to them verbatim. Archie was puffing hard on Woody sucking and blowing as he examined the images, a rage welling up inside him.

Big Cliff sifted through several of the images and heaved a huge sigh before speaking with his deep doleful double bass, "They don't look too happy about being there wherever there is. Some have been taken indoors, others outside. I don't recognise anywhere nor do I know any of those poor ladies. Jeez, nipple clamps and down below. Fuck me! They're sick."

Shelley took a sip from her second vod then lit up. Their snug was fast turning into a murky pea souper. None took any heed as Elvis serenaded softly 'In the Ghetto.' Shelley was now in full police mode lifting one of the images.

"What's with the pair of letters then a group of numbers beside each group of images. Like this set involving this blonde-haired woman, hers is KD12389. God help her she must be in her fifties and she's wearing a wedding ring. Naked tied to a tree, what kind of sick bastard would do that? Look at the misery in her face."

Derek held up an image of a twenty something redhead. She was tied to a bed, heavily mascaraed, she had obviously been crying. Mascara which had been amateurishly applied was smeared over her cheeks. Her naked body was covered in dark blue candle wax, her configuration was BW16290. Derek sighed. "It looks like each set of pictures has its own unique set of letters and numbers all right but what can we do? We have no idea as to who they are and we don't have any complaints to act upon?"

At this moment, Tweety placed a glossy Police Gazette [5] magazine on their table. This particular Gazette was two years old and dated December 1981. Its cover bore a seasonal image of a snowman outside Ballycastle Police Station.

They all looked on as Tweety opened the magazine to a page containing an article relating to a Charity Golf Function at the Glenavon House Hotel in Cookstown County Tyrone. An attractive 50-year-old blonde was presenting prizes following a golf outing at the Killymoon Golf Course. She was referred to as Rhonda the wife of Inspector Wayne Gordon stationed locally. Tweety whispered, "It's the same woman if I'm not mistaken, do we all agree?"

They all nodded comparing the images of the female tied to the tree and the happier Gazette image. Archie wriggled in his seat. "KD. Kilo Delta. That's the Cookstown call sign and I'll wager the number refers to Inspector Wayne Gordon's force number."

George Sewell nodded gravely downing his whisky in one. "Dirty, dirty bastard, what type of low life sicko would do that to a woman. I don't care who she is or where she's from, it's sick and just pure evil!" He let out a huge sigh before catching Paddy's eye followed by a circular sweep in the air with his right hand.

Another round was on its way. "Right Tweety we're all with you. Give us your instructions, where do you want us and what needs done? I'll authorise any overtime for this one. Let's catch this heartless sick bastard."

Shelley raised her glass and proposed a toast, "To the dream team." The game was on.

---

[5] *(The Police Gazette is a glossy monthly publication circulated throughout all of the police stations in the province. Its contents are varied and include any new changes in the law, notable arrests or incidents of good police work. It covered social functions of interest as well as a wide sporting section. It's also used an advertising platform for car dealerships, hotel and restaurants seeking police business.)*

Chapter 12
Courting Disaster

Heavenly made good time that morning and had arrived at Downpatrick Courthouse with 20 minutes to spare, she just loved the place. It was like stepping back in time, the area was steeped in history and folklore. The courthouse sat on an elevated site in English Street in the County Down market town. It was originally built on the grounds of a monastic site in 1735 and took on a neo-classical look. It was rebuilt following a fire in 1855 and sat beside the county jail of Down built in 1796. A one stop shop of the day. Many men were sentenced in the courthouse and ended up in the jail next door.

Conditions then for prisoners were atrocious due to bad diet and filthy squalor. For many of them this was to be their final staging post before penal migration, a brutal voyage of between three and five months which took them to a new life and fresh beginnings far from home. Those that survived the trip arrived in New Holland or Australia as it's known today.

Heavenly slipped her silver Fiesta into a parking spot with a view, she was on top of a hill looking down into the old town below. Downpatrick then was a mixed town with a population of around 10,000 souls. It had its terrorists and as a police officer you had to tread carefully, always mindful of your conversations and not taken in by its apparent charms. She paused taking in the beauty of Down Cathedral where legend has it that Ireland's patron saint, Saint Patrick was buried way back in the fifth century.

Stephanie took a deep breath before checking her eyes out in the rearview mirror, "Ugh, red and blotchy you big cry-baby, come on girl pull yourself together, onwards and upwards." She kicked off her adidas trainers and slid into her black court shoes, apologies for the pun. She then reached into the back seat for her handbag containing her notebook, witness statement and summons, thinking what do we call you then, I can hardly go into the courthouse looking for Mr. Bulgy Eyes on the court list. She took a quick shifty at her summons. Ok then so you're a Mr. Denis McNeice when you're not trying to burn the place down. Last but most essential, yep there you are my company for the day. Thank you, Catherine Cookson, for your services to boring court trials, 'Tilly Trotter Widowed' should do the trick.

Although it was July it had been a cloudless night and even with the morning sun it was still quite nippy. She smiled at the irony as her John Denver cassette tape began playing 'Sunshine on My Shoulders.' Stephanie was a bit out of sorts today, verging on sad, well her heart was heavy. She had come across an article in the C6 or Occurrence Book yesterday when her section had returned from their long weekend off. B. Section had attended a sudden death at 33, Shelbourne Road the previous morning. The deceased was Mrs. Nancy Flynn. Heavenly's heart sank remembering Nancy's kindness to her a short while back, that was the day of lemonade and laughter in her garden shed with that big lig, the Preacher. That was the day of the bomb! Then something else struck her and she began to cry, then there was that other matter she had to get off her chest. The feeling had been going on too long. She had to find out, was it just her, had she been imagining things? She smiled and nodded with grim determination; time to find out girlfriend, let's kill two birds with the one stone, shall we?

The lobby of the Downpatrick Courthouse was full and buzzing as Stephanie glided in. She was stylish in a pale blue blouse, matching cardigan, navy three quarter length skirt and matching tights. She had her hair swept back in a bun with just a few strands floating free as she walked. She had on the slightest application of makeup and looked stunning.

Inspector Damien Dalzell was cruising the lobby trying to look important. He had nothing to offer to the proceedings but liked to pretend that he was there in some official capacity or another. If there was a journalist's camera about, rest assured, he would find a way to get in front of it. He was generally ignored by the real police officers. On seeing Stephanie, he made a beeline for her, "Mmm, Woman Constable Gates, I hardly recognised you out of your uniform. Good to go, I hope, ready to give Queen's evidence and all that?"

Stephanie smiled out of politeness, "Yes Inspector Dalzell, raring to go and ready to answer the call if required."

Inspector Dalzell nodded slowly eyeing her up and down, leaving her in no doubt that he was very interested. "And your colleague, you know the scruffy fellow, has he slept in today or what?"

Heavenly was fast running low on good will, "Eh no Sir, Constable Weaver is giving evidence at a murder trial at the Crumlin Road Courthouse today, his evidence here has been agreed, so it's just little old me I'm afraid."

Double D nodded sagely, double tapping his nose and winking at her, "You'll be alright today. This one's a slam dunker, a home runner of a case. All forensic you see, every contact leaves a trace, glass on his clothing matching glass at the seat of the fire. We've got the top forensic man to take this one home. Just sit back and enjoy the ride, I can't see you being disturbed today. I was just wondering though; I've been thinking about you since last we met and well, I think there's something going on between us. Maybe a coffee sometime or a candlelit dinner for two?"

Double D's mind raced to the notches on his bedpost. He had room for one more, she would soon be fawning after him like the rest. He landed her with his legendary Double D dazzling smile, "Well, what do you say then Woman Constable Gates?" Stephanie wanted to vomit. She sparkled her eyes and flared her nostrils then gave him that seductress smile, well two can play at that game. She winked and motioned him to come closer. Double D gulped, a different side to this one was emerging, and he liked it. He drew close, his ear leaning in towards her mouth.

He felt her warm breath and smelled her sweet perfume as she whispered gently in his ear, "The name's Stephanie Inspector. I can well imagine many women being overjoyed by such an invite but sadly for you, I have to decline, you see, I bat for the other team. If you know what I mean?"

A look of abject horror appeared on his well-groomed face. He looked like a man that had just swallowed a feather pillow whole, he began coughing and spluttering. Stephanie was in triumph holding her seductive pose while the idiot squirmed. When he eventually regathered himself, he threw himself in reverse gear, "Ah good, excellent, sorry about that. Didn't realise you were qu... ga... well you know what I mean. Lovely meeting you again. Very busy here, very, very busy. As they say in Russia, Moscow!" And with that, Dashing Damien Dalzell left Stephanie's world forever.

Stephanie chuckled then made her way over to a 50-year-old man in a suit holding a clipboard. She knew the form, he was responsible for all the police witnesses in the case. "Hi there, Woman Constable Stephanie Gates from Mountroyal."

Looking across the crowded hall, she spotted a tall willowy figure, early forties standing in and around 6 feet 4 inches. He was wearing his work gear, a large black robe and white handcrafted horse hair wig. The wig sat a tad askew shouting forth the message that he was one cool superior dude. His minions stood around him adoringly holding onto his paperwork and hanging onto his every grunt and squeak. Stephanie shook her head thinking on Double D and then this clown, you wait ages on a bus then two of them come at once.

The CID man with the clipboard found her on his list, "Aye, that's you, love. What's that you just said?"

Stephanie giggled, "Just talking to myself. I take it that's our Crown Prosecution Counsel over there surrounded by his lackeys. Do you know if he wants to brief me on my evidence before this thing kicks off?"

The old stager smiled, "I think we're all about the forensics on this one. Hang fire I'll double check for you. Oh, and by the way, yer man there's called Chris Freeland, the DPP's new golden boy. He's a bit too up his own arse for my liking. That's him canoodling with the forensics man. They won't be best pleased at me interrupting them, but I say fuck 'em. Two ticks."

Stephanie waited in splendid isolation and watched as the CID man interrupted Freeland who looked appalled at the intrusion. A brief diatribe took place as the CID man pointed over to Stephanie. Freeland snarled, shaking his head as the CID man nodded and trotted back to Stephanie.

Smiling as he got to her, he said, "That would be a big fat NO, Stephanie love. Fuck me, you would have thought I just asked him to donate a lung. Cheeky bastard, if I was you, I'd grab myself a wee coffee from that vending machine over there and go relax in the court. It's Court Number 1 by the way, sure it's easy money. As they say in the job, when you're marching, you're not fighting." Stephanie thanked him then glided towards the vending machine.

As she drifted across the hallway making room for others, this way and that, a male in a black gown appeared ahead of her. His arms were full of papers and the familiar horsehair wig was sat on top keeping everything down. The male was around 40 and came with a squat bovine build, definitely not fat, the build of someone who lifted weights. Heavenly couldn't make out his face as his back was to her but he had a thick head of grey hair which could very well have passed as the twin of his barrister's wig. She got the feeling they were both heading for the same place and that she was going to be a comfortable second so she eased up as he arrived at the vending machine. She watched as he set his stuff carefully down on an archaic bench then began the all too familiar Morris dance of someone searching for their wallet.

"SHIT, SHIT, FUCKING SHIT, I must have left it in the car!"

Stephanie chewed a smile and bounced in, "Having a wee bit of bother there, are we?" The male spun around and she got a look at his face for the first time. It was a handsome face in a plain kind of way but she was struck with his deep blue eyes and when he smiled then laughed it was a genuinely pleasant face that greeted her.

"Oh, fuck me. I'm terribly sorry for my language. There I go again. I appear to have left my wallet in my car."

Stephanie laughed, "Quit while you're ahead, I'll sub you this time. What are you having?"

The male smiled, "My guardian angel. Coffee, white with sugar and extra cream thanks."

Stephanie popped the twenty pence piece in and pressed all the required buttons. As the machine was doing its thing the male spoke. "Hi, I'm Billy Bolt by the way. I'm Defence Counsel for the arson trial today." Stephanie handed him his coffee and popped another twenty in for her white without. "Pleased to meet you, Billy. I'm Woman Constable Stephanie Gates from Mountroyal. I'm a prosecution witness on the same case."

Billy smiled, "Ah ha. I've read all about you. Listen just to keep things sweet we'll part ways here but I'll see you on the other side. Billy always repays his debts. Toodle pip." With that, he spun around regathering his paperwork and disappeared into Court 1 his black gown flapping in his wake. Stephanie took a seat at the bench and smiled. The jury had yet to be sworn in and nothing would happen until then. Well, he was different, a bit of an open book. Quite pleasant really.

Twenty minutes later, the tip staff appeared in the hallway and announced the jury was sworn in. The Crown Court Arson Trial was ready to start. Stephanie was in no real panic, no need, the evidence was all scientific as she entered the courtroom behind a load of strangers. She took a seat in an area set aside for the prosecution witnesses. She actually selected a whole row to herself; she wasn't there to make friends and after the trial, she would probably never see them again. She checked for her notebook and witness statement one more time. It took a lot of effort to look this cool, all good.

Sitting comfortably Stephanie began to relax and take in the view. She gazed around the old courtroom enjoying its sense of theatre. The judge sat on his bench in an elevated position looking resplendent in his scarlet robes. He looked as though he was eighty and his peruke or wig was made for someone with a larger head. Not one jot did he appear to give. She secretly wondered was he all there at all. To his right were the selected jury, 12 citizens, all good and true. They sat in two rows of six in the jury box. Beneath the judge and facing him were the prosecution and defence counsels and behind them their gerbil gibbering lackeys. Mr. McNeice the accused was sat in the dock accompanied by a uniformed police officer. The witness box which was empty faced both he and the jury.

"Time for Tilly Trotter Widowed," Stephanie whispered as she eased her novel out of her handbag. She began happily reading all the while keeping a lazy ear on the current court proceedings.

It had just gone 11.20 AM when the Clerk of the Court read out the charges to Mr. Bulgy or should we say Mr. Denis McNeice. The charges read were those of Arson and Criminal Damage to the tune of £35,000. The alleged offences occurred at the Texas Home Store located at the Bloomfield Shopping Centre Bangor at approximately 6.00 AM on Thursday, 2 June 1983. Stephanie was heavily into her book throughout all of this blether. She did however lift her head at the point when the clerk asked the defendant how he wished to plead? The courtroom hung in suspense for a few brief moments before he replied in a heavily stammered fashion, "NO. NO! NOT GUILTY SO I'M NOT!"

Stephanie sighed. A wee last-minute plea and a flier would've been nice, but not to be. She was now there for the duration, back to her book. "Where was I, Tilly?" Both counsels gave their openings to the jury but Stephanie was lost in another world. Her page turner was doing its job, killing time and keeping her happily distracted. She was peeled from her pages by the Clerk of the Court calling for a Doctor George Gordon, Forensic Scientist. He was acting as an expert witness on behalf of the prosecution. A male in a large tatty woollen jacket made his way to the witness box and was initially questioned by Freeland. He was largely how you would imagine a Professor Bagshot to look and sound, a man in his early sixties with thick wild unkempt greying hair, slightly stooped at 5 feet 10 inches with a hint of a shuffle in his walk. In these vaunted surroundings, if ever there was a fish out of water, it was he. It was like watching paint dry or maybe we should say watching a sample of paint dry as his considerable credentials were aired to the jury. Between the pair of them and the hot air they produced, they were doing their utmost to send the jury to sleep.

Eventually Freeland got down to the nitty gritty. Gordon was to be questioned about the comparison between the glass fragments lifted at the Texas Home Store and the glass fragments found on the accused body and clothing following his arrest. Freeland turned to his audience the jury then hawkishly glared at McNeice then back to his perceived jury. It was pure pantomime.

In dramatic fashion, he rasped, "Doctor Gordon, my question is a simple one, are the glass fragments recovered from the defendants clothing and person a match for the glass fragments recovered at the scene of the arson?"

Doctor Gordon paused with great effect nodding several times sagely. The jury were now putty in his hands. Heavenly snatched a glance at her watch, her heart fluttered, she could be down the road in half an hour. She awaited his answer along with the rest. The anticipated slam dunker, or Bulgy's 'Coup de gras'. Doctor Gordon didn't disappoint, he smiled leaning back in his chair which creaked in protest. Here was a man sucking the very marrow out of his every second in the witness box. Each member of the jury sat forward in their seats, eyes fixed on his lips. Each one of them begging for release from the chains of anticipation they were shackled in. Doctor Gordon set them free.

Now leaning forward in his creaking seat, he spoke with gravity and utmost sincerity, "I can categorically state, that the glass fragments found at the scene of the fire are a match to the glass fragments retrieved from Mr. McNeice's clothing and person."

The jury visibly sighed, sat back and relaxed. A bag of 'Werther's Originals' was secretly being passed around. *Nicely slam-dunked, Doctor Gordon*, thought Stephanie. She was however a little surprised when Freeland smugly looked over at the defence barrister, a certain William Bolt, and said, "No further questions from the prosecution, Your Honour."

Billy Bolt's head shot up in amazement and that's when he caught Stephanie's mirrored expression. The old judge leaned forward and smiled warmly at Doctor Gordon.

"Thank you for your precious time, Doctor, most beneficial to this case, most beneficial indeed."

Doctor Gordon returned the unctuous smile with his own syrupy effort and responded dramatically, "You're most welcome, Your Honour."

Stephanie cringed at the apparent Dickensian love-in. Doctor Gordon still smiling made a fidgeted attempt to get up and leave the witness box when Billy Bolt slowly rose like a cobra eyeing its prey, "Eh, Doctor Gordon, just a couple of questions from the Defence, if you please." It had the same effect as someone sneaking up behind the old scientist and shouting, "Boo!" He looked up at the Judge as if he'd just been shot! The Judge smiled and shrugged his shoulders. Billy Bolt then turned to his target audience, the jury and smiled with that big open smile he possessed. He let them take in his handsome face and wallow a little in his deep blue eyes.

"Take your time, Doctor, we're in no rush." Doctor Gordon harrumphed as he collapsed back into his seat. Stephanie was intrigued, she gently turned her book face down and waited on the mercurial Billy Bolt's next move. Billy then turned to face the Doctor who was now viewing him disdainfully. Billy then looked at his case files for several moments ramping up the tension and creating an electric atmosphere, he then quickly glanced over to where the prosecution witnesses were seated and ever so subtly shook his head in a manner inferring that they had disappointed him. The jury picked up on it.

The judge broke the aching silence, "Mr. Bolt, your questions for Doctor Gordon if you please." Billy turned to the jury, his newly found besties and gave them that 'Who's been a naughty boy then,' expression. Several of the female jurors positively gushed. Stephanie had to admit it, he was good. Quick as a flash and in chameleon fashion, everything changed. Billy spun around and began a series of quick-fire questions taking the good Doctor completely by surprise.

"Doctor Gordon, you have informed the members of the jury that the glass from the scene of the fire was a match to the glass fragments found on my client, is that correct?"

Doctor Gordon nodded, "Yes, that's correct. We analysed the fragments under our most advanced microscope and concluded that they were a match."

Billy nodded, chewing on the arm of a pair of gold-rimmed spectacles which had suddenly appeared. "The glass for argument's sake couldn't have come from a car headlight or a jam jar for that matter, could it?" Doctor Gordon's patience was beginning to wear thin.

The judge eased in, "Mr. Bolt, direction of travel, where are we going with this line of questioning, please?"

Billy glanced quickly up at the jury who were now intrigued. He gave them one of his old charmer smiles and returned to the doctor, "Thank you Doctor

Gordon, I'm nearly done. Similar pig with a different snout, you see. Is the glass itself a common type, could it be found in maybe window form in properties such as houses or business premises or the like?" Doctor Gordon began to wriggle uncomfortably in his chair. Heavenly glanced over at Freeland and his team who were finger pointing at each other. This flapping spilled across to the police officers involved in the investigation, a mini-Mexican wave of blame began. Meanwhile Billy Bolt remained statuesque, calm, almost stoic with his large blue eyes fixed on the Doctor. The good doctor was shaken, rattled and rolled by the impressive Defence Barrister.

The Judge leaned forward and whispered, Doctor Gordon, if you would answer Counsel's question, please."

Doctor Gordon tensed up and barked, "Our offices were asked by the Police to ascertain if the two glasses were a match and that is what they are. A Match!" Billy Bolt raised his eyebrows and slowly approached the witness box like a matador to a bull. His metaphorical sword was in hand ready to kill off the witness. "Doctor. Gordon. Please answer the question I asked you."

The tension in the courtroom was now palpable. Doctor Gordon's eyes shot this way and that before spewing out, "Yes. It's a common type of glass found in houses and business premises and the like."

Billy Bolt spun around to the jury smiling all the more. With his back to Doctor Gordon, he said, "Thank you, most beneficial to our case. No further questions, Doctor."

The Doctor slid out of the box practically unnoticed. No fawning thanks from the Judge this time around, all eyes were fixed upon the amazing gladiatorial Defence Barrister.

Billy Bolt waited for the Doctor to shuffle out of the courtroom before continuing.

"Ladies and gentlemen of the jury, the glass in question was a common type found in the windows of our own homes, businesses and the like. The accused at the time of his arrest worked in the double-glazing business. The day before his arrest he had spent several hours smashing up old double-glazed windows into a skip. My client hadn't changed out of his work clothes nor had the opportunity to wash himself thus accounting for the glass fragments found on his clothing and person." Billy Bolt then purposefully took his seat. Several members of the jury looked at each other and nodded.

Freeland bounced up and in a pleading demeanour spoke, "Your Honour, the accused had ample opportunity when spoken to by the police to relate those hitherto unknown facts. However, he chose to remain silent throughout. Perhaps the jury should consider those inexplicable omissions and draw adverse inference from them."

Freeland scowled at Billy Bolt on the blind side then gave a cardboardy smile to the jury before smugly taking his seat. Billy Bolt let the dust settle before slowly rising to his feet. Stephanie sensed that he was now quietly in control and waving the baton. He contritely approached the jury with a face full of sadness. My god, were there tears in his deep blue eyes. He then spoke barely above a whisper.

"Ladies and gents, I'm sure it wasn't lost on any of you just how hard it was for my client over there to offer a plea of 'NOT GUILTY'. We all witnessed his struggle to get his words out when challenged by the Clerk of the Court. You see, my client has suffered from a lifelong stammer. He finds it extremely hard to string even the simplest of sentences together, even among family and friends, can you imagine then, just how hard it must have been for him or how he must have felt when he was arrested. Yes, mistakenly by police at Ward Park that summer's morning, the untold stress that put on him. There's no doubt in my mind that his stammer would have been tenfold worse and put a great strain on his mental health, therefore, my client chose to say nothing as a coping mechanism. Sadly, he's been doing this all his life.

"Mr. McNeice knew that he was innocent and therefore had nothing to prove. There is a legal term called Burden of Proof or 'Let he who accuses prove.' My client was and is under no obligation to prove his innocence, but rather it's up to the Prosecution to prove his guilt. So, there we have it all in a nutshell. The glass fragments dealt with, the glass was a common type and my clients perceived silence dealt with, a man with a lifelong debilitating stammer. Your Honour, I move to have this gross miscarriage of justice dismissed. The burden of proof has simply not been met by the prosecution!"

Stephanie glanced over to the jury; several were nodding. The Judge cleared his throat.

"Ahem, Mr. Freeland, any thoughts on the matter?" Stephanie watched fascinated as Freeland and his prosecution team debated the issues heatedly in staccato whispers. This had not been expected at all. McNeice smiled down at his Counsel who remained impassive. After a while, Freeland got to his feet a little less arrogant. Billy Bolt had clipped his wings. "Er, Your Honour, there is always the identification evidence to be considered." Heavenly gasped, "Shit!" She was on the verge of a heart attack. That would be me, she whispered to herself, quickly stuffing Tilly Trotter into her open hand bag. Was it just her imagination or was everyone in the Courtroom looking at her. Then…

"Woman Constable Stephanie Gates to the witness box please."

Billy Bolt had to admit it, Woman Constable Stephanie Gates was a beauty as she glided into the witness box. Standing with a Bible in her right hand she took her oath from the Clerk of the Court then quietly sat down. Billy eyed the jury who were drinking her in. A penny for their thoughts he mused. Lucky for us readers, I can tell you…. several of the male jurors were imagining her naked, one of the elderly females thought she would be a perfect match for her son who was a panel beater and going places. Finally, a female juror just loved her court shoes, had she seen a pair just like them at "Marksies?"

The old Judge then spoke like a jolt out of the blue. Looking to the jury as though they were in kindergarten he smiled warmly then proceeded. "Ladies and gentlemen of the jury, it is incumbent on me to give you the following advice. Before Woman Constable Gates gives her identification evidence to the court you must bear these two things in mind. Firstly, an honest and sincere witness may still be wrong, secondly do not jump to conclusions. I know some of you may find all of this exhausting but please, listen closely to all the facts and then at the end, make your final decision based on everything you've heard, thank you, Mr. Freeland, your witness."

Freeland slowly rose holding a copy of Stephanie's statement. She noticed it was unscribbled and unsullied as did Billy Bolt. The statement he had was a litany of scrawls, comments, question marks and exclamation marks. Oh, and there were a few clouds drawn on as well. There was a dreamer in there somewhere. It was obvious to Stephanie and everyone else there that Freeland was flying by the seat of his pants and that this was the first time he had set eyes on her statement. Freeland stood for several aching moments in the silence of the watching courtroom. He swayed from side to side as his eyes devoured her words.

The judge, now becoming impatient, spoke, "Mr. Freeland. Any time today please."

He then pulled his wig over the front of his face in exasperation causing several of the jurors to giggle. Freeland finally looked up at the Judge and grovelled. "Humblest of apologies, Your Honour." The old Judge nodded.

Freeland then smiled at Stephanie and if looks could talk, hers were yelling, you bastard, you're going to throw me under the Billy Bolt bus. Freeland responded with his own look which Stephanie got immediately, his smug expression said as much, well, it's either me or you and as I'm wearing the wig, tough luck, it's you.'

Freeland's reputation was saved due to the fact that Stephanie's statement was picture-perfect in date, times and in chronological order. Everything relating to the arson was there including Gary's heroics in lifting the plastic bottle minus the top. Mr. Bulgy's appearance, then disappearance. The bottle top and its retrieval. The torn clothing on the barbed wire fence. The identification of Mr. Bulgy to Bangor police at Ward Park several minutes later and finally submitting statements to Bangor CID before returning to Mountroyal and termination of duty.

Stephanie was left with nothing more to say or do with Freeland's questioning and delivery of her statement other than to say, "That's correct, Your Honour." It was done with all the excitement and drama of a teleprinter delivering 12 no score draws on a wet winter's weekend.

His final question to her was simple. "And is the man that jumped out in front of your police vehicle the same man that is in the Dock before you today?"

Stephanie looked across at Bulgy who looked down from her stare and nodded confidently for the benefit of the jury. "Yes, Your Honour, to the best of my knowledge, it's the same man."

A flurry of whispers and nodding could be seen and heard from the jury. Stephanie noted several smiling at her. An elderly female juror sucking on a Werther's gave her a sneaky thumbs up.

Freeland had survived thanks to Stephanie's good police work. The arrogance returned to his face perhaps with a hint of relief but with no hint of thanks, as a matter of fact, if looks could speak his were saying, "Cheers easy, I'm outta here."

He smiled at her like an assassin then spoke as if bored, "No further questions Woman Constable Gates."

Stephanie steeled herself, the worst was yet to come. As much as Freeland was unprepared and flew by the seat of his pants, Billy Bolt she felt would be totally the opposite. She was afraid, very afraid, afraid of this wolf in sheep's clothing. Afraid of this charmer with the big blue eyes wearing the wide smile, fully armed with sharp teeth and claws.

Billy was experienced enough to let them have their fill. When he did stand up, he presented her with his full-on smile. Stephanie waited in dread realising she was gripping her legs as you would sitting on a dentist's chair. Billy then left his lair and slowly approached the witness box all the while smiling. He was giving the jury time to adjust their sets as it were, time to get used to them being together and time to re-focus on the case. If this was to be a dance, then he would be the lead. He snatched a quick glance at her handbag and spotted her, 'Tilly Trotter' hanging out. He looked up at her with a twinkle in his eye. Would he, or wouldn't he? Stephanie gulped. He then turned his back to her and faced the jury.

He spoke. "Woman Constable Gates, you looked rather surprised to be called to the witness box. Certainly, several things have surprised me thus far in relation to the presentation of this case by the Prosecution Counsel."

He fired a glare at Freeland who appeared unfazed. "What length of service do you have, please?" He now turned and faced her.

Stephanie replied quickly, "Approximately eight years Your Honour."

Bolt held her gaze, "And would you be an inny or an outty?"

Stephanie was puzzled. Billy Bolt continued. "I'm aware that due to the fact that they haven't given female officers firearms as yet, many choose to remain indoors where it's most infinitely safer?"

Stephanie took the hit and replied calmly, "I'm fully operational Your Honour. I'm an outty, to use the Defence Counsel's phraseology."

Several of the jury giggled to which Stephanie smiled.

Billy Bolt continued. "As I see it, you are the Prosecution's only chance of securing a conviction in this case. Evidence by identification. Perhaps you would answer the following questions to the jury which would give them some indication as to how alert you were mentally at the time of your alleged identification of my client."

Stephanie sat back in her chair and braced herself for the onslaught. The storm had most definitely arrived. "Woman Constable Gates, would I be correct in saying that the morning in question was in actual fact the last of your weeks night shift at Mountroyal Police Station in East Belfast?"

Stephanie nodded, "That's correct, Your Honour."

Bolt continued, "I understand that the Belfast Stations run a night shift from 11.00 PM to 7.00 AM. Correct me if I'm wrong, but I take it providing you weren't on leave or anything, that would mean seven night shifts at eight hours per shift were completed by your good self. Fifty-six hours answering calls in what can only be described as extremely anti-social hours. I don't for the life of me know how you brave officers cope especially with the terrorist threat. So, you worked 56 hours that particular set of night shifts?"

Stephanie looked up at the Judge, "I'll have to check my notebook, Your Honour."

The old Judge smiled, "Absolutely Woman Constable. Take your time." Stephanie knew where this was heading as she started counting how many hours she had actually performed that week of nights starting from the first night which was always a Thursday. She saw that she had performed three early starts that week, the final one being that last night. She had commenced duty at 7.00 PM the Friday, Monday and the Wednesday nights.

Gazing up at the Judge, she said, "I actually performed a total of 68 hours that week. I had three 7.00 PM starts, the final one was the Wednesday night going into the Thursday morning in question, Your Honour."

Billy Bolt turned his attention to the jury and sighed, "Sixty-eight hours. Unbelievable, and you say you started duty at 7.00 PM on the Wednesday night. Did you get a break that final night Woman Constable Gates?"

Stephanie thought for a moment, "Well our break was at 3.30 AM that Thursday morning. I would say we had about half an hour or so before my Sergeant requested, we run a sick colleague home to Bangor."

Billy Bolt jumped in, "Was that a request or was it an order then Woman Constable?"

Stephanie smiled for the benefit of the jury, "Goodness no, it was a request. You see, the sick colleague was and is also our friend, we were glad to help."

Billy Bolt nodded. "Then after you left your friend's home, it was then when travelling back to Mountroyal. Then, when the male jumped out in front of your vehicle. I put it to you that you must have been exhausted?"

Stephanie nodded. "I would be a liar if I didn't admit to being tired. I was. We both were. But when the male jumped out in front of us, it had the desired effect. Had my colleague, Constable Weaver not been driving so slowly we would have hit him."

Billy Bolt nodded. "How long was he in your sight before he disappeared then?"

Stephanie considered, "Somewhere between two and three seconds at a guess."

Billy swung away and addressed the jury who were hanging off every word and syllable. "And yet your statement goes into great depth when describing this individual, his looks, age, piercings and clothing. For someone who has only snatched a glimpse, your powers of recall are extraordinary. Oh, and the little blue bottle top as well, and if that was not all, you and Constable Weaver come across the arson and have to deal with all those ramifications. Notebook please?"

Billy Bolt held his hand out with eyes that were reaching into the recesses of her being. Stephanie tried hard to appear calm but inside she felt like a bag of spanners. She placed her pocket notebook into his outstretched hand like a child handing in her homework. Her notebook was something she prided herself in and Bolt could find no flaws in it to aid his cause.

He returned it with a smile. "Just one final question before I let you go. When did you make this masterpiece of a notebook entry? Was it then and there at the relevant times? Maybe it was when you identified my client to other police at Ward Park minutes later. Please enlighten us? When was this chronological masterpiece containing all the relevant details of dates, times, places and descriptions actually recorded? You see ladies and gentlemen of the jury in all my years at the bar this is the most flawless notebook entry I have ever had the pleasure of examining?"

The jury's minds were swaying like wheat in a field on a warm summer's day. All were waiting for an answer. Stephanie responded firmly. "My notebook entry was done at the earliest opportunity. I, in fact completed it at Bangor Police Station along with my witness statement that morning before returning to Mountroyal and terminating duty."

Billy Bolt nodded as if his mind were someplace else. "Where in Bangor Police Station did both you and Constable Weaver complete these notebook entries and statements Woman Constable Gates?"

Stephanie smiled remembering Tweety's advice on the morning of the incident. "I completed mine in the Constables Workroom. I believe Constable Weaver did his in the Bangor CID Office."

For the first time, Stephanie noted a hint of disappointment from the young Defence Counsel. Looking to the ground he said quietly, "Thank you, Woman Constable Gates. No further questions."

As Stephanie rose to her feet, she paused then looked at the old Judge and like a schoolgirl gingerly raised her hand which the Judge spotted. "Yes, Woman Constable, you wished to say something?"

Stephanie cleared her throat and spoke, "Your Honour. I was just wondering about the other evidence?"

The Judge took his wig off and began twiddling with it. He dramatically looked at his watch then said, "Other evidence? Do we have any further evidence to place before this court and jury, Mr Freeland?" Freeland went rummaging through his paperwork then awkwardly got to his feet sending the stoniest of glares Stephanie's way.

"Your Honour, I think that Woman Constable is referring to the following. Exhibit GW1 an empty blue plastic bottle recovered by Constable Weaver at the seat of the fire. Upon forensic examination there were no fingerprints found, however traces of petrol were found on it. Exhibit SG1. A blue bottle top recovered by Woman Constable Gates at the location where the male leapt out in front of their vehicle. Forensic examination found traces of petrol on it but as the two exhibits travelled in the same police vehicle back to Bangor Police Station together cross-contamination may well have occurred. A point my learned counsel for the defence would surely have picked up on." Billy Bolt was scribbling throughout and made no response to the backhanded compliment.

Freeland went on, "As for the final exhibit SG2, a strip of material recovered from the barbed wire fence at the location where the male appeared in front of the Mountroyal crew. This was found to be a match with the cream-coloured top the defendant was wearing on the morning of the arson. Glass fragments were also recovered."

The Judge was flabbergasted, trying hard to keep his emotions in check, "And you failed to present these exhibits before the court for what reason? Oh, and thank you, Constable. You may take a seat?"

Freeland was having a kerfuffle as Stephanie exited the witness box with her head held high. Billy Bolt caught her with a wink as she glided by, *Angel with a dirty face*, thought Stephanie trying hard not to like him. The Judge threw his wig down, "Well Mr. Freeland, I await with bated breath. An answer please?"

Freeland spluttered, "Well, Your Honour, I just considered that my learned friend for the defence had dealt with those issues. The broken glass fragments on his clothing and his refusal to answer any questions to the police when arrested. There were no prints lifted from the plastic bottle so I didn't see the relevance."

The old Judge went ballistic, "How's about compelling circumstantial evidence, Mr. Freeland? We have a fire; a plastic bottle is recovered from the scene containing petrol. The scene itself is covered in broken glass. A male person appeared from a hedge and stopped in front of a police vehicle near the scene of the fire at the ungodly hour of 6.00 AM in the morning. Police witness the male throwing a bottle top out of the back of his hand. He then does a runner, pardon my expression, leaving behind a piece of torn fabric on a barbed wire fence. He's subsequently stopped by other police and a positive identification is made by the Mountroyal personnel. Forensic analysis of his clothing reveals glass fragments matching the glass smashed at the scene of the fire as well as a match with his cream top and the torn fabric. The male in question flees from the police and then when arrested does nothing to help his cause by remaining silent. Sit-down, sit-down Mr. Freeland. This jury deserved better."

The judge sat back on his bench. He plopped his wig back on his head and rubbed his eyes like someone who has just woken from a deep sleep. His good form returned like the sun reappearing from behind a storm cloud. He smiled at the jury, "Apologies, good people. I didn't get my Weetabix today."

The jury laughed. "Mr. Bolt, Mr. Freeland, are there any more witnesses to hear from?"

Both men shook their heads. "No more skeletons lurking in your cupboards then Mr. Freeland?"

Freeland smiled, "No. No skeletons Your Honour."

The Judge chuckled looking at the jury before looking directly at Stephanie with a smile. "It's now make your mind up time, folks. You have heard all the evidence and been given explanations you must deliberate over. At the start of this trial, I cautioned you to be wary with regards identification evidence. I suggested that an honest and sincere witness could still be wrong. You have heard from Woman Constable Gates, you have listened to her testimony. You have scrutinised the words of her written statement and now you must decide based on everything you've seen or heard, in your collective opinions, was she right or was she wrong? Is the accused sitting before you in the Dock guilty of the offence of arson? I wish you well in your deliberations. Remember this. A man's liberty is at stake?"

The jury rose to consider their verdict and Stephanie made her way out into the lobby. She took a seat at an empty bench and tucked her paperwork back into the large blank envelope. She smiled at the sight of her 'Tilly Trotter' peeking out from her handbag remembering how Billy Bolt had spared her.

"Ahem!" She looked up to see Billy Bolt smiling down at her. His wig much like boxing gloves, was resting on top of his paperwork. "No hard feelings in there I hope Stephanie. That's what we both get paid for?"

Stephanie couldn't help but smile at the impish grin on his face. "No William, no hard feelings. I thought you did really well unlike our Counsel. What an arrogant plonker."

Billy chuckled, "I can't possibly comment, well at least not about the arrogant bit." They both shared a giggle.

The Clerk of the Court appeared summoning all the interested parties back inside. A mere half an hour had passed. Billy looked up with his professional head back on. "That was quick. By the way, Stephanie, well done in there. I did all I could to rattle you from your perch. Let's see which way the jury swung?"

The courtroom was a buzz of excitement but slowly quietened as it filled. Mr. Bulgy's hour was nigh. When everything and everybody was still, the Judge nodded over to the Clerk of the Court. The clerk stood up and gave a nervous tic of a cough before addressing the jury.

"Ladies and gentlemen of the jury in the case of the Crown versus Mr. Denis McNeice have you reached your decision?" The jury spokesperson rose to his feet. He was a fifty something tiler in his normal world. His hands shook as he looked at the judge and addressed the court. "Yes, Your Honour, we have reached a unanimous decision on both charges." The Judge raised his eyes slightly and nodded.

The Clerk continued, "In the matter of Arson at the Texas Home Store, Bangor on the 2 June 1983. How do you find the accused?"

The Spokesperson looked across at McNeice whose head was slightly bowed. He licked at his lips which were dry before rasping "Guilty."

The Clerk continued, "In relation to the matter of Criminal Damage to the value of £35,000 caused to the same Texas Home Store, Bangor on the 2 June 1983. How do you find the accused? The Spokesperson now a little more assured looked across to the old Judge who had gently steered the hearing to the conclusion.

"Guilty, Your Honour!" A collective sigh went up from the victorious prosecution side. Freeland eased himself back in his chair, a syrupy gloating expression spreading across his face as his back was slapped by his courting minions. He gazed over to Billy Bolt and nodded. Billy returned the nod with cool indifference. The judge thanked the members of the jury and released them from their duties. He then adjourned sentencing for three weeks pending pre-sentencing reports on Mr. Bulgy. He was released on court bail to reappear then but advised by his Counsel, a certain William Bolt to bring his tooth brush.

And that was that. As far as Stephanie was concerned it was all over. One day she was on a beat patrol through the Ormeau Park, another day she was at a Crown Court trial being spit roasted in front of a jury. As she eased out of the court, Freeland tried to catch her eye. She blanked him. She wasn't interested in anything he had to say. Out in the lobby Double D stood and preened like an exotic bird of paradise. On seeing Stephanie's glare, he scurried off into the shadows.

"Plonkers!" she muttered as she stumbled out into the startling summer light. The world had indeed kept on turning and life had carried on. "Beep, beep!" She jumped as a racing green "S" Type Jaguar drew up beside her, the driver-side window eased down, it was Billy Bolt. He was in full tennis gear wearing his full-on cheeky smile. "I'm off to Kiltonga for a game of squash, get some of that frustration out of me. Well done, Stephanie, you swung the case in there today. Hopefully we won't meet in court again but it was nice while it lasted. I still owe you a coffee by the way, a gentleman always repays his debts. Enjoy your 'Tilly Trotter', you wee rascal!" With that, he sped off wheels spinning. Stephanie laughed, noting the vehicle registration plate on his Jaguar… FIB 007!

Billy Bolt was all right.

Chapter 13
Starlight, Star Bright

Strangford Lough was flat and calm, its surface as a mirror for the setting summer's sun. The sky was a thick red and golden marmalade colour. It looked just like a fleshy Van Gogh canvas all heavily applied. Drip, drip, tiny droplets of water carelessly fell from the Preacher's body as he rocked aimlessly on his old wicker. His eyes were fixed on everything and nothing in particular. He was chomping away on raw carrots and occasionally took a sip from a pint glass containing his favourite yellow pack orange cordial. He sometimes carried his rocker, his luxury item, out to the end of his jetty.

There he would sit and chill, sometimes worry, other times dream. He was worrying about tomorrow and his fated appointment with the infamous Detective Chief Inspector Bartholomew, of Complaints and Discipline infamy. Had he been too aggressive with Mr. Prentass on the day of the bomb? A clatter of employee witness statements seemed to think so, but the bomb which blew the front out of the Wyse Byse store was just seconds away from going off. Folks may well have been killed or injured not least himself and of course the beautiful Heavenly.

A smile followed then a shrug of his massive shoulders, Heavenly, '*big tough guy*' he thought, '*you haven't even got the guts to ask her out for coffee. But what if she doesn't see me in that way?* It would ruin that special thing they had going between them. "Aaagh!" Bud was lying beside the rocker chewing on his carrots. He was drenched from the swim he and his master had just had, he would take hours to dry stinking the smoky cottage out with his damp musty fur, neither cared. A small price to pay for quality time. He could sense his Master's agitation but knew that being there with him was support aplenty. Suddenly his ears pricked and his head spun back, "RUFF, RUFF, RUFF."

The Preacher surfaced from his thoughts to see Bud bounding down the jetty with his tail wagging barking wildly with excitement. Pete looked to the ground, "Must be serious, the big fella's abandoned three carrots." He slowly stood up to see what all the fuss was about. If it was the Provos he'd better start swimming. Pete was standing basically naked save for his shorts and a half-chewed carrot for protection, hardly licensed to kill. Then from behind the wooded area to his cottage, a gleaming silver Ford Fiesta slowly appeared, he watched as it carefully skirted ruts and potholes that were strewn along his time weathered drive. Pete's heart skipped a beat, it was Heavenly arriving all unexpected.

He groaned, "Just great. Look at the cut of me. Note to self, cancel the coffee invite, you haven't a chance big time loser. Guess it's just friendship then?" He popped a carrot in his mouth in cigar fashion then tip toed his way down the jetty towards dry land. What was the purpose of this surprise visit from the woman he lo… he was very good friends with?

Heavenly had been returning from Court when the impulse took control. She would let on she was telling him how it went and the result but that wasn't it really, there were a couple of other things. She would act all friendly the way they always were with each other, but this was not how she truly felt about the enigma that was Peter Majury. Bud arrived first as she parked up beside his clapped-out moss green Citroën Dyane, the green was there somewhere behind the mud and rust. Peter was most definitely not a car person. Stephanie eased out of her shiny Fiesta carefully placing her new trainers on lush grass avoiding the mud at all costs. She was still in her court outfit and her look was classy cute. A massive ball of soaking fur bounded up to her barking excitedly with a tongue licensed to lick.

"Aww Bud. How are you, big fella? Oops!" Bud bounced up, his front paws were now on her shoulders, the canine fur ball began furiously licking at her face. Stephanie surrendered to the delirious slobbers gazing hopefully in the direction of the lough and jetty for salvation. The sun was now at its lowest point on the horizon and was casting a huge golden silhouette of the Preacher as he ambled towards her. She couldn't help thinking, if thinking was the right emotion capturing her feelings, that he resembled a Greek God descending from Mount Olympus. Six feet four plus of highly tuned muscle dark eyes and today wet curly rebellious hair, oh, and as he drew ever closer, she spotted that he hadn't shaved which really suited him and really worked for her. As he approached, she saw him smile while chomping on a carrot. Her knees went a little weak.

"Thanks for letting me know you were calling Heavenly; I would have dressed for the occasion and bought a cake. Well, how did your arsonist case go?" Stephanie was inwardly relieved there was no awkwardness between them and felt way overdressed standing next to this Tarzan.

Looking at his face while enjoying the rest of the view, she said, "Sorry Peter. I just took an urge on the off chance. Court went well. Mr. McNeice was found guilty by his peers on all counts. It's a way for pre-sentencing reports, chances are he'll be doing some prison time or as the yanks call it (giggles), some bird."

She squinted looking up at him, her nose pinched as the sun finally dipped below his shoulders. "Yours truly was in the box for over an hour, not nice. Freeland the Prosecution Barrister threw me under the proverbial bus and that bus was a certain Billy Bolt. He was brilliant. I have to give him his dues, I also have to confess he was actually quite nice outside the ropes. Anyhow, we got her over the line."

The Preacher nodded, "Pardon me for saying but you look a tad crestfallen. Is everything alright with you, pard? Tell you what, why don't I make us both a cuppa. I've baked some oatmeal biscuits, they're a little dry but we like 'em, don't we, Bud?"

Bud wagged his tail and went "RUFF!"

Stephanie smiled, "If it's not any trouble, I'm gasping. Can I take a pew in that rocking chair out at the end of the pier?" Stephanie for the first time, really took in the view. "Wow, it's really beautiful out here. It's so amazing and so quiet."

Pete was quietly chuffed, "Absolutely. Bud, keep Heavenly company fella, I'll quickly pop on a top and get the tea made. Give us five!"

The Preacher's heart was pounding as he dashed into the cottage. A fresh top, something without a tear or stain. Ahh, you'll do. Pete grabbed his pale blue 'Popeye, the sailor man' T-shirt from his spartan ironing basket and quickly threw it on. He watched out from the kitchen window as the two loves of his life strolled down the old jetty. Bud ever the gentleman trotting by her side, they were a good fit. A kettle was filled and placed on his Aga to heat, he then gathered a selection of his least burnt oaties onto a chipped blue and white Spode plate, this was his best plate. The kettle whistled and the tea was made in two shakes, he knew how she took it, white, with half a sugar. He gave himself a quick once over in the cracked mirror hanging above the open fireplace.

"Ehhh, could do better me old son. Nevertheless, a faint heart never won a fair lady. At least Bud's keeping her sweet. Good work fella. Well, here goes to nothing."

Several minutes later they were relaxing at the end of the jetty watching the final death throes of a magnificent sunset. Pete had brought a tatty old deck chair up from his work shed and was happily plonked. The tea and oaties were good as well. They watched on as the 'crunchie' coloured sky dipped below the horizon giving way to a pillow soft star encrusted night. The surface of the lough was flat calm and became a mirror to the millions of stars above, the horizon was lost in stars. Pete realised that he was totally besotted with her, she was pure perfection like the evening itself. Mother nature had pulled out all the stops for him.

The setting couldn't be any more perfect yet inside he felt like he was going to explode. No that wasn't it, he was going to spontaneously combust with stress. She was so close.

A voice within was yelling, "Do something, you'll never get a better chance than this!"

Then another voice was yanking him back, "What if she sees you as just good friends. Don't rock the boat or you'll lose her! Then what?" Then his heart suddenly gripped as he saw tears silently fall down her gossamer cheeks.

He waited a while then whispered, "What's up. This isn't like you?" She sniffled, reaching for two sheets of kitchen roll lying on the Spode plate, he'd used them as serviettes for the oaties. She then abruptly blew her nose with such volume that Bud leapt up from his slumber, it sounded just like a fog horn. The surface of the lough exploded with all manner of wild fowl fleeing and squawking. Heavenly was oblivious which was one of the things Pete loved about her, she was completely and utterly unpretentious. She smiled at him with large blue puffy eyes.

"It's just that, well, it's just so unfair. I'm just sick with the worry about tomorrow." She looked at him with a pleading expression. "You know, it's the fact that I feel so helpless and can't do a thing about it."

He smiled; she was worrying about his appointment tomorrow. "Stephanie, stop worrying, something will turn up, but thanks for your concern. It really means a lot." He noted a puzzled look on her face. "Peter, I'm sorry, but you've lost me there me there. What are you talking about?" He smiled, "My C&D appointment with Detective Chief Inspector Bartholomew's tomorrow. I'm either for the gallows or walking the plank. I could end up in jail, lose my job or, at best, get blocked to good old Crossmaglen. Then I'm thinking, what will happen to this place and old Bud here! So, pray tell, what were the tears for then, if it wasn't for little old me?"

Stephanie shook her head, biting her bottom lip, "Preacher, how clumsy of me. It's nothing really. It's just that I've fallen in love."

Pete's heart crashed and burned; he did all he could to feign concern. "Oh, and is there a problem with that?"

Stephanie nodded, "It's just that he's used to the quiet life and the great outdoors." Pete nodded slightly puzzled. More trumpeting and tears. "Well, he's so old. Nobody will want him and tomorrow he's going into a shelter. I feel terrible that I can't keep him. Oh, it's all so hopeless."

Pete tried not to smile as she innocently bulged away. He didn't have a clue what she was on about. "Sorry, I'm totally lost, shelter, outdoors?" Stephanie now became aware that her present blotchy eyed look and blubbering could not in any way be construed as attractive. She morphed back into something like her old self.

"Men! You're all the same. MONTY, MONTY, the cat, the day of the bomb. Nancy Flynn. The accident sketch outside 33, Shelbourne Road. The summer house, the lemonade!" Stephanie could see Pete's cogs whirring and the blank expression changing as the penny finally dropped. "Yes, yes, the lemonade. Awk, and the big ginger cat, Monty. He was gorgeous, wasn't he?" Bud looked up disapprovingly.

Stephanie went on, "Nancy got her wish. She passed first, she actually died the day before yesterday. Her next-door neighbour found her. I came across the incident while going through yesterday's occurrences in the C6 this morning, that was just before heading off to court. Now OUR Monty has to go into a cat's home. Like I said, he's so old no one would ever take him on. I can't take him, no pets allowed in my block of apartments."

Then she lovingly smiled up at him fluttering her eyelashes for comical effect. "I don't suppose you would know of anyone who would take an old ginger moggy in, well Mister Preacher man, what do you say?"

Bud looked up, anxiety setting in. He could see his Master going all goofy eyed. Pete let out a laugh. "Ha! You wee vixen, so that's what this was all about. Little Miss I just took an urge, hook line and sinker. Ya got me. YEESSS, OK, fine. Me and Bud will take old Monty in, won't we, fella?" Bud woofed, tail wagging.

Stephanie screeched with excitement and leapt into his arms squeezing him tight. The Preacher spontaneously combusted or as near as. "Oh Peter. Thank you, thank you. I'll pay for his food and visit here often. I promise!"

Pete was liking this new arrangement as he held her for the first time. She was on cloud nine and could happily have stayed there for the rest of her days. Eventually she went "Would you just look at the state of us?"

Pete smiled widely down at her and laughed. "Yep Stephanie, just look at us."

She whispered to him, "Oh you've got something on your cheek there, Mister. Lean down a sec." Pete leaned down as she raised herself forward and kissed him powerfully on the lips. His knees buckled as he happily surrendered. He was now floating high amongst those stars and didn't ever want to come down. She was the one for him, his final missing piece. When Stephanie pulled away, she bit her bottom lip. "It wasn't all about Monty Peter, it was about all of us. Me, you, Bud and Monty and about you asking a girl out on a date. She's got tired hanging around. Rumour has it she loves a flat white and a cherry scone with raspberry jam. Well, what do ya say to that, Mr. Preacher man?"

Their dusk had given way to nightfall and their past had given way to promise. A clear sky revealed a clean heaven full of brightly polished stars. A harvest moon lit the wooden jetty as good as any lantern. Pete gulped as the universe held its breath.

Bud woofed, "Don't fluff your lines."

He stuttered, "Coffee? I mean, would you be free for a coffee sometime soon?" The universe continued on.

Stephanie smiled. "Are you asking me out on a date then?" Pete squeaked like a mouse, his eyes mirroring hers with joy.

Of all the words he could have used in the English language he chose, "Yep?" She laughed. "Tomorrow it is then, right after work, SD Bells, Upper Newtownards Road. Then we'll go fetch Monty for our, his new home. Deal?"

Pete stammered back, "Deal." She gave him a squeeze then whispered into his ear, "You can set me down now, Tarzan, I've got to be on my way."

Pete gently set her down. He now saw a change in her, a lightness, a waspish joy. Stephanie's tragic past was now behind her. She was free, released from the chains that had held her following the tragic death of her fiancée.

The pair walked in silence down their moonlit jetty with bud padding quietly behind. Their hands touched and then held, it all felt so completely natural. As she got to her car, she spun around and quickly whispered, "You won't change your mind, will you?"

Pete laughed, "About Monty?"

She looked to the ground, "About me and Monty, I mean."

He sighed, "Stephanie I've never felt happier in my life. Don't you dare change your mind on me. Deal?"

She laughed. "Deal. Oh, and by the way, about that plonker Bartholomew tomorrow, our Tweety's on the ball. If I were Bartholomew, I'd be the one worrying. Fear not hot date. Oh, and you can buy the coffees and cherry scones, I'll pay for old Monty and all his worldly needs." And with that she was gone leaving the two amigos standing in silence under a beautiful starlit canopy.

Pete broke their bromance, "You got to admit Bud, when I go for something, there's no stopping me."

Bud gave a double take and raised an eyebrow. He then gruffed, "A CAT. We're getting a cat?" They sauntered back to the cottage; this had been one very special day in their lives. Fingers and paws crossed for all of their tomorrows.

Especially TOMORROW!

Chapter 14
Vilfort and the Dublin Port

Dublin Port is found on either side of the famous River Liffey. It's the major seaport of Ireland and is approximately 500 acres in size. Around two-thirds of Ireland's modal or container traffic passed through this port making it the busiest port on the island of Ireland.

It was a pleasant Friday evening and the July sun had just enough in its tank to offer a balmy softness to the captain and crew of The Oceana Perla or Pearl. The old dowager was inconspicuously moored up in Dublin Port. She was looking every inch her age among the other newer more modern container ships laid up there. The Pearl had sneaked in largely unnoticed on a flat calm sea that morning. Her schedule had taken her from the Port of Mersin in Turkey then Rotterdam and finally to her present mooring in Dublin. She would be berthed there for two days as pressing maintenance was required to the tired old guts of her engine. Meanwhile her Irish bound containers were in the process of being removed. Two such containers were destined for Northern Ireland; both were shown on the Pearl's manifest to contain 'Vitra' ceramic bathroom ware from Turkey. There was nothing unusual as this was a regular delivery.

As the containers were off-loaded, they made way for other containers due for onward transport to either Rotterdam or back to Turkey. This was their scheduled return leg. It was a never-ending cycle of commerce and trade. Each of the Pearl's multinational crew knew their jobs inside out and these procedures were performed with the utmost efficiency.

On these occasions, Captain Lars Vilfort, the Pearl's Danish Captain was seldom if ever bothered. His mantra was, "Call me if there are any problems." He would remain hidden in his cabin either listening to his classical music or reading. At that moment, he was lying on top of his bunk with his shoes off reading. He was a big Clive Cussler fan and had gotten his hands on his latest page turner 'Night Probe'. It also helped that his number two, Dimuth de Silva the quietly spoken Sri Lankan loved the 'Hurdy Gurdy' of this loading and unloading process.

Lars would happily admit that as far as the 'Hurdy Gurdy' went, Dimuth was far more capable than himself. Dimuth possessed social skills and an endless supply of patience which were sometimes found wanting in the old Viking Sea Dog. Lars was trying desperately to convince himself that he was relaxing. Mozart was playing softly in the corner of his cabin while the pages of his 'Night Probe' stared blankly up at him. He had read the same paragraph three times but the incessant banging and clanging caused by the portal ship-to-shore gantry cranes removing and depositing containers was doing his head in. If that wasn't bad enough the "league of nations," or his crew were, chattering, shouting and erupting in laughter with their Irish counterpart's dockside.

"Enough. Fucking enough! Drink. I need a drink. You lot, shut the forever fuck up!" He was well aware no one could hear him but it made him feel better anyway.

Lars felt his mood suddenly improve as he approached his drinks cabinet. It was positioned perfectly beside his rattly companion fridge which he'd had for years, this thing just refused to die. On opening it wide matching his grin, he hummed, "What's it to be then, whisky or… WHISKY. To the untrained ear, this all sounded more like VISKY?" His choice was simple, three bottles of golden nectar faced him.

First, there was his day to day go to bottle of Irish Black Bush single malt. Nice, but today not nice enough. Second was a Scottish Macallan 18-year-old single malt, very, very nice. Finally, he creaked at his goddess, a bottle of 25-year-old triple cask Macallan single malt, orgasmic! From left to right, he was looking at £30, £200 and £1,700 a bottle. For no other reason than "Fuck it!"

Lars made a grab for his 25-year-old goddess while at the same time flinging open his fridge door. He plucked out his Tyrone Crystal whisky glass which was ice-cold to the touch, then from his freezer nabbed an ice cube for good measure. Now the magic would begin.

"No, no stop Lars, special occasions only. Special occasions!" He just couldn't go through with it. "Not today. I am so very sorry my precious love, another time my princess." He then most reverentially placed the £1,700 bottle back into the cupboard. He was now settling for a shot of the 18-year-old gold which was carefully poured. Lars now grinning then paddled over to his armchair glass in hand. He knew the form, the golden nectar needed time to stir, to come alive, to breathe. He smiled to himself in excited anticipation, stealing a smell of its rich peaty perfume relishing in its dance as it seduced his senses. "Eine kleine Nachtmusik" was adding to the allure as he slowly closed his eyes and raised the glass to his puckering yearning lips.

BANG, BANG went his cabin door causing him to leap. A tenner's worth of whisky swept down his shirt. Gunter the ship's chef barged in like a tornado, oblivious. "Ola Lars. Eff you seen ze boy on your travels. I know that he sometimes plays the chess wiz you. He vas to help me vis the potatoes for tonight's Irish stew. Do you like it, ze Irish theme?"

Lars was in a state of shock before the anger kicked in. "Fuck you Gunter, you've made me spill my drink over me. An 18-year-old single malt to be exact!" Lars glared up at Gunter as he pointlessly flicked away at his tatty T-shirt. Seeing the familiar huckleberry hound sad face staring back at him he climbed down from his icy glare. A soft sweet fragrance of wacky baccy hovered around Gunter and his doleful eyes looked ever more soulful as he slowly swayed from side to side. He was clad in his chef's whites which were far from it. His long stringy balding hair was begging for any form of love, a cut or even a wash it pleaded.

"I'm so very sorry Captain Lars. How vos I to know you were about to 'ave a drink of your whisky. I hope it vasn't the really good stuff?" Lars laughed. Gunter was just Gunter, one of life's triers. Some men come just short in life. Gunter was not one of those unfortunates. He wouldn't have made the short list for the "just short list".

Dimuth appeared with his usual minimum fuss or fanfare. Lars laughed slowly seeing the funny side of it all. "Aghhh, Dimuth, care to join us, the more the merrier?" Dimuth smiled quietly offering Gunter a nod taking in the sweet embrace of his narcotic aroma. He then glided over to the fridge and lifted out a bottle of ice-cold water. Screwing off the lid he snatched a quick sip then screwed the lid tightly back on again. Seeing the troubled brow on the swaying ship's chef, he ventured, "Is everything ok gentlemen?"

Gunter spoke, "It is ze boy, we can't find him. He vos here for breakfast vis ze crew but zat vos ze last time I that have seen him. He vos to help me vis my potatoes."

Dimuth nodded. "I saw him laughing later this morning with the crew on top deck. It was just as the containers were being lifted off by the cranes. Now that I think of it, he had his bag over his shoulder. I never thought anything of it." Lars nodded a sense of foreboding creeping in. Whispering softly, he looked at Dimuth. "Go check his cabin please." A quick nod and Dimuth was gone.

Lars smiled at Gunter seeing the worry on his normally self-absorbed face. In the short time Ozan had been with the ship's company he had made a big impression. It was the kindness in his ways. If he could be of any help he was there. Gunter the chef, normally cold and aloof, had softened in the boy's light. A more human side to this German fridge was defrosting. There was in fact a happy Gunter lurking somewhere among the thaw. Wherever Ozan went, happiness followed. Lars had lobbied the crew as to what action to take about the boy shortly after he was discovered. To a man, they voted that he did nothing and that on return to Turkey they would spirit him back to land. Such was his popularity, some even suggested that he be recruited onto the crew if it were possible.

Dimuth returned, his face solemn. Lars wringing his hands while looking down at his table croaked, "Well Dimuth, tell me the worst?"

Dimuth wasted no time, "Captain Lars, Ozan's cabin is empty, the boy's gone."

Gunter exploded in a Wagnerian rage, "Mein Gott! Was werden wir tun? Der Junge?" (My God! What are we going to do? The young boy?)

Lars raised his hands in supplication, "Gunter, Gunter, calm down. What can we do? The boy doesn't officially exist. Certainly not on any of our records. No one knows that he's missing in Turkey. He has no family, no home and no friends. We're probably the nearest thing to family the boy's had, and that's not saying very much, is it? This is what he wanted, to go to Ireland, to start a new life. If he has jumped ship, the good people of Ireland will have no record that he's there. I for one, pray that he's safe and that all his hopes and dreams come true. Dimuth, let the rest of the crew know immediately. They are to take no action whatsoever. Our silence is imperative to Ozan's chances!"

Dimuth nodded, "As you wish, Captain Lars. He was a good boy and our friend. You can count on us all."

Dimuth quietly slipped away. Gunter stayed put. Lars could see tears welling on his bloated face as he swayed staring out of the cabin window. "Captain Lars, but I shall miss him." Then came an outpouring of tears and blubbering, "I shall really miss my Ozan. Why, why, why?"

Lars gently led the big chef to a seat and then got another whisky glass out. Without pause he reached into his whisky cabinet and respectfully lifted the goddess out. He'd never shared her with anyone before, until now, this moment was not lost on Gunter whose eyes widened in wonderment as the golden glory was poured, no ice this time, that would have been a violation, a mortal sin. As the two glasses breathed, Lars looked over at the bloated mass facing him. Gunter, the Germanic iceman was a slushy mess.

He thought quietly for a while then spoke. "Gunter my friend, you are upset and sad, we all are. Our little Ozan is gone, a stowaway, a boy whose worldly possessions fitted into a tiny canvas bag. A boy with poppy seeds in his pockets. A boy who had known much sadness in his short life. But I tell you this, Ozan Karaki had the biggest heart I have ever seen. I don't know how his legs could support it. His heart was full of kindness, caring and love. The crew to a man each thought that they were Ozan's favourite. Look at the state of you, Gunther, crying like a baby."

Gunter smiled as tears eased down his bloated cheeks then burst out crying again. Gunter stalled mid-blubber as Lars raised his hand. "A toast!" Two glasses were raised by two friends while outside the world went noisily on. "Here's to Ozan. May he find health, hope, happiness and love. To Ozan."

The goddess delivered. It was late afternoon as a lorry carrying a container bound for Belfast eased its way out of Dublin Port. From the sanctuary of its cabin, ghastly pop music was blaring to the delight of its driver. The container's cargo was all Turkish, from high-end bathroom ceramics, to cannabis and then to a certain young frightened stowaway.

Chapter 15
Directions to Shangri-La Please!

The dream team was on their way, and what a team they were.

Detective Inspector Archie Brown was at the wheel of his highly polished brown Ford Escort. A 'James Last' cassette was churning out soothing Strauss Waltzes but wasn't having the desired effect. His accomplice sat demurely by his side. Her nose twitching from the sickly-sweet scent of three orange blossom air fresheners. These dangled from the rearview mirror inches from her face. Archie was in his usual brown attire jabbering away with smatterings of small talk. His antlike frame was thrust as far forward as his car seat would allow. His shiny bald head was practically pressing against the misted front windscreen. It was raining in splat fashion and the windscreen wipers were going at full pelt. A lesser pelt would have sufficed. Shelley spotted that his thick lensed specs were well fogged up. The thought of an early death by way of road traffic accident elbowed in but "hey-ho," he had survived to sixty-plus driving this way. They were doing 45 mph on a 70-mph motorway. Had it not been for the rain, Archie would have sunk the boot to the board, hurtling the pair along at a more death-defying speed of 50 mph. He could be a rebel that way.

Shelley just adored Archie. She always found him to be Disney cute. He'd never changed in all the time she'd known him. Five feet nothing, eight stone wringing wet and always dressed in brown. The wee DI was as bald as a billiard ball save for the sides. Then there were his seriously thick spectacles which made his brown eyes appear huge. When he spoke, his voice was slightly high-pitched and nasally. His words came at you as if fired from a 'Gatling' gun, pop pop pop.

Archie Brown was a legendary figure amongst his CID colleagues. A lion in the interview room with a razor-sharp mind. Shelley knew all that but still found her week chauffeur Disney cute. She spoke, raising her voice against the waltzes, wipers and hot air.

"Well Sir, do you think we'll get all three done today?"

Archie chuckled, "Shelley love, I promise you this. One of these a day is more than plenty. These sorts of situations, scenarios if you like are exhausting. At the end of our first one you'll know exactly what I mean. (Cackling to himself.) I'd rather be interviewing a terrorist or a serial killer at the Castlereagh Holding Centre than be doing one of these. Hey and less of the Sirs, missy. It's always been plain Archie to you. I've told you that from day one."

Shelley smiled, "I know Archie, it's just that you're a legend that's all."

Archie roared with laughter which sounded more like an aardvark's mating call. "Legend. Legend, my arse, Shelley love!"

Their mission was taking them to Cookstown, County Tyrone. It's a pleasant looking market town with a 60/40 Catholic to Protestant ratio. Both its communities are polarised regarding their political aspirations. A strong nationalist one facing an equally strong Unionist one. A strained tension sat gnawingly just beneath the town's surface. There's little hope for reconciliation when even the children are kept apart at school by virtue of their religion. Both sides exist by politely blanking each other in the street. In ostrich fashion, if you like, pretending none of this murder and hatred is actually happening. Besides, they're all good God-fearing church going people and my god's the real one by the way.

Cookstown and its outlying areas could best be described as dangerous with a capital D. Cookstown RUC Station was the Sub Divisional Headquarters of 'K' Division. It had a patrolling area of 140 square miles. The majority of its roads were unmarked and had to be learnt from maps, your colleagues and local knowledge. It and its satellite stations of Coagh, Stewartstown, Moneymore and Pomeroy were seriously dangerous stations to serve in. In 1983, a large and very successful IRA network operated there. Land mines, shootings and murders of security force members was a very common occurrence.

The town itself is located around 55 miles from the city of Belfast. It was a journey that would take the average punter about an hour. With Archie precariously at the helm, maybe an hour fifteen. The rain continued to clatter down causing huge blobby splodges on the windscreen and windows. Visibility ground to a big fat zero. Shelley gave up on stressing over Archie's driving and opted to zone out. If this was to be the day she was going to meet her maker, then she chose to make his acquaintance zoned out. *Rather out than in*, isn't that what folks say? The waltzes ground on as Archie turned his car heater up from nominal to full blast. He'd decided to clear the fog on his front windscreen not realising that his vents were directed straight at Shelley.

Given the choice, Shelley would have preferred standing in the Gobi Desert during a huge sandstorm. At least there, Strauss wouldn't be playing adding to her misery. Maybe she was dead and this is what hell looked and felt like. Archie was none the wiser regarding her pressing thoughts on eternity. As far as the little DI was concerned, they were having a ball. Archie was quietly amazed at the turn out of his partner. Tweety had given her a look to go for and she hadn't let him down. Her thick black hair was carefully swept back in a bun.

Shelley's usually slightly over the top look was gone. She had that look of an administrator or a tax inspector. Her blue eyes were modestly framed with the faintest silver eye shadow and her normally scarlet lips were now a rose pink. He approved of her white silk top with matching grey blazer and skirt. All finished off with plain black low heeled court shoes. He'd his doubts when he first saw her strut into the Hop House a couple of evenings back, but that was then. This was a very different creature altogether. Tweety could always pick a winner.

The pair were destined for an 11.30 AM appointment at 22, Lomond Heights, Cookstown. The home of Inspector Wayne Gordon. Wayne had done 24 years on the job and was well respected throughout the rank and file. He played with a straight bat. Sometimes firm but always fair. With Inspector Gordon, everything was by the book. His only weakness was perhaps his kindness which he tried unsuccessfully to keep under wraps.

The arrangements had been made discreetly between George Sewell and the K Division Sub Divisional Commander. As always, when officers in plain clothes were operating in another Division the boys at Special Branch had to be informed. This was much more than a courtesy. Covert Operations could be compromised and lives put in jeopardy. If the boys in the branch said "NO", then that was it. No also meant no questions asked. Their say was always final.

Wayne had been puzzled about the circumstances of the visit, not least by the fact that his wife Rhonda was also asked to be there. It was just the thought of strange police calling at his home with their smoking mirrors that had him on edge. Rhonda hadn't taken to the news well either. It had upset her. Stressed her out.

The brown Escort arrived at Lomond Heights with 10 minutes to spare. Archie pulled in at the top of the street then switched everything off. Shelley sighed. She was exhausted. "Thank fuck. We're finally here." Her face felt as dry as the dead sea scrolls and she was gasping.

Archie smiled over, "Y'all set, Shelley love. Ready to rock and roll?"

Shelley fidgeted in her clobber. This wasn't her usual gear. She adjusted her skirt for something to do with her nervous hands. She then flashed one of her smiles. "I'm dreading this so I am, Archie. Just think what this is going to do to them. Fuck it. I need a fag. Care to join me? We've five minutes yet." She raised her eyebrows and puckered her lips in pleading fashion. It never failed. Archie was a gift. He reached for Woody, his pipe. "Good idea, wee pard. It will not do us any harm."

The rain had stopped and the air was light. The soft blue sky had a Garden of Eden feel about it. The rotten weather was slowly turning pleasant as the pair hopped out of the car taking in the fresh County Tyrone air. Both began puffing in strained silence, each aware of what lay ahead.

Lomond Heights was in Monopoly speak the Mayfair of Cookstown. Modern detached and semi-detached des res all with sprawling lawns and immaculate driveways. Archie, now finished, patted Woody down and gave his specs a quick polish. He wasn't relishing this one at all.

"Let's go, pard. That's number 22 down there. The one with the 'Shangri-La' sign dangling on the gate post."

Shelley nodded, exhaling her final puff. "Fuck it Arch. Let's do this."

The doorbell rang causing Rhonda to jump. She was in the kitchen preparing freshly baked scones and tea for their anticipated guests. She heard her husband Wayne at the door letting their visitors in. Muffled conversation, a female voice then a smattering of laughter. Ah, that was good. She found herself wringing her hands. Moments later, the kitchen door was quietly tapped. In walked a beautiful twenty something female. She was striking in an executive kind of way. She carried with her a black leather briefcase. She smiled at Rhonda holding out her free hand. "Goodness me. Those scones smell gorgeous and what a beautiful home. (now winking) I take it you're the one with all the taste. I'm Constable Shelley McCann. Please call me Shelley, it's Rhonda, isn't it? I've seen pictures of you presenting prizes in the Police Gazette, you're just as glamorous in the flesh."

Shelley gazed at the 50-something female with the long blonde hair. Everything about her was modest from her make up to her attire. A quiet elegance if you like. With the slightest tweak, she would look stunning but that was not her way. She was softly spoken with a Tyrone lilt. She smiled at Shelley then laughed, "I wish. Wayne tells me you need to speak to me about something. Nothing serious, I hope. (A nervous giggle.) I don't think I've broken any laws recently."

Rhonda clasped her hands tightly as Shelley took a chair at the kitchen table. It was then she picked up on the anxiety on the young officer's face. Shelley looked up at her biting her bottom lip. Rhonda's chest tightened.

"What is it, Shelley love? Please tell me. Is it Wayne? Are we in some kind of trouble?"

Shelley smiled her eyes deep with sadness. She motioned Rhonda to join her at the table. Rhonda pulled up a chair and began breathing in short, trembling gasps. Shelley placed a hand on Rhonda's shoulder then whispered softly. "Rhonda, we desperately need your help. There's no easy way about doing this, so please be strong. I have some photographs to show you. They're not very nice."

Shelley reached into her brief case and retrieved the buff envelope containing the exhibited stills. She placed the envelope on the kitchen table and swallowing hard, whispered, "Are you ready for this, Rhonda?"

Rhonda was now trembling as she slowly mouthed "Yes."

Archie stood in the front room gazing out of the window, his eyes seeing nothing, his nerves jangling for Shelley. Wayne had poured him a Bushmills neat from an elegant Tyrone Crystal whisky decanter. It was just what he needed, not that Wayne knew. What was going on in the kitchen? His thoughts were with Shelley and her open-heart breaking surgery.

Wayne broke the silence. "Any chance telling me what all this is about, Archie. This here's all very unusual?"

Archie turned from the window and placed his empty glass on an ornate card table. Looking at Wayne he could see a man in his early fifties. A man fit and strong, his body belying his age. He was handsome too with greying wavy hair, blue eyes, swarthy complexion and a strong square jaw. Archie could see or feel an openness about the man. A countrified openness if you catch my drift. There wasn't a lie in him. Wayne looked worried and Archie felt for him. He smiled softly but his tiny brown eyes were deadly serious behind his bottle top lenses.

"Ya ever come across a Detective Chief Inspector Bartholomew Wayne; name ring any bells with you?"

Wayne nodded back with a puzzled expression. "Aye. He dealt with a complaint against me a year or so ago. Why?"

Archie knew the answer but asked anyway, he was playing for precious time. Time for his wee partner in the kitchen. "Ahem, just wanted to hear your side of it all. Sometimes, the facts get watered down when the pen hits the paper. What was the gist of it all then. In your own words, if you don't mind?"

It was like yesterday to Wayne. Nodding back with raised eyes he began, "Fuck me Archie, how could I ever forget. It was some handling so it was. I was out this night enforcing licensing laws at the Greenvale House Hotel just on the outskirts of the town. There's never usually any trouble there. Family-run place, pro police you know. I had a probationer Constable out with me that night, a good lad too, not long out of the depot. Wee bit wet behind the ears, we all were once, you know what I mean."

Archie nodded. "It had gone just after 10.00 PM and we were stood at the hotel reception having a chinwag with Ronnie the manager. Known him for years, went to school together. His books were all in order, as per usual. Suddenly a female member hares out of the function room screaming fight, fight, some fella's getting a hiding. Surprised, I made an urgent RT (Radio transmission) requesting immediate back up. Me and the cub then dash towards the madness pushing past punters scurrying the other way. When we get to the function room it was pitch black apart from the flashing disco lights.

"As for that thumping bumping music, what the young ones listen to today (chuckled.) Anyhow, it was then I spotted a fella taking a serious pasting from three other blokes. They were all over him punching and kicking away, he was helpless, curled up in a ball and squealing like a stuck pig. I yells at them to stop, identifying myself as police. The next thing is a beer bottle's winging its way towards us. I catch sight of it at the last moment and duck. It misses me but clocks my partner on the head sparking him out. Their leader, he then turned on me. He's huge. A big farmer from Dunnamore. Recognised him straight away. All 6 feet 4 of him and 23 stone of prime cut County Tyrone beef. He's farmer fit and hard as nails. His name's Ryan, Fergal Ryan or Fergie to his mates. He's in his mid-twenties. His family aren't exactly pillars of society but nothing terrorist, more fuel smuggling and the like.

"Well, I can see he's way drunk. He's swaying all over the place and his eyes are hanging out like dogs' balls. I call him out, by his name, letting him know that I know who he is. I'm shouting, Fergie enough, enough now. He then charges at me with his huge fists swinging like a windmill. I'm telling you this Archie I was shit scared, if one of those big bastards had connected, I was a goner. Now I was a handy boxer back in the day. I mean my army days and just as he's on me I quickly step to his inside and out of pure desperation throw a huge right upper cut. Bang! He staggers back squealing. I broke a knuckle on the big bastard's chin, still hurts when I'm gardening. With all the commotion I didn't even get a chance to draw my baton, it all happened so quickly."

Archie chuckled. Wayne continued, "What else was I to do, then suddenly they're all on me and I'm getting a proper hiding and I'm thinking to myself is this is how it all ends. Then mercifully, the K1 MSU boys (Mobile Support Unit) arrive just in time to save my bacon. If they hadn't showed up you and I wouldn't be having this conversation. Thank God, I says to myself. Fergie and his mates were all scooped. Firstly, for the assault on the punter on the ground. He had a broken jaw and wrist by the way. Secondly, for the assault on me and the young probationer and finally, for the pile of damage to the hotel property. So, there you have it all and what's more, a nice smelly **DPP**[6] file for yours truly to do."

Archie shuddered, "Jeez, you were lucky enough that night, Wayne. It could have ended worse for you pair, couldn't it?"

Wayne nodded then motioned over to the crystal decanter offering a wee top up. Archie declined but held Woody up with eyebrows raised. Wayne nodded again pouring himself another settler as the old chimney was fired up. Wayne took a sip regathering his thoughts then continued, "Well the victim, the fella on the ground and the wee probationer were whisked off to the South Tyrone Hospital in Dungannon for treatment. Muggins here goes back to Cookstown Station with the three amigos. They're all pissed as farts so they can't be spoken to until they're sober. A night in the cells for them. Then Fergie's lovely face swells up, courtesy of my upper cut so he has to be medically examined. My right hand begins to ache and soon resembles a catcher's mitt so in the end we both have to be seen by a doctor. Here's the rub of it.

"While he's being medically examined by the Force Medical Officer (FMO), he alleges that I assaulted him. He tells the good Doctor that he'd done nothing wrong and his two mates are there to back him up. Then it gets even worse for me. The fella on the ground. The guy I rescued. He declines to make a formal

---

[6] (Any incidents involving assaults on police were known as DPP files. These were handled by the Director of Public Prosecutions headed by the Attorney General for Northern Ireland.)

statement of complaint. He's very apologetic and all but he's more fearful of reprisals from our Fergie and his mates. So, all of a sudden, I'm left hanging out to dry and it's my word against theirs. You couldn't write it, Archie, honest to God. Then after a couple of weeks Detective Chief Inspector Bartholomew waltzes into my life. One afternoon I find him sitting all resplendent in my office.

"He's looking like a tailor's dummy and grinning at me like a Cheshire cat. He introduces himself to me, informing me that he's the designated Investigating Officer from C&D. Complaints and Discipline and it's to do with the Greenvale incident. He had a formal complaint with him which he served on me. You could have knocked me over with a feather. Then he noticed a picture of Rhonda that I keep on my desk and starts to chat about marriage, partnerships and the importance of sharing. I think he was trying to put me at my ease after the shock news you know, just small talk. Nothing serious. He then shows me a copy of Fergie's statement of complaint along with the two supporting witness statements. He allows me to read them which really surprised me.

"All of their statements were completed in fine detail but certainly didn't read fine as far as I was concerned. A crock of lies, I can assure you. All the while he's coming over all sympathetic towards me. This visit in his own words was just a 'courtesy call.' Archie, to me, he came across as a bit of a smiling assassin; you know the sort."

Archie nodded. "But I was well and truly fucked and he knew it. Anyhow he suggests that if I cough up to the assault, he'd see what he could do for me. The good options were is how he put it, "Maybe get me a block to another station or a demotion." If I didn't throw me hands up, the not good options were he'd be forced to arrest me for the assault. A GBH assault no less. Grievous Bodily Harm Contrary to Section 20 of the Offences Against the Persons Act 1861. I could feel my world spiralling out of control. Arrested. Suspension from duty. A criminal trial in front of a judge and jury. If all that went against me, I'd be sacked, with the loss of my police pension after 24 years. Now who's going to employ a sacked 50-year-old peeler with a criminal record?"

Archie nodded grimly, biting hard on Woody. Wayne continued, "Look he's very apologetic and being nicey-nicey about it all but I just had the feeling he was enjoying every second. He urges me to talk things through with Rhonda stressing how serious the consequences would be for her and of course us. Quite the philosopher, suggesting the decision should be a joint one, as it affected us both. He had a point, I suppose. He then leaves me with a week to make my decision. I was in no doubt as to what my options were. I had to tell Rhonda of course. We've no secrets between us."

Archie's stomach tightened causing him to cough as smoke from Woody charged down the wrong way. He held his hand up apologising. Wayne went on. "She was devastated, really devastated. Everything we had together, worked for, our hopes and dreams, our future was on the line. She stuck by me though. Then out of the blue it all just went away. The day before our arranged appointment, I gets a phone call from him stating that there would be no further action from Complaints and Discipline regarding the assault. It was a case of my good character against their bad and on the night in question they were all wasted and I was sober. Also, that I was responding to a request for assistance regarding the fight in the function room. He urged me to tell Rhonda straight away, he even remembered her name. A man who remembers the small details, I like that. And here's me thinking he was gunning for me. I guess I got him all wrong and I'll admit to that. We or should I say I, sent him a Christmas card that year. I've since heard stuff about him, but as far as my dealings with him went he looked after me the best."

Archie winced drawing hard on Woody for he knew that a storm was coming. He cleared his throat and piped in while his pipe was out. "And how did Rhonda take the good news then?"

Wayne smiled. "Archie, when I rang her, she burst into tears what with the shock and relief I suppose. That week she was very strange though. She was snappy, didn't want me anywhere near her, which wasn't like her. Actually, now you mention it, she was down for several months. It really must have knocked the stuffing out of her."

A long squeal like the wail of a banshee followed by heavy sobbing came from the kitchen. Wayne spun around his face a picture of panic. "In the name of Good God Almighty, what's going on here, Archie? What have you pair brought to our home?"

Archie walked over and gently placed his hand on Wayne's shoulder. "Sit yourself down brother. Your lovely wife has a few tears to shed. Detective Inspector Bartholomew is no friend of the police family, no friend or colleague to you and has been an absolute monster to your lovely wife and other wives. We've been sent here to put an end to all that."

Rhonda suddenly burst into the room and threw herself at Wayne's feet. She was distraught, her face streaked in tears. She looked up at him sobbing, "I feel so filthy. Can you ever forgive me, Wayne? I did it for you, for us. He promised me it would only be the one time and that he could make everything go away."

Wayne stood, paralysed in shock. His beautiful wife sobbing continued. "That cursed day. What he made me do in that god forsaken field. It was terrifying Wayne. The outfit he made me wear. Those dreadful clamps, how crudely he put them on and then how hard he yanked them off me. Then he's groping me roughly while click clicking away at his camera. All the while he's sneering at me. The bastard revolted me, I just felt like killing myself. Afterwards, he told me to keep my mouth shut about it all and the complaint would disappear. Then I had to go home pretending nothing had happened. Trying to be cheerful for you. Keeping everything normal, when all I wanted to do was curl up in a ball and die. I avoided your touch until the bruising was gone or you'd have suspected something. Then the wait to see if he was true to his word. That day you rang me with the good news, I felt physically sick. I was even more mortified when you sent the bastard a Christmas card from us."

Shelley appeared from the kitchen holding the brown envelope. The normal upbeat fire cracker was positively grey. She looked at Archie who gave her a subtle nod. Rhonda slowly got to her feet. Her head was down, her long blonde hair covering her face. Wayne was white with shock. Rhonda felt ashamed, a woman stripped of all dignity.

She reached her left hand back and whispered, "Photographs please, Shelley."

Archie quietly nodded; Shelley obliged. Rhonda held the envelope forward then whispered, "Everything stops here until you look. I can't carry this burden on my own any longer. Be strong and look. I need you to look. I want you to see what that bastard did to me and what I did because of our love. If you don't look then, it was all in vain and we can't go on. Wayne, I need you to please look just one time. For us."

Wayne nodded, with his hand trembling he took the envelope containing their tomorrows and looked. Tears began to flow as he carefully and deliberately viewed each grotesque image. Having to look at his childhood sweetheart, the love of his life and his beautiful wife depraved at the hands of the twisted and cruel monster. When he had finished, he stood up and gently took hold of her. Drawing her face upwards he stroked her blonde hair back revealing the beautiful heartbroken face.

Wayne then quietly whispered, "I'm so very sorry my love. I had no idea." His tears fell onto her cheeks and she smiled, her secret shame now gone. They embraced, then began to sob uncontrollably in each other's arms.

The grandfather clock in the hallway chimed twelve times marking the hours. Shangri-La was restored.

Rhonda was now strangely happy. A huge weight which to her felt like a lie had been lifted. She turned to Shelley and smiled, "Do you mind if we have a cup of tea first Shelley love, before I give you my statement. I'm all of a tizzy at the moment and my face is a bit of an 'Eton mess'?"

Archie spoke, "Rhonda love, you pair have been through the mixer. We can call back tomorrow when you've gotten yourselves settled."

Rhonda smiled at the little man. "Archie, I'm doing the statement today and then we can move on with our lives can't we, Wayne? Wild horses won't stop me. Let's go Shelley. You pop the kettle on while I fix my face."

With that, the girls disappeared into the kitchen leaving Wayne and Archie. Without asking, Wayne leapt up, whisking Archie's empty glass from the coaster. Looking at Archie, he got himself a glass and reached for the Bushmills, quickly pouring two healthy measures. "I don't normally, but today I'll make an exception."

Handing his glass to him Archie could see the anger burning in Wayne's eyes. "I wish to propose a toast!"

Archie went, "Oh?"

Wayne continued, "I propose a toast. Here's to you guys catching that perverted bastard and stopping him doing any more of these hateful acts."

At that, the ladies entered wheeling a trolley of freshly baked scones and tea. Mrs. Gordon had her face on and looked beautiful. Rhonda, seeing the pain in her husband's eyes, walked over to him and gently took the glass from his hand. She rarely if ever drank but that day she downed the whisky in one. Wayne was gobsmacked. Then he burst out laughing, shaking his head.

Looking around the room with her new defiance she said, "I'll drink to that! Now let's have some tea, shall we?"

The dream team left Cookstown for home by a different route, always mindful of avoiding patterns. They would return to Belfast via the shore of Lough Neagh.

Lough Neagh is the largest freshwater lake in the British Isles covering some 150 square miles. It's breathtaking in its beauty and is a haven for wildlife. Their drive would take them via Coagh and then onto Ardboe, a beautiful but dangerous stretch. Then through the town of Toome famed for its eel fisheries and finally onto the M2 and home.

It was now 3.30 PM and Shelley was exhausted. Her eyelids felt heavy and the music was now strangely soothing. The soft heat on her face was also nice. She had spent two hours with Rhonda in the kitchen recording her written statement of complaint. She carefully teased the horrifying memories from mouth to page pausing when the tears fell. There was a depth to Shelley from which Rhonda garnered strength and encouragement. Nothing, no matter how painful, was omitted. No tortuous stone left unturned. Bartholomew had indeed been a meticulous planner and schemer.

Archie looked across at Shelley whose eyes were now closed. She was asleep, a sleeping Snow White. Today, she had been exceptional in every way and yet was so very young herself. They had two more to do. Two more days of this emotionally exhausting work. The old detective smiled a fatherly pride pricking at him. He gently turned the music down as the Escort took them home.

Chapter 16
Justus Is Served

Bud sensed something wasn't right with his master that morning. He was agitated as he left for work at 6.00 AM. There had been no play time, no scratching of his soft woolly coat and no chasing of his busted ball. All he got was a quick "seeya fella" before climbing into his clapped-out Citroen car and away. Buds old heart was heavy. There would be no sniffing through moist summer grass, no chasing of rabbits or gazing in wonderment at the butterflies. No not today. He would lie on their wooden porch and fret until his return.

It was Thursday, 28 July 1983 and a more beautiful summer's morning in Belfast was hard to recall. It was a soft 16 degrees as a lazy sun quietly rose from its slumber. Schools were off and the traffic, like the morning air, was light. People were in great form out on the streets. "'Bout yees" and "Mornin' till yee naes" were in plentiful supply.

At 6.45 AM, 'A' Section, Mountroyal paraded for duty. Sergeant Tony Speers briefed the section and detailed the crews. He purposely detailed the Preacher and Shelley McCann out on a beat patrol, their call signs were AM30 and AM30 alpha. Everyone in the station party was anxious that particular day, from the station cleaners all the way up to George Sewell the Sub Divisional Commander. Each knew that today at 10.30 AM Pete had a date with destiny. Today was the day he would encounter the infamous Detective Chief Inspector Bartholomew or "Black Bart" from Complaints and Discipline fame.

The section felt each other's pain and as a unit became more agitated as Pete's hour drew nigh. Tony had stuck Pete out on a harmless beat patrol with Shelley the Section "Upper". They had left Mountroyal that morning heading country wards for Castlereagh Station for breakfast. They checked the lock ups on their way. Shelley could see that the Preacher was down. He still moved with the same ease, smiling at the punters but the natural light had gone from his eyes.

At Castlereagh canteen, Shelley had her usual full Ulster fry with a mug of builders' brew. Pete played with a bowl of muesli; semi-skimmed milk topped with honey but his heart wasn't in it. He had so much to lose, his chest was aching. Shelley decided to let him be with his thoughts. Outwardly loud and brash, there was also a depth of perception and compassion in this young woman's heart. The pair left Castlereagh shortly after 9.30 AM and slowly they made their way back towards Mountroyal and destiny.

Pete's stomach was churning as he relived the Wyse Byse incident over and over in his head. Could he have done things any differently with the store Manager, Mr. Prentass? Should he have initially apologised, better explaining his actions? Had there been any other way? His notebook entry was woefully inadequate and his statement of evidence even worse. Should he make that statement of apology which Bartholomew had suggested? Would that make it all go away? The Preacher just wanted his old life back. If he lost his job a job that he truly loved, what would he do with himself and then of course there was Heavenly. His heart ached. Then he would replay the entire loop of thoughts and emotions through his head again and again.

Pete briefly paused to gaze at his miserable reflection in a toy shop window. He then caught sight of a child's rubber ball. It was like a dagger to his heart remembering how he'd ignored his bestie that morning. Bud would be upset and Pete was the cause. He felt totally lousy. The Preacher's heart was well and truly in his boots. He was oblivious to the fact that Shell was quietly watching him, her hero, from across the road. She felt so helpless.

Pete's hand-held radio crackled into life. "AM30 from AM, over!" Pete jumped inwardly recognising Tweety's voice, then responded, "Alpha Mike from 30, send over."

Tweety's voice was calm and void of his usual upbeat tone, "Roger 30, your 10.30 AM appointment's been put back to 11.30 AM, over." Pete's heart sank glancing across the Cregagh Road at Shelley who was rolling her eyes.

Pete wearily shook his head and responded, "Roger on your last Alpha Mike, out."

By the time, he'd finished his radio transmission Shell was standing next to him. He'd failed to spot the mischief in her eyes. She quickly tucked her arm under his and escorted him into the sanctuary of the nearest entry. Checking that the coast was clear she grabbed his flak jacket and pinned him hard up against the wall. Pete was in a state of shock, Shelley could pack a punch.

Looking up at him she then gave him her full-on gorgeous smile, "Right Mister Sulky Plug, we've another hour to kill. Ormeau Park for a wee chill, what do you say? Sergeant Speers says I have to do whatever it takes to cheer you up."

Her eyebrows bounced up and down, she was giving it her all. "Let's go then you big tube. I'll even buy you a lolly."

The Preacher burst out laughing then they both laughed. He thought to himself, "What a wee gem." Smiling he said, "Shell, what would I do without you? Right, you're on then, mine's a 'Choc Pop' since you're offering."

Shelley laughed triumphantly, she'd broken through his fug, "Greedy Pig! Get the arm in Preachy, why don't you. Let's go then." Keeping to the alleyways, the pair eased up Ravenhill Avenue via a short detour to the Delaware Stores in Delaware Street. A couple of minutes later they were sucking their lollies on a secluded park bench behind a copse of silver birch trees. They had their flak jackets off and for 15 minutes enjoyed the heat of the sun accompanied by the cooling breeze from the River Lagan. They made the most of that aching hour as High Noon approached.

Wee John was perched in the high stool of the Mountroyal Sangar when Black Bart's blue Rover Vitesse pulled up at the station barrier. It was 10.15 AM, 15 minutes early. Wee John calmly double clicked on the station tannoy a warning signal for the relevant players to assume their positions. He then leaned forward looking out of his 3-inch-thick security window, inviting Bart to produce his warrant card. At the same time, Derek Grant who was in his office removed Miriam's photograph from the window ledge and placed it in his desk drawer. He then locked everything there was to be locked before hastily exiting his office and trotting upstairs to the CID Office, there he found a DMSU Crew (Divisional Mobile Support Unit) quietly bagging and labelling exhibits. It had that 'morning prayers before Mass' feel with occasional whispers and muted coughs. Derek knew from experience when to chat and when to keep his big gob shut.

Archie and Big Cliff sauntered out from Archie's office; nods were exchanged. Woody was releasing a soothing St. Bruno cloud as the wee Detective Inspector poured over a Search Record making sure every detail was 100 per cent correct. He had no worries on that score, Big Cliff didn't do mistakes. He along with the DMSU Crew had carried out an evidential search of a private dwelling that morning. Derek took himself out of everyone's way. He took a seat beside the rear car park window and enjoyed the soft summer's breeze pushing in from a barely opened latch.

Catherine the Office Manager appeared from the kitchen carrying a tray full of mugs of tea and coffee and a large boiled cake ready sliced. She spotted Derek and smiled, mouthing, "The Boss Cat's on his way." She then glided over to a large table at the centre of the office and placed the refreshments down, "Right fellas, tea, coffee, cake, you've earned it."

Archie dispelled any hesitancy, "Right lads, take yerselves five and enjoy. Yez have been up with the larks this morning. It's a case of more haste less speed isn't it Catherine love?"

Big Cliff leaned over Catherine and lifted a mug of coffee and a slice of cake. "Mmm, (growling bear like) lovely bit of cake, cheers, Catherine." A pressure valve had been released in the office as tired bodies helped themselves to Catherine's delights. A brief chuckle ensued for several minutes and then it was back to perfecting records, namely, the bagging and labelling of numerous exhibits. This was followed by the writing of thorough witness statements fully corroborated by notebook entries.

Black Bart thrust his warrant card in the direction of the Sanger. Moments later the security barrier rose. A minute later he was standing in the reception area of the Enquiry Office feigning important impatience. Tweety was waiting at the counter, Vic was pretending to be on the phone, Wee Mo was in the radio room, legs shaking, listening.

Tweety looked up smiling, "Morning Sir, if you don't mind me saying that's a lovely belt you've got on. It matches your shoes and tie, nice, very nice indeed."

Bart detested familiarity from the lesser ranks. He had grown a disliking to this one from the day and hour he'd clapped eyes on him. He glared at the smiling guard, "I'm Detective Chief Insp…"

Tweety continued beaming, "Bartholomew from Complaints and Discipline. We've been expecting you Sir. I've been told to escort you down to Inspector Grant's office. Follow me please." Tweety was suddenly beside Bart. The partition door buzzed and the pair headed off. Derek's door was open. His desk was clear and his drawers were locked. "There you go Sir. Thank you now." Tweety turned to leave.

Bart was pissed, "Constable, constable," his soft usually whispering voice raised a notch.

Tweety turned, "Sir?"

Bart locked on to Tweety with one of his glacial glares, "And what do they call you?" He snarled trying to strike fear.

Tweety smiled, "Constable Sweetlove Sir. THEY call me Constable Sweetlove, SIRR." The smile remained, fixed. Bart was incandescent. He couldn't make a dent in this dopey bastard. Probably too thick and those fucking dark blue lenses, he couldn't see his eyes, the mirror to his soul. "Mmm, Sweetlove, any signs of your Inspector Grant or Constable Majury, the reason for my attendance in this (Pausing for his sarcasm to bloom to its fullest.) LOVELY station of yours today?"

Tweety gulped, "Sorry Sir. Inspector Grant told me to tell you he's called to an important meeting but feel free to use his office, Sir." Bart hummed.

Tweety turned to leave which was bloody infuriating, "AND MAJURY?" Tweety chuckled, "Sorry Sir, he'll be right with you at 10.30 AM as agreed.

He's on a beat patrol this morning. He's awful nice Sir so he is, just saying."

Bart sneered. "Mmm, I'm quite sure he is, AWFUL nice!" Tweety turned again to leave. Bart just couldn't resist, "Oh, Constable Sweetlove!"

Tweety turned, "Sir."

Bart's slim lips hissed as he gently nodded, "I won't forget your face!"

Tweety smiled, "Sir, thank you Sir, awful nice of you to say so Sir." Then he finally left. What Bart didn't or couldn't see from behind was that the genius was chuckling.

Bart was now alone in Derek's office, in Derek's seat. He was well used to this, sitting in a strange office. This wouldn't take long. He had a pre-prepared written statement sitting in a plain green DPP cardboard file cover which he eased out of his expensive briefcase. It was a grovelling apology of a statement which he would get the Constable to sign, he had Majury bang to rights. "Same old, same old."

Bart sniggered then softly whispered to the silent office, "This is so unfortunate for you, for the force. The pressure you uniformed types are under every day. Joe Public just doesn't understand. Sign here. I'm on your side. I'll do my best for you. Crocodile tears matching my shoes, shirt and tie." Bart had already his final report and recommendations written regarding the Wyse Byse complaint. His recommendations were that Constable Majury should be prosecuted for the assault on Mr. Prentass. This was to be contrary to Section 20, Assault Occasioning Grievous Bodily Harm, under the Offences Against the Person Act 1861. The Preacher was facing the sack and possible prison time.

Bart leaned back in his chair checking his nails. He was getting them done at 1.00 PM. The king was in his castle and all was well with his world. He looked down at the green folder reading the name MAJURY. He briefly wondered what he was like. Then he realised he didn't give a jot. Sadly, this one was single, no fun and games to be had here. He glanced over to the window ledge where he had seen a framed photograph of a beautiful woman the last time he'd been there.

Now, she was just his type, "Mmm." A puzzled expression followed, "Where'd it go? Where was the photograph?"

Wee John leaned forward from his stool in the front sanger. He heard the unmistakable snarl and burping of the powerful Tangi Land Rover engine first. Smiling he spotted it as it roared up the Woodstock Road. Members of the public froze to the spot as the war wagon roared by. He recognised the number plate immediately; it was a Strand vehicle and it had been in the wars. Its grey body was smeared in white paint and its front window grills bore the unmistakable black and treacle smudged charring from petrol bombs. The Tangi was up to the barrier in seconds which rose in perfect tandem.

It belched thick grey exhaust fumes as it sped on in its engine roaring and growling like a big hungry cat. It had no sooner pulled to a halt when the twin back doors clanged open and out skipped the boss Chief Superintendent George Sewell. George spun round and gave a quick thumbs up to the crew. The rear doors slammed shut again with a heavy metallic clang. The Tangi abruptly reversed back out onto the Woodstock Road with all the airs of an unwelcome guest. Then, with its huge engine screaming it roared off like a bat out of hell. Wee John got a nod from George whose mind was elsewhere as he was buzzed into the station.

Tweety was at the counter as he entered, "Sir."

George smiled, "Well Tweety, how'd the search go?"

Tweety smiled, "Really well, did you get the two envelopes?"

George nodded tapping on his breast pocket. "Where's the Preacher?"

Tweety looked up at the Enquiry Office clock. "Him and Shell are due back in ten minutes. Shell's going to cover me while WE take care of business."

George nodded, "Speaking of business?"

Vic shouted over their shoulders, "That loathsome bastard's festering in Derek's office."

George nodded, "Good, good, I'll pop upstairs and get the paperwork sorted. See you in a bit Tweety." George, resplendent in a grey Saville Row suit was buzzed into the main building and could be heard skipping lightly up the old wooden stairs.

Tweety turned to the grim-faced Vic, "Not long now, Vic, me old son. Not long now."

The Preacher and Shell arrived wearily in the Enquiry Office at 10.25 AM. Tweety had just left. Vic was on his lonesome. He looked up at the gloomy pair and smiled. "Fuck me kids, has someone just died? The only thing missing with youse pair is a piper playing a funeral dirge."

Shell pouted, "Na Vic, just feels like it doesn't it, Preachy, babe?"

Preacher shrugged, attempting a smile, his heart was back in his boots. Vic beamed which wasn't helping the gloomsome twosome. "Come on kids, things have a way of turning out. Good things happen to good people, didn't mean you there Shell by the way."

Shelley smirked, "Whatever, Vic!"

Vic carried on, "Skipper says that you have to join me in here Shell, 'til Tweety's finished some job with the boss. Preacher, you have to go up to the CID Office immediately, no detours and no faffing about, comprehendi?" Pete shrugged and quietly nodded. Shelley slid into the Enquiry Office adroitly flipping her flak jacket off followed by her green Dartex raincoat. Vic buzzed the weary Preacher into the main building and watched as he slowly clumped up the stairs. Shell appeared beside the musing Vic; an open box of Embassy Regal fags was thrust under his chin.

He looked up at the snow-white cherubic face and smiled, "Thought you'd never ask, wee pard."

They lit up and inhaled the first few drags in silent mode. Her Majesty gazed down from the Enquiry Office wall. Vic could have sworn she had that gasping for a fag look about her. Radio 2 quietly stirred the pot in the background. A certain Nat King Cole was crooning, 'Let's Face the Music and Dance!'

Shell spoke first, "I hope the Preacher's gonna be okay, Vic, I hear your man's a real bastard."

Vic quietly nodded then after a couple went, "Tea?" Shelley smiled, "I've never been known to refuse."

Vic had by now disappeared into the radio room. On clicking the kettle, he chuckled, "So I've heard, Shell, so I've heard."

The partition door sprung open and the ever so hunky Sergeant Tony Speers sauntered in trying to look as cool as. He had someone's Accident Report Booklet tucked under his muscular arm making him look purposeful. Shells face lit up, "Ya joining us for a cuppa, Skipper?"

Tony smiled, "Sounds good Shell. My nerves are shot today. I just want this whole Preacher shit put to bed."

Vic shouted out from the cubby hole, "What's yer poison, Skipper?" Tony pulled a stool up with his back to the reception counter, he always gravitated there. The Accident Booklet was now rolled up like a fly swat then morphed into a drumstick as Tony began rat-a-tat-tatting his nervously jigging thigh. Shouting back over the screams of the boiling kettle, "Coffee, milk and two sugars, cheers Vic. So Shell, how's your love life going?"

Shelley had taken up residence in Tweety's chair. She had just lit another and sighed as smoke escaped from her 'Betty Boop' mouth and nose, "Not as good as yours, hot rocks." Vic appeared carrying a tray with three steaming mugs. Shell and Tony gave each other a grinning double take before Shell blurted out, "And the rest 'D'Artagnan', where's the 'choccy' biscuits, we both know where you hide them?"

Vic laughed, "Oh I, silly me. Forgetsies!"

The Preacher wearily approached the CID Office door at the top of the stairs. It suddenly burst open causing him to swiftly give way. His boss, George Sewell was charging grim-faced towards him like a man on a mission. Their eyes collided. The Preacher's stomach lurched, was that face like thunder all for him?

He gulped, "Morning Sir."

George's face changed, he momentarily broke into a smile then patted him on the shoulder as he whizzed by, "Ah Peter. Sorry don't have time for a chat." George was knee deep in a cunning plan Tweety had hatched and didn't need any distractions. Agitated, he shrilled, "I've left an envelope with Catherine for you. In you go now, there's a good chap. There's tea and a lovely slice of boiled cake waiting for you. Toodle pip!"

Pete spluttered, "Sorry Sir, you see I have an appointment with C&D in fi…"

George stopped him in his tracks roaring over his shoulder as he 'Fred Astaired' it down the stairs, "Change of plans, Constable Majury, change of plans. Read the letter man, just read the bloody letter!"

The Preacher entered the office; to say he was bewildered would've been an understatement. The office was now empty bar Catherine Mercer the CID Office manager who was at her desk 'admining.' An old radio was playing ghastly classical music in the background. It sounded to Pete like two cellos falling down a set of stairs. Could his day possibly get any worse? He was drawn to voices coming from the DI's Office and recognised the dulcet tones of Pinky, Perky,

Derek and Tweety. Catherine looked up and smiled at him, her eyes twinkling. She could sense the gentle giant was all beat up, "Aww, well isn't it the handsome Constable Majury."

Pete smiled from behind clenched teeth. Catherine got to her feet holding an envelope. "Take a seat here young man. I'll get you a cuppa and a slice of cake. The Boss asked me to give you this." She handed him a sealed manilla envelope. The address on the envelope leapt out at him like a jolt from a Taser. Complaints and Discipline. Lisnasharragh RUC. Belfast, his heart sank and his palms began to sweat.

Catherine smiled, "I'll leave you in peace; while you open that, Peter." She then disappeared into the CID kitchen humming quietly to herself. The radio sensing the moment showed compassion and played 'The New World Symphony' by Dvorak. (That's the theme from the 'Hovis' ad to us lesser mortals.) The Preacher took a deep breath as his huge hand gently nursed the envelope open.

Black Bart looked up from behind his highly polished nails as the office door abruptly opened. A sixty something male entered, he was well groomed and wore an expensive looking tailor crafted grey suit. His jade green matching silk tie and hanky were sublime against his white linen shirt. Oh, and the black barkers, classy, interesting. Superior or inferior, pranced through Bart's grey matter. These things were always vitally important to him.

The grey-haired man smiled then whispered crisply, "Morning," then took a seat facing him.

Bart glared at the male but got no reaction. He was unsure as to where his land lay. He leapt from his ledge of indecision clearing his throat like a bark,

"Ahem, excuse me, but I have booked this office for an interview in a couple of minutes." The grey-haired male's eyes sparkled oblivious to the glare. "Quite remarkable, so have I!" He continued in a flat tone, "Mine's one of those horrible ones that you dread, they're not pleasant but you know they've got to be done. Rights have been wronged, just wish it wasn't me doing all the righting or writing for that matter. (Chuckles to himself.) You must know what I mean, surely?" The stylish interloper then fixed Bart with a death stare. He then leaned back in his chair and stretched out looking at the ceiling completely unperturbed.

A few anxious moments passed while Bart mentally bobbed around in his sea of doldrums and uncertainty. Then he snapped, "Have you any idea who I am. I'm Chief Inspect…" Suddenly the office door crashed open, causing him to jump. In reversed that one-eyed twit from the Enquiry Office banging and clanging. With his back still turned, he croaked, "Morning all. Sorry, I'm a fraction late." He was lost behind a pile of clear plastic evidence bags.

Bart, now furious, slammed his soft white fist on the table, his pain far outweighed any authoritative gesture, "Constable Sweetlove, (exasperated.) what's the meaning of this, what's going on? This gentleman says he's booked this room as well. Do we have any explanations? I'm waiting!"

By now, Tweety had taken the seat beside George. He had carefully placed all the evidence bags in a particular order on the floor beside him. Then their eyes met. The jabbering buffoon was gone; Bart's glare was met with a friendly calm. The male in the grey suit raised a hand exposing a silver-tone Onyx 'Montblanc Man' cufflink. Bart began to sense for the first time that things were not as they ought to be.

The grey suit spoke, "Detective Chief Inspector Bartholomew, let me introduce myself to you, I'm Superintendent George Sewell. I'm the Sub Divisional Commander of Strand SubDivision. I'm instructed to formally serve this on you. It's from Detective Superintendent Stephen McCormick, your boss at C&D. You are to open it immediately and read its contents carefully. Take all the time you need." George calmly handed Bart a sealed manila envelope marked 'Private & Confidential. Complaints and Discipline.' Lisnasharragh RUC Station, Belfast.

Bart coldly tore the envelope open then read its contents. He glimpsed Constable Sweetlove biting on his bottom lip, a picture of apparent concern. A bead of sweat found its way past his now raised eyebrows as the narrative in the communication slowly sunk in. His eyes darted up at the pair sitting quietly opposite him. He heard himself roar, "What the hell's the meaning of all this, hand me that phone, I demand to speak with my boss immediately. How dare they or should I say he. That Detective Superintendent McCormick's a real piece of work, swanning around, being nice to my face and to all in sundry. The staff all love him, you know. The department's gone soft since his arrival last year. No backbone, no moral fortitude. He encourages the staff to lean on the side of mercy. What's that he always brings up, "If you're big, be merciful. What tosh. Listen here, our job's a tough one, it's as tough for us as it is for the boys out on the ground." George and Tweety exchanged a swift side-on glance totally disagreeing.

"We've got to make tough decisions. My reputation is gilt-edged. I perform my duties conscientiously and with the utmost professionalism. I've never brought myself under any notice and my figures are the best in the Department. It's outrageous that I now find myself, SUSPENDED! Suspended from duty without the slightest explanation other than I'm under some sort of criminal investigation. Professional jealousy and backstabbing, that's what this is all about. Heads will roll for this. Mark my words!" Bart felt himself shaking with rage. An animal inside him had been unleashed and he felt powerful. His nostrils flared as he gazed at the two idiots opposite him.

George unfazed sighed. "Mr. Bartholomew (Bart hated that!), I fully appreciate you're emotional at this time but I can assure you that professional jealousy has nothing to do with this, quite the opposite in fact. The job doesn't treat the suspending of any senior officer lightly. Although your immediate suspension has been authorised by Detective Superintendent McCormick, it has also been approved by our very own Chief Constable. Your suspension comes as a result of a criminal investigation relating to allegations against your good self. All will be revealed to you, that's why we're all gathered here today. Oh, and by the by, Constable Majury's complaint has been fully dealt with by your C&D department. Just thought you'd like to know."

Bart's stomach tightened, feeling his Babylonian walls of superiority crashing down.

George in a weary monotone continued, "Now that you've been formally suspended from duty, kindly hand me over the contents of your briefcase. They're after all property of the Crown. While you're at it, hand me over your police warrant card as well. You won't be needing that anymore either."

Bart's hands trembled as he handed over his briefcase. His blustering had now slowly fizzled out. Constable Sweetlove offered him a sympathetic shrug whispering, "Nice case, Sir."

George continued, "It's now my onerous task as your superior officer to formally arrest you for THREE separate alleged offences. They're the reason for your immediate suspension from duty. They were all committed over the past few years and have just recently come to the light of the police. They were allegedly committed by yourself while engaged in the capacity of a Complaints and Discipline Investigative Officer. They each relate to the blackmailing and assault of police officers' wives. Each done at a time when you were investigating separate criminal allegations against their husbands. The women all allege that you made contact with them on an innocent pretext. You then coerced them into lewdly posing for you and had them wear deviant outfits while you photographed them. These outfits were supplied by you. You made them wear nipple clamps and other degrading torturous items, again supplied by you.

"They allege you coerced them into performing sexual acts and activities of your choosing. These acts also caused them great pain and humiliation. You threatened them with their husbands' futures. You placed them in real fear that their husbands faced the sack and or imprisonment, in essence destroying their family lives and future. Faced with these threats, they felt compelled to comply with your vile demands. Their complicity in exchange for their partners' complaints being favourably resolved by yourself."

George snarled contemptuously at Bart then folding his arms tightly, looked across at Tweety. "My colleague, Constable Sweetlove will now caution you in relation to these allegations. All three females concerned have made written statements of complaint and are quite happy to formally identify you."

Bart blustered in, "A mere constable interviewing a detective chief inspector, I don't think so. I demand to be interviewed by an officer of no less than equal rank. Certainly not a bumbling plod like him, I know my rights." Black Bart was now sweating profusely. Every pore was betraying his internal panic. What had they got on him? Were they bluffing? Constable Sweetlove was smiling warmly at him. George chuckled.

"A PLOD you say. How wrong you are. Constable Sweetlove here is not only a police constable but he's also a highly qualified barrister at law. His legal stature is in no way undermining your lofty rank, so you see, SUSPENDED Detective Chief Inspector Bartholomew, you're being interviewed by a superintendent and a barrister at law. Oh, and another thing, I should also point out, your home was searched this morning by a crack DMSU (Divisional Mobile Support Unit) search team."

Bart tried to swallow but his mouth was dry. George, smiling coldly continued, "They've seized a swathe of evidential items, some are in this room as we speak. For today's purposes we have a camera. A Kodak EK300 to be exact. Nipple clamps. Female S&M clothing and other assorted items for female pleasure." Tweety then quietly placed three exhibited envelopes on the desk.

George nodded before setting the envelopes in datal order from left to right. He then stared coldly at Bart before speaking. His eyes were a mix of ice and anger, "And finally three sets of photographic stills relating to each of the three blackmailed wives. All these images are formal exhibits. This morning's search unearthed further photographic images containing as yet other unidentified females. These poor unfortunates can clearly be seen wearing the same S&M gear and subjected to the same cruel ordeal as the wives we're here to interview you about. I have no doubt in my mind that thanks to your remarkable referencing system, we will be able to locate these new victims and obtain further statements of complaint from them. The pain and suffering you have caused to these innocent women, not to mention the cruelty beggars belief."

George's voice was rising with fury as every word hissed from his lips. Bart inwardly squirmed as home truths arrived in bucket loads. George suddenly leapt from his seat and screamed at the cowering suspect, "Even turning up to formal events following your wicked deeds. Parading yourself in front of these poor women. (Head now shaking.) Bartholomew you are one sick and sorry individual."

Bart looked over to the one-eyed constable who stared anxiously back, quietly shrugging his shoulders. George then calmed a tad turning to his interview partner. "Tweety, or should I say Constable Sweetlove, let's not let this loathsome tail wag the dog any further. Caution him and let's present our evidence." Bart's world was collapsing all around him. He could hear the cautions being administered to him, but it was all a blur. Looking at the floor, he could see the contents of the individual evidence bags, his camera, nipple clamps, garish S&M clothing and then the photographic images of the three women all wearing the same clothing and clamps, all images taken with the camera in the evidence bag. Then there were more charges to come. He knew the bitches could all identify him; he began to feel weak. He looked down at the crotch of his trousers noting a fresh warm damp stain. He had pissed himself. Oh, and the smell or was it his 'BO!' Quickly looking up, he became aware that the other two were staring at his shameful predicament. This is what rock bottom looked and felt like.

"Blackmail you say?" He stuttered…

Upstairs, Pete quietly read. The majority of the letter was procedural jargon. He arrived at the closing paragraph. "This department finds that your swift actions taken at the time of the alleged complaint were wholly appropriate under the extreme circumstances you were placed in. A bomb was seconds from exploding and Mr. Prentass, the complainant was obstructing you in the execution of your duty and in your efforts to preserve life. The force used on Mr.

Prentass was appropriate and in no way disproportionate under the extreme circumstances. Lives were saved by your prompt and heroic actions. It is the opinion of this department that you should be commended for your actions as opposed to complained against. No further action will be taken with regards this complaint. A letter of our findings has been sent to the complainant and to your Sub Divisional Commander. Your personal file will be updated accordingly. Should you have any queries regarding our findings do not hesitate to contact us on the number below. Detective Superintendent SJ McCormick 16336, C&D Lisnasharragh."

A tear found its way down Pete's cheek accompanied by a huge wave of relief. Bud came to mind causing another tear. "Oh, me of little faith."

Catherine returned with his cuppa and cake. She smiled at the big lump sitting by the desk with the crumpled letter in his huge hand. "Good news, Peter?"

The Preacher looked up and smiled, "Yes Catherine. NFPA. No further Police Action."

Catherine smiled, "Never in doubt Peter. Here's a tissue. There's something in your eye, mine as well." They laughed and hugged.

Tweety nodded at Bart sighing. Bart sensed a hint of sympathy unlike his snarling boss. Constable Sweetlove went on, "Yes, Blackmail. Section 21 of the Theft Act 1968. 'Making unwarranted demands with menaces with a view to making a gain or causing a loss.' It carries a 14-year prison sentence and…"

George blasted in, "And Bartholomew, the long and short of it all is, that you coerced these poor females into carrying out your vile demands under threat. You threatened them that their husbands were facing the sack and or prison unless they acquiesced." (His turn to slam his fist on the table.) "We've got you bang to rights, you despicable human being. You're a disgrace to the force!"

Tweety meekly interjected, trying to avoid any unnecessary bloodshed. "Ahem, Mr. Bartholomew Sir, do you wish any legal representation at this juncture or are you happy for us to crack on with a **Q&A**[7] interview under caution?" He then offered up a sympathetic smile. Bart now found himself

---

[7] *(Question and Answer interviews were carried out prior to tape recorded interviews. Entire interviews were carried out in a written question and answer form. At the end of the interview the suspect was permitted to read the documentation, sign each page and sign the final page attesting that the documentation was a true and accurate account of the interview.)*

unwittingly engaging with the one-eyed constable. He was much nicer than his snarling boss.

A subdued silence followed. Bart gazed across the table at the pair facing him. One would have hung, drawn and quartered him given half a chance while the other, well, he was more understanding, after all, nobody was killed, were they? Bart eventually sighed, "Constable Sweetlove, let's just get it over with. I assume if I throw my hands up things will go better for me?"

George leapt in, "Whatever better means. It didn't go better for your victims, did it?"

Tweety quietly shrugged, a look of understanding in his eyes. "Well; okay Sir, it's up to you. If you're entirely sure." And so, they began their Q&A Interview. Tweety did all the asking and writing while George sat back glaring and snarling. Bart found himself strangely opening up to the lines of questioning at no time feeling judged. Before long, he found himself quietly championing the shrewdness of his actions, salivating over his cunning and guile. Constable Sweetlove appeared to be in awe of him.

Simple questions flowed as he gently probed and clarified the pearls that eschewed from Bart's self-perceived brilliant mind. Graphically, he answered everything put to him. Bart soon felt a real sexual high especially on seeing the excitement in the Constable. Here was someone who really seemed to get him, at last someone who could see how cunning and clever he really was. This really spurred him on, the serial manipulator purred like a Cheshire cat.

Tweety's plan was to flatter the narcissist at every corner and turn. His fawning adoration against George's opposition had worked a treat. A fuller confession could not have been recorded. When all was done, he signed each page agreeing them to be a true and accurate account of the interview. Tweety had been magnificent and Bart the popinjay was none the wiser. He had been led by the nose by the master.

George looking on from the sidelines pondered on the good work that had been done. His dream team had delivered. Their faces flashed before him, what a bunch. He smiled unnoticed, a particularly rotten apple had been caught and could do no further harm. The Preacher had been saved and well, it was all down to Wee Mo who had the courage to do the right thing. George strangely now much calmer, excused himself and lifted the phone. He made a brief call to the Enquiry Office. A minute later, the door knocked quietly.

George answered. "Come in, come in Woman Constable." Bart had been quietly chatting with his new confidant when suddenly he was stopped dead in his tracks. His jaw fell open and he gasped. A woman police officer entered the room carrying a parcel, it was Maureen, his Maureen wearing a police uniform.

She smiled at the open-mouthed monster then handed George a prisoner's boiler suit still in its wrapper. The air was thick with tension. Tweety quietly set his pen down on the desk and along with George watched on as the drama unfolded. Bart clasped his hands tightly together stopping them from trembling then quickly threw them on top of his damp patch. It was all too late.

He nodded then stuttered, "M-M-Maureen. Maureen, was it you? Were you the one that? I mean did you?"

Maureen smiled a smile that neither George nor Tweety had ever seen from Wee Mo, it was a smile filled with guttural hate and loathing. "Oh, my goodness, is that you J, or should I say your full name, JUSTUS Bartholomew." She glared at the beast for several seconds releasing several years of pent-up anguish and frustration. Bart pissed himself some more feeling the moist heat on his thighs. Maureen nodded, giving a smile of gratitude to both George and Tweety.

As she was turning to leave, George spoke, "Maureen, would you let Aggie know this place will need a clean after we're done here, a wee accident occurred, as you can see."

Maureen wasted no time. "Pardon me Sir, that's not a wee accident sitting there, that's a big fucking accident! Right, you be, Sir, I'll let her know. Sorry for the outburst, I couldn't help myself just like that sick bastard sitting there." Maureen left the room.

Tweety bit his bottom lip and shared a raised eyebrow moment with his boss. Bart was then relieved of his fancy attire and got himself tidied up. He then got into the less fashionable prisoners boiler suit and black rubber gutties. His days of fancy click clacking and Saville Row suits were over. Black Bart, the slayer of police careers and arch blackmailer had entered the building, an hour later Justus Bartholomew, police prisoner was deposited in a Mountroyal prison cell. The following morning, he would appear in cuffs before a Magistrate who would remand him in custody pending trial. No bail applications were made. The rest of his life would start or should we say stop. His case would subsequently go to a Crown Court Trial where he pleaded guilty to all of the charges. This was all done at the earliest opportunity. He would receive an 8-year concurrent prison sentence pertaining to all matters.

Justus would do his prison time at the Maghaberry High Security Prison. There were never any visitors. It took him a while adjusting to prison life but eventually, he joined the camera club. Click, click. He now had to settle for inanimate objects, stones and sunsets were his new favourite subjects. JUSTICE for JUSTUS was finally served and our Preacher got his life back. Bud was pleased. What's that they say about revenge being a dish best served cold, Wee Mo would tell you, "Better late than never."

Chapter 17
Bye-Bye Baby (Baby Goodbye)

The thick chain to the Industrial Estate gates is wrapped in a fashion. Its security padlock has been discretely unlocked but left in place. It gave the illusion to a man on a galloping horse that the site's secure. A large blue and white Bedford TK Container truck is parked up way back, the murmur of its powerful diesel engine barely audible as it idles melodically with the evening breeze. On the passenger side of the big truck is a cartoon image of the Looney Tunes Road Runner bird, it also sports the caption "Beep Beep!". On the driver's side door is a further caption, "Loons till I die!"

The truck is hidden behind a row of derelict outbuildings and empty containers. Its headlights are off. This is the usual place, the handover spot. We're at the Greenbank Industrial Estate on the outskirts of Newry, County Down. It's located just over the Irish border, this is where for some, the easy monies are to be found.

It's gone just shy of 11.00 PM and inside the bouncing cabin of the truck 'Beller' was having a ball to himself. His speakers were up full blast and his favourite tape, the 'Bay City Rollers Greatest Hits' was belting out. Beller or should I say Ricky Bell didn't have the greatest set of pipes on him but he was giving it his all. When I say giving it his all, I mean for a man hampered with a ham and tomato crusty bap in his mouth. Shrapnel was flying everywhere. His muffled performance was being sloshed down by a warm, slightly out of date can of 'Iron Brew'. Ricky was wriggling and writhing desperately in his seat, trying to adjust his imminent need for a pee to the rhythm of the music. "Shang-A-Lang, Shang-GAA- Lang, Shang-GAAA-Laangggg, OHHH Wee aaahhh!"

Ricky also had his large eyes on the Industrial Estate's front gate. Multi-tasking was a thing he excelled at. He was expecting a shiny green van with the

'Fields the Love' logo on its sides. "Any minute now fir fack sake. Hurry up ya bastard am busting fir a peeeee. La, tra la, tra la, Sommer love sinnsationnnn!"

Ricky Bell, Beller or Bell End depending on how you stood in his affections was a 35-year-old Scot. He stood at a pasty 5 feet 8 inches square. When I say square, I mean packed tight with muscle. He had Popeye forearms and shoulders for which an ox would have given blood. Whenever he found the time, he pumped iron, even when he was out on the road. He kept a set of free weights stashed in the back of his cabin; he found that they helped with his anger management issues, not to mention his burgeoning testosterone. His head was sort of owl-y in shape with no discernible neck to speak of. It was absorbed into his huge back and shoulders. A hangman's nightmare, some might say. Beller's eyes were like deep black pools enhanced by his long blinking eyelashes, these perched just above his short beak-like nose. It was quite mesmerising when he was looking directly at you. Maybe he'd been an owl in a previous life, "twit tawoo."

He was trapped in that 'Should I stay or should I go' predicament with his hair. It was fine and wispy but falling out in clumps. What remained exuded a ghostly cobwebby effect. To do something or nothing about it was a pointless exercise and would have simply exuded a different form of ugly. Beller hailed from Angus in the Highlands of Scotland where he lived with his widowed mum, that's when he wasn't out on the road. He was a man with three passions in his solitary existence. Firstly, his life on the road driving. Secondly, his unbridled love for the Forfar Athletic football team or the 'Loons'. The 'Loons' had just won promotion from the Scottish second division that year and Beller was, pardon the pun. "Over the Loon."

Finally, and far from the least of his three loves he was a man mad keen on the opposite sex. A stash of German 'Treble X' Porn 'mags' attested to this. He always kept these handy underneath his driver's seat, just beside his box of 'Handy Andy' tissues. I know what you're all thinking but keep it to yourselves. Our Beller can hardly play 'Snap' by himself now can he. He's had to find other distractions to pass the time of day away. Let's face it, the open roads can be a lonely place folks and who are we to judge.

Ricky left school at 16 with minimal qualifications and joined the army. There he learnt several trades one of which was driving heavy lorries. He enjoyed the driving and its hours of quiet contemplative solitude; it was during those times that he was at his most content. Beller would have explained these moments of idyll a little differently, "Fuck the bastards, they cannae get at yee when yer oot on the rood!"

Thank you Beller; succinctly put. When he left the army after ten years of slipping and sliding, he took up with the long-distance lorry driving. It suited his personality down to the ground or should I say road. There he found his life to be as dull as dishwater except sometimes a bit murkier. He had a dot-to-dot approach to most things and was a man to be trusted to get on with a job. A man that would ask no questions if you asked him not to, nudge-nudge, wink-wink. He enjoyed the perks associated with stuff falling off the back of his lorry as well other stuff mysteriously falling onto it. Beller enjoyed a bit of excitement from the norm of his hum drum world. For him it wasn't just about the money, he relished in the risk and tension of it all.

Puff, back in the room! Which is why he's here tonight at a desolate industrial estate just on the outskirts of Newry. The poor fellow's wriggling and writhing for all his worth. Our favourite Loon is now caught up in a very different "should I stay or should I go" moment. "Fir feck's sake mannn. Hurry oop. Am gonna pee maselll!"

At the point of bursting, he leapt out of his cabin and scurried round to the front of his truck. "Zip, zip. I cannae find ma zip. Arghhhh!"

He's now writhing like the world hula hoop champion while his butt cheeks are clenched like a choir boy at his first confessional. Finally, he found the errant zip, "Haaaaaaaah!"

In the twinkling of an eye, he whipped his 'mister' out. Bell End then power hosed his front nearside tyre. "Bye-bye baby" gushed from his tape while his eyes rolled white like a character from the Exorcist. He got the irony. Such was his nirvana that he failed to notice a stiff breeze blowing back into him. It's a score draw folks, Loon trousers 1, nearside tyre 1.

"Nae more of that Iron Brew for you, Richard." Beller allowed himself a chuckle. Just then he spotted vehicle headlights approaching the main gates. He smiled, "Ochh, thank fuck I got ma business done just in the nick of time. It's aboot bloody time Mister. Fields the Dreeem!"

Oli Fields quietly removed the padlock before sliding the chain free. His large hands trembled as he eased the creaking metal gates open. Don't be taken in by this magnificent specimen of manhood, he's actually quite cowardly by nature. You see, Oli's a lover not a fighter. He just wanted this to be over. His eyes darted anxiously around the dimly lit site. "Where the fuck is he?" His heart's pounding and his mouth's dry. He's sensing monsters in every shadow. A stiff breeze throttled ageing trees and hedgerows causing them to creak and groan like lost souls. He shuddered then heaved a sigh of relief seeing slowly flashing headlights at the far end of the site.

"Pull yourself together, dick head. Let's just get this over with." Oli slid back into his van quickly checking himself out in the rearview mirror. He's been in better form as he gently dabbed at the right side of his jaw, the swelling was gone but the pain killers were wearing off, "Ohh!" it was agony to the touch.

Snarling, he replays the earlier incident back in his mind, "Judas bastard, your trainers have mud on them he says till me. Should have seen it coming." He's referring to the one punch knockout by the Provo heavy earlier at the monastic site. The last thing he remembered is looking down. Then whack! "Fucker." He turned off his 'Air Supply's Greatest Hits' then thumped his steering wheel.

"Come on son, we can do this." He filled his lungs full to capacity then exhaled long and slow. He engaged first gear and like a lost soul searching for salvation made for the light.

The green van pulled up in front of Beller's truck and is left stuttering with its engine on. A scragging gust suddenly blows as a tall handsome male confidently steps out. His head's tilted against the snarling breeze. He approached the driver-side door of the lorry, Beller grinning winds his window down. "Well, aren't you just one handsome bastard. What do they call you then?"

Oli glares up with his doorman's death stare, "Cheers Mr. Looney Tunes but TMI. Where's the gear?"

Beller was slightly wounded, "What the fuck ya mean ba TMI. I was just being friendly?"

Oli snarled, continuing with his macho front, "No offence but what if the police were to stop you? It's better you don't know who I am. My firm wouldn't like it anyway. Comprendi!"

Beller erupts, "Aye right ya be, Einstein. They would nae get too far with me telling them that you are one handsome bastard or that ya drive a big girly green van with 'Fields the Dream' on the side."

Beller chuckled on against Oli's glare and the heavy gusts. If looks could kill. Beller now realised they don't share the same sense of humour. He quit while he was ahead, or more accurately while he still had a head. "Whoa there,

Mr. Grumpy, I was just pulling your plonker. Settle yourself now, I'm Beller by the way, now, have you a wee envelope containing the two large ones for me?"

Oli nodded, tapping at his inside pocket. "Gear first. Good Holy fuck what's that racket coming from your cab?"

Oli hits a nerve ruffling Beller's owl-like feathers. Growling from his nest, sorry cabin, he snarled, "Fuck you. Leave the greatest group ever tae come frae Scotland out of this." Oli shrugged, releasing a smile.

Beller continued, "Right then, this is how it's going tae be. Reverse your van up to the back of mine and open yer rear doors. Then walk back to me. I'll hop oot, get the three cases and set them into the back of your van. When I return, you pay me."

Oli thought hard on this. Beller tutted, "Any time today son, I've other places to be and people to see." Oli creaked. He used to be indecisive! "Seems like a lot of toing and froing to me."

Beller sighed, fast becoming impatient. "No offence handsome but I don't know you from Adam and I have an aversion to being stroked. I promise I'll not nick any of your paint unless of course you have any Forfar blooo. (He cackled hysterically.) A minute should do it then we'll be on our merry way. Happy enough?"

Oli looked up at the prickly Scot subliminally being mesmerised. This was turning into his worst nightmare. "Mmm. I suppose." He reversed his van to the back of the container then opened its rear doors. He just wanted all of this to end. He shuddered then walked back to the front of the truck. A smiling Beller then theatrically popped on a pair of luminous yellow rubber gloves. This done, he flung his driver-side door open and powerfully launched himself out of his cab.

As he headed for the rear of his container, he hooted, "Ye cannae be too careful. I dinnae want ma dibby dabby doos found all over thae bags. Ya ken what I'm saying handsome?"

Oli whispered from under his collar, "Scottish Prick." For all their blether, the switch took only a few seconds. Oli marvelled at the cut of the mad Scot then sniggered on seeing his damp stains. "Come on fuckwit!" His eyes frequently darted over to the front gates as a grumbling breeze fussed up like a snarling dog ruffling at his hair. He heard clunking coming from the container then in a flash Beller was by his side.

"Job done, ma envelope if you please?" Oli smiled looking down at the Scot, "Just need to check I've got all three cases, I like my knee caps just as they are."

Beller nodded, "Suit yourself." All was as it should be. The pair returned to the front of the lorry. Beller was becoming impatient. There was a hint of nastiness, "Right ya be. It's pay me time!"

Oli yawned handing Beller the envelope. "Fair enough. Here take it." Beller snatched, quickly tearing it open. He then began to melodically count out aloud while fingering crisp twenty-pound notes. His large tawny brown eyes sparkling with delight in the blustery moonlight. The only thing missing was a Tu-whit tu-whoo!

Suddenly a thump from the back of the container caused Oli to jump. "What the fuck was that Oli son. Did you hear that, Beller?" Beller looked up from his operatic counting and began laughing hysterically, "Oooooh, so it's Oli is it now. Are ya scared of things that go bump in the night? Dinnae fuss yersel man, stuff's always shifting aboot the back of them big containers. They're never loaded right half the time." Beller stuffed the envelope into his trouser pocket then in a flash closed up his container. As he walked back to Oli, he twanged the rubber gloves off with a huge smarmy grin on his face.

"Oliver son, I'm thinking you're a bit too highly strung for this line of work." Reaching up he gently patted the meatloaf on his broad shoulders then whispered, "Stick tae what yer good at, the painting. Well, that's me all ready tae rock and roll. It was nice doing business with you lot as usual. Ochh, I sure hope the police disnae stop me, Mr. Oliver Fields. You were a hard nut tae crack. No hard feelings then, big man?"

Beller offered his hand for the briefest of handshakes. Oli wearily accepted then winced at the huge power coming through. He caught a twinkle in the Scot's eye as he bounces back up into his cabin. A cushion of heat escaped caressing Oli's tired face. It felt good. He heard the clunk of the gear engaging, then the large lorry slowly inched forward. The driver-side window slid down releasing an onslaught from the Bay City Rollers and Beller's head popped out for the final time. "Ahh just love this one, Ba ba baybee baybee goodbaaaaa! All the best to ya, Oli and dinnae forget to lock the padlock to the site on yer way oot. Bye the noo!"

Oli watched on as the blue and white lorry disappeared from view. He allowed himself a chuckle. Beller was a head case but there was worse than him out there. Now in splendid isolation he slowly made his way back to his van. He was dog tired, his eyes heavy and as for his poor jaw… too much adrenaline for one day. It would take the guts of an hour to get back to Belfast and then that fucking church job tomorrow. He would be glad to see Monday, there was a wee living room job with that tasty blonde in Loopland Drive; she had used him before and had never complained about his strokes. "Stick tae what yer good at Oli son." A quick check of the rear van doors and he'd be on his way. He casually reached for the handles then opened. "Ahhhhhyyyeeeeee!" The scream was out of him before he knew it.

A dark figure leapt at him crying, "Greetings my name is Oza…" Oli's punch was instinctive, he struck the advancing figure hard on the jaw, knocking him out. "Fuck, fuck, fuck. What am I going to do? Where did he come from?" Oli panicking spun around. Had anyone heard him? He began wringing his large hands as a frantic breeze clawed at the hedgerows. "I didn't sign up for this, Jesus, have I killed him?" He had punched the lifeless body backwards into the van. Panicking, he quickly felt the neck for a pulse and let out a huge sigh of relief. "Thank fuck for that. You've got this, relax, settle yourself."

On checking, Oli realised that the figure was barely a man, 16 years old at most with black hair and a swarthy complexion. A further rummage revealed a battered holdall containing scraps of clothing and other items of little value. Fifty Turkish lira was found rolled up in a tiny green purse in his back pocket. Oli quickly got to work. He bound the figure with masking tape then stuffed a linen hanky in the mouth, he then carefully hauled the body fully back into the rear of the van covering it with tarpaulin. His final act was to secure the site. Carefully, he reset the thick chain around the heavy metal gates then locked the padlock. Oli was now wide awake and in full panic mode. What if he was stopped by the bastarding peelers with an unconscious body and the drugs in the back. PRISON, PRISON, PRISON and years of it.

Chapter 18
That Phone Hasn't Stopped Ringing All Night

It had just crept past midnight that Saturday night Sunday morning and the downstairs lights were still on at number 11, Roseberry Gardens. The Gardens is a quiet little street verging on picture postcard. Tonight, we find it snuggled under twinkling stars in the bosom of East Belfast. You would never describe Roseberry Gardens as working class or middle class either. Not even if it was straining on its tippy toes. It languished somewhere in between. It's formed in a cul-de-sac and its houses are painted white and adorned with bright green euonymus hedging to the front. The street is well kept and a sense of pride pervades unlike most of its surrounding younger neighbours. The houses were built in the 1920s just after the First World War and come the 1980s, most of its residents are elderly.

Apologies, I'm rambling on. Let's take a peek at the night owl in number 11, shall we? The lights are on in the front room. The good room is what they call it in these parts, and what a good room it is. The mustard drapes are drawn tight, a tulip shaped orb hanging centre ceiling cast a soft glow from its 60-watt bulb. Aww, that's nice, soothing sounds oozing from an old Phillips radio crackling in the corner. I think it's the Radio 2 'Night Ride' show.

Very chillaxing. "Aw, Max Bygraves, 'Underneath the Arches.' Lovely."

A glass fronted wooden cabinet is the show piece in this charming room. In it are displayed hand me down dinner sets with matching cups and saucers. Ghostly heirlooms from family long since gone and sadly forgotten. These objects of worship are all of fine bone china and are too good for mere mortal lips. They are seen as status symbols as if anyone living in the gardens needed one. They would only be used if the Queen ever called round for a cuppa, which was never. Sets such as these like vestal virgins remained untouched and untarnished over many generations save for the odd reverential dusting whenever the need arose. Sadly, a forgotten part of our past when stock and status were measured by good rooms and fine bone china tea sets. These sets would end up in builder's skips during house clear outs in the 2000s, their time now past and status measured by other possessions such as motor cars, televisions, music systems and foreign holidays. (Oh, and even further on down the line the size of your ass, boobs and TikTok following)

Life can be a twisted bitch, can't it?

A framed photograph took pride of place on the mantelpiece. The image is worn and sun bleached but I can still make out a man in an army uniform. My, how proud he looked, so big and strong with his arms folded looking the camera square in the eye. I wouldn't like to mess with him, he reminds me of someone, in looks anyway. Now who is it?

Plonked in the middle of the room making it feel much smaller than it actually is sat a large dining table. Its legs are dark, nearly black in colour and maybe Georgian in design. The table itself is protected by a pitted olive-green oilcloth. On top sat a huge jigsaw puzzle nearing completion. Oh, there's the box in the corner, let's see now. Holy moly, it's a thousand piecer! What's it say on the cover, ahh, "The Hanging Gardens of Babylon." Hey, weren't they one of the Seven Wonders of the Ancient World listed by the Hellenic culture? Folks, you'd find me hanging if I had to tackle that monstrosity. If the jigsaw was a gift, then it came from your worst enemy. If you bought it for yourself then do yourself a favour, stick to the self-flagellation. It's way cheaper and burns more calories. Oh, here he comes now sliding in from the kitchen.

I'm sure you've already guessed, it's our Malky. In case you've forgotten, Malky or Malcolm Mackie is the tag team partner of Aggie Patterson, this dynamic duo made up the cleaning team for Mountroyal Police Station. Evening there, Malky. How's it going? I've noticed something about our Malky, he always looked down as he passed his dead father's image. Bob Mackie was killed at the Battle of Monte Casino in April 1944, a terrible affair, one of 55,000 casualties; poor Malky never got to meet his father and the loss destroyed his mother. Crosses for our station cleaner to bear. He's always been terrified by that image from behind the glass. Sad isn't it. You can find out a lot about a person in the good room. Sorry for digressing, one of my many bad habits.

Back to our Malky. He knew how to party the night away. What ya got on your tray there, partner? He's just rocked in with a cheese and piccalilli sarnie accompanied by a pint of full fat milk. His dark eyes widen and a broad grin appeared illuminating his usually doleful face. He's on a roll, it's as if his crazy night couldn't get any better. What's that I hear canoodling from the radio? It's only the Righteous Brothers singing one of his all-time favourites "Ebb Tide."

Malky sat down at the old table and quietly tucks into his midnight feast. He has seen to his elderly mother and she is down for the night. He settled slowly, becoming absorbed in his hanging gardens. Only a hundred pieces or so to go, way to go Malky son, you've got this.

A short distance away a telephone rang on a bedside drawer. We find ourselves at number 13, Donard Street; although both dwellings are a short spit apart, they are in a different universe with regards to what's going on inside. The phone rang incessantly like a brat child. Somewhere out in the wilderness, our Oli's shitting himself. His stress levels are 11 out of 10 and rising.

"Come on, come on, pick up you big useless bastard. Why's it always fucking me!"

He'd stumbled across the old red telephone box out in the middle of god's nowhere, turned out he wasn't far from Crossgar but how was Oli to know? It's pitch black outside and a stiff breeze nagged at his jacket collar. A flickering light in the old box feeds his anxiety.

A naked sixteen-year-old blonde dramatically swings the shower doors open releasing a cloud of warm steam. She's been lathering her perfect form fully aware she's being ogled at. "Would someone care to answer that fuckin phone, it's doing my head in, so it is!" She stuck a tongue out then pouted for effect; her watcher grinned. Giggling she returned to her lathering. Finally with a snarl, he picked up but immediately set the phone on his pink fleshy lap. Here's a man that's happily distracted.

Our voyeur is a certain Darren Boyd or Dazbo, we've met him before, haven't we? He's the UVF Commander for East Belfast. You might also remember him as Mr. Pissy Pants from the Nendrum Monastery affair. Well, it turned out that number 13, Donard Street is his stinky ashtray of a home. Pride is not a word to be used when describing this fleapit.

We find our leader lying on his king size bed taking in the sumptuous view. Dazbo is flying high and he's feeling 'sweet as'. As far as cool is concerned, he's daddy cool. Several spliffs and a load of vod have taken him to where we find him, enjoying the frothy perks of his job. Darren has a thing for teenage girls and even younger if truth be known.

Tonight, he's entertaining two of them. Tracey, she's sixteen, the blonde bit in the shower. She's an old hand at this game and knew where his buttons are and how to press them. Tracey is a Dazbo groupie of sorts. When she looked at him, she doesn't see ugly, sweaty or stinky like the rest of us, Tracey saw status, power, money and drugs. Tracey fancied a slice of that cake. It's her favourite cake. Yummy!

She's brought her mate over tonight by special invitation. Lecherous Dazbo noticed how well she looked in her Ashfield school uniform earlier in the week. Just like 'June' in the musical classic our Charlene was 'bustin' out all over'. She had been innocently waiting at a bus stop with her more pipe cleaner shaped pals as he and his goons drove by. Our Dazbo has a soft spot for the innocent looking ones and this one was perfect, just peachy. Charlene's a wee brown-haired stunner, a nice girl from a good family. She's a Grade A student and is currently studying for her O-Levels. Her parents have high hopes for her future and have smothered her with love. Charlene hasn't quite matured as fast as the rest of her body and while that in itself isn't a crime it can lead to catastrophic consequences. I take it we're all on the same page here?

Now who's been a naughty girl then? Well, it's our Tracey since you asked, she's tricked poor Charlene. There's only ever one winner when 'streetwise' and 'gullible' hook up. A meeting with an unknown male admirer was the hook that done for Charlene. You see our Tracey's gone that extra mile regarding Charlene's makeup and style. Her style for the meet turned out to be decidedly flaunty by the way. I'm sure she looked stunning. Where is the little princess now by the way? Ah, but of course. Do the needful there, Dazbo, lift the duvet cover there's a good chap. Oops, apologies folks, avert your gaze, Charlene's as naked as a jailbird and out for the count. Unfortunately, it's been her first time for alcohol and the wacky baccy, not a good combo. I'm guessing she's had lashings of encouragement from Tracey, what with being a novice and all, what a pal. With friends like Tracey, who needed enemies.

As for our leering UVF boss, tonight he's got it all, power, drugs and women. He's like the cat that's gotten all of the cream. As for the kitten bit, well that's not very nice. Not very gallant at all is it? Hardly the actions of a knight in shining armour there, Sir Dazbo. Hope you don't have to pay for that somewhere down the line. Oh good, he's finally placed the receiver to his ear.

"Whaa?" He listened to a screeching voice at the other end as his roving eyes enjoy the titillating Tracey show. His free hand occupies itself with the forbidden fruit under the sheets.

Dazbo's slowly blinking eyes suddenly widen then he burst out laughing, "Oli, you're fucking kidding me, you've what? A body wrapped up in the back of your van. How the fuck did you manage that? Are you Hit Man now, a one-man nutting squad, is this your new job on the side you big wanker?"

More laughter. The screeching continued as Dazbo listened on half-heartedly. He found it hard to concentrate what with his current state of nirvana and eye-popping distractions. A tired boredom crept in and when the screeching finally stopped, he croaks, "Where the fuck are you anyway, ya big wanker?"

Tracey then appeared in all her seductive glory wrapped up in a cloud of steam. She beckons him into the shower with a sexy dance, it never failed. He held up his free hand with a pained expression mouthing, "One minute, love." She tutted then disappeared back into the piping mist.

From the flickering phone box, Oli blurted out his story. It came out like an explosion in a paint factory. He'd half expected Dazbo to go apeshit but strangely his boss had found it all hilarious. Oli's still not getting it. Drink and drugs are now making themselves right at home in Dazbo's addled brain, he listened as euphoria slowly sunk in gently shooing away his sexual cravings. Oli's frenetic jabbering is beginning to ruin his bliss though. Dazbo's suddenly very tired, all he wanted to do is sleep. Mentally though, he's a few steps ahead. He cut the meatloaf off mid-sentence, "Right Oli, ya listening? We've a contingency plan for shit like this. Stop your panicking, you big girl's blouse. Right when you get back to Belfast drive your van around to Stan's. I'll call him. He'll fix your wee problem for you. I'll have him gather up our two packages while he's at it. He'll leave the other one in your van for you and your wee fenian friends, you know, for tomorrow morning's hit in Castlereagh Street. You've not forgot about it, I hope? Ah ha. Nooo problems. By the time you get up for church tomorrow your van will be sitting out front of your gaff." Dazbo's eyelids feel like lead, his speech is stumbling like a drunk on a cobbled street. He briefly came around, "Here you, don't forget about the Glentoran top and newspaper. Yep, that's right, just leave her parked up at the end of Cluan Place with the back doors unlocked. Aye, they'll do the rest. You got all that fuck wit? Don't worry yourself about the body, from here on in, it's got fuck all to do with you. Never you talk about it or bring it up ever again. Come on now, dry yer eyes Oli son, sure it's all sorted, don't I look after ye? Remember this, shit happens. What's that you say? Hey don't be a lazy cunt, sure it's only five minutes' dander from Stan's front door to yours. The walk will do you the world of good, help you with your stress and all. Stop your flapping, that's an order. Right off you go, then. YESSS, no sweat, sweet as. Big Stan will be expecting you. Now fuck away off and get your shit together, it will all be over soon. Sure, I'll see you at the Longfellow tomorrow night for a few jars, on me and all, no arguments. A wee double celebration if you like, getting our hands on the drugs and getting the peeler popped by the Provos. Yeowww, now fuck off, I've had enough of ye this night. Bye nae."

The line went dead at the other end and a very weary Dazbo made the call to Big Stan who thankfully take's it all in his stride. "Sweet as." Dazbo slammed the phone back into the receiver. "Oli, you're one stupid fucker, so you are."

Exhausted he crumpled back onto the mattress as his eyes orbit like a sputnik in space. His stinky mouth opened ever so slightly and he wheezed through the drool, "I'm fucked, so I am." Dazbo's eyes close for business.

Moments later, a naked Tracey emerged from the bathroom followed by a whiff of heady musk. She's drying her bleached blonde hair vigorously with a filthy black towel. She saw there's no need for anymore sexy dancing. She giggles at the big-time UVF boss who's snoring heavily and seriously 'Ali Bongoed'. His gold encrusted mouth hung open like a portcullis exposing a pitted tongue which is an unhealthy mixture of slate grey and orange. A stench of dead cannabis and vodka flees from his rattling lungs. Charlene's cherubic face has surfaced from beneath the filthy sheets, she's still unconscious. Tracey filled in the blanks and smiled.

"Happy days. No smelly sex with Mr. Tiny tonight." She leaned over the slumbering brute and stroked Charlene's angelic face then whispered into her ear, "As they say in Russia, Moscow pet!"

Tracey brazenly helps herself to £60 from his wallet then pilfers a £10 deal from his wacky stash. She's not bothered, he went through the stuff like wildfire. She slips into her clothes then quietly lets herself out. "Easy money!" As for her mate Charlene, she's on her own now. I just pray she wakes up before he does, don't you?

The phone rang and wee Geordie jumped up from his bed wide awake. His father Stan answers with a growl then everything turned to whispers. Geordie knew by the muffled tones that it's serious. He picked up snippets, words, crumbs of conversation, something about a van on its way he has to get sorted. With each crumb, a picture formed in his tiny mind, "Hit on the peeler in the morning as he's walking to church."

Wee Geordie grabs his 'Roy of the Rovers' colouring in book and started scribbling for all he's worth. This is important. The phone call ends and he strains as his father made another call of his own. He spoke with a Tommy, something about a job up in the hills. He laid back on his pillow wondering what to do. He can't sleep, he started scratching at his hands and arms, it's a fear thing. Ten minutes later Geordie jumped again when the front door bell rang; with a dry mouth he scurried from his bed and looked out onto the street from his bedroom window. A bright green van is idling under the street lights. He can just make out the word 'dream' on the side. He scrawled this onto his book. Green van, 'Dream!' He then crept to his bedroom door which is barely open. His frantic scratching became frenzied.

He's shaking with fear but listens for all he's worth. From where he's stood, he can see the back of his Da standing by the front door. He's in muffled conversation with another man who's talking very fast. His Da's trying to calm the man down, trying to make him speak softer. He heard, "Settle yourself Oli son. I'm sorting all that out for you. I've got it you wanker. Leave it with me. Now where's our two bags then, I've been told to fetch them?"

He then steps out into the street; a warm gust of wind invites itself in. Seconds later he returned carrying two large cases. Geordie heard these being set quietly in the cupboard under the stairs. His tiny heart's pounding, he swears he can hear it beating. If his father cottoned on, he would be in for it. This fear, this dread made him close his bedroom door all the way over, but he continued to listen all the harder. Nothing he heard made much sense but he scrawled everything down in different spaces on two adjacent pages of his colouring book. Little clumps of whispers. Cluan Place tomorrow morning. Leave van with rear doors unlocked. Fenians do the rest. Maroon Volvo, something 1690 (Geordie scrawled purple car!). Glentoran top, newspaper. Follow the black bastard a bit when he walks out of the Mount. Then that was it.

Geordie heard the front door quietly close then everything went completely silent. He cranes his ear to the door listening for his Da's footsteps, ready to scurry into bed and pretend to be asleep. But Stan, his hateful father, has gone. He heard the van door slamming shut and then the rasping of gears. Quickly he dashed over to his bedroom window just in time to see the bright green van turn right at the end of the street. What to do, what to do? Geordie sensed something very bad was going to happen but what could he do? He knew his Da will be back soon and then it would be too late to do anything.

There was only one way he could think of. He quickly pulled his tattered red jumper on over his pyjama top then slid into his threadbare slippers. Next he gently tears the two pages out from his colouring book carefully folding them so they fitted easily into his tiny hand. Pushing hard against his fears, the boy ghosts out the back door into the blackness of the unseeing night.

Geordie hated the darkness; it held the keys to untold terrors that his vivid imagination generated. A scurrying breeze caused hedges to rustle and surge, these spectral shadows dance wildly against the faltering street lights as dogs howl in the distance. Geordie's terrified but keeps on going. He's now too afraid to stop. Then he heard a high whining sound approach him steadily from the rear. A tinkling ball of light came out from the clawing shadows and groaning breeze. It closes in on him fast then he is illuminated in the glare of its bright lights. His eyes lose all focus but he ran blindly on.

Then he heard soft whispers coming closer and closer, "Geordie, Geordie, wee man, it's me. Stop for God's sake. Are you in any kind of bother wee man?" Geordie now exhausted, stopped and turned to face his fate. A smiling figure all in white appeared from behind the bright lights. Geordie has never been so relieved in all his life.

"Deano, you scared the shite outta me, so you did." The milkman smiled, "What's up wee man?"

The phone rang and Malky is stirred from the delights of his 'Hanging Gardens'. It's as if he's been brought out of a trance. He yawned, then gave a puzzled look at his 20-year-old Timex watch. He's had the strap replaced six times so far you know. It's a green one at the moment. He's doubly puzzled as he stretches himself because the old phone never rang. "Who's calling this hour of the night. Probably a wrong number, dears oh, it's 1.30 AM, so it is"

Reluctantly he left his jigsaw puzzle, which is nearing completion. Defeat has been snatched from the jaws of victory. He nervously picked up the black Bakelite receiver, he hated talking on the phone, correction, Malky hated talking. "Hello." He jumped back like a startled rabbit, recoiling at the screeching coming from the other end. "MAALLKKYY, MAALLKKAAYY. The poor wee mite."

Malky's jaw drops open like a trap door. It was Aggie.

"Heaven bless us all, Malky. Deano's delivered more than my milk this god forsaken hour. The child was banging away at my front door so he was. Got me out of my bed so he did, what a scare he gave me. It was Wee Geordie Magee, you know him, the footballer. 'The Pearl.' Sure, he's only 11, Malky. (Malky gulped and took a sip of water.) God help him. Got me out of my bed so he did. I didn't even have time to put my teeth in, oh heaven bless us all. The look of terror on his wee face. Malky it's not right, it's just not right. That's no life for a young boy."

Malky finally got a chance to speak, "Aggie love, what you on about. You been at the communion wine or something?"

Aggie won't be denied, "I'm coming round to yours. He's given me two pages to give till you. Thank the good Lord for our Deano, he's running the boy back home now in his milk float. I just pray his parents are none the wiser. I'm mortified that good-for-nothing father of his will cotton on that he's been out. Wee Geordie says you'd know what to do and all. I'm putting my coat on now, five minutes, be with you in five, right you be nae, Malky love."

The line went dead and Malky shuddered. He gently set the receiver down and the heavy hand of anxiety started pressing hard on his chest. The radio crackled right on cue and Max Bygraves is crooning 'You Need Hands.' which for Malky at that moment is 100% spot on. "What can I do about this? Why me Aggie, Why me?"

He spun around and faced his father staring him hard in the eye from the mantelpiece. Malky buries his head in his hands. "Daddy stop looking at me like that. All my life you've given me that look. You're right alright, I'm good for nothing. I'm useless!" He turned at the sound of a light rap a tap-tap on the window. Malky quickly rubbed at his moist eyes then ran his fingers through his thick hair in anxiety. The last place on earth he wanted to be is heading for the front door. Sighing he opened it slowly, Aggie bustled in, nearly knocking him over.

A cloud of nervous anxiety clung to her spotless pink overcoat. "It's a terrible business so it is. Wee Geordie thinks something terrible's going to happen tomorrow. On the Lord's Day too. Here's the two sheets he asked me to give till yee. I can't make head nor tail of any of it."

Malky sighed following her fluster into the good room. He now reluctantly held the pair of torn sheets. His eyes examine the child's scrawls, nothing made sense. He looked at Aggie who has perched herself on his armchair. Her old face was fraught with worry. "Well Malky, what d'ya think pet?"

Malky laughed, "Aggie love, what do I think? HELLO! I'm Mr. Stupid in case you forgot. I'm no genius, I'm no Tweety Pie!"

Aggie's face lights up. "Oh, Malky love I knew you had the answer in you. That wee boy was right about you. Go on then." Malky's face is blank, "Eh, what you mean Aggie?"

Aggie shrieks, "Malky, you're a geg, so you are. Well, go on then, phone him." The penny drops. "You have his number, don't yee. Please don't make me run back round till mine?"

Malky smiled, "Course I've got it. He gaved it to me for important emergencies. I reckon this counts but I don't know what to say to him. Say he's in bed or something?"

Aggie shrieks, "That Tweety one never sleeps at night. He's like yer man 'Count Dracula'. A creature of the night. Ring him, you'll see he'll be up. Go on then!" Malky recovered the number from his special note book. This is important. His special friend and child footballing prodigy needed him. Malky's hour was nigh. As he's dialling, he's looking his father square in the eye. Aggie watching see's exactly what's unfolding and smiled, whispering under her breath, "'Bout bloody time, Malky love."

The phone rang in the hallway. In the back living room, a log fire crackles its last in an open grate. On its mantle two large candles blink and sway casting shadows this way and that. The floor is weathered herringbone covered by a luxuriant Persian rug. A record player well used is turning, a diamond stylus bites into a slow spinning vinyl record. 'Clair de Lune' by Claude Debussy massages the senses of the male figure sitting on a deep green leather recliner. His eyes are closed. One of them permanently. A Tyrone crystal glass containing Ramos Pinto vintage port sat cupped in his long fingers. Tweety is lounging in his pyjamas. His deep blue Harborow dressing gown staves off any chill. The large green eye opened. He was half asleep, maybe a tad under. He made his way to the hallway and lifted the receiver.

"Sweetlove residence. Ahh, Malky, me old son. Yes, I knew it was you, stop apologising about the lateness of the hour. What's up?"

Malky nodded down at Aggie who claps her hands in excitement. She whispered, "If anyone can, our Tweety can." Tweety wanted to know everything that's occurred leading right up to the phone call. He wanted to know all about wee Geordie, his mum then his thug of a Da Stan. Fortunately for Malky, Tweety knew all there was to know about Stan Magee including all of his paramilitary associations and activities. Malky then went on with the child's roughly handwritten sheets. The green van with 'Fields' written to the side. The church hit. The purple car with the 1690 numbers. Cluan Place. Glentoran top and the newspaper. The phone was handed to Aggie on occasions who though highly agitated was fit to state the level of emotional control the child was in. Tweety needed no pens or sheets of paper. He was filling the gaps to this particular jigsaw and a very deadly canvas was slowly emerging.

When fully satisfied, Tweety whispered softly to himself, Ubi est, mors, stimulus tuus? (Latin for, Death where is your sting?)

Malky, confused said, "What you say there, Tweety, didn't make you out?"

Tweety smiled, returning to the moment. "Pay no heed Malky, me old son. You pair have done an amazing job. I'll take it on from here. Get yourselves off to bed and sleep well."

Tweety returns to the living room and slumps onto his ancient recliner which groaned in protest. The room is all but silent and the fire out. The music has ended. Patiently the stylus sat on the slowly spinning vinyl depositing a soft repetitive pip from the crackling speakers. Tweety noticed but lets it be. He drained the remainder of his port then laid back with his eyes closed. He knew the value of breathing calmly. His huge brain carefully assimilated the crumbs of conversation recorded by an 11-year-old boy. The fact that the boy sensed the danger and felt compelled to act upon it is not lost on him. A boy who had crept out into the darkness aware of the consequences to himself.

Several precious minutes passed, Tweety's eyes open, he is now ready. He stepped back out into the hallway and lifting the receiver began calmly dialling a familiar number. His 'Charles Howse' Longcase grandfather clock with pendulum crudely clunking faces him. To Tweety, it's in countdown mode and it's warning him that it's just shy of 2.00 AM.

As the line rang, he whispered softly in Esperanto, "Perle de plej granda prezzo!" A pearl of greatest price has been given to him by an 11-year-old boy. Priceless information that could save a human life!

As for our Malky and Aggie, they were too excited for their beds. They had a cuppa and a slice of Battenberg and together the 'Hanging Gardens' were finally finished. This particular dream team had proven themselves.

The phone rang like a defibrillator shock. A darting hand surfaced from beneath a dark grey duvet. It poked and padded along the sleek surface of a modern black drawer until it found an equally modern bedside lamp. A click later and the bedroom is lit, the bulb is far too bright for the hour of the night.

George Sewell had gone to bed at 10.00 PM the previous evening. He had decided on a new regime, healthy body healthy mind. "Early to bed early to rise makes a person healthy, wealthy and wise," well according to Benjamin Franklin anyway. George's crumpled face now resembled a battered sausage that had been well and truly battered. His alarm clock told him it had just gone slightly after 2.00 AM. Yawning, he lifted the receiver and rolled over onto his tummy. He recognised the caller's voice immediately then mumbling with the gravelly frog in his throat he growled, "Tweety, this better be fucking good!"

He then listened quietly while the genius at the other end calmly replayed the night's events, then all is silent. George sighed thinking to himself, "Here we fucking go again!" He scourged the recesses of his mind looking for any other way out of this cluster before blurting out. "Tweety, are you fucking mad? You're asking me to lay my nuts on the line on the word of an 11-year-old boy. For Christ's sake, he could be a fucking Walter Mitty!"

At the other end, Tweety smiled picturing the angst George Sewell is going through but go through it he must. He softly delivered the 'coups de grace'. "I'm not asking you to do it for the boy George, I'm asking you to do it for Derek! Before you ask, I've tried calling him. There's been no answer. The local plods have also been out, they've banged on his doors, no lights on and no signs of life. Yes George, we'll all keep trying. By the way, I feel your pain but sometimes that's the way it is."

George is now very wide awake, at a from the ceiling level. "Tweety, I fucking hate you. But you already know that. There goes my career, poof. Up in smoke again. Fuck away off now. I've urgent phone calls to make!"

Tweety laughed, replacing the receiver, "Night-night, George."

The following morning in every parade room in every police station in the province the following was read out to the officers reporting for duty by their section sergeants.

"Area OOB (Out of Bounds) until further notice. Castlereagh Street, East Belfast. From the Templemore Avenue junction, city-wards to the Short Strand."

Chapter 19
The Pearl Earring

It had just gone 8.00 AM that Sunday morning, a view to die for, he mused. From his elevated site, his eyes lapped up patchwork quilted fields bound by weathered dry stone walls. Each was different, all were higgledy-piggledy and haphazard in design. He smiled at cattle grazing lazily as their tails swished unconvincingly at pestering flies. Distant moos could be heard like echoes from afar. Darting blue dragonflies caught his eye hovering just above the succulent green grass. The temperature was sneaking up into the mid-twenties as the summer sun rose unobstructed into the clear blue sky. He removed his jacket enjoying the cooling breeze offered up by the lough. This was the final touch, its gentle caress marking perfection on that sumptuous July day.

"As usual you were right my love; this is simply wonderful. What a glorious day you've laid on and what a stunning view."

This was to be his last port of call. He had driven down from Belfast the previous day; it was a drive he always enjoyed. No speed limits were ever threatened. Two hours of memories, two hours of quiet reflection. On arrival in Enniskillen, he pretended to shop, quietly cruising up and down the main street mingling with the locals and the animated tourists. This is in fact where he got his yearly supply of woollen socks. He then dined royally at the famous 'Horse Shoe Bar', a traditional pub with a cracking atmosphere.

Burger and chips if you must know accompanied by a couple of pints of the black stuff. It was where they first met in 1947, he a probationer constable and she the beautiful farmer's daughter; theirs had been love at first sight. Sitting in a quiet corner he took a sip of the black stuff and smiled. He loved it there, he loved the anonymity, the solitude in a crowd and the fact that he would soon be with her.

She was a Fermanagh lass from the village of Lisnarick in the Civil Parish of Derryvullan. Her hair was as black as a raven's wing with large searching eyes to match. When she spoke, her voice was light like a summer's breeze and as gentle as a spider's web on the morning dew. No bad ever came from her only good. Admonishment was a sigh and her love which she only gave to one man was indeed his pearl of greatest price.

He had stayed at the Manor House Hotel, Killadeas on the shores of Lough Erne, the previous evening. He had done so the same time last year and the year before. There he had enjoyed a steak dinner with all the trimmings, yes pepper sauce as well. He would also splash out on a top of the range bottle of chardonnay to mark the occasion. No, he wasn't alone, not in the physical sense anyway, there from his secluded corner table he would gently pull out a solid silver cigarette case. He hadn't smoked in years however this is where he kept something very special.

On opening the case, he would read the engraving then smile through glassy eyes, for nestled among the deep blue velvet inlay was a single pearl earring. It had been hers. He would leave the case open smiling absent-mindedly at it while his feet tapped in time to the local fiddly-dee-dee band. A brandy nightcap was always his last order from the bar, this he would take back to his room for comfort. There, while lying in the darkness of his hotel bed, he would reach back into his memories for a hug and with every turn of the page Derek Grant would quietly sob bittersweet tears.

Derek inhaled the morning air resting a hand gently on the cold grey polished granite surface. He was sharing this stunning vista with his wife Miriam and his hand was on her headstone. He was standing in the graveyard of the Killadeas Priory Church to be precise. Miriam had passed three years ago and it had been her final instructions to him that he should get on with his life and live. Visiting her grave was a strict no-no but she had relented, allowing him one visit a year.

Derek then whispered to Miriam not wishing to disturb peaceful solitude, "I think it's time for me to step down. I've done my 30 years and the rest. The job will survive without me and well, my friends will always be my friends won't they pet. A trip to Tasmania to visit our son and our grandchildren seemed in order, eh, what do you think? A wee retirement treat to myself. Well, that's that settled then, I'll let George know on Monday morning, he won't be amused. A month's notice maybe? No, not fair. We'll retire on a first, give him time to get a replacement in. Mmm, the first of September seems a reasonable enough notice to me, that's it then, the first of September it is." Derek nodded; he had always listened to her advice.

Reaching into his breast pocket he retrieved the silver cigarette holder containing the pearl. Her pearl, Miriam's pearl. He placed the cigarette holder on top of the headstone and read its engraving softly into the morning air. 'If I should die and leave you here a while, for my sake turn again to life and smile.'

Derek smiled. Seeing the same words on her headstone, he gently opened the silver case and kissed the tiny pearl, a reminder of their vast unquenchable love. Derek caught the time on his wristwatch and gasped, "Gracious me, is that the time. I'm late, I'm late. I'll be late." He quickly popped the holder back into his breast pocket and blew her headstone a kiss. Laughing as he went, "Yes, I hear you, Miriam. I'd forget my head if it wasn't screwed on." Then off he scampered like the famous white rabbit to meet his own very important fate. Birdsong and a soft summer breeze eased back into the old graveyard leaving a slice of heaven for those who were already there.

Oli Fields closed the amaranth pink front door at 12 Ampere Street quietly behind him. His ma's a light sleeper and asks way too many questions of her precious son. Oedipus is going on in there somewhere. "Thank fuck for that. It's back.

This is fucking shite. That's me. No more! This is the last time I'm running errands for those shower of cunts. They're lying tucked up in their fucking beds while I'm collecting and delivering drugs for them. Oh, and let's not forget being part of a Provo nutting job today. I'm looking at twenty years in the slammer while they're looking at The Sun, page fucking 3! Not what I signed up for. They can go fuck themselves so they can, I'll settle for the painting and riding on the side."

His chartreuse green Escort van bearing his 'Fields the Love' logo is parked daintily outside. He spotted the car key in the ignition; it's slightly obscured by the shocking pink hair of a gently rocking 'troll doll' keyring. Fear and trepidation gripped as he walked out into the Sunday quiet street, a mixture of warmth, birdsong and far-off traffic. He crept around to the rear of the van and tentatively opened its doors. His heart's pounding and his nerves are jangling. Next came a huge sigh of relief, the van's empty barring his decorating gear and the Turkish package. It's just gone 10.30 AM.

The morning sun's bright glare is one of the many things pissing him off. Oli's not shaved which isn't like him. He's wearing his bright green Glentoran footie top, a pair of tattered grey jeans and his favourite paint-stained Puma trainers. Oli's feeling very sorry for himself. He hasn't slept a wink with all the shenanigans of the previous evening, he's dog tired and felt rough as a badger's arse.

"An hour should sort this cluster out, then back to bed or someone else's bed," he muttered, hopping into his van. "This is the last time Oli, you fucking dickhead!"

His face is a blend of Sangria and Crimson red according to his colour charts and constant mood swings. Oli's a man on a mission, well two actually. Firstly, he has to park his van in Cluan Place with its backdoors unlocked enabling the Provos to collect the Turkish stash, this bit is pretty straightforward. Secondly, he's to plant himself in Castlereagh Street facing the Mount with a newspaper tucked under his arm for around 11.00 AM. He's to keep an eye out for a maroon Volvo Estate with numbers like TIJ1690 or was it TIJ9016. He'd know it if he saw it. The vehicle was expected at the Mount somewhere in and around that time.

All Oli has to do is follow the punter as he left the Mount on foot into Castlereagh Street. He's to walk behind him discretely for about 10 to 15 yards, then simply turn and walk away, mission completed. This simple task would let the nutting team know that the man in front of him was their target. The peeler would be none the wiser making his way to church. Pity he would miss the service, no worries, he'd be meeting his god 'mano a mano' sooner than expected. That's if everything went according to plan, or was it God's great plan? Just who was our Oli working for that day? The Taigs would do the hit and that was that, he hoped he'd be offside before the killing bit. He didn't like upsetting his gnawing conscience, after all, Oli was a lover not a fighter.

He quickly checked himself out in the front mirror. "Ughh!" Then he started the engine. His form started to pick up as his van eased out of Ampere Street into Ravenhill Avenue. A good day can have that effect on one, can't it? He found himself breaking into song though singing isn't his bag, no definitely not. "What did Delaware boyz, what did Delaware? Tra la la boyzzz." Ahh, there's the Freudian connection. His chariot stopped at the Delaware Stores.

It's a one stop corner shop located just off My Lady's Road. It has everything the big stores have except it has everything packed into six square feet of space. Oh, not forgetting the knock off fags and booze, oops, caught me out there, our Oli's in and out like a fiddler's elbow. Yep, there's the newspaper, I'm sure it's the Sunday Times or Telegraph commensurate with his enquiring mind and high intellect. Oh surprise surprise it's the Sunday World a local tabloid catering for a very select clientele. Its discerning readers are interested in who's riding who, who has been nutted by who, what King Billy had for his breakfast and what the Pope had for his tea. Oh, and big titties.

The green van moved off, a minute later it's parked up in Cluan Place with its engine off. I would love to say it's invisible but it's chartreuse green. It's now gone 10.50 AM; it will take our Oli 30 seconds max to walk from Cluan Place to Castlereagh Street. There he'll choose a spot looking up into the Mount. When the time comes, if it comes, he'll Judas Derek Grant to his killers, still, he has five minutes to go yet. What now? Smiling, he opened his salacious rag, "Aghhh, titties!"

Minutes later, a black Honda motorbike with rider and passenger on board glided city-wards down Castlereagh Street. It drifted past a male wearing a green Glentoran top, he's casually reading a newspaper. It then slid by the Free Methodist Church to its left. Strains from an old church organ drift out onto the Sunday quiet road, vainly it called out to a long-gone generation. An agitated gust from the River Lagan tore up the road tossing old newspapers and takeaway cartons this way and that. The motorbike is in no hurry, the rear passenger is none other than an excited Slugger who's invisible under his crash helmet. A Walther PPK pistol is stuffed down the back of his jeans, this is to be his big induction day.

A scruffy yellow NIE (Northern Ireland Electricity) transit van is parked up on a footbath in Cluan Place. It slipped in at 10.00 AM that morning, its windows are blacked out. No one has gotten in or out and no one's any the wiser. It merges in like a smudge, not looking out of place amongst the other third and fourth-hand wrecks in the street. From the front, it saw down Castlereagh Street and from its rear all the way into Cluan Place. This however is no ordinary NIE van, this is an RUC covert van, it's call sign's Purple Zero. Inside, its occupants are keeping a detailed log and reporting any activities to dedicated response crews.

"Purple Zero to all Purple call signs. Can confirm the green van's in Cluan Place. No one's come near it, its driver, Glentoran man with his Sunday rag's standing in Castlereagh Street facing the Mount. Still no signs of the target vehicle. We have however a suspicious motorbike with a rider and rear passenger. It's done a couple of drives-by already. It comes back as registered in

The Markets area. It's stationary now in Paxton Street looking down Castlereagh Street. We'll keep eyes on. Over."

George Sewell is stressed as he paces around the Strand station yard. He's clutching a Motorola hand-held radio. "Where the fuck are you, Derek, son? Whatever you do, stay away from church today please? I can take a block!" He looked over to the genius and raised both hands into the air then continued pacing. Tweety smiled, he was standing in his scruffs by the loading bay with his arms folded. Both men felt helpless. A palpable tension gripped the morning air. An unmarked dark blue Ford Sierra with blacked out windows was idling its nose facing the station gates. Its occupants the highly motivated, super fit, super prepared and armed to the teeth HMSU or the Headquarters Mobile Support Unit.

Directly behind the **HMSU** vehicle growled a paint splattered Land Rover containing Sergeant Nigel Norwood and his Strand crew. Their call sign is Alpha Sierra 19. (AS19) Its rear doors were hanging open allowing what cool air there is to enter. Two of its crew are leaning out the back trying to escape the heat and thick fumes from its growling engine. One's armed with an SMG (Sterling Sub Machine Gun) the other's cradling a Ruger Rifle. A pacing George Sewell glared over to the leather faced Doc Halliday, the officer with the Ruger. A fag's dangling ash laden from his bottom lip. No amount of his chesty coughing can dislodge it.

George stressed, let rip, "Fuck's sake Doc, you know the Standing Orders about smoking in Police vehicles?"

Doc looked up, he has that Stig of the Dump look about him, I suppose you would if you'd spent the best part of your working life wedged in the back of a police Land Rover. Doc smiled from behind deep hazel eyes, his face morphing into a thousand creases. Seeing the strain on his boss's face he carefully burrowed in behind his filthy black flak jacket pulling out a packet of crumpled fags, "Want one?"

George smiled at Doc then laughed out loud, "Go on then, you cheeky bastard." Tweety smiled, shaking his head. George lit up and inhaled winking up at Doc. He then joined Tweety at the loading bay. "Well maestro, do you think your plan will work?"

Tweety gazing heavenward sighed, "Wish that bastard would show up somewhere, anywhere but here today, fuck him, he's always creeping off to this place and that."

George took a quick drag then spoke through his exhaling fumes, "'scuse me maestro, it's called having a life, try it, why don't you?"

Tweety nodded, conceding the point, "Well George, it'll be tight, we have the OP van (Observation Point) keeping eyes on, backup responses both here and Mountroyal. If the balloon goes up roughly 30 seconds to a minute to get to Castlereagh Street.

The drugs in the van are secondary to Derek's life, everyone's ready and know the score. By the way, nice one, I see you've got the 'A' Team involved."

George smiled, "Aye, no use in having favours if you can't call them in once and a while."

Both men glanced at the **HMSU**[8] vehicle knowing they'd done their level best. Tweety whispered, "Life's but a walking shadow, a poor player."

George spun, "What's that you say Tweety?"

Tweety smiled, "Nothing George, just talking shite. It's the waiting and not knowing, isn't it?"

George glanced at his watch stubbing his fag end out under his mirror polished shoe. "We'll find out soon old friend, we'll find out soon enough."

Derek's frantic, road works on a Sunday, on the Lord's Day of all days. "Fucking disgrace if you ask me." BJ Thomas was singing gospel on the radio and fighting a losing battle. God's great love and infinite kindness was lost on him at that precise moment as he sped through the Sunday quiet Belfast City Centre. Derek needed a break, a few actually.

"Thank the good Lord for that." He's now on the Lower Newtownards Road, a run of green traffic lights would give him the faintest of chances. He took a right onto Templemore Avenue. "Yesss. Praise be." The lights are with him at the Templemore Avenue, Castlereagh Street junction. He raced on into Castlereagh Street now heading city-wards towards the Mount. He failed to notice the motorbike at the Paxton Street junction or the yellow NIE van at Cluan Place. He does spot the big Glentoran man in his unmistakable bright green top as he swerves hard left into the Mount. All this furious driving done without once bothering his indicators, a screeching lurch of tyres followed as Derek brought his vehicle to an abrupt halt with a hard stop. His mind's now on Mr. Glentoran

---

[8] (The HMSU were an elite unit within the Royal Ulster Constabulary formed in 1977. Their primary role was to combat terrorism with "firepower, speed and aggression". Its members were recruited by Special Branch and intensively trained by the SAS. If the HMSU were involved, an extreme situation warranted it.)

man as he whipped his seat belt off. "Should be at your fucking church ya goat, plenty of time for the Glens six days a week!"

Derek's mood's on the up as he reached into his glove compartment retrieving his well feathered Bible. "Let's go then."

Stepping out into the street he's met with a less than glorious view. His surrounding area has seen better days, Victorian shabby without the chic, it was certainly no Lough Erne. He skipped down the Mount into Castlereagh Street feeling the morning sun on his face. The pungent odour from the River Lagan arrives as expected, strangely he enjoyed it, it was like meeting an old friend you bump into on a regular basis. Humming softly to himself he scurried on, there it was 200 yards down the road to his left, his place of worship. Gentle organ strains reach out to him on the soft morning breeze. He's going to make it on time after all. Smiling, he whispered, "Never in doubt Miriam, my love." Derek patted his breast pocket. Life indeed was good.

Chapter 20
A Time to Live
A Time to Die

"There's the bastard nae. Them's his wheels." Slugger nodded. He has no idea who his rider is nor does he care, that's how the Provos worked. Teams or cells were formed for jobs then broken up. The less you knew the less you could tell, this was a one off. Slugger, his real name's Michael O'Prey by the way, but keep that to yourself, that's if you like your kneecaps where they are. Slugger lifted the back of his black bomber jacket then reached into the back of his jeans. He pulled out a Walther PPK semi-automatic pistol, a favourite of the day. Slugger then deftly flicked the safety to off, it's now his time. He pulled back hard on the sliding mechanism; this is known as 'crashing the slide' feeding one round into the chamber. The rest will load automatically. His magazine held eight rounds, more than enough, every sinew in his body is alive. Adrenaline's exploding in his veins like a Handel's Messiah firework display.

Leaning forward he growled, "Right cunty balliks, no fucking about, we're getting one go at this. We go when I say we go, nice and steady. No fucking Steve McQueening. When we get up to the bastard glide in nice and slow. I want to plant at least three in his chest for good measure, got that?" His rider nodded. They watch as Derek appeared from the Mount and moved down Castlereagh Street. Glentoran man crossed over and followed.

Slugger whispered, "It's him alright". He decided to go early, tapping his rider on the shoulder. "Pronto Tonto, let's go!" His rider half turned, "But Glentor…"

Slugger cut in angrily, "Fuck him, he's not getting shot, is he? MOVE!"

Oli sighed. A smile of relief, does a runner, his job's done. He turned to cross over the road when he spotted the motorbike slowly exiting Paxton Street. Transfixed he watched as it glided into Castlereagh Street heading in his direction. He became grotesquely fascinated by the unfolding events. He looked at the Peeler and then back to the bike several times. He's having one of those slo-mo moments except this time no drugs are involved. He knew he should "get the fuck out" but he's now rooted to the spot.

A gold Ford Montego now exited the Short Strand from the opposite direction. It moved innocuously up Castlereagh Street; its occupants have a package to collect in Cluan Place. To a man on a galloping horse, everything is Sunday quiet and Citadel sweet in Castlereagh Street, how wrong could that man on a galloping horse be?

George Sewell jumped as a radio transmission abruptly blared from all the radios in the Strand station yard. "Purple Zero to all call signs. GO GO GO! Motorbike's on the move down Castlereagh Street. Rear passenger has a hand gun over! Repeat, all call signs, GO GO GO!"

George got it and immediately felt sick to the pits of his stomach. Derek has turned up for his own execution. The station gates of both the Strand and Mountroyal are flung open and the response vehicles burst out leaving thick diesel fumes in their wake. George, quick as a flash, transmits down the radio "All call signs, BLUES and TWOs, BLUES and TWO's boys!"

Looking over at Tweety he thought of the courageous boy. A boy searching for help in the blackness of the night. It's come down to this moment. George prays it all won't end in tears.

The soft velvet breeze infused with the strains of the church organ are suddenly hijacked by wailing sirens. The gold Montego alerted quickly aborts its mission, and glided by Cluan Place attracting no attention. Derek now heard the pitchy scream of the motorbike and spins around; his killers are 50 yards away and closing. He saw the passenger leaning out from behind the rider and then the handgun taking deadly aim. Derek smiled, he wouldn't have long to wait, it was his time at last, time to be with his Lord and time to be reunited with Miriam.

The motorbike slowed right down as it approached. Death for Derek is but moments away. Slugger can't believe what he saw next, the Peeler turned and faced him, then oddly he smiled. He then looked skywards while raising his arms aloft Bible in hand. Slugger blinked, momentarily blinded by the gilt-edged pages shimmering in the sunlight. The Peeler's lips move as he opened fire from 15 yards. It would be the last thing Slugger would ever see.

A whispered prayer escaped from Derek's lips just as the round's dispatched, "For to me to live is Christ, and to die is gain." (Philippians 1:21.)

The explosion to his chest snapped his head back causing him to gasp. His eyes stare skywards as he tumbles like a rag doll to the ground. The Bible toppled awkwardly from his hand landing beside him. Pages flutter in protest against the fury. A pool of deep crimson blood seeped from Derek's chest onto the cold hard pavement. His breathing slowly became shallower, a figure wearing a dark blue balaclava suddenly appeared kneeling beside him. The figure breathed heavily; an emergency patch is applied to his chest as he's eased into the recovery position. Derek smells gunshot residue from the improvised weapon he's carrying.

"Inspector, Inspector! Open your eyes Sir, stay with us. Help's on its way. Inspector, can you hear me. Stay with us." Derek weakly smiled as the church organ plays on. He then caught the kneeling figure's next words, "Jesus, Mary and Joseph. What the good fuck is this?" Derek slowly blacked out. Like banshees, the sirens wail on.

George and Tweety listen helplessly from the now deserted station yard. They'd both jumped at the sound of the first shot quickly followed by the short sharp staccato-ed automatic brrrppp. George shuddered. The second automatic discharge was unmistakable. It came from the elite HMSU.

"Purple Zero to all call signs. Man down, man down. Request for two ambulances urgently. One fatality to date. The shooter's confirmed dead. One handgun seized. His rider has gunshot wounds to both legs but should pull through, the lads on the ground are treating him. Glentoran man's been scooped. He's on his way to Castlereagh Holding Centre. He was sobbing like a baby so he was, his wee green van's been seized for forensic examination. We're waiting on the pick-up truck to arrive. Castlereagh Street's been cordoned off at both ends pending SOCO (Scenes of Crime), Forensics, Mapping and Photography. Guess what, the fucking press have just arrived. Over."

George trembling now transmitted, "Purple Zero. Any news about Inspector Grant please?" Silence followed for what seemed like an eternity then his radio crackles into life. It was Sergeant Nigel Norwood, "Alpha Sierra from AS19. Re: your last transmission. The HMSU boys are administering first aid. Nothing further over. I'll update when the ambulances arrive over."

George nodded. "Many thanks AS19. Out."

Tweety was cleaning his blue lensed glasses vigorously with a cotton hanky like a nervous twitch. He always looked completely different with them off but today at that moment he looked wretched. His one green eye was red and filled with moisture. He glanced up at George, his voice shaking, "I'm sorry boss, maybe I missed something? Jesus. Anyone but Derek. Not Derek."

George smiled, placing his arm around the reluctant genius. "We did our best Tweety. From the wee boy all the way to the HMSU. Whatever's done is now done, it can't be undone. Besides, there's now one less killer on the streets to worry about. Let's get up to my office. We can run the rest of the show from there with our fingers crossed. Maybe a wee whisky for our frazzled nerves?"

Tweety nodded, replacing his deep blue glasses masking his heartache. The pair wearily trudge up the metal fire escape stairs. Both exhausted. George's radio transmits incessantly from call signs involved at the scene. Derek's scene. Church bells pealing in competition from near and far add to their gripping tension.

A pale blue Bakelite phone rang stubbornly in the downstairs hallway of Number 3, Vulcan Court. It's the home of Martin Rooney the head honcho of the Strand and Markets Provisional IRA. Oblivious to the phones pleading he saunters out from the upstairs bathroom. When I say sauntered, I should also mention a splash of light boogying. Well, sure nobody's looking and he's got a Kriss Kross to die for. A cloud of perfumed steam followed his wibbly wobbly gyrations out into the cooler air. Martin's wrapped in a fluffy pink M&S towel and is none the wiser. Life for Martin up until this exact moment is 'sweet as'. A ghetto blaster in his boudoir pounds out 'Relax' by the group of the moment and gay iconic band Frankie Goes to Hollywood. Eventually he paused mid-drying his carrot top with a separate peach hand towel.

"There's the phone. Typical!" He discos it down the stairs sweeping up the receiver in a smiley flourish, "Helllooo. Rooooney residence, Martin speaking."

His smile is short lived, his eyebrows suddenly rise and his tiny mouth formed a perfect O. "Slow down, slow down for fuck's sake. Let's have all that again?". He gulped, "Slugger's dead! The Peelers shot him? What d'ya mean special peelers? Holy good fuck. What about Bruno then? He's shot as well ya say? Not dead yet? Off to hospital. Right, and the drugs? Yer kidding me on? The peelers have lifted the Prod's big fruity green van. What? He's been scooped as well? Glentoran man, yer man with the crystal chin? What an almighty cluster. Has any good come out of this balls up? Yep. Slugger took the bastarding inspector out. Bullet to the chest, OK. At least that's something. Ok, ok. Is that it? Right, ring me if you hear anything further. Ok, right you be. Cheers now. Bye."

Martin's dazed. He zombies into the back living room, collapsing in a heap onto his white leather recliner. His mind's racing. Martin eventually arrives at two simple and elementary conclusions, his first conclusion is one based on self-preservation; he's now under extreme scrutiny after this cluster, questions would be asked. He must be seen to be strong, a man of action, a leader. Secondly, he hisses. "Some proddy bastard's been touting, an eye for an eye DAZBO? An eye for a fucking eye." Martin glanced at his watch. It's ten-to.

Chapter 21
How Times Flies and Still the Poppies Blow

No horizon exists between the Black Sea and the night sky as the Oceana Perla quietly eased her way towards the Turkish Port of Mersin. The Mediterranean was a glass mirror to myriad stars dancing impishly on her surface. Lars Vilfort the ship's Captain, sat quietly at his desk. He felt its engines softly shuddering as the Pearl gradually reduced speed on her final approach. His paperwork is complete. The manifests are in order, all shipshape and in Bristol fashion. Looking through his salted porthole, he sighed as twinkling harbour lights ease into view. "Ahh terra firma, dry land. Once more you bring me home again Madam Pearl. I give you my eternal gratitude and that of my merry crew."

Returning to Mersin always made him think about the boy. Maybe this was his eleventh, or was it his fifteenth time since. A line from a poem he'd read somewhere crept into his melancholy mood,

"How time flies and still the poppies blow."

He gazed down at the cabin floor smiling, "Ha, the seeds. The poppy seeds." Then moving over to his trusty porthole, he wistfully gazed up at the stars and whispered, "Ozark, Ozark."

The stars hear and cast their light towards the Lisnabreeny Ring Fort. We find it located on the highest point of the Castlereagh Hills just on the outskirts of Belfast. It was built by early man sometime between 500-1000 AD. Its purpose was to protect life and livestock. The fort commanded magnificent views of the city and beyond. In truth it's a raised mound surrounded by aged and weather-beaten trees. It's a nice place on a nice day which isn't very often. When it rains up there, it pours and then when the wind blows it would cut you in two. A small car park welcomed the occasional dog walker, jogger and future 'dogger'.

However, a strange phenomenon occurs beneath the old fort each May and June. Three hundred yards below, looking in the direction of the yellow crane Goliath and Belfast City in the distance lay a rough patch of ground. It's about fifteen yards square consisting of wild gorse and hawthorn hedging. Why the farmer left this unkempt carbuncle in the face of carefully managed fields is a mystery. Folklore, fairies and superstition perhaps. It's at this very time of the year when the scrubland is overwhelmed with choruses of poppies. They're to be found nowhere else. They grow and thrive in defiance of their drab surroundings. They cover the earth like a huge red banner demanding the eye. When night fell, these scarlet hearts gently weep as they bob and curtsy to the stars, weeping for innocence lost as they have wept many times in Ulster's inglorious past.

A groaning breeze laments raising a cold finger to its lips whispering, "Shush, Ozark sleeps. Let him sleep. Shush, shush."

Ozark sleeps now. At peace, forever in the land of his dreams. The fort quietly nodded to the bobbing hearts, the chastening breeze and to the night stars.

"I will watch over him. I will guard his secret."

The cabin door knocked. Dimuth entered carrying two coffees. He found his Captain stargazing by the porthole with his hands in his pockets. Cupped in his right hand is a poppy seed. The Captain turned, smiling his eyes betraying his melancholy mood.

"Aw Dimuth my old friend, what would I do without you? Thanks for the coffee. How long before we dock?" Dimuth's now gazing star wards out the porthole with his Captain. Both men gently sway to the sea's timeless caress.

"Ten minutes to go, Captain."

Chapter 22
Ten Minutes to Go!

Ernie Vale the United Captain trotted over to the Russian referee as a mixture of roars and boos greet the young replacement. "How long's left, ref?" The stopwatch is checked and the answer's brief, cold war brief. "Ten minutes to go, then extra time if it is necessary."

Ernie nodded and turned to his team, "Ten minutes fellas, come on, we can do this." A glance at his teammates doesn't fill him with much hope. They're out on their feet. Desperate defending can do that to you. The whistle blew and the game restarted barely audible against the tympanic torrent. Geordie glided on to a pitch fast turning into a vast puddle. He shouted encouragement to his teammates, clapping at them. "Come on lads. Let's get in till 'em, we've got this, they've got nothing, just get the ball to me!"

Danner heard the call to arms and sneered. A sheet of lightning ripped through the black sky followed by a boom of rolling thunder. By the time the Pearl arrived at the halfway line he's drenched. But Geordie's more than ready for his moment and has the battle scars to prove it. Much blood sweat and life's tears have carried him to this spot.

Belfast is frozen in time as one of their own takes to the pitch. Those that know their football appreciate the significance of this moment. The Pearl is on.

Back in 11, Roseberry Gardens, Malky's delirious. He'd no idea the Pearl was even on the subs bench let alone playing. Tears are tripping him seeing his lifelong friend gliding around the pitch as if he owned it. An abandoned cheese and piccalilli sandwich sat discarded on a chipped black plate. His tele's up full blast and Malky's nose is pressed hard against it.

"Come on wee Geordie. Show the bastards what yer about!"

A hopeful ball is punted from deep defence towards the halfway line where the Pearl awaits. He has company, three burly defenders have him covered. The ball disappeared as a huge crack of lightning dazzled the eye against the downpour. The ball reappeared and the crowd gasped in concert with the booming thunder. The Pearl is gone along with the ball, searing pace, sublime balance and unerring control are captured in this unique moment in time. The world watched; its mouth open in awe. The Edgars Builders yard sign clanged in rapture as the wind ripped and jigged through its abandoned spaces. Cart horses chase the thoroughbred. He's 25 yards out with only the keeper to beat, everything's against him, the horrendous conditions, the soaking pitch. Why he's hardly had a touch.

Mac clenched his fists and gritted his teeth. "No Geordie, son. Not now, you'll not beat the keeper from there!" But Geordie's already pulled the trigger. The ball flies from the outside of his left boot with power and precision heading for the top right-hand corner of the net. It carries with it ten yards of late swerve leaving the keeper rooted to the spot. By the time the world blinks, the ball's crashed into the top right-hand corner. Stunned silence momentarily follows as the crowd take in what they've just experienced, then the stadium erupts as one. They have just witnessed one of the greatest goals ever.

A stunned Maxi shook his head in disbelief. He can't believe what he's just seen. Bobby and Mac bounce up and down doing a ridiculous jig from their dugout. Bobby hugged Mac and screamed, "tactical genius, Mac. That's us, never in doubt mon."

Mac laughed pointing to the pitch. "Look Bobby. Who's having who for dinner?" The Pearl has just nutmegged our Maxi who, enraged tried to cut him in two with a scything tackle. Perfect balance, blurring skill and control saw the Pearl skip the tackle and power towards the German superstar. Maxi's feet have deserted him, he felt like a cart horse wearing diver's boots. He screamed out, "Gott hilf mir!" Everything about the kid is at 100 miles an hour. Maxi found himself nutmegged again and dumped on his backside.

The stadium roared, "Nein." The boy single-handedly rejuvenates his team and for the rest of the match they grow an inch taller and find their swagger. When the final whistle blasts against the pummelling rain Manchester United are crowned the new European Champions. As the trophy is being presented, Beer, the Bayern manager caught Bobby's eye. He then raised his hands to the heavens and applauded. Bobby found himself filling up and returned the gesture. It's a hackneyed cliché but both men know that football had been the winner, they had also been privileged to witness a new superstar stepping up onto the world stage.

Moments later, Bobby noticed Mac watching the jubilant United players performing the traditional lap of honour. Tears are tripping him. He shouts over, "I guess our wee secret is finally out of the bag then Mac?" Both men laugh then embrace. They have reached the top of their mountain. They spot Magee, their number 7, he's alone on his hunkers at the halfway line lost in a world of memories. Some good, a lot bad. He suddenly felt a pat on his broad shoulders and turned from his thoughts. It's our Maxi, a dazzling smile followed. Geordie stood and the pair shake hands. "Pleased to meet you Maxi, I've watched you on the tele a lot. You're a smasher so you are."

For once, Maxi is lost for words, eventually he stuttered, "WOW. We didn't know anything about you. Where have you been hiding. (laughed) I am never wanting to play against you again Geordie Magee. I am thinking you are the new king. YESSS?"

Geordie laughed back hard at the German legend, "Na mate. Not me. Where I'm from I'm just wee Geordie Magee. They call me the Pearl, the Pearl Street Pearl."

Back in Roseberry Gardens, Malky sunk his teeth into his cheese and piccalilli sandwich. Plain Ormeau loaf with the thick crust. He chomped in triumphal silence. He then reached for his glass of milk and drained it in one. A forced burp followed. He then got up from his tattered recliner and looked out the front window. Malky cast his gaze out into the darkness and in the direction of Edgars Builders yard. A floodgate of memories open and rush in. The old cleaner sniffed back a tear then whispered, "Told yez!"

Wee Geordie versus the Wall, the Ball and the World.

Chapter 23
Ten Minutes to Go ... Finally!

Vic's on a major sweat. He checked his trembling Casio watch, 10.50 AM, 10 minutes to go.

"Fuck you, Tweety Pie, and all who sail in you. How did I get myself talked into this gig?" He'd just slipped into **SD Bells Coffee Shop**[9] by the rear car park entrance.

Such was Vic's dread that he failed to notice the amazing aroma of the roasted coffee beans. He was ashen faced as he made his way into the main coffee shop. Unwittingly sporting his little boy lost look. Nothing could 'perk' our hero up.

His trusted partner, Tweety had coaxed him into a cosy threesome with Wee Mo the previous night shift. Today was a Monday Rest Day and the 'A' Section gang were all off. Vic's stomach lurched like a learner driver on a ropey clutch. He had developed feelings for Wee Mo. In his heart of hearts, he knew that today she would discover the cold harsh truth. The truth being that if you plucked Vic away from the safety of his work surroundings you would quickly discover that he really was a sad boring bastard. His best friend Tweety had alluded to that many times which wasn't helping Vic one iota at that exact moment.

Now don't get me wrong, if Vic was going down, he was going down fighting. He'd made a supreme effort, pulled out all the stops. Let's have a look at the cut of you, big fella? Oh dear! Humphrey Bogart eat your heart out.

---

[9] SD Bells or 'Bellsies' is an iconic pit stop located on the Upper Newtownards Road Belfast. It's the place to go to if you want a classy cup of coffee. Bells is a unique family-run uber-friendly place. If you want it, they've got it. Their coffee comes to you in many varieties. It's been tickling the palate of coffee aficionados for generations. It must be good because they've been grinding away, beans that is, since 1837.

Vic looked as though he's just stepped out of a 40s film noir movie. He's wearing a tan overcoat, you know the one with the coat hangers in the shoulders, a white dress shirt just out of the packet, creases included. No tie. Black shiny trousers and black rubber shoes. Did you get dressed in the dark there Vic? Oh, and he's gone all out on the Old Spice. Poo yuck. There goes that sweet coffee aroma folks. As for his hair, brylcream? A regular Teddy Boy aren't you bud? My heart bleeds for you Wee Mo, it really does.

"Yoo hoo. Yoo hoo!" A young waitress chewing gum is 'Yoo hooing' in Vic's direction. She's carrying a tray of goodies. His stomach's now reincarnated into a butterfly farm. She's no more than sixteen and could pass for Sam Fox's better looking twin sister. Vic should know. Her face is stunning, raised a level by natural innocence. Blonde shoulder length hair cascaded off her tiny shoulders. But still she came. Vic's trapped in the headlights of her glare, surely, she's not *Yoo hooing at me,* thought Vic. He quickly glanced over his shoulder to see if Roger Moore's standing behind him then swiftly looked back.

She's now masticating for all her worth right in front of him. Beautiful blue eyes and a lovely pair of baps meets his eye, on the tray cheese and ham and tuna and onion. They're destined for table number 5 you hallions! She smiled widely mid-mastication. "You're Vic, right?"

Vic gulped, "Yep, how'd you guess. I've never set foot in this place before, luv?"

She giggles, "I'm Libby by the way. Tweety told me what you'd look like. Like, it was uncanny. I knew it was you the second you set foot in the place. Your lot have taken over the big table by the front window."

Vic stuttered, "My, my lot?"

Vic's wondering what the fuck's going on as he casually made his way to the front of the shop. He has that look of a mafia hitman. He then tried for all his worth to hide his amazement and act casual at the sea of familiar faces now staring up at him. All of 'A' Section are there including Malky and Aggie. Shelley had kindly picked them up under instructions from Tweety. She knew better than to ask. Everyone was there except the aforementioned genius, of course. Vic mused to himself that Tweety was a bit like God, he moved in mysterious ways, his wonders to perform. Lionel and Gary Weaver were at the far end of the large bench squeezed up in the corner. Billy Porter and Arnie Savage were facing them, they were all engrossed in the Daily Mail sports section. Shelley, gorgeous as ever, is sniggering between the two cleaners, Aggie and Malky. She has the table in hysterics with her Humphrey Bogart impression at the sight of poor Vic's approach. Malky chuckled looking down at the floor.

Aggie hooted, "Stap it nae, Shelley love, I'm going to wet myself. Ahh, Vic love, you scrub up awful well."

Vic flustered, searches for somewhere safe to hide. He spotted the Preacher and Heavenly, they appear together mid-bench. They're blathering excitedly about Monty, a rescue cat or something. Maybe the locker room rumours are true.

Tony Speers is at the end of the bench swivelling on a stool. The Sarge is chatting with Wee John. Tony is scruffy chic, wild unkempt wavy black hair, designer stubble, black capped t-shirt and large muscular arms. Oh and matching black jeans to finish off his look. Females of all varieties and ages try to catch his eye, married, single, divorced and the ever so religious types. You see, Tony has that sex factor, he was born with it. Commiserations, Tony, such a cross to bear. Our babe magnet's chuckling at Wee John's acerbic wit while swaying this way and that. Tony just loved to swivel. He's after a wee homer, no, not a woman, not today anyway. Keep it clean. A set of shelves needed putting up in his bachelor pad, and after all, Wee John had been a carpenter in his previous life.

Vic's heart suddenly leapt, and there she is. Vic's 'raison d'etre.' His reason to be, his Wee Mo. She sat to the left of the Preacher, hidden away and out of sight, all but lost behind his huge frame. Mo then peeked forward and on seeing Vic, her face lit up. She dazzled him with her face on, her thick brown hair is a mass of soft curls, plum lipstick generously applied contrasts perfectly against her olive skin. Vic's heart exploded like a Catherine wheel. His eyes are saucer wide. Mo's wearing a moss green silk blouse with the top two buttons undone. For the first time Vic realised this woman is in full possession of ample cleavage. He struggles to keep his mouth closed. Where in the great God of good heavens had she been hiding those? Giggling, she quickly thumped the Preacher on his huge arm. He turned to her smiling then leaned all the way down to her elfin face. The pair quickly nodded.

Vic soared as Heavenly precisely mouthed, "Looking well there Vic," a heavenly wink followed. The Preacher smiled looking up, motioning Vic in with a thumbs up.

Everyone on that side of the bench then shuffled to the right making the necessary room. Room for Vic to sit with his Wee Mo. Seconds later, they're together neither avoiding each other's closeness. It's out before he realised it. "Err, you look lovely today Maureen so you do, just saying."

Heavenly, Shelley, Aggie and Wee Mo share a look that only the women can see. Mysterious nods and half smiles follow; ancient signals forever invisible to the Neanderthal male eye. Maureen fixed Vic with a smile while under the bench she gently placed her hand on his unsuspecting thigh and squeezed. "Thank you, Victor, that's awful nice of you!" Victor is in eighth heaven; he is now loving the absent genius from the bottom of his exploding heart.

Libby appeared and momentarily paused mid-mastication. She's just started on three fresh Bazooka Joes and would dearly love to blow a bubble the size of her face and pop it.

"Right, you lot. Tweety's just off the phone. He's running about 10 minutes late so he is. He says you're all to start without him. Fill your boots. Because he says he's picking up the tab. He said for me to tell all of you that ALL will be revealed in the fullness of time! Whatever the fuck that means. Oh, and the big boss is on his way as well. So, let's have your orders folks, please."

Right on cue, George Sewell breezed in through the front door. He placed a hand on Libby's young shoulder and planted a smacker on her cheek. Jaws dropped like trap doors at a magic circle convention. "Hello Libby love, how's your mummy keeping. Is she over the flu?"

Libby beamed, "Aw, me old Uncle George, are you their boss then?"

George smiled, "Depends, love. On whether they've been good or not. I'll have the usual please." While Libby's taking the orders, George drifted over to Tony and whispered into his left ear, his right ear still isn't 100% after the bomb blast. Tony's eyebrows raised, then nodding, he smiled. The pair are up to something.

George then squeezed in beside Aggie who gave him a quick kiss on the cheek. "Aw George luv, you've been going through a rough time of it. I don't know how you do it, I really don't."

George smiled. "Aggie love. I'm just the tip of a very large iceberg. I've got a huge team working beneath me. Your good self and Malky here have proven yourselves to be part of that team. Team Mountroyal!" While the group watched the George and Aggie show Tony nipped over to an empty table and quietly plucked three swivelling stools. He then placed them side by side beside his own stool at the head of the table.

It was always slightly awkward when the boss from upon high was in your midst, even George. He picked up on their nervous vibe. Smiling at the group, he said, "Whoa team. I've been summoned here the same as the rest of you by Tweety. I'm as much in the dark as yourselves."

Tony smiled at George's cherubic face. George kept going. "Though it would be remiss of me while I've got you all gathered here today not to offer my sincerest thanks. Thanks to all of you for the fine work you've done as a section over the past wee while. A couple of your team deserve a special mention in dispatches. Who among us will ever forget the terrorist explosion on the Woodstock Road. What a day. What a nightmare. Firstly, Preacher, your prompt actions in clearing the Wyse Byse store in the nick of time. Then your good self, Arnie Savage, well done, in picking up on the ringer van at the scene, pure genius, especially when the area was about to be declared a hoax and safe. Precious lives undoubtedly saved by both of your courageous actions. Just to let you know, I've submitted reports recommending you both for the Queen's Gallantry Award."

The Preacher blushed. Heavenly found herself getting teary. Arnie beamed his heart swelling with pride, no longer the section turkey, the eagle had returned. From sinner to latter day saint. Their boss continued. "Gary Weaver and Wee Mo, I've also recommended you pair for commendations. Your selfless courage and swift actions in clearing the immediate area prior to the blast was crucial. A very well done to both of you." Wee Mo beamed. Could her day get any better? She felt Vic's hand on hers and a gentle squeeze followed.

George smiled and went on. "Regards the drugs seizure following Inspector Grants, err, unfortunate incident, a case containing cannabis was seized from a green decorator's van in Cluan Place. All this was intelligence lead of course.

(Aggie smiled winking across at Malky.) Its driver was arrested at the scene. We think he was a look out of sorts. A chap by the name of Oliver Fields, a painter and decorator by day and UVF enforcer by night. When scooped, he was conveyed to Castlereagh Holding Centre. There he had the pleasure of our very own Pinky and Perky. Turned out the chap had a conscience or was it the prospect of 20 years at Her Majesty's pleasure. Well, when it got to the interviews, he started talking, they couldn't shut him up and the rest as they say is history. He pointed us in the direction of Pearl Street where a further two cases were seized. The male occupant of the house was arrested, a chap by the name of Magee!"

Aggie jumped in, "Good. He was a scoundrel so he was. Oops, sorry. Excuse me." This outburst raised puzzled looks from the group. Aggie blushed, Malky cocked an eyebrow as if to say "Shut up!" She did so, sucking hard on a Werther's Original. She always carried a packet in her good hand bag.

George leaned in to the gathered group and whispered on, "The drugs were shipped in from Turkey of all places. The cases were hidden among high-end bathroom suites. The experts say in total the street value off the stuff was three million quid give or take. Ouch. (Smiling.) The Paramilitaries won't be terribly happy. Mr. Fields was finally handed over to the Special Branch boys. As for the nuggets he's coughed up, well, all I can say is that numerous arrests have been made on the strength of them. The Prod side obviously. Their drugs operation has taken a temporary hit. All in all, I'd say we're up in points today but tomorrow, well that's another day, isn't it. As for 'Mr. Fields the Dream', he'll probably be plying his trade further afield. Most probably Australia or Canada, maybe even the States. No longer Oliver Fields, he'll be given a very different nom de plume to get by on."

Arnie nudged in, "Aye, but he'll always be looking over his shoulder, worrying about a stranger's glance, wondering if he's been found, wondering if his cover's been blown. A forever stranger in a strange land. No family contact nor nothing. He's welcome to all of it. He can shove it all right up his orange arse, that's what I say after what those bastards did to Derek."

Arnie growled garnering gathered nods, "Hateful fucking murdering bastards." George remained silent while a moment's festering took place. Fears and frustrations were exhaled. He took a quiet sip of his coffee then closed off. "So once again, thank you all."

Shelley cleared her throat then dived gently in. She spoke softly, in reality speaking for all of the gang. "Any word on Inspector Grant, Sir?"

George slowly shook his head, "Tweety keeps me posted on that front. He was to report to me today, oh and while I'm dishing out the praise, congratulations go out to you in nailing that evil blackmailing bastard Bartholomew."

Shelley beamed. "I'm pinning very high hopes on you, Woman Constable McCann. The bastard was one of our very own, who would've thought it. Scumbag!"

Wee Mo looked down and cringed. George noticed. His eyes sparkled then his face lit up now smiling at Wee Mo. "Silly me, totally forgot, must be all the excitement of the past few days. I got word to collect an item of post from Knock Police Headquarters this morning. I have it on me here, though it's not addressed to me. Tony, would you kindly do the honours in handing this manila envelope to Woman Constable Morrison. Our Super Sleuth of the bacon thefts."

Tony smiled receiving the brown envelope from his boss. "My absolute pleasure Sir. Wee Mo, this is for you with all our love and heartiest congratulations."

Wee Mo felt herself tremble as a muted cheer rang out among her friends. Looking at George, she whispered, "Sorry Sir, there must be a terrible mistake. I'm only a full-time reserve officer."

George laughed. "Just take the bloody envelope woman and open it." Wee Mo was now all of a tizzy. "Oh dear. Oh, dearie me folks."

A chuckling Vic leaned over and quietly whispered, "Now's not the time to let the boss see that you're a Muppet Maureen. Just open the fucking envelope!" Maureen nervously took the envelope then quickly tore it open. She retrieved a single sheet of paper headed Knock Police Headquarters Recruitment Branch. Her hazel eyes slowly scanned its contents. An agonising silence hung over the bench as everyone waited expectantly. George and Tony shared a smile. Shelley would always be the first one to snap. "Well Wee Mo, AFC, any fucking chance? Don't leave us all hanging here."

Moist eyes glistened followed by large blobs of salty tears. They gently made their way down Maureen's olive cheeks onto the single page. Then the familiar squeak. "Eeeeeek. I'm in, I'm in. I start the regulars on 11 December. K Squad. Enniskillen Depot. Yipeeee to meeee. Oh Vic, I'm so thrilled. Ohh thank you Sir for all you've done for me, getting me in and all."

George was taken by complete surprise as a tsunami of gratitude enveloped him. Wee Mo spontaneously launched herself at him knocking him back against the large glass front window. A mixture of strangulating hugs and teary embraces ensued. The gang were in hysterics. George did all he could to breathe. "There now Maureen. All this is of your own doing. My bit was easy. Congratulations to you, well done, a very well done to you. I hope you'll consider coming back to us at Mountroyal. We're always on the lookout for good officers?" Cheers of approval rang out amidst reams of excited silly banter.

Then came a sudden deafening silence. It was like someone pulling the plug out of the tele just as the announcer was saying, "And the winner is…" George could feel Maureen's tiny frame freeze and tense. Mouths that had seconds previously been filled with laughter now hung open wide. Each paralysed in shock gazing wide eyed over his shoulder. His ruse was over. He turned smiling at the figure now standing before them.

It was Derek. Derek Grant back from the dead. He looked like a celestial being for he was dressed in white from head to toe. Shelley began to blubber incoherently whispering, "Derek, I mean Derek Sir. We all heard you were shot in the chest and that there was very little chance of …" Now sobbing. "I mean how is it that you're standing in front of us here right now. And for fuck's sake, what's with the whites. Are you trying to freak us all out?"

Arnie for once was lost for words. His mouth hung open like an ashtray on a Vespa scooter. All. All he could manage was a dry gulp. Derek smiled at his section. "Cheer up, you lot. You look as though you've seen a ghost." A dapper Tweety now appeared all in beige save for his green fedora. He was followed in by Doctor Chloe, who was ravishing in faded denim jeans and shirt. Her long brunette hair draped her fine shoulders and her gorgeous face was immaculately applied. She nodded at the gobsmacked gang and winked over to George. She then took up a swiveller beside her hunky boyfriend Tony.

He pecked her cheek and whispered, "I see you got him out Doctor. Well done."

She smiled, "He's one lucky man, as are you, Tony Speers. Another inch and…"

Tony playfully whispered into her olive cheek, "It's always about another inch, Doctor Chloe, isn't it?" He received a fiery dig to the ribs for his troubles.

The mastication princess bounced in planting a smacker on Tweety's cheek, "Uncle Tweety, love the fedora hat, really suits. Usual, flat white and a cherry scone, my love?"

Arnie couldn't resist, "Can anyone be your uncle Libby pet?"

Libby shook her head fiercely. "Sorry love. Only men that's seen me naked, isn't that right, Uncle George and Tweety?"

George laughed, "I'm her real Uncle. Her mum's my sister. Tweety's her honorary Uncle. We've looked after this wee monster since the day and hour, haven't we, Uncle Tweety?"

Tweety chuckled, "I'll never forget the nappies, ugh. Gross!"

Libby shrieked with laughter skipping off towards the kitchen, "TMI boys, TMI." Tweety took his seat and placed his moss green hat on the table in front of him. The genius looked tired. Derek sat to his right with Chloe to his left. A sea of expectant faces anxiously stared back at them.

Tweety spoke, "Well Lazarus, you should by all accounts be seriously dead. Tell us how you did it. Tell us how you mugged off the grim reaper that fateful day?"

Derek smiled. "Simple really. It was a miracle. Nothing more nothing less. I had absolutely nothing to do with it."

Preacher whispered, "Amen."

Aggie exalted, "Praise be to our Heavenly Father."

Lionel piped in from the far end, "So what you're saying is while the man above's been miracleising you, he's allowing the Provo hitman to get rubbed out by the HMSU?"

Gary Weaver followed on. "Aye and his funeral was the other day up in the Whiterock. Hundreds attended. Men, women and children all paying their respects to an Irish martyr. The usual. It all kicked off when the masked Provo cortege tried to fire a three-volley salute over his coffin. The DMSU crews intervened and the usual riot followed. Injuries to both sides and multiple arrests. The media loved it."

Derek sighed. "All because of me, Gary, a bloke going to his church. When will this madness ever end?"

Heavenly spoke, clearing a tear from her eye then trumpeting into a strangled tissue. Preacher chewed a smile. "Well Sir, it's a terrible thing for anyone to die. But in the grand scheme of things, we're glad it was him and not you. He was there to murder. He lived by the sword and in the end, he died by it. So, what really happened, pray tell. How'd you cheat death?"

Derek nodded then reached into his trouser pocket and placed the silver cigarette case beside the fedora. Everyone gasped, it had clearly taken a huge thump from the bullet. The outer case had imploded and was twisted to one side. The heat of the strike had charred its surface which now bore a deep blue patina. Much of its delicate engraving was lost. The precious pearl had been obliterated.

"The bullet struck the cigarette case which was tucked in my inside jacket pocket, unwittingly it was covering my heart. When the bullet struck it deflected low and right. Although it physically entered me much of its energy was spent. It exited here, (points), just above my right hip, so there you are, that's about it, isn't it, Doctor Chloe?"

Chloe nodded, "Yes, Derek love. That's about it in layman's terms. You're one very lucky man, though you'll not be hammering in any garden posts for a while!" Derek remained silent for a moment while the effect of the cigarette case took hold on the group.

Shelley was sobbing. Her streaming mascara and smudged eyeliner now a perfect match for the case, "Oh Derek love, you were so very lucky."

Aggie shoved a paper tissue into her blubbering hand. "Stop it, Shelley love. You'll be starting me off with the tears."

Derek smiled. "Settle yourselves, ladies. I'll explain all. And he did. It was the Derek and Miriam love story and a cigarette case bought for him over 30 years ago. Love had saved him from beyond the grave. It had indeed been a miracle."

By the time he had finished, all four women were blubbering, even Doctor Chloe. Tony was amazed for he had never seen her wobble, not even during a Lassie movie. George looked at the gathered group. They appeared all beat up. A strange family of sorts. Each is different in their own way. Each with invaluable skill sets. Each totally reliant on each other. That was their only chance of survival during those deadly times. He was a proud boss and proud to be one of them. This had been a close call. Too close. He gazed outside and sighed. His mind momentarily elsewhere.

Tweety was in like a shot. "What's eating at you, big boss man. It's written all over your face?"

George smiled at his good friend. "It's that pervy kiddie flasher, we're no nearer in catching the bastard. I hate loose ends, that's all."

Tweety laughed, "Fuck me George, is all of this today not good enough for you. This lot has produced the goods and by the grace of God, we're still all here in one piece. Fuck him. He'll rear his ugly head again, mark my words George he'll come again."

George's eyes twinkled then he burst out laughing, "Tweety were those two quickfire puns intentional you genius bastard?"

The penny dropped and Tweety roared, "No flies on you, George," pointing at his trouser zip. More laughter followed between the pair. The gang joined in not knowing what the joke was. Laughter can do that to you, can't it?

Finally, they all settled and George sensed that the timing was right. The beloved boss took a deep breath, "One final thing you forgot to mention there, Derek?"

Derek laughed, "Oh the whites. It's President's Day at the BBC. The Belmont Bowling Club. The good Doctor says I'm allowed to play as long as I don't overdo it. Pinky and Perky are meeting me there later if any of you would care to join us?"

George chuckled. "Are you sure the bullet didn't hit you on the head, you great big numpty. The other thing for fuck's sake!"

Derek paused then felt himself fill up as he absorbed the A. Section faces one last time. He lifted the cigarette case from the table and gently kissed it before tucking it back into his trouser pocket. "That's me team. I've retired. That last episode was a real wake up call. I should really be kicking up the daisies but I've been spared. I've been given one last opportunity and I'm going to grab it with both hands. George here has kindly placed me on gardening leave until I reach my official retirement date which is the end of next month."

Aggie butted in, "Awful glad for ye, Derek love but will you not get bored all on your lonesome all of a sudden? The place will not be the same without ye scurrying around with all your files and craic?"

Derek laughed, "Awk Aggie love, I've a son in Tasmania and his wee family to see. The travel's booked and from then on, we'll take it day by day."

Tweety patted him on the shoulder and whispered, "Hear, hear, Derek son." Derek had finally retired after 30 plus years on the job. He was lucky, for he had survived. Others were not to be so lucky.

Arnie, as the senior man in the section, felt duty bound to speak. He stood up and gave a quick cough from his wheezing chest. "Well, this is one cup of coffee I'll not forget. I can now call you Derek as opposed to Sir or Inspector which is nice. Just that I speak for all of us when I say you were the absolute best and always had our backs. We wouldn't be half the section if it wasn't for you at the helm dishing out the praise when it was due as well as the odd well-deserved kick up the arse. And I've been on the receiving end of both, let me tell you."

Lionel piped in, "More arse than praise, Arnie son."

Arnie chuckled at his mucker. "Well, if the cap fits. Anyhow, I'm not good at all this speechifying. Whoever the bloke is that's replacing you, well, he'll have mighty big boots to fill, won't he, gang?"

A chorus of "Hear hear" followed. When the fizzling energy softened, George winked across at Derek, who chuckled silently. He then spoke six words which left the gang gobsmacked.

"WHO SAID ANYTHING ABOUT A BLOKE?"

Derek laughed out loud. It was to be a perfect ending for him. George had involved him in the hunt for his replacement. He was delighted. He turned to his former colleagues, tears of laughter tripping him and said, "The only advice I can give you all is to hold on to your hats. She's an absolute belter and has my fullest blessing!" Tweety, like the wise old owl that he was, just sat and smiled.

The section is on Lates this Monday. Who can predict what befalls them? From mundane to murder, it's all in a day's work for our intrepid gang. Wonder what the new Inspector's like. A she? Well, I never?

"Care to tag along, Pard?"

I trust you all enjoyed these pearls from Mountroyal. Catch you at the next shift!